BEAVER CREEK BOTTOMS

By Herb Edson

Cherish Your Memories H

Prairie View Publishing, LLC. Indiana, USA
P.O. Box 0045
New Carlisle, IN 46552
www.prairieviewbooks@earthlink.net

Herb Edson

1

Preface

This book is dedicated to the memory of my wife Alice. Without her and her input, it couldn't have been written.

I consider this, a book of fiction. Although many of the events herein actually happened, perhaps a little different than the way it is told.

Many of the places still exist though they too have changed with time. I have used some of the names of towns and communities as they really are to give the story authenticity. The names of the people have all been changed to eliminate any possible embarrassment to living relatives.

Please look upon this work as a product of my own imagination.

CHAPTER 1

Around the turn of the twentieth century, Belle Prairie was a thriving community that sat on a sprawling hilltop overlooking a fertile valley. It was miles off the main highway and although somewhat isolated, was a pleasant place in which to live and grow up. The main street, which ran through the center of town, was lined on each side with two mercantile stores, a barbershop, a feed and harness store and other businesses.   The blacksmith shop was at the east edge of town. Although most farmers did their own shoeing, there was still plenty of work to keep the smithy and his helper busy, what with repairing various pieces of equipment and tools such as plows, wagons, etc.

The land in the valley that surrounded Belle Prairie was rich enough that most farmers were considered prosperous. Of course, there were some exceptions to this rule.   There are always those who are not destined to become successful in life.

The Reynolds family was one of those families. It was a family of many children that lived on a farm three miles across the valley. They were an honest, hard working clan, but even in good years, they never seemed to get ahead.   The children learned their three R's in the one room schoolhouse, and that completed their formal education. Whatever else they learned was somewhat less formal, but far more useful to their well being and livelihood.

Lawrence Reynolds, or Law as he was known, was the oldest boy. Lucille was a year older than Law and besides being brother and sister, the two were steadfast friends all of their lives. The younger brothers and sisters looked up to Law and followed his leadership in all venues of play and derring-do. Often this devotion was disastrous to some participants, but never the less, he continued to be their idol and leader.

As were most other young and old men of that era, Law was accustomed to hard work. His days began at daylight or before, and ended after it became too dark to see. It was a practice that he continued throughout his life.

During wheat harvest season, it was his lot to take the threshed wheat in to Belle Prairie to the mill.

The Homestead Flour Mill was a large wood and metal structure, two blocks off the main road, sitting on a hill overlooking the valley. It was here that most farmers sold their wheat. The best grain was stored here and used as needed and then ground, refined and made into a high quality flour that was well known all over the central states as one of the best products of its kind.

Law always looked forward to this season of the year because it provided him with an opportunity to relax and rest beneath the giant oak and maple trees that surrounded the mill. Most of all though, it gave him a chance to visit and talk to friends driving other wagons.

On this day he was distracted and soon lost interest in his friends' bantering. The face that he saw through the open window of the

4

mill office held his attention and caused him to shut out everything else. It was that of Delcie Graves, who he remembered from grammar school. Law stood beside his wagon staring at her from a distance, oblivious of those around him. She was still a small girl with delicate features, almost frail, even as she had been in school. Her skin was pale and white, and the long black hair that framed her face gave her the appearance of a pixie. Yet, she was considered to be a beautiful girl.

Delcie's father owned and operated the mill, and was by far the wealthiest man in the village. She had been given all the advantages that were available to the better class of young women of that time. Her parents protected her from the hard rigors of country life and discouraged young men of lower means of calling on her. She learned to accept and appreciate the finer things in life. Law remembered her from grammar school, and even then, she attracted the attention of little boys. When other children finished grammar school and went to work full time on the farm, Delcie went away to a girl's school; for refinement, some said. Others opined it was to find a suitable husband.

Nevertheless, Law had not seen her for a number of years and although he was surprised to see her now, and working in her father's office, she had not changed much.

When it was his turn, he unloaded his wagon and went inside for his voucher. Delcie was writing in a big ledger when he entered, and he stood staring at her. She looked small and pale and beautiful.

Finally, she looked up and held out her hand for the weigh master's slip.

"Hi, Delcie," he said, a little awkwardly.

She looked at him a moment and then smiled in recognition.

"Oh, hello Lawrence," she said. "That is right isn't it, Lawrence Reynolds?"

"Yeah, that's right," he replied, pleased that she remembered him.

"How have you been Lawrence?" she asked politely.

"All right, I reckon. I ain't seen you around lately."

"No, I guess not. I've been away."

"Yeah, I heard you was away to one of them fancy schools, some place."

"My parents think I should have a proper education."

"Well, they ain't nothing wrong with education, just so long as it don't get the best of you. They's only so much a person can learn and make use of. After that, it's just a waste of time."

5

"Yes, I suppose you're right," she reflected soberly. "Anyway, I'm home to stay now, for awhile at least. I plan to help out here for my father for the time being."

"Good, maybe we'll be seeing each other some time. I come to town here pretty often."

She smiled again, "Maybe."

Holding out her hand again, she said, "May I have your weigh slip, please!"

"Oh, yeah, sure, I forgot."

She made out the voucher and handed it to him. He started to leave, then turned to face her.

"Hey, Delcie," he said, "They're having a big barn dance at the community center next week. Will you go with me? I'll come by and pick you up in my Paw's buggy!"

"I'm sorry Lawrence, but I have already promised to go with someone else," she answered.

"Gosh, that's too bad," he said. "Well, anyway, I'm glad you're home for good now. I'll probably see you at the dance."

"Probably," she agreed.

The side door opened and Mr. Graves came in. He was a big, tall man, and muscular from hard work. His shirt and hat were stained with sweat and chaff dust from the wheat being unloaded.

"Hi, Mr. Graves," Law greeted. "I was just talking to Delcie here. I'm glad she's home."

"Yes, that's good of you, Lawrence. Her Mother and I are also," Mr. Graves said. "How is your father? I haven't seen him lately."

"He's just fine," said Law. "How's Mrs. Graves?"

"She's fine too, thank you."

"Well, I better be going, I'll be seeing you. We had a pretty good wheat crop this year." He hurriedly left and climbed up on his wagon.

Law felt exhilarated, all the way home, letting the team have it's own way, while he day-dreamed about the future. On this day, he arrived at a decision that was completely unlike him. For the first time in his life, Law was in love. He had been out with girls before and some he liked, but none had affected him in the way that Delcie Graves had. He couldn't accept the fact that he was in love, that was an admission that was foreign to him. Love was something one just didn't discuss, even in the far reaches of his mind. Yet, this was more than mere infatuation that he felt. It was a feeling he had never experienced before and there was only one thing to do about it, and being a young determined man, he set about in his mind making plans that included the young lady.

That night, he disclosed his intentions with an announcement at the supper table. "I've decided to get married," he told his family.

Everyone stopped eating and stared at him in stunned silence, openmouthed. Not a word was spoken for a full thirty seconds. Then, all his brothers and sisters began talking at once, asking questions and teasing.

Sidney, who stood nearly six inches taller and was fifteen months younger than Law was the first to make himself heard about the issue. "Who you fixin' to marry Law?" he asked.

"I didn't even know you were going with anybody, Lawrence," said Lucille. "You've been mighty secretive about it."

Ethan, being the youngest, led the pestering and the others joined in. Law chose to ignore the questions of his younger brothers and sisters and almost wished he had kept his news to himself.

"Come on Law, who you fixing to marry?" asked Sidney. "I bet it's that Hornick girl over at Carmel, ain't it? I seen the way you looked at her that day, when you thought nobody noticed."

"No, it ain't the Hornick girl." Law replied. "The girl I'm going to marry's got her beat, all to thunder."

"Yeah, I bet," scoffed Sidney. "Why they ain't no girl in the country can hold a candle to her."

"Well, this one can. She's the prettiest girl I ever saw."

"Ha, how come I didn't know nothing about it then," Sidney scoffed. "I know just about ever' thing you do."

"You don't know so much," Law told his brother. "You ain't seen this girl lately."

"Then how come you never told none of us about her, if she's so great," Sidney wanted to know.

"Yes, we'd like to know who the girl is, and when you plan to get married?" Lucille said.

"Well, I don't know when. I ain't talked to her about it yet," Law answered.

"How do you know if she'll marry you, if you haven't asked her yet?" Lucille asked.

"She'll marry me all right. She has to."

"How do you know?" Sidney persisted. "I bet she don't even love you." Sidney seldom spoke the word love and it sounded unnatural coming from him and embarrassed Law.

7

He recovered quickly however and responded, "Maybe not, but she will."

Law's mother, who had been watching and listening quietly, now said, "What's the girl's name Lawrence?"

He hesitated a minute before answering, as all eyes were focused eagerly on him. Then, he announced proudly, "Delcie Graves!"

The younger ones had never heard of Delcie Graves, but the older ones exclaimed her name almost in unison.

"Boy, you sure can pick 'em," Sidney said. "I remember her from school. She was kinda skinny though."

"Well, that don't matter none. She's all grown up now and even prettier," Law said.

"I thought she was away to school some place," Lucille said.

"She was, but she's home now. She works for her old man, I seen her today," Law informed them. "She's going to the barn dance, next week."

"How you know?" Sidney asked.

"She told me so, dummy."

"She going with you?"

"No, she's going with a friend from Fairfield," Law said, "but she said she'd see me there."

"How come you think she'll marry you?"

"Cause I got my mind set on it and I said so."

Although the teasing and questioning continued through the rest of the meal, there was no doubt in the minds of Sidney and the younger children that they would have a new sister-in-law. They had the utmost confidence in their older brother, for he usually accomplished what he set out to do. Their mother and father however, were more apprehensive and harbored serious doubt about the matter, viewing their son's predictions with skepticism.

Later, when Law was out in the barn feeding his team, his father, who was a quiet man that talked little, felt concerned for his son. Ordinarily, he would have been happy at such an announcement, because Law was old enough to be thinking and planning such things. After all, it wasn't good for a young man to wait too long to start a family. He needed to have children growing up to help with the work and he needed a place of his own. That was natural. He had been showing signs lately of the need for a woman but if Law was going after who he thought, then he was wasting valuable time.

"Son," he said, "about this here gal you been talkin' about, is she the Graves girl that owns the flour mill?"

"Yep!"

The older man clucked his tongue and advised, "You best shy away from her son, you ain't got no business with a gal like her."

"What'd you mean Paw, she's just as good as we are!"

"That ain't the way I mean, Law. That family's too high-class for the likes of you. They ain't exactly our kind of people."

"She ain't like that a'tall, Paw," Law argued. "She ain't stuck up or nothing. Why she's just as friendly as anybody. She talked to me this afternoon, the same as she would to anybody."

"You best stay clear of her anyways. You're liable to wind up gettin' mighty disappointed. Her Paw didn't send her away to school so's she could marry up with somebody from Belle Prairie."

"I don't care what you say Paw. I'm gonna marry her, you wait and see."

"You'll be sorry son, she just ain't our kind of folks."

"She will be!"

"I'm glad you got marryin' on your mind but you best go after some other gal. What's wrong with that there Hodge girl you been chasing? I hear she's been making moon eyes at you."

"That Sidney's been talking again, ain't he?" Law demanded. "He's got a big mouth. Sides, ain't none of his business. I'm gonna marry Delcie and I don't care what nobody says."

The two entered another barn and began pitching hay into the cow manger.

"I hear tell this here gal is on the puny side," observed the elder Reynolds. "She wouldn't be much help on a working farm."

"I reckon she might be just a mite on the skinny side maybe, but it don't matter none," said Law.

"I don't figure on her working in the field like no hired hand. She can keep house and raise my family."

"Ain't you getting the cart before the horse son?" his father said. "Peers to me you got this here gal all married up and you don't even know that she'll have you. I think you got your sights set too high."

Law replied, "She'll have me all right. I could tell by the way she looked at me today. I tell you Paw, I'm a'gonna' marry her, you just wait and see. I'm gonna' start courtin' her right after the barn dance."

The old man, knowing how head strong and determined his son could be, didn't pursue the matter any farther. He was twenty years old and should be taking on a bride and settling down. It was all part of life. He, himself had married at about the same age, but the boys mother was of sturdier stock and had worked right along beside him before all the children came along. Then they gradually replaced her in the field and she took care of the house and garden. Mr. Reynolds doubted that the Graves girl could ever adjust to real farm life. On the other hand, he doubted if his son would ever have the opportunity to find out.

All the Reynolds family looked forward to the big barn dance with anticipation for various reasons. A barn dance was always a big event in the lives of country folks. It provided them with an excuse to get away from home for a spell, for getting together with old friends and meeting new ones maybe, for fun and frolic and having a good time. It was a time and party where everyone could join in the festivities and kick up their heels, young and old alike. It was the highlight of the year for many. For the Reynolds brood, it was all these things, plus the eagerness of being able to watch their older brother start the courtship of the girl of his choice. The younger ones had never seen Delcie Graves, so they were anxious to see the girl who was, according to Law, soon to become a member of their family. They talked and joked about the event often, while the older members looked upon the affair as fantasy that would surely pass in due time.

Law and Sidney rode their own horses to the dance. The rest of the family went in the big wagon, which was pulled by a team of workhorses. Behind the seat a wide plank had been placed for the older girls to sit on. The younger children sat on straw in the bottom of the wagon bed. Excitement ran high among the children for this was one of the rare occasions when they went anywhere together.

The big wooden community building located at one end of the street was decorated inside with autumn leaves, corn stalks and the like in keeping with the season. Bales of hay were strewn about to be used as seats, along with the wooden benches around the walls. At the front of the structure, a platform had been erected where the musicians would play for the dancers. Already the violinists and the accordionist were warming up their instruments in the chords, to make sure the sound was just right when the time came. Just inside the door, on the left, tables had been set up where one might go for a cool drink of refreshment, such as punch or apple cider. Stronger drinks were usually kept outside where some men might go for something a little more to their liking.

Mr. Reynolds guided his team into one of the lots and tied the halter rope to a post. The lots were filling up fast, an indication that the turn out would be good. Folks would come from as far away as Mt. Hebron to the west and Fairfield to the north.

Many of the smaller children would run and frolic in the area around the building until they wore themselves out. Then, they would climb up in their wagons and fall asleep in the hay, without ever going inside to watch the grown-ups and the dancing.

Some of the young men congregated at one of the wagons, in sight of the entrance, close enough to watch the young ladies arrive. There was much talk and speculation over each new arrival. Sidney joined this group.

Law sauntered over to the door of the building and let his eyes wander over the crowd already inside and was a little disappointed that Delcie Graves was not in sight. Reluctantly, he went back outside and joined Sidney and the other young men at the wagon.

Sidney watched his brother as he scanned each horse drawn vehicle that arrived, noticing the disappointment. He wanted to kid Law, but knew better for letting the others know of his feelings could cause a heap of trouble. Law was not one to be kidding about such things lightly.

The young ladies were the object of more than casual scrutiny as they arrived and entered the building, casting shy, side-long glances towards the group at the wagon. There was snickering and good natured jesting among the men. Sidney soon joined in with his companions in welcoming them, in their own boyish fashion.

The first dance was almost ready to begin when Delcie arrived with her escort. The buggy, drawn by a team of bays was tied at the far end of the lot, since all the choice places were taken.

The young men watched as the animals passed and emitted some good-natured cat-calls and whistles as Delcie was helped down from her seat. The young man at her side walked like a gentleman as he extended his arm and she placed a small hand, just below the elbow, on his forearm. They walked past the onlookers silently, perhaps somewhat embarrassed by the attention. Delcie had her head high, looking neither to the right or left, pale and beautiful in the waning twilight.

Law took an immediate dislike to her friend, who had the appearance of breeding, which he detested. He was a handsome young man who dressed well and walked with the baring to someone in control and sure of himself.

Watching Law, Sidney knew that these two would tangle before the night was over.

At the sound of fiddles, the group drifted inside the building, where they scattered about, choosing partners for the first dance. Law stood just inside the big open door and watched as couples formed the circles and the dance began. Twice, young ladies came to him and offered to dance. Each time he mumbled that he didn't feel like dancing and they left him.

He stood there, through two squares, his eyes never leaving Delcie, as she whirled around the floor. He felt longing for her that couldn't be dispelled as he watched her flushed face and smiling eyes.

There came a break then and before the next square could begin, he pushed his way through the crowd and up to the couple.

"Hi, Delcie," he said. "How about this dance?"

"Oh, hello Lawrence," she said and looked up at her companion. "Fred, this is Lawrence Reynolds. We went to school together."

Fred stuck out his hand and Law took it loosely in his. It was a hand that belonged to a merchant or banker, soft and delicate rather than one hard and callused like a farmer's, and he held it no longer than necessary. Fred's eyes reflected superiority and disdain for the other, and a sardonic smile played around the corners of his mouth. Law could feel anger seething inside him as he turned his attention to Delcie.

"You want to dance with me?" he asked.

Before she could answer, Fred put his hand on Law's arm and said, "She came with me and she'll dance with me."

A look of anxiety came over the girl's face.

Law ignored Fred and asked again, "How about it, Delcie, can I have this dance?"

She looked at him and then at Fred.

"I'm sorry, Lawrence, but I suppose Fred is right. I did come with him."

"I sure would like to dance with you. I don't see why one dance would hurt, everybody else changes partners," Law persisted.

"You heard the lady, you clod-hopper, she doesn't want to dance with you. Why don't you go join your other plow-boy friends and leave her alone," Fred told him, pulling on his arm.

It was all the encouragement that Law needed to vent his resentment and anger on the other, would-be-suitor. Details of the fight that followed are sketchy after all these years, but it was very intense, although short lived. The other young men were delighted at the prospect of a good fight but several of the older family men stepped in

12

and separated the two before any great damage was done and held them on opposite sides of the building until they cooled off.

Delcie fared worse than anyone, being the center of attention, and the embarrassment to her was considerable since the ruckus was over her. Mr. Graves and his wife made some apologies on behalf of their daughter and took her home, leaving Fred alone to lick his wounds.

After that incident, Law took up his quest in earnest. Nearly every day he found some excuse to go to Belle Prairie, whether it be to buy a bridle-bit or horse-shoe nails or merely to stop at the local restaurant for a cup of coffee, and usually, he managed to get by the flour mill. When he saw Delcie working in the office, he rode by slowly so she would see him and wave. Before long he mustered up enough courage to stop to talk. At first, she was not very responsive to his visits, but after awhile they became friends and talked together and discussed things.

As time went by, he began his courtship, wooing her in his own fashion. She came to care for him and soon they were talking of marriage and the future. Her parents were very upset over the matter and tried desperately to discourage the friendship. Her parents offered to send her away on a trip with her mother, to give her a chance to forget the farm boy and meet someone more suited to her upbringing. Their efforts were futile and their pleas fell by the wayside, for the two had already fallen in love.

Law, who was always tight with his money and squeezed every penny out of a dollar, managed to get together enough money to make a down payment for a small nearby farm.

In the spring of 1900, Lawrence Reynolds and Delcie Graves were married. It came as a great surprise to most of the neighbors, but her parents had, by that time, reconciled themselves to the fact that they were to have a poor dirt farmer as a son-in-law.

After the wedding, the couple took up residence at the groom's newly acquired home and settled down to everyday living.

Delcie was what one might call a corner cleaner when it came to keeping house, for no dust ever settled for long on the furniture. She kept her house spotlessly clean and was an excellent cook and seamstress.

She was not meant for the rigors of farm life, and realizing this, Law protected her from the drudgery and hard work that most women accepted as part of their life. He worked in the field and tended the livestock and garden, leaving her to her duties indoors. She went to visit

13

with her mother every few days and the couple was very happy, especially after she learned she would have a baby.

But, all the care, love, and protection that Law could give her was not enough to shield her from the harshness and demands of farm life.

Barely ten months after their wedding day, she died in her parents home, while giving birth to a baby boy. Although, the doctor was present, as well as a mid-wife, it proved too much for her frail body to endure.

Law was heart broken over the loss of his beloved wife and in his grief, vowed to never again love another woman. It was a vow that he kept to his dying day.

It was several days before he would allow himself to even look at the son that she had given up her life for and then only after much persuasion from her mother.

His resentment was so strong against the baby that it was weeks before he would accept him as his own. He named the boy Leonard, the name Delcie had wanted, after a favorite uncle, and took him to his own mother for awhile. Then, after his pain had eased somewhat, he began to care for the baby himself, not out of love or pity but a sense of duty and obligation because he was a part of Delcie. He never forgave his son for the injustice he had done. There was always to be a barrier between them, even after Leonard became a man. He was treated with tolerance and indifference, much like a hired hand.

As time passed, Lawrence became a strong disciplinarian who would not tolerate laziness or inefficiency, feeling there was no excuse for either. Punishment for such offenses was dispensed with intensity, in the form of whippings or going without a meal or with extra work.

He learned to bury his grief in hard work and in due time felt the need of a woman's companionship and a housekeeper. It wasn't too difficult to find a suitable wife because he was now becoming a man of means. This time, he chose a young woman of sturdier stock. She was the very opposite of Delcie in every way. Her name was Bessie Hunsinger. She had grown up on the farm and so was accustomed to the hard life. Her voice was often coarse and loud, especially when excited.

Although Bessie Hunsinger bore no resemblance whatsoever to Delcie, she was still a handsome figure of a woman. Everyone decided that Law had made a good choice, and he was envied by every man in the valley.

Bessie bore Lawrence no children and she took little Leonard as her own, up to a point. Her husband was first in her life and although the boy was raised as her own, he was still subject to his father's discipline. However, Bessie still pampered him in her own backward way and protected him as best she could from the wrath of his father.

Lawrence and Bessie were well suited for each other and worked and prospered together, along with the boy.

It wasn't long before Law realized that his farm could not expand in the way he would like. All the neighboring farms had been in families for generations and were likely to stay that way.

So, in order for him to prosper, he must sell his farm and relocate to another area.

CHAPTER 2

Beaver Creek Bottoms was a fertile valley, perhaps the richest and most productive farmland in that part of the state. Stretching for more than fifty miles across the lower part of the state, it accumulated topsoil for many generations from the surrounding uplands that eroded and washed down into the bottoms. The gentle rolling hills of the higher ground sloped so gradual in some places, a man hardly notices he was entering the valley.

Running through the valley was the Little Wolf River, winding its way, first on one side and then crossing over to the other, finally emptying into the Wabash River far down stream. Compared to most rivers, the Little Wolf was unlikely to rate as a major stream but was considerably larger than Beaver Creek which helped in its small way to supply water to the larger waterway. These two streams, small though they were, played an integral part in the welfare of the valley, for they carried away the run-off water of heavy winter and spring rains.

However, often during the rainy seasons, the Little Wolf and Wabash were unable to carry away the water fast enough and the entire valley would flood. Sometimes, the water could be seen for days in the fields as the river overflowed its banks and spread out over the land. Farmers could only watch and wait and pray as it moved closer and closer to their homes. It was a time of great despair, for there was no defense against this act of nature. During such times, the farmer would load up his wagons with family valuables and necessities and head out to higher ground, driving his livestock before him.

Then the Federal government dug a large drainage ditch through the Bottoms in hopes of alleviating the problem. Since then, there had been no heavy rains that the normal drainage couldn't handle and no one was anxious to find out if it worked or not.

At one time, not too long ago, the Bottoms was thickly settled with small farms, mostly under forty acres, on which the owner eked out a living. Many of these people were leftovers from the prosperous logging days, who had either worked in the forest cutting logs, or at one of the many sawmills. Some drifted here from railroad jobs and just didn't move on any further. Others came for the reason that they liked it and never bothered to leave.

Before the farms, the entire Bottoms was covered with nearly impenetrable hardwood forests. This brought the first white hunters and trappers to the area. Before that, Indians lived peacefully in the vast valleys. There was little reason for them to roam too far from home in search of food and they apparently were satisfied with their way of life. Traveling the creeks and small rivers by canoe and boats, they were able to cover most of the area by water. There was little reason to go elsewhere until the white man came and forced them to search for new hunting grounds.

Most of the early settlers came because of the abundance of prime timber. The forests consisted mainly of several varieties of oak, elm, hickory, walnut, maple and others, all the very best for lumber to build. Numerous lumber camps and sawmills were scattered throughout the country for as long as the trees lasted.

Sawmill Hill was one of the largest and better known mills in the area. Situated on the highest point around, it provided a view of the surrounding valley to the south and east and was the source of most of the prosperity of the village of Aden. During times of high water, loggers cut the trees, trimmed them and then floated them down the waterways and to the sawmills. Here, the trees were cut into rough lumber and shipped out by rail to destinations all over the country, to mills that would plane and finish the product.

After the forests were somewhat depleted, the swamps were drained and the land cleared little by little for homesteading and farming, making it some of the richest soil in Southern Illinois. The major crops of these counties were wheat, rye, oats, and corn. Tons of potatoes were shipped out and at one time tobacco was raised. Another big money crop of the higher ground was fruit, such as apples, peaches and plums.

Even now there was plenty of wild game to be found for the hunter with good dogs. One could go out any time for rabbits, squirrels, quails, and an occasional turkey or pheasant. Also, there was an abundance of small fur bearing animals. Wolves still roamed the bottoms, and a brown bear was seen in the distance more than once.

As the logging era drew to a close, most of the old time loggers moved on to new locations. But, many of the younger men stayed on where they were, having bought a few acres of ground while working. For the most part, these men were not lazy or lacking in ambition and although they were accustomed to hard work, farming was a far different kind of labor. There was no remuneration at the end of the month to live on. The work was hard and the hours long, with very little to show for their efforts. In order for these men to be successful, they had to have a little nest egg to live on until their crops matured and could be gathered in. Even then, there would seldom be enough to sell for cash money. The ground must be cleared and plowed and planted, then cultivated and harvested. Very few knew enough about farming and the prospects were dim indeed, what with families to feed and care for.

Preparing the land for farming was a tremendous task. Even small children and women folks were required to work alongside their men in clearing the ground of stumps, vines and all types of brush and undergrowth before plowing could even begin. Local blacksmiths worked steadily repairing broken plowshares and other types of equipment damaged while tearing up the ground and turning the rich loam. Fire and black smoke were a common sight in the bottoms where land was being cleared, leaving open spaces for farming. Good seeds for planting were scarce and hard to find. Each year the best of the crop was saved for the following season, but that was often needed and used for food for survival through the harsh winter. Sometimes, mice and rats found and ate what had been put aside for seed.

Many homes were little more than crude replicas of houses, built of logs hewn on the site, mostly one, two or three room structures, heated by a large stone fireplace in the main living room. A well or cistern in the backyard supplied all the water needed for drinking, cooking and washing, and of course, the inevitable little outhouse with a path, out back. Every home was blessed with the usual number of livestock, such as a cow or two, a horse or mule, goats, chickens and various other fowl and of course a hound dog for hunting. Most families had a new edition to their brood each year or so with a new baby, making it even more difficult to feed and supply all the necessary needs.

Maybe the old-timers were the lucky ones. They had no dependents, for the most part, other than themselves. They lived in the log or clapboard hotels or rooming houses in the settlements and villages that had sprung up wherever the mills were. They were hard working men and lived just as hard as they worked, drinking and gambling their money away. When one job was completed, they simply moved on.

There was one man, however, who abandoned his life as a logger and turned to farming. He proved to be more ambitious and laborious than his contemporaries. His name was Jeff Quigley. Now Jeff Quigley was a man who believed in hard work, which was necessary to survive. He also had many sons, five to be exact, who he felt must work just as hard as he himself. Even as small boys they were appointed chores to do and these tasks were carried out with very little objection. As the boys grew in age and size, so did the chores. At an early age, they learned to shoulder the burdens placed upon them; scubbing sprouts, cutting trees and clearing the land by hand was back-breaking work and then plowing this newly cleared root bound land was no less easy.

Although these five sons grew up to be husky, stalwart fellows, accustomed to hard work, they had no desire to kill themselves for such a diminutive amount of rewards. So, one by one, as they reached adulthood, they left the family farm. Three of them bought farms of their own, farms up on the higher ground that were already established. There, life was still hard, but not as in the Bottoms in the new ground, and the work was more rewarding. The other two boys went to St. Louis to work in factories.

When the three Quigley daughters married and moved away, leaving only Jeff and his wife, the upkeep of the homestead took on tremendous proportions. Jeff continued to work just as hard as before. Still clearing land and planting crops, he maintained a fairly decent living for the two of them. He lived only a few years after the last daughter left, keeping up with his crops, until his land was nearly all cleared and the farm flourished. He died one hot August day of a heat stroke while digging up a robust tree stump, the last in an otherwise cleared field.

The widow Quigley stayed on for nearly three years, on the farm where she had lived most of her life, raising eight children and burying four others. The sons and daughters who lived in the near vicinity kept a close watch on their mother, at least one or the other coming by every day or so. The sons took the livestock to relieve her of the care of such, leaving her with a milk cow, her chickens, a goat and two dogs for company. The vegetable garden, fruit trees and berries gave her plenty to do and provided her with most of her food.

Finally, it became evident that it was no longer feasible for the widow to remain there alone, what with her advanced age and the rheumatism in her joints. After much persuasion on the part of her children, she agreed to move in with her younger daughter in the nearby town of McLeansboro, providing the farm could be sold at a fair price and to a man who would appreciate all the years of hard work gone into it.

Once Lawrence Reynolds realized he had to move out of the valley in which he lived if he expected to grow and expand, he was determined to do so as quickly as possible. But, he would not be in such a hurry as to buy a "pig in a poke." He would be patient, up to a point, and find a place he liked and give him the room he needed to grow.

So, began his quest! He soon became familiar with farms, roads and farmers all the way from Fairfield to McLeansboro and beyond, a distance of at least thirty miles, which was quite a feat in those days of poor roads and no accommodations along the way. The horse he rode on those excursions began to think its master was a circuit riding preacher, what with all the miles they covered. But one had to admit that walking along a rutted road was much easier than pulling a plow or wagonload of logs. Occasionally, Law's younger brother Sidney rode along with him for company when his own work permitted, but more often than not, he rode alone.

He looked at dozens of pieces of land and farms, only finding a couple that he considered at all, then changing his mind. It's not to say there was nothing available, because there was. Many plots of ground were for sale, some partially cleared and some covered with brush and vines and trees. Most of the so-called farms with dwellings were constructed of logs and dilapidated clap-boards and few usable out-buildings.

One day they went over to near Belfield, a hamlet of about fifty or so, to look at a place Law had heard about. It had some potential and Sidney couldn't understand why his brother showed little or no interest in it. They rode along for quiet awhile before he finally broke the silence.

Sidney pulled a package of tobacco from the bib of his overalls and stuffed a big quid in the side of his jaw, automatically offering the pack to Law, knowing full well he didn't chew.

Law declined, as Sidney knew he would, but offering a chew or a smoke was habit among all users.

"You know blamed well I don't chew," Law admonished his younger brother, "So why do you keep asking if I want a chew?"

Sidney rolled the wad around in his mouth a moment before spitting out a long brown liquid stream to the side of the road.

"Reckon it's just habit," he replied with a grin. "Most men take me up on it."

"Most men will take anything that's free whether it's good for them or not," Law said sardonically. "I don't see why you ever started chewing the stuff. It's a bad habit anyway you look at it. It's bad for your health and it's nasty, having to spit all the time."

"I know, but it gives me something to do and besides I like the taste of it. I think maybe next year I might set me out a few tobacco plants so I won't have to buy any. I know two or three fellers who raise their own."

"Well, that's a habit I don't want to get," retorted Lawrence.

"A little tobacco never hurt nobody," Sidney returned, spitting again. They rode along in silence for awhile. "What'd you think of the place we looked at today?" Sidney asked.

"Didn't like it much," Lawrence answered.

"Didn't think so, from the way you lost interest in it before we was halfway over the place. Me, I thought it looked pretty good."

"Reckon it was all right for some people, but not for me."

"Why not? I didn't see anything wrong with it!" Sidney queried.

"It's just not what I'm looking for," Lawrence returned.

"Dang it, Law, I just don't understand what you're looking for. That place had a pretty good house on it, better than the one you're living in, leastways. I admit the barn and sheds ain't much but there's more land than you've got. I'm not faulting you or nothing like that, it's just that I'm not sure what we're looking for. And I'm not saying I don't like riding with you whenever I can, because I do."

"All right, Little Brother, I'll explain it to you," Lawrence grinned. Although Sidney was at least five inches taller and heavier than his brother, he was still two years younger and Lawrence often referred to him affectionately as Little Brother when explaining a particular plan to him as he now did. Admittedly, Sidney rather liked the reference, feeling the approval in Law's voice. He too, was married now and had a family started, but still looked up to Law.

"I'll tell you what I'm looking for," Lawrence said. "That place wasn't even close to what I'm going to buy. I grant that the house is a little better than mine, but that's as far as it goes. Ain't interested in a good house, at least not now. Later, maybe!"

"Why not? I thought that's why we been looking so hard."

"Nope, you're dead wrong about that. Barns and sheds is what I need so's I can get more livestock and store my grain until the price gets right. Living quarters ain't important at all, just yet," Lawrence explained.

"Oh, I want a decent place for me and Bessie and the boy to live in and we'll find that. Most of all, I need land. Land for the livestock to graze on and land to plow and raise crops. That place we looked at today had land all right but, most of it still had to be cleared of timber and brush. Why, that only had a few acres of tillable land. Not near enough to make a living off of. We'd all starve to death before I could get it cleared. Nope, I want land that's already cleared and ready to plow. I don't want it all cleaned off now, just enough to plant to use while I clear the rest."

"You see, Little Brother, I can plant a crop and clear some more land while that crop is growing, but I need enough to get started on. Simple isn't it?"

"I reckon, if you say so," Sidney replied thoughtfully. "It'll take awhile though, won't it!"

"Yep, it'll take awhile. Look at it this way, I've got the rest of my life to do it in. It won't take that long to do it, though. Why, in ten, fifteen years I'll have me the best farm in these parts, just you wait and see."

Sidney glanced sideways at his older brother, at the glint and determination in his eyes. He didn't doubt him a bit. From all the years they had been together, Lawrence had never failed to accomplish what he set out to do and that's one reason Sidney admired him so much. Even as a little boy he was headstrong and determined.

"I don't plan on being a poor dirt farmer all my life like Paw is."

"Paw hasn't done too bad," Sidney defended. "He raised all us kids and he don't owe nobody nothing. We should be proud of him."

"Oh, I ain't bad-mouthing Paw, Sid, you know that. He's worked hard all his life and is one of the best men I ever knew, but he's still dirt poor. Why, I bet he couldn't raise two hundred dollars in cash money if his life depended on it."

"Well he's honest and he owns his own farm and that's more than most folks can say. He's respected too. His handshake is worth a lot."

"I know that, Sid, and I'm proud of him too. The thing is, I want better and I'm going to have it some day, by planning ahead and hard work."

"Yeah, I reckon you will, at that," Sidney said. "You sure do some planning about your work. I never seen Paw nor nobody else that plans ahead the way you do, when it comes to farming."

"That's why there's so many farmers that don't make any money," replied Lawrence. "They don't plan anything, they just keep doing the same thing the same way, every year, instead of trying to improve their lot. You understand what I'm talking about, Sid?"

"I think so," conceded Sidney. But, he would never plan and contrive to better his life to any great extent. This was one of the main differences between the two brothers, other than size. While Lawrence was of medium height and wiry stature, his younger brother was close to 6 feet 3 inches tall, weighing about 200 pounds. The contrast between them was significant. Lawrence was very energetic and ambitious whereas the younger sibling was lacking in both. He was strong and dependable. He would work, hard when necessary, especially when helping out his older brother. He wasn't lazy, not exactly. There just wasn't any get up about him. Most folks called it lack of ambition, finding it easier to drift along with the current. That may be why the two made a good team.

Two weeks later, Lawrence went into Belle Prairie to purchase some horse-shoe nails. Coming out of the general store, he met Bill Floyd, an old friend from school days. They stopped on the boardwalk to talk, as all farmers do when the opportunity arises, with nothing better to do. After the usual amenities about the weather and crops, etc., and bantering back and forth about their private lives, Bill said, "Say, Lawrence, you having any luck about finding you a place or did you just give up?"

"No, I didn't find a place yet, and I didn't give up," Lawrence replied. "I'm still looking and one of these days I'll find it!"

"Good. I been meaning to go see you about this place I heard about a couple days ago."

"Where is it?"

"Over 'round Blairsville," Bill replied. "I was over there the other day and got to talking to a man I know, there in the store. My Paw and his Paw used to log together, down in the Bottoms. They quit logging and started farming. His name is Quigley. His old man died awhile back and his maw stayed on the farm until now, but she's getting older and the kids don't want her staying way out there alone. So she's going to sell it, if she can get enough for it."

"That's over in Beaver Creek Bottoms, ain't it?" Lawrence said. "I've heard that's some of the best land around these parts once it's cleared off."

"I reckon so," Bill Floyd said. "I've seen some of the corn over there, and it's a lot taller and better looking than ours."

"How many acres are there?"

"I think about sixty as far as my friend knows."

Lawrence felt his pulse quicken. "Is it cleared?"

"About half of it," he said. "The rest of it is in good timber and pasture," Bill told him.

That much sounded good. Thirty acres was about all he could plow and plant the first year anyway.

"What about the house and barn, are they any good?"

"I guess there's a house, since my friend was raised there and his mother still lives there, but I don't know anything about it or the barn either, for that matter. I just didn't think about it at the time."

"How come you're not interested in it?" Lawrence asked.

"Who me?" Bill laughed. "You know me better'n that boy. Me and Bev are satisfied right where we are, living with my folks. This way, I help with the work and Paw does most of the worrying. Besides, I'll get the farm one of these days, when he dies. Nope I'll just stay where I am. If I was you though, I'd get over there as soon as I can. It might be just what you want."

"Sounds pretty good," Lawrence said thoughtfully. "Can you tell me how to get there?"

"Sure, that's easy, if you've ever been that way before."

"I've been there a couple times."

"Good, then you shouldn't have any trouble finding it, if you've been to Blairsville."

"I've been there," Lawrence repeated.

After having received directions from Bill, Lawrence shook hands with his friend. Both hands were brown, hard and callused from long years of gripping plow-handles, axes and other tools of the trade.

"I sure do thank you, old friend," Lawrence said sincerely. "I'm going over there in a day or two, just as soon as I can."

"Good luck, Law, hope it's just what you want. Let me know, will you!"

"Sure thing!"

Riding back home, Lawrence mulled the situation over in his mind. Although the possibilities seemed to be there, he had had good prospects before that didn't pan out. Not wanting to be carried away by false hope, he still remained optimistic. Knowing very little about the place, he still had a deep down gut feeling that wouldn't go away. By the time he reached home and put away his horse, his mind was made up.

In the house, his wife Bessie, was cooking supper. Little Leonard was playing just outside the back door with a puppy that had wandered into the yard a few days before.

Lawrence crept up behind her, turning her around to face him, drawing her body up tight against his own and running his hands over her ample bottom.

"Land sakes, Hon, what's got into you?" she giggled, holding the long handled spoon out away from them. "What happened to you in town, anyway? You haven't been sampling nobody's home-brew, have you?"

"Nope, nothing like that," he grinned sheepishly. "I just feel good, that's all."

"Well, we can't do nothing about it right now, not with the little one right outside the door. He might come in any minute."

"We could lock the door," Lawrence said.

"Too late," Bessie told him, looking over his shoulder, "He's already in here."

"Oh, well, maybe later." He swatted her on the behind and released her, looking down at his son.

"When you cook Sunday dinner tomorrow, you better fix some extra," he said.

"What in the world for?" she wanted to know.

"Cause we'll need it Monday," he said. "We're going on a trip over to Blairsville."

Staring at him questioningly, she asked, "What in the world for?"

"To look at a place Bill Floyd told me about. It sounds pretty good and I want you to go with me. We'll take the wagon and supplies we'll need. If we can't stay all night with these people, we'll camp along the road. It'll be an overnight trip, since it's nearly fifteen miles one way."

A little bit stunned by this sudden offer, Bessie considered it for a full twenty seconds. She hadn't been that far from home in nearly a year and that was to a funeral of an uncle that she hardly even knew, but went only for her mother's sake. That was the only time she was away from Law and home since her marriage. Not that this didn't have it's merits, she would love to get away for a day or two and all the objections that come to mind soon dissolved into nothingness.

The one objection she voiced was, "But Hon, Monday's wash-day." Everyone knew Monday was wash-day; that was common knowledge all over the country. All women had that day set aside for the sole purpose of doing the family wash and nothing could or would change it.

"The world won't come to an end if you don't wash on Monday," Lawrence retorted. Do it on Wednesday or Thursday or leave it 'till next week. The clothes will still be dirty."

Since Bessie wasn't that fond of washing anyway, she wasn't that hard to convince and she did relish the idea of going someplace different for a change.

"What about Leonard?" she said, "He's too little to make a trip like that. He'd be fussing all the time."

"We'll leave him with Sidney. They're always wanting him over there," Lawrence told her. "Him and Reuben will have a good time together. It won't be a problem."

So, the matter was settled and they each began making plans on what to prepare. Lawrence noticed that Bessie was humming as she worked and felt happy about going.

There was a nip in the air as the wagon rolled out of the yard on Monday morning. They were both bundled up in heavy jackets and warm clothes, to ward off the chill of the early autumn. Bessie also wore overalls and had a horse blanket over her knees. All these clothes would only be needed for a few hours, until later in the day when the sun come out. Then it should be very pleasant, indeed. Neither of them really needed the extra wraps as they started out, since loading and preparing the wagon had raised their body temperature considerably. But, once the wagon was out on the road, that would change and the extra protection would surely be welcome and it would be hours before the sun afforded any great deal of comfort.

Sidney and Lottie had been happy to have the boy, Leonard, yesterday for a couple of days and in return he seemed to be just as happy to be there with Reuben.

It was a good three hours before sunrise and Bessie couldn't understand why anybody would leave home so early until her husband explained it to her.

"It will take most of the day to get there," he said. "Riding horse-back would be a lot quicker but, if I rode, then you couldn't go now, could you?"

"No, I'm not going traipsing around over the country on top of no horse," Bessie replied. "Why I couldn't sit down or walk for a week."

"That's why we're taking the wagon and that's why we're leaving so early," Lawrence explained. "It'll take most all day to get there and I want enough daylight so I can go around over the place and see everything good in the daylight. I won't buy a pig in a poke. I want to go over everything. We can come home the next day and not have to leave so early, see!"

So, they had gone to bed early, just after dark the night before and were up at the appointed time. Now, the wagon jostled noisily along the rutted road, the springs creaking in the still, dark night. The big bay team moved along quickly pulling its burden effortlessly, having rested well and anxious to be on the move. A lantern glowed dimly from the upright pole fastened to the side of the wagon, just to the left of Lawrence. It was not designed for the purpose of lighting the way, because very little light reached out more than six or eight feet in any direction It served merely as a beacon or warning to any other traveler who might be traveling along the same road. It was highly unlikely that at this time of night this may occur, nevertheless, the possibility was there. As a further precaution, a cowbell dangling on the side rang loudly whenever a wheel hit a rut or other object in the pathway. Not that this was of any great value, because each time a bump was hit the occupants in the wagon knew it immediately, anyway.

For Bessie, it was a rather long and tiring day, what with the bouncing and jostling around on the wagon seat, but, being healthy, young and exuberant, it might be considered almost delightful. And it was never boring. The young couple talked together about many things that had seldom been discussed before. Law pointed out objects and the people that lived in them. He knew most folks and considered them to be friends.

Just before dawn a cold, damp chill and dark quiet pervaded the valley. In a little while the sky in the east began to turn pale. The lightening grew until it pushed the darkness away, and was followed by the glow of the autumn sun rising over the treetops. The warmth of the sun was more than welcome to them, and before long Bessie and Lawrence shed much of their extra outer garments, causing them to relish the bright new day.

After crossing on the old wooden bridge over the Little Fox River at mid-morning, Lawrence pulled the team off the road under a giant sycamore tree, commonly used by travelers and passersby.

He fed the horses a small bit of grain and let them drink the cool, clear water from the stream. Bessie, with solid ground under her feet, walked back and forth in the shade of the tree, stretching her legs, until her husband was ready and then offered him a sandwich made of smoked ham, set between two slices of thick, home-made bread. They ate silently for the most part, Bessie savoring the circulation being restored in her aching legs and Lawrence for a more fundamental reason, to be on the move again.

Although this was the main road, running east and west through the Bottoms and normally well traveled, only a few wagons and horsemen were out on this day. Usually, people stopped to pass the time of day but Lawrence had more important things on his mind than carry on a lengthy conversation about the weather or how his crops were doing and merely spoke and waved cordially. Bessie perhaps, would have relished talking to people for awhile, since her social life was practically nil and she did enjoy talking, even to strangers, but she too was anxious to arrive at their destination.

The road began to rise slowly as it meandered along the edge of the foothills. Soon they could see out over the valley between the smaller trees. Small houses and cabins spotted the countryside with plots of corn ripening in the cleared fields and livestock grazing among the trees. There was a lot of virgin timber here, mostly scrub oak and elm and sycamore not worth logging for profit. Some day probably this whole valley would be cleared and put under cultivation. That prospect was many years away. On the higher ground, the leaves were beginning to take on the annual fall colors. The oaks and hickory and maples cast off the yellow hues that they were noted for and in another two weeks the hillsides would be brilliant with red and gold.

The road continued along the outer rim of the valley, gradually rising upward until it reached the Blairsville Road. Here they turned south, going through the village of Springerton , named after the founder. Springerton was a community of some thirty or forty homes, two stores of general merchandise and a feed store. Situated atop a hill of a modest incline, the ground beyond was considered the up-lands for the next three or four miles until it reached the downward swing back into the same valley.

Bessie sat up a little straighter on the wagon seat, going through Springerton. She smiled and waved to folks outside the stores and in the yards. Her greetings were returned by people whose awkward, shy response was often mistaken for being backwards in their ways and yet friendly enough towards those who gave the first encouragement of greeting.

"This is a nice place," she remarked. "The people are friendly."

"People are friendly, most ever place, if you give them a chance," Lawrence told her. "Sometimes it takes somebody else to show the first signs of friendliness. I'm glad you like it here, because if we buy that farm, this is where we'll do most of our trading."

Bessie smiled. "You mean we haven't got much farther to go?"

"Two, three miles, I reckon, 'cording to Bill Floyd."

The roadway on the higher ground was hard and more firm so that very little dust escaped from under the horses' hooves or the wheels of the wagon. The vehicle squeaked and jostled on the rough surface. This road, commonly known as the Springerton Road, stretched from Springerton through the village itself and on to the Fairfield Road, some eight miles distance in all, thus connecting many otherwise isolated roads and neighborhoods.

The mile long stretch, along the lower part of the hills, going back down into the valley was so gradual that it was hardly noticeable. Reining-up the horses, Lawrence stopped the wagon in the middle of the road and looked around in all directions.

"This must be where we turn off," he said, satisfied with what he saw. "'Cording to Bill, this has got to be Haw Creek School over there." He nodded towards the one room building over to the north of the road where children were playing in the yard and then back to the other side of the road. "And there's the house on the southwest corner. And down the road there about half a mile where them wagons are would be Blairsville. So, we're just about there," he concluded with a flick of the lines across the horses backs, geeing them at the same time, heading down the narrow tree lined road to the south. After a quarter mile and the last crossroad, they turned left just a short distance from the clearing with the Quigley farm.

Both of the Reynolds were wide awake and alert now, coming closer to the house and surrounding vicinity, taking in every detail. There was nothing outstanding or particularly impressive about the place and yet each seemed to be drawn to what they saw. The low roofed house and all the outbuildings were constructed of logs, with minute detail given to endurance.

Two mongrel dogs came running out to greet the strangers, barking furiously. A loud command from one of the sheds quieted them and they walked around the wagon, sniffed the wheels and trotted off, in search of something more interesting to occupy their attention.

A young man, though a little older than Lawrence, came across the yard as Lawrence helped Bessie down from the high seat.

"Howdy, I'm Tom Quigley," he said, extending a hand that gripped Lawrence's own in a firm hearty grip. As most hands were, that had been accustomed to years of holding plow-handles and axe-handles. "You must be Lawrence Reynolds and his woman, from what Bill Floyd told me the other day!"

"That's right, I'm Law Reynolds alright, and this is my woman, Bessie."

Tom Quigley grinned as he shook hands with Bessie. He was a pleasant enough young man and both the Reynolds liked him at once. Bessie smiled shyly and rather awkwardly at the introduction, not being accustomed to meeting new folks.

"Let me call Maw," Tom said and called loudly, "come on out here Maw, here's them folks I was telling you about the other day."

An old woman came out of the house and walked toward them, eyeing the company up and down as she did so. She moved slowly, with a slight limp due to rheumatism in her right knee. Gray hair hung down over one side of the face, from beneath a bonnet whose strings were untied and hanging loose. She was a thin woman, but far from frail and at first glance appeared to be much older than she really was. Her advanced age was not entirely in years, being just only on the dark side of fifty, but in the years of long, hard labor.

Wiping wet, callused hands on the dirty apron about her, she smiled as she drew near and Bessie realized that the woman's son favored her vastly in that respect. They both had the same friendly, infectious smile, and she noticed too that Mrs. Quigley had nice, friendly eyes set in the wrinkled face when she smiled.

"I'm glad I happened to be here when you came so I can show you around the place," Tom said. "I didn't know when you'd be coming or if you'd even come at all. Bill Floyd just said he knew somebody that's looking. I live over there a ways on the up-land. I got a farm there. I come by every day or two to check on Maw to see if she's all right."

They talked a few minutes and Tom, seeing that Lawrence was anxious to get on with it, suggested they go in the house first and then the two of them go outside and look things over, knowing, that that was mostly where Law's interests were.

Naturally, he wanted to see the house, but after a few minutes he was satisfied. He did admire the way the house was built, solid and strong to last for many years to come. There were four large, spacious rooms with the living quarters much larger than the rest. In this main room, there were two fireplaces which provided heat in the winter, located on opposite sides of the room. It was much better than most log houses of the day, perhaps because the man who built it was more of a craftsman, working in timber and wood products all his younger life and also because he took pride in his work. When the last two rooms were added onto the first original ones some years later as the family grew, there was no noticeable difference between them, the work was so well done.

Reluctant to spend any more time inside, Law went back outside, leaving the two women folks to discuss whatever it is that women like to discuss. He could tell that Bessie had fallen in love with the crude house and had many questions to ask.

There were no barns, in the general sense of the word, as we know barns, but several low roofed sheds in diverse sizes, all constructed of logs, neatly stacked atop of one another and fastened together by notching the ends. Some had two sides open, while others were closed in on all four sides with heavy doors on home made iron hinges. Each had its own use and purpose for being there. Lawrence inspected each one, asking questions as to the purpose of each one.

After having received answers to each of his many questions, he decided there was an out building for all of his needs for a long time to come. A long structure, open on the south side to receive the warm sun in the winter, would shelter all of his meager number of live-stock, at least for the time being until his holdings began to grow, as he planned they would. A long, open tool shed next to this was large enough for all the farm tools that he now owned. There was also a grain shed and tool shed for smaller garden and carpenter tools and a poultry house. Off to one side was the pig-run, situated so that rain water ran away from the rest of the buildings.

"Your Pa was quite a carpenter," Lawrence remarked on one occasion, with a sweep of his hand to include all the buildings.

"He was, at that," Tom Quigley returned proudly. "He could build just about anything, given the material and time to do it in. He never did like to hurry. He always said if a job is worth doing, it's worth doing well. He learned most of the trade he knew about while logging. He helped build a lot of the saw-mills that used to be around here and some of the loggers cabins, before he decided to give up logging and settle down to farm. It's a shame he didn't have the time and money to go into the construction business. He probably could've done pretty well."

"It 'pears to me like he did pretty good with what he did," Lawrence said. "He might have been happy doing something else, since this seems like what he wanted?"

"I guess you're right, maybe," Tom agreed. "He had a pretty good life, he just worked too hard, that's all, and he expected us kids to work like he did. Lord I don't think any body could work like he did."

He gestured with a sweeping wave of his hand. "Take this field here, it looks pretty good now, don't it? Well, Paw like to've killed us all, digging stumps and hauling them over to the side and burning them," he said grinning. "And then plowing the ground the first time with all the roots and things to contend with. Lord Gawd, that was work. But, I ain't sorry for any of it. Paw was a good father and we always respected him and we learned how to work and do things."

They stood on the edge of an open field. Most of it was covered with tall weeds, but there was one small plot of tall corn. Law went to it and gazed up at its height.
"That's a lot taller and better looking corn than mine is, and I thought mine was pretty good," he said. The stalks and leaves were turning a golden brown and each stalk produced two large, firm ears.

"It's better than mine at home too," Tom agreed. "This is probably the best soil around here. I came down and planted this little patch. It's all the time I had after planting on my own place. We used to plant this whole field after it was cleared, when Paw was living." Pointing over to the west side of the field, he said, "Paw cleared most of that all by himself, after us boys got married and moved away. We'd come back and help him some, when we had time, but he done most of it. It's never been plowed, not really. Not deep down plowed anyway like it has to be to do good. That first time is going to be kinda' rough, with a root of some size every few feet, but it'll be worth it after the first year."

"See that stump over there, that's the last one that came out of this field. That's the one that killed Paw," he said sadly. "He shoulda' left it and plowed around it. It wouldn't have made much difference. But, if you knew Paw, you'd understand why it had to come out. He didn't want anything obstructing his furrow, so it had to come out."

They reached the huge object and stood there before it, each immersed in his own thoughts about it. What can be said about such a stump, except it's big or little, Tom Quigley had his own thoughts about it. His feelings were almost those of reverence. To Lawrence Reynolds it was an inanimate object that meant nothing to him until Tom spoke again.

"I drug it over here out of the way," he said, kicking dirt away from between two big roots that were exposed to the sun. I wanted to leave it here as a sort of memorial or monument to him. It seemed the least I could do for him, it cost him his life."

Lawrence had a sudden feeling of tenderness towards him and thought he detected some tears in Tom's eyes before he turned his head. Facing Lawrence again he was grinning, "Guess I got carried away there," he said.

"That's all right, sometimes I do too. Tell you what I'll do. If I buy this farm, I'll leave this stump right where it is."

"That's mighty nice of you to say that," Tom said with emotion, "But you don't need to do that."

"I want to and that's a promise I'll keep."

"Thanks, Lawrence. I hope you do buy this farm. I'd like to have you for a neighbor, and a friend," he added.

The pasture, which was encircled with a hand-split rail fence, was grown up with lush, thick grasses that had turned brown now with the approaching fall.

"There's enough grass in there to graze several cows and horses in the summer," Tom offered.

They continued to walk around, Law apparently smitten with what he saw, asking questions and receiving positive answers.

Finally, satisfied, they started back to the house.

"One thing I don't understand, Tom. Why don't you or one of your brothers move in here?" Law asked.

"That's a good question, but there's a simple answer to it. We've all got our own place and have had for quite a spell," Tom said. "Me and Kate worked hard to build up our place and we're satisfied with it and she don't want to leave it. My brothers and sisters feel the same way about theirs. We all decided that if we could get the right folks to buy this, who'd appreciate all that Paw did here and take care of it, that'd be the best thing to do. I personally feel you and your wife belong here."

"Thanks, Tom, I already feel like I belong. I bet Bessie will feel the same way too. We'll talk it over when I get back to the house."

It was easy to see that, after spending the last two hours or so with Mrs. Quigley, Bessie felt pretty near the same as he did about the place. The old woman, who by nature was slow to take up with strangers, had found Bessie almost like one of her own daughters and the two developed an immediate friendship. Bessie, who was outgoing and talkative after the initial introduction to anyone, usually became unreserved and very candid. This case was no exception. They liked each other and Bessie learned many things about the life of the Quigley family, about the beginning of the man and his wife and the long years of struggle and hard work and the hardships that accompanied such a life. It wasn't told as a narrative, but in bits and pieces along with explaining about various objects and items of furniture or fruit trees and gardening, etc.

"It's different from any place I ever saw before," Bessie said later when they walked around the yard alone to discuss the matter. "I've never seen a place with so many sheds and buildings and a nice big house and all made of logs."

"You mean you like it?" Law joshed, knowing full well what the answer would be.

After some discussion on the pro's and con's, very little was left in the matter of deliberation, so it was mutually agreed that they buy the Quigley farm.

Back in the house, when the matter of price was offered, Lawrence had a little difficulty refraining from quibbling over it and offering less than the asking price. After all, he was a horse-trader, just like every other farmer and man in the county, and couldn't give in too easily. Trading or buying wasn't done that way! He knew the asking price was a fair one and rather than agree at once, he began to dicker over how to pay for it. The Quigley's however, were agreeable to his offers and Bessie breathed a sigh of relief when the deal was made. She was afraid that her, usually head-strong husband might argue with these nice folks about the price being too high and embarrass them all.

They shook hands on the deal, all around and that was as binding as any signature on any piece of paper. When the debt was paid off, the deed would be turned over.

"Maw is the one you have to deal with and make payments to," Tom explained. "She's still the head of the family."

Shaking the hands of Lawrence and Bessie once more, he prepared to take his leave. "I'm glad we'll be neighbors," he said. "Well, I gotta get home and do my chores. They won't get done by theirselves. My boys are a help, but still too little to depend on all together." Kissing his mother on the forehead, he went out to the waiting horse that had been eating grass during the long stay.

There was no question about them staying the night. "I reckon you'll be wanting to get an early start back home in the morning," the old woman said, as more of a statement than question. When Law assented, she said, "You two'll sleep in that room. I'll fix some vittles, while you take care of your horses. There's feed in the long barn, help yourself."

Lawrence was grateful of the fact that he lived in a place and time when folks shared their food and lodgings with others. This was just considered a matter of common practice and courtesy in the rural areas of the day and much more comfortable than having to make a camp alongside a lonely road.

After tending the horses, he returned to the house to find the two women busy with the supper and chatting about things that held no significance whatsoever to Law. The fare was very simple, but satisfying and adequate.

"I like your Tom," he observed once during the meal.

"Pears he must like you, too," Tom's mother returned, "Else he wouldn't've let me sell you the farm. He don't always cotton up to some people if he don't like them. There was a man come by the other day that acted like he wanted it. Tom didn't like him and wouldn't let me sell. Tom said the man didn't understand all the work that went into it and he didn't want him for a neighbor. There was another family come out from town and Tom didn't like them either. So, I reckon you and him will get along."

While the women went about doing the dishes and cleaning up, Lawrence sat down in one of the big chairs and regarded the room reflectively for the first time. The original dirt floor had long ago been covered over with rough, oak boards, worn smooth by years of wear from many feet running and walking back and forth. Boards a trifle smoother covered the walls, hiding the log exterior and making the house a little homier looking.

Although all the furniture was hand made by Jeff Quigley himself and durable enough to last a life time, it lacked a lot in comfort. The coarse covered corn shuck cushions helped immensely, but there was

35

no softness under them, just plain hard wood. The cane bottom chairs were much better. The long table they had eaten at was scuffed and worn, with sturdy benches on either side. A wood burning cook stove had replaced one of the fireplaces for cooking meals. When this had been purchased and placed in the section of the room serving as the kitchen, Mrs. Quigley felt as though a great burden had been lifted off her shoulders. This added luxury was a thing of beauty and extravagance to her, for a long time to come and she had used it extensively during it's early years, cooking things that had been forbidden to her in the past. She especially liked baking bread in the big oven and became quite adept at mastering the craft.

The bed on which they slept that night was a duplicate of the one beside it. They were made of oak, like the other pieces in the house. The side rails, notched out on the ends, fit snugly to the head and foot boards, holding the bed firm and solid. A very thick straw-tick served as springs and mattress over the solid portion of the bed.

A hand braided rug on the floor separated the two beds. A wild cat hide adorned one wall and a hand painting, apparently done by a child, across the room were the only efforts of decoration. The only other furniture was a crude chair and a wash stand with a pitcher of water, leaving very little room to move around in.

Shortly after sunset, they retired for the night. Despite the fact that they were many miles from home and in a strange bed in strange surroundings, Lawrence and Bessie slept like the proverbial log, probably due to the long tiring wagon ride.

Going home took about the same length of time as the day before going in the opposite direction. The sun was setting, because, having left home so much earlier it pushed their arrival that much later in the day. The trip home seemed shorter as they each had so much on their minds, such as things to do and plans to make.

Passing through Springerton again, Bessie sat a little straighter on the seat than before and acknowledged the greetings of the few early rising residents who were up and about. Feeling friendly towards these people came automatically, knowing this is where she would be doing most of her scanty trading in the future. She liked this little town, situated on the hillside, with its maple and walnut trees.

Once out of the town they turned westward on the main road, for the long stretch across the valley. Gradually, they began to talk intermittently, not so much to each other or at least not expecting answers, but mostly to themselves, like thinking out loud.

"Hon, did you see that vegetable garden plot?" Bessie said thoughtfully at one time. "Why, that's big enough to feed an army. Looks like I'll be hoeing weeds all summer."

"I reckon they had to raise enough to almost feed an army when all the family was home. That sure is a big one though," Lawrence said, "You'll have plenty to do alright."

"And all them fruit trees. There's all kinds of them and you know how much I like fruit," she went on. Back where they lived there were several good sized orchards but they consisted mainly of apples and peaches. "We'll have apples, peaches, cherries, and red and blue plums and pears and there's a quince tree. I never ate a quince but, I'll bet they're good, and there's plenty of grape vines too." Stopping to think for a minute, she said, "You know Hon, I'm goin' to be spending a lot of time hoeing in the garden and canning. I hope Mrs. Quigley leaves that nice big stove, I could do a lot of canning with a stove like that."

Her husband laughed. "I think she will leave it, it's so big, her kids don't need it," he said. "That garden is too big for us. We'll plant about half of it in vegetables and put the other half in sunflowers for chicken feed. Don't count too much on all that fruit. I know there are two or three of each kind of tree, but they're old and I imagine by now the fruit will be kinda' scrawny. Oh, there'll be some alright, but we'll hafta' replace them trees the first chance we get."

"Hon, do you think she'll leave some of her furniture?" Bessie asked.

"Probably leave some of it, I reckon." It ain't too comfortable though, not like our own. Even with that thick straw-tick on it, that bed was hard with no give to it."

Bessie giggled. "It was kinda' hard wasn't it! I like springs on my bed so I can sink down a little bit. I slept good tho', didn't you?"

"Yeah, I was tired."

They rode along in silence for awhile, then Law began to plan, half aloud with Bessie paying little attention to what he was saying, engrossed in her own private thoughts.

"You know what I'm going to do. I think I'm going to buy me a team of mules and sell these horses. Oh, maybe I'll keep one more to ride and use with a buggy that I'll buy some day and to use for light work around the house," he thought out loud. "I know this man over around Horse Creek and he said mules is all he uses because they're stronger, and can work longer and can take the heat better and everything. Yes sir, that's what I'm going to do, just as soon as I get moved and settled.

Maybe even before then if I come across a good looking team." He pondered this until it was settled firmly in his mind, then on to the next phase of thought, excited at the prospect of the future. "There's enough land there already under cultivation to last me a couple of years maybe, but I aim to plant all that next year and clear off all I can and then the following year I'll have more to plant. I aim to keep clearing and planting and then buy more land if I can." He had big ideas and meant to carry them out.

"There is one thing about moving," Bessie interrupted his train of thought. "We'll be an awful long way from home."

Law laughed, "When we get all our things over to the new place, we won't be a long way from home. We'll be home! That's where we'll live."

"I know, but you know what I mean," she responded sheepishly." We'll be so far from our folks and all. I've never been away from them very long at a time before. I won't hardly ever get to see them."

"Thunderation, Bess, you don't hardly ever see them anyway," Law retorted. "It's just in the next county. Not like moving to another country, or even another state. They can come visit us any time they want to and we can go visit them whenever we want. Nothing will change that much."

"I know, but fifteen miles seems like a long ways." She sat brooding a few minutes, then brightened, "I guess I was just being childish," she smiled. "After all, we'll have a new life in a new home, won't we Hon?"

"That's right, you should be happy."

"I am," she enthused. "I can't wait to get in our new home. When are we gonna' move?"

"Just as soon as we can, but it'll take a while to get every thing over there."

When Law asked Sidney the next morning for help in moving, his brother was agreeable as usual. The conversation was taking place on Sidney's front porch, where many problems were solved and many other issues were discussed, some important and others not.

Lottie appeared in the open doorway and stood leaning against the doorframe, her legs slightly apart for support, for she was becoming large with their second child. Her first born, a boy named Reuben just under two years old, was playing in the yard. She sipped black coffee from a cracked granite cup. Her disheveled hair hung loosely around her face. She had grown up on a farm and was used to hard work, where the life will soon remedy any kind of beauty a girl may have had. Sidney and Lottie Hufstutler had married shortly after Law's wife Delcie died. They had lived in this rented three room house on the small farm from the beginning, where Sidney tried to make a living.

"Keep an eye on Reuben, will you. He's kinda' little to leave outside alone," she said and went back inside, knowing the boy played outside alone most of the time, but it was something to say.

Lottie was a large girl. Not large in the sense of being fat or over weight, but tall, about an inch more than Law and big boned. The kind of woman that birthed babies well. Her skin was already coarse and brown, as was the custom of most girls reared on farms at that time, when cosmetics and lotions were unheard of. Her facial features were rather attractive and she was a good wife to her husband.

Sidney sat on a straight back chair, leaning against the house. His feet were hooked over the rung of the chair and his legs being so long, pushed both knees up almost under his chin. Law sat in an old rocker next to him. It was a favorite spot to rest, visit and watch an occasional neighbor pass by.

The brothers sat watching the baby objectively for several minutes as he played in the dirt of the yard. He picked up a small stick, but dropped it almost immediately in preference to a hard shelled bug that happened to cross his path. Holding it in his open palm, he studied it very carefully until it crawled over and fell to the ground. Reuben bent to pick it up again when a large, more interesting subject came into view. The big Rhode Island Red rooster, that he longed to catch and play with and feel the coarse red feathers and big waddle came around the corner of the house.

Reuben began muttering to himself or to the rooster, one couldn't be sure which and tottered towards the subject with both hands out-stretched. The rooster chose to ignore him at first, until those little hands almost touched him. It half turned and walked along close to the house.

Sidney perked up and grinned, letting the front legs of the chair settle down on the porch floor. "One of these days that young'un is gonna' grab aholt of that big, red bird and get the day-lights flogged out of him," he said. "He keeps on trying every time he sees him."

Law started to get up to rescue the little boy. Sidney laid his hand on his arm in restraint. "It's all right, just leave him be."

"But that rooster could get mean and hurt him. It's as big as he is," Law protested, indicating the long talons on the back of its feet." Look at them spurs, it could tear him open."

"I don't think so, just wait and watch."

He rolled the chaw of tobacco around in his mouth to work out more juice, his eyes glittering in anticipation. He was grinning broadly by the time the rooster came along the edge of the porch with Reuben closing in. Sidney waited patiently until the time was just right and the quarry was directly in front and beneath him. Letting go with a long steady stream of brown liquid juice, it caught the unsuspecting rooster full on the side of the head.

It jerked its head upright in surprise at the sudden impact, looking in all directions to determine what happened. Then a strong burning sensation began in its eye as the acid flavored juices entered around the eyeball. Turning around two or three times, it bumped into Reuben, knocking him down. The big rooster began to twist and jerk and flop around erratically and run in circles, squawking in pain.

The bewildered little boy sat watching in fascination, trying to decide if he should cry. Realizing he was not injured, he rose slowly to his feet, with his diaper hanging precariously down around his knees. With a slight twist of his little body, the garment fell the rest of the way to the ground, leaving him standing in the morning sunlight, naked, pointing a finger at the antics of the bird, wonder and confusion in his eyes.

After perhaps two minutes, the big, red bird settled down. It jerked its head a few times, its wattle and comb swinging back and forth, then ruffled the feathers all over his body. When they had settled smoothly back into place, he drew himself up to his full height, his head high in the air, turning toward the porch, it stared at the two men. Satisfied or not satisfied at what it saw, it walked proudly away, clucking to itself.

All the while, the two brothers laughed uproariously.

"I think that's the funniest thing I ever saw," Lawrence said.

"Me too," Sidney laughed, wiping the sweat from his face with his cap. "I wasn't sure I could hit him just right, but it looks like I did. That tobacco juice must've burned like the devil."

Lottie came out on the porch. "What in the world is so funny out here?" she wanted to know. Before either man could answer, she spotted Reuben in the yard. "My God," she exclaimed, "What happened to Reuben? Why he's stark naked. What happened to his clothes?"

"He didn't have nothing on but a diaper," Sidney told her laughing, "And he lost it somehow."

"Reuben, go get your diaper and bring it here," she ordered.

The baby picked it up and brought it to his mother, grinning broadly.

When the incident about the rooster was related to Lottie, it lacked most of the humor of the actual event.

"I think we'd better have that bird for dinner Sunday, before it does hurt the boy," he concluded. "There's a lot of meat there, so Law, you and Bessie come on over for dinner."

Lottie nodded in agreement. It was always good to have someone for a visit and a meal, and she and Bessie had become good friends, though they didn't get together nearly as often as their husbands.

Law spent the next few days repairing his equipment and preparing things to move. Moving his belongings wasn't going to be the major problem that he had anticipated, mainly because he owned a lot less equipment and furniture than he realized. Not being married and on his own long enough to accumulate a great deal of possessions, he supposed he should be thankful that he had so little. Once in his new home though, he could begin the building process in earnest.

When he decided that he was ready, he notified his brother, who brought over his own wagon. Loading equipment, such as plows, harrow, disk and other tools on one wagon, it added up to a pretty full load. A few pieces of furniture they didn't need and the remainder of knick-knacks made up the other load.

After it was all loaded, at least what was going on this trip, the two men sat on the edge of the back porch, drinking black coffee.

"My Gawd, Law, you ain't got much more in this world than I have," Sidney said.

"I know, but I aim to have a lot more than this afore long," Law returned. "Just you wait awhile until I get going on my new land. I'm going to have me a fine place over there, soon's I get more land cleared."

He took a big swallow of coffee. "I'm through renting," he continued. "From now on it's all down hill."

"It don't sound like down hill to me," Sidney exclaimed. "It seems to me you're just to go up hill with all that work you been talking about."

"Sure, there'll be a lot of work but all I do from now on, will be for me, not on somebody else's property. I'll be working for my own future.

You know, Little Brother, maybe you ought to buy a place of your own and quit renting. Some day you'll have it paid for and it'll all be yours."

"I reckon I'll buy a place some day," Sidney said thoughtfully. "It's hard to save any money right now though, for a down payment. It takes everything I make just to keep going."

"I know it's hard, but it don't take a whole lot," Law declared. "Why I bet you could find a pretty decent place for two or three hundred down. In fact, I know you could. My down payment wasn't much more than that so, I know you could do it. I aim to have mine all paid for in three or four years."

"It sure sounds good," Sidney said. "Maybe I'll do it."

"I hope so, 'cause if you don't you'll just be a poor dirt farmer all your life with nothing to show for it."

Sidney stood up and stretched. "I better get home and do my chores, 'fore it gets dark," he said. "I'll see you in the morning at sun up."

That night Law and Bessie went over their plans again.

"Me and Sid will take these two loads over in the morning and come back the next day. If the old woman has moved, then we can finish moving right away. If she hasn't, I'll find out when she is leaving and we'll know how to plan," he explained. "At least, we'll have this much out of our way and won't have much more left. I figure one wagon load will do it. All we'll have is what little furniture is in here and the chickens. We'll put them in crates and tie the cow on behind the wagon. Just be you and me and the boy."

"What about the corn, you ain't going to leave that are you?" Bessie asked.

"Lord no! We wouldn't have no feed or seed for next year or nothing. I'll come back and pick it up in two or three weeks when it's ready. I'll put some sides on the hay wagon, it's bigger than the other one, and haul what I can in two trips over to the other place to use. I'll sell what's left for cash money to live on this winter. In the spring we'll be ready to start fresh."

"You're not leaving the pigs, are you?"

"No! I'll have to make cages and put them on one of the loads of corn," Law replied. "I'll keep the old sow for breeding and two others to butcher this winter. Sid can have the other two for helping me."

It was late afternoon when the two brothers reached the Quigley homestead with their wagons. Going down the lane, before even reaching the house, Law could see it was deserted and he felt a pang of relief at the prospect of being able to return with Bessie and Leonard, at once. He reined up in front of the log house and got down.

Sidney stopped behind him. He had taken in the buildings and all the surrounding landscape as he came in and liked what he saw. He pushed the cap back on his head and jumped to the ground.

"By Gawd, brother, it looks like you done all right for yourself," he exclaimed, with enthusiasm. "I like this here spread. Look at that there log house! I always wanted a log house. I'll bet it'll be plenty warm in winter time."

"Law looked around outside and then knocked on the door, just to be sure there was no one here. When there was no answer and he noticed the heavy lock on the door, he turned away.

"Looks like Mrs. Quigley has already gone," he said to Sidney. "Guess we might as well go unload these wagons."

While they were unloading, Tom Quigley rode up.

"I saw the wagons when they turned the corner back there and figured it must be you," he greeted Law.

Law shook hands and introduced the two men.

"I'll help you unload the tools out here and then we'll put the rest inside the house for the time being," Tom said. "Ma left day before yesterday so, the place is yours. I've got the key to the front door."

Law found that several pieces of the rough oak furniture were still in the house.

"Ma took all she could or wanted," Tom explained, gesturing around the large main room. "Whatever's left is yours, if you want it. If there's something you don't want, you can get rid of it. All us kids have got all the furniture we need, but Ma said, since you and your wife are still young, maybe you don't have everything you need yet. I will say though, I took a couple things I wanted to save and of course we already moved all the tools and equipment."

The main thing that caught Law's attention was the big cook stove, the one Bessie liked so well. It was still in place.

"Bess will be tickled about that stove," he said grinning. "She's been hoping your Ma'd leave it."

"It's been a good one over the years. I guess Ma has cooked and canned tons of food on it. It's too big to move and besides my sister, the one that Ma's living with, don't need it. I'm glad your wife wants it."

There were two other items of note. One was the long table where the family had eaten and the other was the bed where Law and Bessie had slept. That last piece would have to go. He remembered how uncomfortable it had been and he liked his own better. Sidney ended up by taking it home with him when they left the next day, since he liked that type of furniture.

After the business at hand was settled, Tom said, "I gather you fellers will be going back to your homes in the morning!" When Law assented, Tom said, "Well, come on up to the house when you get ready and have supper with us. I know you're hungry and Kate wants to meet her new neighbors."

Sidney was more than anxious for a good meal and they agreed to go as soon as they cleaned up a bit.

"Good! You go back down this road and instead of turning at the corner, go on straight. It's about half a mile at the top of that long hill. You can't miss it," Tom directed. "You can't see it from here because of the trees."

Riding towards Quigley's later, after having washed up a bit, the two brothers felt starved and in need of good nourishment.

"That Tom Quigley seems like a nice feller," Sidney remarked. "I like him."

So do I," replied Law. "I think we'll get along good together as neighbors."

"You know, Law, I like here," Sidney said. "I like the lay of the land. This is gonna be a great place to live. I think maybe I might come over when I get time and look around. Maybe I might find me a place."

"I wish you would, Little Brother," Law said sincerely.

"I'd like to have you closer. I'll keep an eye out for a place. There should be several abandoned farms scattered through the Bottoms."

The Quigley farm seemed to be pretty much what Law expected, everything was neat and orderly, only the house wasn't as large. There was a large barn and two smaller sheds. Beyond that, the trees obstructed the view. The house itself was typical of the time and region, small, three rooms and built of rough-hewn clap-boards with a small porch on both the front and rear.

Inside, the house was neat and clean, and smelled of good, wholesome food cooking. The furnishings were plain, but strong.

Law would learn later the reason that Tom didn't want the heavy oak furniture of his mother's was because Kate absolutely refused to have that rough, hideous stuff in her house.

Kate said, "I'm glad to meet you Mr. Reynolds; Tom talks so much about you."

Law replied awkwardly, "Me too, but my name's just plain Law."

Kate was a little shy at first, not being accustomed to having strangers around. She soon warmed up to the guests and grew talkative and encouraged Law and Sidney to eat more. They ate heartily and Law liked the woman, as they became friends. He felt that she and Bessie would likely become good friends also, though there would be little opportunity for visiting and developing a close friendship.

Law could never guess the ages of children, though the three Quigley's, two boys and one girl, were small indeed, in the early grades at school. As could be expected, they showed signs of discipline and good manners. They watched the two strangers shyly from lowered heads, not having much to say.

Wanting to get back to his own place before dark, Law made ready to leave as soon as the meal ended. They both thanked Kate for her hospitality and went outside with Tom.

"We'll be leaving at first light in the morning," Law told him. "Hope to be back here with my family to stay, in a couple of days."

He thanked Tom for all he had done and they shook hands all around.

Later, in bed, lying in the pitch darkness of the log house, Sidney said, "I mean what I said Law about moving over here. If you hear of a place, anything at all, let me know, will you?"

"Sure, Little Brother, I'll find you a place," Law said drowsily.

Within a week, the Reynolds family was settling into their new home. Bessie was happy as a lark, humming, slightly off key, putting things in order, realizing this would be her permanent home from now on with no uncertainty about having to move again. Owning a place gave one such a nice feeling of security!

Law was just as happy with his prospects. Now that he owned his own place, he answered to no man. It would take a long time and much hard work on his part to get things in order, but he was a determined young man and he set about the task before him with vigor and aplomb.

There was a woods down the road, west of Law's house. He was passing these woods one day when he espied an object setting back among the trees that he had not noticed before. The leaves falling from the trees had left a small cabin exposed to view. He went down the narrow lane for a closer examination. Sitting there among the vines and brush and brambles was a small cabin of sorts. Drawing nearer, Law knew it had once been a dwelling for someone. It appeared to have been abandoned for some time from the growth around it. Walking around the building he ascertained that it had indeed been home for some one. Four windows allowed light and ventilation, two on the front, one of which was broken and one on either end, with none in the rear. However, a door was fastened on rusty hinges that opened to the outside world, with no porch. The front did have a very small porch, in need of repair. The house itself sat up off the ground on cinder blocks, two high, and open underneath. The roof, being corrugated tin, was rusty in spots, but all in all, it seemed to be firm.

Pushing open the solid frame door, he entered the main room, kitchen and gathering room, pulling the cobwebs away. The floor was littered with papers and broken glass. The other room was much the same. Law surmised this served as a bedroom. Tar paper and newspapers covered the walls of each room. He decided that a broom, a bucket of soapy water and scrub brush, along with a large amount of elbow grease would almost make the place livable.

The two sheds outside didn't amount to much, but could serve as shelter to animals for the winter, until something better was built. There were also some signs of a garden in the distant past.

That evening he paid a visit to Tom Quigley. Tom was not aware who the present owner of the property was.

"The man who built the cabin was a logger, named Bert Faust. He worked in the swamps with my Pa," Tom told him. "He married a girl from over Carmi way, I think. They had a baby and then one day the girl and baby both caught the fever and died. Mr. Faust moved away when the logging business died out. I don't now what happened to him after that. Later, another family lived there for awhile, but I don't think they owned it because they left after a short time and it's been sitting empty ever since. Clem Hurley over at the Blairsville store'll know. The store has only been there three or four years, but ol' Clem keeps up with ever'thing that goes on around here. Ask him! If he don't know, he'll know who does."

Clem Hurley was a thin, hawk beaked man who liked a bit of gossip or information and was willing to share what he knew. He eyed Law over the top of his spectacles as he entered the store. When Law told him his name, Clem stuck out his hand after wiping it on the side of his pants.

"Ah, yes, you must be the young feller that bought the Quigley place," he said. "Wondered when you'd come by. Heard all about you."

"Been pretty busy, getting settled," Law replied, embarrassed. "I haven't needed anything from a store yet."

"Don't feel bad about that, young feller. I understand! Folks only come in when they're in need of something I've got." Clem said. "Look around and if you don't see what you want, just ask for it. That's what I'm here for. Always glad to help out."

Law looked around at the well-stocked store and decided he'd have to bring Bessie by, one day soon. There was plenty here to interest her.

"I'll bring my wife in afore long," he said. "I don't aim to buy anything today. I just want some information. Tom Quigley said you could give it to me."

"Tom's a good man. I hope I can help you. What is it you need to know?"

"Well, there's a cabin in the woods, just west of my place and I wonder if you know who it belongs to," Law said.

"Yes, I know the place. You're not interested in that, are you?" Clem asked.

"Not for me," Law replied. "My younger brother might be, though. He's looking for a place over here in these parts. He likes it around here and aims to farm some. Do you know who owns it?"

"Reckon I do, maybe, but there's nothing there to farm. It's just that woods and no other land to do anything with."

"I guess he could rent some ground from somebody or hire out," Law replied. "He's a hard worker, and a man would be lucky hire him. Will you tell me who owns it?"

The store keeper studied thoughtfully for a full minute, then said, "I guess I'm the man you want to talk to."

"You mean you own it?" exclaimed Law.

"Well not exactly, but I am authorized to rent or dispose of it any way I choose," Clem informed him.

"I don't understand!"

"Let me explain it to you," Clem said. "Bert Faust bought the land and built that cabin on it way back in his logging days. He got married and they had a baby. After awhile his wife and baby both died of the fever. Bert stayed on there for a while, but never remarried, at least not while he was around here. When the logging ended, he moved on. Me and him had worked together off and on and got to be friends. Before he left, he came over to my house one night, that was before I had this one, and said that he might come back sometime. Never came back, though!

He said if I ever collected any money from it for rent or anything, I was to keep it for him and one day he'd come by and we'd settle up."

"Well, I did rent it out one time. It was to a deadbeat family that never took care of anything. They stayed there a couple years and I did collect sixty-two dollars from them, all together. I've still got it, too! They skipped out one day, taking everything that wasn't nailed down tight. That was three or four years ago. When I heard they had left, I went over there to look at the place. When I saw the condition they left it in, I decided I wouldn't rent it any more. I'd just wait until I heard from Bert and see what to do with it."

"Well, a couple years ago, I heard that Bert was dead, killed in an accident down in Arkansas, so," Clem continued, "I guess I'm still in charge of that cabin and woods. I never heard of any relatives he had."

"It looks like you own it then," Law remarked.

"I don't know about that," Clem said, "But I guess I am still responsible for it until I find out something different."

"Will you rent it to my brother?" Law asked.

"Yes, I reckon I will. You look like an honest, upright young man to me and I've heard good reports about you. If your brother is anything like you, I think it will work out alright."

"What about rent?"

"Tell you what I'll do," Clem said. "If your brother will fix it up and take care of it, he can have the first year free. After that, we'll see what can be worked out. Does that sound fair to you?"

"It sounds more than fair," Law said. "Can he take over right away?"

"Sure! It's been sitting empty too long now. If somebody doesn't get in there soon, it'll be beyond repair."

Bessie was happy that Lottie would be living so close by. She was already missing the companionship of her sister-in-law and friend. The following week Law went back to his old farm to harvest his corn crop and relate the news to his younger brother.

Sidney was jubilant about the prospects of moving and slapped Law on the back in thanks.

"You better not thank me until you see the place," Law told him. "You may not want to move there."

"I guess if you recommend it, it'll be good enough for me," Sidney proclaimed.

"Wait a minute now, Little Brother," Law advised, " I didn't say I recommended it. I only said you might want to look at it. It's gonna take a lot of work to even get livable."

"That's good enough for me," Sidney repeated. "As soon as we finish picking our corn, we'll move."

Law knew there was no use in trying to dissuade him, so they planned accordingly. After helping each other harvest their corn, they prepared to move Sidney and his family and belongings.

Lottie and little Reuben were made as comfortable as possible on the floor of the wagon among the bedding and cooking utensils, with pieces of furniture piled high around them. It was not a pleasant ride for her because of her condition. The constant jar and jolting of the vehicle gave little solace to her body, and Sidney stopped often to ease her aching joints and stomach.

They went directly to the home of Law and Bessie, for darkness had already fallen. Although it had only been three weeks since Bessie left home, the two young women were overjoyed at seeing each other and had much to talk about.

The following morning, Law took his brother down to view his new home. Sidney looked with his mouth agape at the structure before him.

"My Gawd, you wasn't kidding when you said it needed some work, was you?" he exclaimed.

"I tried to tell you not to get your hopes up. But look Sid, we can fix it up pretty good. Me and Bess will help."

Sidney never stayed daunted for long and his sense of humor returned and he grinned.

"Well, I guess there's only one way to go from here and that's up!"

He and Lottie stayed with Law two more nights while the cabin was made livable, then they moved their things in and settled down. The women worked mostly inside, scrubbing and cleaning and giving it the feminine touch while the men repaired doors, floor and roof. They even found a replacement for the broken window.

After that, they all settled into their own normal routine, each helping the other when needed.

CHAPTER 3

Bessie Reynolds was baptized into her role as a mid-wife a few nights later.

They were awakened from a sound sleep by loud yelling and pounding on the door.

"What in tarnation is that?" exclaimed Law, sitting upright in bed. "Sounds like Sid yelling."

"It is Sidney."

"What's wrong with him? Why is he hollering like a wild Indian?"

"Stop and think a minute and you can guess what's wrong."

She jumped out of bed and went to open the door. Sidney stood there, out of breath, pale and excited.

"I guess I know why you're here, I can tell by looking at you."

"Yeah, you'd better come quick. Lottie's time has come."

"Let me get dressed."

"Hurry!"

While she and Law dressed, Sidney paced back and forth across the big room, urging them to hurry.

Walking as fast as possible to the house in the woods, Bessie told Sidney, "When we get there, you saddle up and go get Mrs. Hunter.

She's a mid-wife who lives about a mile away and she already knows about Lottie. She just don't know when." As an afterthought, "No, let me check with Lottie first, before you go. It may not be time yet and we don't want to drag that old woman clear over here for nothing."

Going into the bedroom and seeing Lottie lying on the bed in her convulsive state, she knew that even now was too late for Mrs. Hunter. She appeared to have already begun her contractions.

The two brothers crowded into the room and stood gawking, first at Lottie on the bed and then at Bessie, expecting her to know exactly how to handle the situation.

Lottie moaned loudly, pressing both hands down hard on her swollen stomach.

"Shall I go get Mrs. Hunter?" Sidney asked.

"No, you fool, it's too late for that. You should have done that hours ago. Or at least come and got me!"

"I know that now, but I wanted to be sure before I bothered anybody," he replied meekly. "You got to help her Bessie."

"My Gawd, Sidney, I never delivered a baby before. I never even seen one born. All I ever saw was calves and horses."

"Well, I don't see why a baby would be any different. They all come out the same way don't they?"

"You idiot," she exhorted. "A woman is a lot different than horses and cows. She's your wife and we need to get that baby out of there as easy as possible, but I sure Lord don't know how. Reckon it will just come natural once it starts. From what I hear, nothing can hold it back then."

Lottie uttered a cry of pain and grabbed Bessie's hand, squeezing it firmly.

"Oh, help me, Bessie," she pleaded and Bessie knew then that it all depended on her.

"All right, you two, get out of here. Go outside, I don't want either of you in the house," she ordered, "And don't come back until it's all over. No, wait Law! Put some more wood in the stove and stoke up the fire. And put a kettle of water on it. I'll need it hot afterwards."

Sidney picked up Reuben, who had been crying in the doorway, and took him outside. After Law had a brisk fire going, he joined them on the porch.

Bessie found some clean rags in a box that she felt might be needed and sat down on the side of the bed, taking Lottie's hand in hers. Her hand was hot and her pale face was sweating profusely.

"I'm sorry Bessie that you got stuck with this."

"That's all right, we'll manage!"

She grimaced with another spasm of pain. "Do you know what to do?"

Bessie started to lie, then decided the truth would soon come out anyway. "No," she admitted, "I've never seen a baby born before."

"I'm sorry it had to be you and there wasn't Mrs. Hunter," she paused squeezing Bessie's hand. I'm not sorry either. I'm glad it's you Bessie.

"Me too, Lottie. We'll make out all right. Just tell me what to do when the time comes."

"I won't have to tell you. When it comes out, just wash it off real good. I won't be able to. Besides it'll come natural to you. It won't be long. Maybe some day I can help you with yours."

Bessie felt she should examine her and raising Lottie's gown was the most embarrassing moment of her life. She had never looked at another woman like this before. Her face turned flame red with self-consciousness. Lottie smiled at her discomfort.

"It's all right, Bessie. Don't feel too bad, I felt the same way the first time I went through this. When this is over you'll be a real live mid-wife."

For some unknown reason they got tickled and held hands laughing as two giddy school girls at a private joke. This seemed to set off new constrictions in Lottie's body.

The brothers looked at each other incredulously in the dim light thrown out from the lamp inside the house.

"What's wrong with them crazy women anyway?" Law said.

"Must not be too bad, if they can laugh like that."

Immediately, the laughter ended and the painful ordeal began. From that point on, they could only speculate as to what was taking place inside. Bessie talked a lot, probably out of apprehension and they understood very little of it.

"You go ahead and yell all you want to, nobody can hear you, but them two on the porch and they sure as dickens don't count. Go on and holler. It'll make you feel better and maybe relieve the pressure some."

They sat on the edge of the porch, listening silently. Sidney jostled Reuben up and down on his knee. He pulled a plug of tobacco from a pocket and bit off a good-sized chaw.

"I wonder if I should go fetch Mrs. Hunter?" he mused.

"Wouldn't do no good. By the time you got there and roused her up and hitched up her buggy and drove back here, it'd all be over."

"Reckon you're right."

"Don't worry, Bess'll take care of her."

"But, she's never done that before."

"I know, but she learns quick."

Another scream! "Oh Bessie, it's going to kill me. I don't think I can stand it!"

"Yes you can, Hon," came as assurance. "You can do it. Go ahead and holler, it'll help."

Law slid off of the porch and walked down the lane, disappearing into the darkness. He had to be alone at a time like this, it brought back so many memories, both pleasant and unpleasant. Sitting down on a stump, it all came back to him and he re-lived that long dreadful night some three years earlier when his beloved Delcie died while giving birth to their son.

As he so often did, Law sat and reflected on the past. Hearing the screams of pain from Lottie did that to him.

He sat quietly, letting the events and memories of them flood his mind and being. Delcie's face swam before his eyes, so sweet and delicate. He had never seen anyone as beautiful. He fell in love with her that first day he saw her in her father's office and that love would never change, even in death. Knowing that her parents disapproved of him as a son-in-law, he tried even harder to be successful in farming. They envisioned their daughter, with her superior education and more desirable back ground, being married to a young man of wealth and similar circumstances. It hurt their pride when she settled for a poor farmer who had nothing whatsoever to offer but himself.

Law could never fully understand this because he worked harder to give her happiness than anyone else ever would. And when they were courting, he always walked up to her door and escorted her out to the buggy, not like some of the better educated beau's who sat outside and yelled or whistled for her to come out.

As much as the Graves' disliked Law, they arranged an elaborate wedding in the First Baptist Church in Belle Prairie. It was the social event of the year and Delcie was extremely radiant and happy. Law's own family was somewhat less exuberant, feeling out of place in such lavish proceedings.

They were very happy during that short time they had together. Law worked very hard to be a good husband and give his wife some of

53

the things they wanted and she, in return, was a good wife to him, maintaining a spotless, well organized household. She was an excellent cook, often concocting fancy dishes that he had never even heard of.

Perhaps their greatest joy came when she discovered she was going to be a mother. Her own mother and father, however, did not share in their enthusiasm. Mrs. Graves, being aware of her daughter's delicate body, feared for her well being. Law worked even harder and helped in the house work as often as possible to relieve Delcie of much of the burden. They laughed and joked together and made plans for the future, happy beyond reason.

Two weeks before the baby was due, Mrs. Graves persuaded Delcie to come home to her house where she could take care of her and monitor her condition. With some reluctance, she and Law agreed that it might be better that way.

When the time arrived, the Doctor as well as an experienced mid-wife were present. They had been at the house all day, waiting. Only the baby survived that difficult birth.

Law, who was waiting in the swing in the yard, couldn't believe it at first when the doctor came out to notify him of his wife's death.

He said simply, "She didn't make it son. She just wasn't strong enough for child bearing. You do have a fine son, though. He's healthy."

Law was dumbfounded and didn't know what to say. He felt so sure everything would go along so well. He'd only heard Delcie cry out once, but of course, she was not one to exhibit a display of emotions. She would suffer alone and in silence.

The Graves held Lawrence totally responsible for the death of their daughter and never spoke to him again after that night. They also blamed the baby, who in their eyes was just as much to blame as the father. One would think that grandparents would covet the baby and want it as a small compensation in their daughter's memory. Not the Graves! They were through with everything that bore the Reynolds name. As far as anyone knows, they never saw Leonard again.

A scream from the house brought Law back to the present reality. In that moment of re-awakening, he was glad that the boy was staying with his own mother and sister, Lucille.

Walking slowly back to the house, it came to him that as much as he had loved Delcie, she was dead and he must forget her and the past. She could never live in a log house in the way he was doing now or couldn't stand the rigors and hard work that lay ahead to get things in order. He was not one to live in the past and for the first time in a long while, he felt a burden lift from his shoulders.

He thought of Bessie, alone in that room with Lottie and the responsibility that lay in her hands. He suddenly realized that she was a good wife and felt a certain tenderness towards her. Lord knows she isn't as pretty or dainty or quiet as Delcie or as good a housekeeper or knew how to cook fancy dishes but, she was strong, resourceful, energetic and kind hearted in her own disconcerting way. In other words, Bessie was almost the ideal helpmate for all the work that lay ahead.

Sidney, still sitting on the porch with Reuben cradled in his arms, sleeping, asked, "Where have you been?"

"I just wanted to be alone for a spell, I had a lot of thinking to do" Law replied. "I guess nothing has happened yet?"

"Nope!"

Then the real labor began. They heard Lottie groaning loudly.

"Bessie, don't leave me. Promise you won't leave me here to die!"

"Of course I promise not to leave you. And you ain't going to die. Just settle back there now and get busy. We have to get that young'un out of there."

"Oh Gawd, it hurts. I think it'll kill me."

"Why even a baby squirrel couldn't get through there."

"Oh Gawd, Gawd, Gawd."

"Go ahead and yell, it'll help."

"Damn that Sidney for getting me like this. Damn him anyway! Oh, damn, damn, damn. From now on, he can sleep in the kitchen. He'll never get in bed with me again."

Sidney grinned sheepishly, glad that his brother couldn't see his face in the faint glow from the lamp inside.

"Come on, Lottie, I can see it starting to come out," Bessie said urgently. "Press hard, hon, push."

Lottie grunted and groaned loudly.

"Oh, it hurts. Damn, damn, is it out yet?"

"Not quite. Keep pushing. Oh, it's coming. There it is. It's out, hon."

Law and Sidney got up and walked out in the yard seeking the cover of darkness.

After awhile Bessie stood in the doorway, hair hanging loosely about her face, holding a disheveled bundle in her arms.

"You can come in now. It's a girl," she informed them proudly.

The baby girl was named Gertrude, after an aunt of Lottie's. Inevitably, she was dubbed Gertie, or sometimes just plain Gert. She grew to be an exuberant, happy, rollicking girl who enjoyed life to the fullest.

Lottie soon forgot her promise to keep Sidney from her bed. She later gave birth to eleven more children and ten of the total of thirteen, lived to reach adulthood and middle or old age.

The episode spread around about Bessie delivering the baby and she became the focus of attention when babies were due in the neighborhood. While she was naturally proud to have been able to help Lottie who was her sister-in-law and whom she loved, she was far from anxious to become a mid-wife for anyone else. She vehemently resisted bringing a new life into the world for several reasons. One being, it was some one else's instead of her own. She would like to have a child she could really call her own but would never be able to. Another reason, when a baby died in childbirth as they often did in those days, she felt responsible. Even when the mother died, as they frequently did. She would dream of that still, lifeless mother for many nights afterwards. So, when asked, Bessie always referred the mother-to-be to Mrs. Hunter, who everyone knew and trusted. On occasions when the older lady was not available for some reason or other, then she provided her services. There were times when she provided her services to assist Mrs. Hunter if the delivery was expected to be a difficult one.

The years ahead were good to Lawrence and Bessie in many ways. They worked very hard and prospered accordingly. The farm grew in size and value, as did their reputation. The Reynolds name became one to be reckoned with and respected. Many came to him for advice, as time passed, and also for money when crops failed. If his crops failed, which only happened once or twice, everyone else's did also and hard times hit the valley. But, often, others failed when his flourished. He seemed to have a certain knack for knowing when to plant his corn and wheat and exactly when to harvest. He rotated his crops so that the earth didn't become sluggish and stagnant and he plowed deep, one of the many secrets to good farming.

Good hired help was always plentiful when it was needed, and Law took advantage of those who were willing to work for wages. He hired Sidney when he was available. After his first good crop, he was able to begin to clear more of his land. It was hard, back breaking work, but most men were accustomed to that sort of life. Gradually, trees were cut, stumps dug up, land cleared and put in cultivation and money crops planted.

Sidney gained himself a nickname that he carried for the rest of his life. He took Reuben with him to the Blairsville store one day. Now, the little boy was fond of licorice sticks. When he spied a box of that candy in the display case, he immediately began to wail.

"Lickrich, Poppa, lickrich, Poppa," the boy pleaded, as he only recently learned to talk.

His father ignored him at first, but Reuben grew insistent, pulling at Sidney's pants leg.

"Poppa, lickrich, lickrich Poppa," he fussed while gazing longingly at the delectable candy.

Sidney grinned to himself and teased, "You don't like that candy, boy, it's not good for you."

"Yes, Poppa, I want candy."

"I don't think you need it. You'd just eat it and then you wouldn't have it any more."

The boy looked dubiously up at his father and contemplated this illogical argument. Not completely understanding and in no way deterred, he set up a new wave of entreaty. Finally, after some ado, Sidney relented and handing the store-keeper a penny for the slender, black, twisted stick of gummy goodness. He held it in his hand observing the texture. Reuben watched his father impatiently, with his little hand out stretched and his mouth drooling.

"Tell you what I'll do, boy," Sidney said. "I'll put this in my pocket and if you can get it out, it's yours." So saying, he stuck it in the front pocket of his overa1ls.

Reuben's eyes lit up in anticipation as he grabbed the side of his father's pocket and yanked downward. But, the pocket was too high for him to reach down inside. Standing on his tiptoes, he pulled and struggled, all to no avail. He just wasn't quite tall enough!

The other three or four customers in the store watched his antics with some amusement. Holding onto the pants leg, Reuben tried jumping up and putting his hand into the pocket at the same time, but lust couldn't quite reach it. Becoming frustrated with a sense of chagrin and anger, his eyes filled with tears.

"Pockets too high," he blurted out. "High pockets, Poppa!"

Sidney gave in then and took the piece of licorice from his pocket and handed it to his son. Reuben held it in his hand just long enough to admire this delicacy very briefly before sticking one end of it in his mouth and biting down on it. Pulling at the other end, he managed to extract a large chunk of it into his mouth. He smiled, as he savored the delicious juices that emitted from it.

The onlookers were still smiling, when one of them said, "By George, you know the boy is right, Sidney. You have got mighty high pockets."

When the others studied the tall frame, they agreed that he did indeed have mighty high pockets in his overalls.

They all laughed good-naturedly and the name stuck. Before long he became known as High Pockets Reynolds.

When their third child was born, Sidney decided to move. There was no more room for growing in the very small house and it was difficult trying to make a living on the small acreage. They moved to a larger farm over near Springerton, where they remained for several years and where most of their brood came into the world.

When the elder Mr. Reynolds died, it left Lawrence's mother with a huge burden. Two children under working age still remained at home and were dependent on her. A daughter Carrie who had contracted infantile paralysis at an early age was her main concern. Being confined to a wheel chair and crutches limited her chances for earning a living in her own right. However, the Gods were smiling on the family and provided a way.

Mrs. Reynolds heard of a small hotel for sale in the village of Ina, some forty miles distant, south of Mt. Hebron. Having had plenty of experience of being around people, her family mainly, and cooking and cleaning, she felt qualified for that part but knew nothing of the business end.

Lucille, the oldest of the children had more education than the others in her family and possessed a certain aptitude for figures and a good business sense. Persuading her mother to sell the farm and live stock, it provided them with enough money to purchase the hotel. It proved to be a profitable venture for the mother. Not profitable in the sense of monetary value, perhaps, but it gave them all a home and security.

Carrie soon found her own independence when a telephone operator was needed in the village. It was an opportunity well suited for her. Renting a nice house on the main street that ran east to west, a switch-board was installed and she became the telephone operator for the community for many years to come. She later bought the house, where she lived until her death. To supplement her meager income,

Carrie made ladies fine hats which she sold at reasonable prices to ladies from all over the county, making her independent of any other support.

The hotel, which was a large two-story house, provided many drummers traveling through the area with a night's lodging. Mrs. Reynolds did the cooking and she and Lucille served, washed and cleaned. Lucille also managed the books and records and the money, what little there was. Occasionally, they took in a boarder for a few weeks. Sammy helped clean and ran errands. It all worked out very well.

When Lucille heard that her brother Lawrence was going to live in a log house, she immediately sent word to him to bring little Leonard to the hotel to live, at least through the winter. As she would have argued, everyone knows how draughty and cold log cabins are in winter. Bessie was reluctant to give up the boy, even for a short time but, Law had no such qualms. He said, they had a lot to do and could get along for awhile much better with him out of the way. In the end, Leonard went to live with his grandmother and aunt and uncle for a short time. He would not return home for nearly five years.

Shortly before Leonard's eighth birthday, his father sent word to send him home. He figured that the boy was now big enough to help with the chores around the farm and with all the work that Bessie was saddled with, she needed some help. They had grown very fond of him in Ina and he had become helpful around the hotel. They were reluctant to lose him but, had no choice in the matter. Leonard was even less anxious to return home to live with his father and stepmother. He hardly knew either of them any more except by name. Having spent most of his young life with his grandmother and aunt, it had become home to him. Though the big rooming house was not a real hotel in the literal sense of the word, it had been a happy place for him. Lucille assigned small chores for him to do, such as running errands, carrying out garbage, bringing in fire-wood and dusting the furniture in the big main room of the building and other things a small boy is capable of doing.

It was a cheerful, happy place for a small boy. He met many people, those who spent a night each time they passed though town. They were mostly drummers, selling their wares to local businesses and just happened to end the day in Ina. Leonard loved sitting off to one side of the room, listening enthralled to the experiences of these world travelers in the evenings after supper. Most salesmen remembered the little boy from one trip to the next and often brought him a bit of candy, which he loved and looked forward to. He even went to school and learned his three R's before returning to his real home in the country.

Back on the farm, he soon became accustomed to the hard work as he helped his mother with the many chores assigned to him. He learned to milk a cow and feed the pigs and chickens. He also learned to work in the garden and draw water from the well, though at first the bucket was so heavy he dropped it back into the well twice and it had to be fished out. The first time his father spanked him for his carelessness. The second time Bessie retrieved the bucket herself and never mentioned to her husband.

As Leonard grew in age and stature, so did his work and responsibilities. Thus, he became a farm boy in the truest sense of the word.

At least one of Lawrence's predictions came to pass when he paid off the debt early to Mrs. Quigley and owned the title to his farm. He also bought a span of fine mules for the rigorous work, a feat of which he was proud, but others thought foolish, since they had always used horses or oxen, mules being too ornery to be dependent.

The time came when Law needed more acreage for his crops as the number of livestock grew and he wanted to enlarge the buildings. The problem of course was finding farm land close enough to work without having to travel too far. Most of his neighbors were satisfied and unwilling to sell.

He waited, a little impatiently, until one day Muley Seles happened to stop by. Muley owned the forty acres adjoining Law's farm on the west and hadn't heard that Law was looking to buy. In conversation, he mentioned that he was thinking of selling out and going over around St. Louis to get a job in one of the factories there. At once Law became alert. He began questioning Muley without appearing too anxious.

"You wouldn't want to buy it, would you, Law? It'd make a nice addition to your place!"

"Well, I don't know," pondered Law, hardly believing his good fortune. "I might be if the price is right."

"If you think you'd want it, we can come to terms on the price," Muley said.

"Why are you wanting to sell out?" Law wanted to know.

"I'm tired of farming and working my tail off," Muley told him. "And what do I get out of it! Work seven days a week from sun-up to dark and after and I just keep getting deeper in debt and all worn out. My wife too! She ain't had a new dress or pair of shoes in a coon's age."

"Why would she need a new dress? There's no place to wear it except maybe church and a woman don't need new clothes just to show off on Sundays."

"That ain't the point Law! A woman likes something new to show off once in a while. It helps her ego or something, whatever that is."

Not wanting to queer the deal before him and maybe losing the sale or upping the price, he refrained from further disagreement and let the matter drop.

"You say you're going to get a job in a factory of some kind?" Law asked.

"Yeah! My wife's cousin works in one of them chemical plants in Granite City. He says he can get me on there, too. It'll sure be nice only working ten, twelve hours a day, five, six days a week and having all that other time off to do whatever I want to, and getting good wages for it too. And not have to worry about if it's going to rain enough this year, or rain too much and ruin my crops. Or wade out in the middle of the night in a snow storm to see if my chickens or calves are all right." A dreamy look came over his face. "Just think, I'll have nothing to worry about 'cept laying in bed as long as I want on Sundays thinking how to spend all that money!"

Law gazed at the man dubiously feeling a touch of sympathy, but again kept still for fear of causing Muley to change his mind. He found it hard to imagine anyone giving up farm life to move off somewhere in a city to work indoors for wages, totally dependent on someone else for their livelihood. Such a thought had never entered his mind before. He decided to drop reasons for Muley's leaving and get back to the business at hand.

After some discussion, a price was set and Law readily agreed, because it was even lower than he had figured. He went down and checked the place over, already knowing it to be worth more than he had agreed to pay. The small house and meager outbuildings were irrelevant to him; all he wanted was the land. That acquisition added considerably to his farm because, most of it had already been cleared which would save him money and weeks of hard labor.

Over the next several years, Law acquired other pieces of land, some of them adjoining his own, while others were as far away as a half mile. Most were small homesteads where families lived and either gave in to hard times or just decided to relocate. It became known that he was always ready for a quick loan and he became a sort of lending bank to some of his neighbors. He was shrewd in his dealings and required some form of collateral or compensation in return. This came in various forms, such as good animals or a piece of machinery or work that he needed. Always though, the loan was for much more than the worth of the collateral, giving him the edge in the transaction.

As the bottom rails of his fences began to rot and deteriorate thus allowing the animals to get out, he replaced those rails with a flat faced barbed wire. Eventually, all the pasture was enclosed with the wire fence instead of the rails, fencing the livestock in much more safely and worry free.

The long sheds also were gradually replaced with finished lumber and corrugated metal, making them more accessible and convenient to use. Then went the log barn. It was dismantled, cut up into firewood and replaced with a large modern barn that would make any man proud to own. A long alleyway ran through the center with stalls on each side. A large grain bin built half-way in the middle made it easier to transfer feed. There was a hay loft overhead with loading doors and hay hooks at each end and windows all along the sides of the barn on hinged doors to allow good light and ventilation. Law was proud to show it off and he often sat and marveled at his accomplishments.

Through the years Law and Tom Quigley remained close friends. They stopped to pass the time of day when meeting on the road, to inquire after the health of the other's family or about the other's crop or ask or give advice concerning a certain problem. And they often lent a hand to each other in time of need. That friendship however, was stretched almost to the limits when Law decided to demolish the log house and replace it with a modern, up to date home in keeping with the better homes in the area. Barns and sheds for grain and livestock have always been more important to a good farm than a dwelling for the family, so the house was to be the last major improvement after all others were completed.

When the out buildings were replaced, they were done so by allowing much needed space for a larger garden and yard. Everything was moved well away from the house that would then sit back aways from the road, which wasn't there when the log cabin was first built.

The simplest and easiest way to get rid of the house was to burn it to the ground. Being all wood, there should be very little debris to move or clean up afterwards. So between Law, Bessie and Leonard they moved all their belongings from the house and into one of the larger sheds, where they planned to live while the new house was being built.

Carpenters were scheduled to begin work as soon as the rubble was cleared away.

Law decided the best time to burn would be day break when dew covered the earth. Flying sparks were not likely to ignite other buildings in the dampness. There would be no breeze and the air being so light, it offered very little chance of the fire spreading.

One morning, up on the hill, the Quigleys got up at their usual time. Going outside to draw a fresh bucket of water, Kate stopped in her tracks, halfway to the well. Down in the bottoms, some half mile distant, a bright red glow filled the sky. At first, she thought it was the sun rising. But no, this glow was in the west. Turning, she saw that the sky was beginning to pale for dawn in the east where it should. Horrified, she realized that it came from the Reynolds home, though it couldn't be seen through the trees. As she watched, flames and sparks shot skyward.

Screaming at her husband, he came stumbling out onto the porch and stopped, staring at his wife and then saw the fire.

"I think it's the Reynolds place," she said. "Come on, we'd better get down there and help them."

Tom stiffened and walked out in the yard. His jaw set and anger filled his eyes. He made no effort to obey his wife.

"Come on, Tom. The whole place will go in a few minutes if we don't help them."

Tom stood gazing out across the tree tops as flames grew higher, and still he did not respond to his wife's plea.

"What's the matter with you, Tom? We've got to help them," she urged. "They're our friends."

Still he did not move, standing there stolidly. "For crying out loud, what's wrong with you any way?"

Kate said exasperated. "Are we going to go help them or not?"

"No," Tom replied. Kate was flabbergasted! "No, not now!" She gaped at him. "For what I might say or do to him, if I saw him right now."

His voice was shaking as he turned and walked out to the barn. "I'll go down later in the day."

Later that morning he hitched up the buggy and he and Kate drove down to the Reynolds farm. Law and Leonard were busy with shovel and rake, moving smoldering wood into little piles of flaming embers. They were doing the job, as there would soon be very little to show for the efforts put out. Since wood left hardly any ash, it would be easy to dispose of the remnants of the house, leaving nothing to show it had ever been there.

Tom sat for a long moment, staring at the dying embers and at Law, and a trace of tears filled his eyes. Kate got down and went inside the shed with Bessie. They seldom had a chance to visit.

"I thought you were my friend," Tom said quietly.

"I am!" Law replied.

"No, you're not or you wouldn't've done this."

It was for this very reason that Law had refrained from telling Tom he planned to torch the old log house. There was too much sentiment in the place for Tom to handle ahead of time and Law was determined to have a new house, so to him at least, it was the sensible thing to do.

"I had to get rid of it to make room for a new house!"

Tom got stiffly out of the buggy while looking at the great expanse of openness. "I knew that you was doing this when I saw the fire this morning. I couldn't believe you'd stoop to this."

"I'm sorry I had to do it this way Tom, but there just wasn't any other way. You should see that."

"You didn't have to burn it down. There's nothing at all left, this way. I'm glad Ma isn't still alive to see this. It'd just about kill her."

"Hell's bells, Tom," Law exploded. By now he began to get rankled. "What'd you expect me to do, preserve it in a can of oil or something? Logs just don't last forever. The bottom ones on the ground had rotted and I sure as thunder couldn't replace them. Before long the whole place would've fell in."

"It wasn't that bad." Tom argued. "It still looked pretty solid to me."

"It was so that bad. You said yourself you was born in it and you're more than forty years old. They don't last forever."

"I still don't think you had to destroy it. That's the last thing my Pa built and now there's nothing left. You already tore down all the other buildings he made."

"If you thought so much of the confounded place, why didn't you keep it and live here?" Law retorted.

" I would've but Kate didn't like it. I thought you'd take care of it."

"I did take care of it all these years I've lived here, but I have to move on. I paid for it and it belonged to me. I can do what I want with it. I know you had a feeling for it and I understand that, but it served its purpose. I sure as devil didn't want that old monstrosity sitting in my front yard blocking my view."

Their voices had become much louder now than before and luckily this heated discussion was brought to an end by Bessie's vociferous voice as the two wives emerged from the shed.

"That's enough out here," she told them sternly. You two are acting like a couple of little school boys, yelling the way you are."

The surprised men looked at her. Kate nodded in agreement. "I agree with Bessie. Why don't we go home Tom and end this visit right now!"

The men glared at each other sullenly. "You all come for supper tomorrow night," Kate invited.

After awhile Tom realized it was no longer any of his business what happened, but being stubborn as most men are, the subject never came up again. The incident was more or less forgotten. The new house had a hip roof and gables, a far cry from the square, dreary contrast of the log house.

Leonard was twenty-one years old when Mabel Stanton came to work for the Reynolds family. She came from over around Mill Shoals, not far from where Law and Bessie were raised and was hired as a housekeeper and helper. With very little housekeeping attached to the job, she was expected to keep the house in order. It was mostly a jack-of-all-trades sort of job, job description being unheard of in those days. A person hired, automatically knew it to be for whatever needed to be done. On a farm there was plenty to do besides straightening up a house that would only get messed up again.

By this time, Law had two hired men working almost steady, especially during the planting and harvesting seasons. Besides, he often had additional help so, this required more help for Bessie as well because of the extra cooking and cleaning. The two steady men lived on nearby farms and walked to work and back home again each day.

Bert Schulty was a wiry, thin man somewhere between forty and fifty years old. Being a hard worker, he stood perhaps five feet, nine inches tall and walked with short quick steps, his arms held almost rigid at his sides. He lived across the field over on the main road.

Clint Wheeler, the other hired hand, was tall and thin, nearly six feet, three inches. He had a long, swinging gait, long steps, stretching his arms out before him as he walked. He lived about a quarter mile up the hill behind Bert. Since he had to pass the Schultz home, he whistled as he approached and waited for Bert to appear in the doorway. Then the two walked down the long lane together in the early dawn light. Though they looked odd walking along together, they were good friends and worked well together. The two always ate dinner at the Reynolds house, as did all others who did work there.

Mabel Stanton had grown up in Mill Shoals and never lived on a real farm. But, as most girls of that time, she learned to cook, sew and clean house at an early age. This being considered by many as a formal education, though Mabel did attend the local grammar and high schools and achieved a certain amount of knowledge of the outside world.

Being a willing worker, she tried hard to please, this being her first real paying job. Bessie let her have a room, all to herself, since the job required full time employment. She was expected to be available at all times if needed. The salary was minimal but, she had room and board, which to Law's way of thinking was substantial. Plus the fact that she got to go home for four days each month! Her duties were varied and wide spread. Besides helping to cook, wash dishes, wash dirty clothes (on the board) and hang them out, she also helped can fruits and vegetables, worked in the garden, fed chickens and gathered eggs and slopped the hogs, helped milk the cows and did any other chore that came along.

A normal day for the women began well before dawn when they got up and started a fire in the cook stove and cooked breakfast as the men arose and prepared to start their own day's work. Usually, Bessie and Mabel milked the cows and returned them back to the pasture across the road before doing the dishes. On busy days, they often left the breakfast dishes all day until after supper. The day seldom ended for them before well past sunset when they fell into bed, dead tired.

Leonard had lived a somewhat lack luster existence, showing little interest in the opposite sex. He attended local barn dances, along with other young men of his age and knew most of the neighborhood girls. None stirred any physical desires in him however. None, that is, until Mabel Stanton came to live and work in the Reynolds home. He was truly smitten with her the day she arrived in her father's buggy. Her father delivered her along with the few belongings she brought and left immediately thereafter.

Leonard just happened to be coming in from the field when he saw the buggy pull into the yard. Though knowing that his father had hired a girl to help out with the housework, he was reluctant to meet this one after seeing her standing beside the buggy. His first impulse was to hurry inside the barn before being spotted, but he did not move fast enough.

"Leonard, come on out here and help this young woman with her things," Bessie shouted, loud enough to be heard clear up on the hill.

Changing course, he walked slowly out to meet the new arrival. By way of introduction, Bessie merely said, "This here is my boy Leonard. Grab them things and take them in the house."

Them things consisted only of one valise and a couple of cardboard boxes, which he picked up and carried into the house, barely glancing at the girl. Just feeling her presence there was enough for him to feel uncomfortable. Quickly, he put the baggage down at the appointed spot and went back out to the barn to contemplate this new addition to the household. He hated meeting strangers, especially girls. He felt inferior and clumsy around them. This one appeared to be different from all the others. Even though he hadn't looked directly at her during their brief encounter, he had seen her in his mind rather than his eyes. As he sat on a railing inside the barn, away from prying eyes, he visualized her in his mind. She was shorter than he, by at least two inches, which was a point in her favor. Being about average in height and rather slightly built, after his real mother, he often became aware of his size when in the company of girls, especially while dancing and being on the same eye level. He had noticed her height at once but, that alone didn't attract his attention. What impressed him even more was her shy demeanor. She hardly looked at him, whereas many girls would have smiled and exerted a false sense of modesty.

Supper that night proved to be another uncomfortable meal for Leonard. Almost unconsciously, he had washed his hands and even his face more thoroughly than usual and combed his hair down slicker. Eating in silence, only once did he dare look at the girl openly in an effort to form a mental picture of all her features in his mind. Her round cheeks were a bright pink and he couldn't tell if it was from a tint of rouge or from signs of shyness caused by being in a strange house among strange people. Deciding that the latter was more likely the case, he continued his evaluation. He noticed the bobbed hair instead of braids or the long hair rolled into a bun on the back of her head, as his mother wore. It accentuated the round cheeks and Leonard liked what he saw and he couldn't tell if it was from a tint of rouge or from signs of shyness caused by being in a strange house among strange people. Deciding that the latter was more likely the case, he continued his evaluation.

Bessie did most of the talking during the meal, which was quite normal for her, explaining the girl's duties and what would be expected of her.

Lawrence ate heartily and finishing his meal, ran his fingers over the handle-bar moustache he had grown over the years and pushed back from the table. Belching, he patted his stomach as a contented man and rose to his feet.

"Reckon you better get to bed before long, Boy," he said to Leonard. "Got to get up early in the morning, lot to do." Leonard's face reddened. He detested being called Boy by his father, when he had a real name. Glancing out the window, he saw it was barely dark. Going to bed early and getting up early was nothing new, he had always done that! His father enjoyed ruling other people though, it being a trait he'd picked up years ago while acquiring some of the lands he now owned. Leonard felt that his father liked loaning money to hard up neighbors and then taking over their farms when they couldn't pay back. It seemed to give him a feeling of power like nothing else could. Leonard knew all of Law's faults and tried to accept them as a son should and he never openly criticized him or talked back.

Leonard began daydreaming on the job, seeing visions of Mabel's face before him, in any direction, in any object he looked at. He found himself trying to hurry the mules in an effort to complete each task, so he could go to the house. But, once there, it became a difficult situation when he came face to face with the new hired girl. It was soon obvious even to his parents that a change had come over him. He wanted to change his overalls and shirt more than twice a week, which Bessie decried, as it meant more work for her. Washing his face and hands became a ritual that could hardly go unnoticed as he scrubbed these parts relentlessly to get away every speck of dirt before sitting down to eat. Lawrence would eye his son humorously, remembering the days of courtship with his mother.

Mabel seemed not to notice the change in Leonard, not having known him before this time, thinking his cleanliness was quite normal.

One morning, Leonard harnessed his team and was idly checking to make sure it was all right, when Mabel came out of the house and crossed the road for the waiting cows. He hurriedly ran over to help open the gate.

"Let me do that," he offered, swinging the gate back, and going around behind the animals, he drove them out into the road. He closed the gate and walked along beside her, driving the cows to the barn.

Lawrence, who had witnessed this display of chivalry, yelled out to his son, "come on, Boy. Leave the milking to the women folks, we got work to do."

Leonard blushed and without glancing at Mabel, he went back to his team.

When she went home for her time off, it was the longest four days of Leonard's life. He grew sulky and irritable.

One day while cultivating corn, his mind was miles away, immersed in his own private thoughts, known only to himself, but likely concerning Mabel. He was jarred out of his reverie by a shout from his father from across the field.

"Hey Boy, what in the tarnation are you trying to do over there? Get them mules back on track, before they plow up all our corn."

Automatically, Leonard jerked on the lines to stop the mules. Looking back down the field, he saw that he had plowed up two long rows of corn with the small cultivator shovels. Law pulled up his own team and walked over to his son.

"I'm sorry Paw," Leonard muttered.

"You better quit that mooning around and get down to business," Law admonished him.

"I don't know what you mean."

"Of course you do, else you're a danged fool. Everybody else knows what's wrong with you. That girl has been here for a whole month now and you ain't hardly said a word to her. You better get some gumption in you and take the bull by the horns before some other young feller comes along and takes her."

Leonard flushed a deep red. Flicking the lines over the backs of the mules, he pulled them back into the rows, anxious to get away from his father. His mind was in such a turmoil, he could hardly think straight.

By the time Mabel returned, he had determined to "take the bull by the horns and let the chips fall where they may."

When he asked her to ride to the store with him in the buggy, for a soda, she readily agreed. Since it was a Saturday evening, she wore her bonnet with an artificial flower on one side and tied with a ribbon under her chin to keep from blowing off.

The bobbed black hair that showed just below the bonnet accentuated the bright rosy cheeks. Sitting on the far side of the seat, she projected a very pretty picture indeed.

Leonard's pulse quickened when he saw her and helped her into the high seat and it continued to race for the rest of the evening. Setting his cap, the one he saved for Sundays, jauntily on his head, he mounted the buggy on the opposite side, careful not to dirty his clean overalls on the buggy wheels and settled on the seat as far away from her as possible and clucked to the horse.

The sun was still hot, though sinking lower in the west. Upon reaching the main road, they were facing the sun and the buggy top did little to dispel the heat rays. Moving along at an easy gait, the wheels kicked up puffs of dust that drifted lazily along in its wake. The three quarters mile ride to Blessey's store in Blairsville was made almost in silence, with an occasional idle comment about something of little importance.

Blairsville had grown somewhat since the old days when the Reynolds had first arrived. There were now at least a dozen houses in and around the community, with two stores, one across the road from the other and two blacksmith shops. All this was necessary to supply the needs of the surrounding farms.

Leonard hadn't anticipated so many other people having the same idea as he, about taking a girl to the store for a soda. But being Saturday, several young men came with the same thought in mind. There was quite a gathering in the village, divided between the two stores. Four or five families had also arrived to do their weekly shopping and trading, leaving the children free to romp and play with friends that they otherwise only saw at school.

Being more interested in those nearer his own age, Leonard's eyes searched out the few who had horses tied to hitch racks and buggies tethered in the shade. Pulling in between two other buggies that he recognized, he hobbled his own horse on Blessey's store side of the road. Helping Mabel down, his eyes roved over the young folks until he saw his cousin Reuben. He liked this cousin, who was just a little younger than he and they got along well together, though Reuben had a tendency to be a little more daring and out going.

The two spotted each other at about the same time and Reuben waved and came to meet the new arrivals, pulling along a young girl by the hand.

"Hi cousin," he greeted. "You ain't been sick or something, have you? I haven't seen you around lately."

"No, I'm all right. Just been kinda' busy, that's all," Leonard replied.

"Hey, that must be that new girl I been hearing about. I heard Uncle Lawrence hired a housekeeper."

"Yeah, this is Mabel," Leonard said embarrassed. "This here is my cousin Reuben."

Reuben whistled through his teeth. "Boy, she's the prettiest house-keeper I ever saw, course, I'm not sure what house-keepers are suppose to look like, but I wish my pa would get us one."

They all laughed, good-naturedly. He pulled his girl friend around in front of him. "This is Lorna, from over by Bedford. She's visiting some of her family over here."

Lorna was a tall girl, taller than Leonard but, not nearly as tall as Reuben, who took after his father, in that respect. Her dress was a little too short, showing the shapely calves of her long legs. The low neck line exposed the ample breast to the white that the sun never reached to tan. She had a jolly laugh that drew people to her but, she wasn't what you would call really pretty. All in all, Leonard decided, she suited Reuben to a T, because she had a forward, outgoing personality, the same as he.

While the two girls talked and got acquainted, Reuben pulled Leonard to one side, well out of hearing from the others.

"Say Leonard, after it gets dark, let's take the girls out to the woods," he suggested.

"What do you mean?"

"I mean let's all four of us drive down the road to a place I know, in the woods. I've got an extra blanket in the buggy I'll loan you."

"Do you mean you've done that before?"

"Sure, lots of times!"

Leonard stared at his cousin, dubiously.

"No, I don't think so," he replied.

"Why not? It'll be so dark we can't even see each other."

"Mabel's not that kind of girl. She wouldn't do that."

"How do you know if you don't try! Hey, I'll bet you have tried, haven't you?"

Leonard felt his face turn brick red as he turned away. "You did try, didn't you? I'll bet you already tried and she turned you down, didn't she. Come on, admit it. You can tell your ol' cousin. I won't let on, own up. Boy, that's really handy, living in your own house. Was it in the house or barn?"

Leonard turned to face him violently. "Shut up Reuben. That's enough out of you."

Reuben stared at him, aghast. "Gosh didn't mean to get under your skin that way. I just thought that living in the same house with a pretty girl, it would be natural to try to get next to her. I know I would."

"Well, I'm not you," Leonard retorted. "And I wouldn't try anything like that with Mabel."

Reuben stared at him curiously for a minute. The good natured grin returned to his face. "I'm sorry cousin, honest. I guess she is kinda' special to you, ain't she! I can sure understand why, she's a real pretty girl. Come on, let's go buy our girls a bottle of pop. You're buying, aren't you?"

He put his arm over the other's shoulder and Leonard felt his spirits rise and the happy mood that he'd felt earlier returned. When they reached the girls, Reuben was still grinning broadly, as he put his arm around Lorna's waist.

"Let's go inside and get some pop. My cousin's buying."

They entered the store and Reuben opened the soda cooler. Very little ice remained in it but, the bottles lying down in the water looked cool and refreshing.

"Do you like orange pop?" Leonard asked Mabel.

"Yes, that's my favorite."

"Good, mine too!" He pulled out two big bottles and opened them on the side of the box, handing one, dripping water, to Mabel.

"I like grape myself," Reuben said, dipping his hand into the water. "What about you Lorna?"

"Grape is fine with me," the girl replied, "But I like all kinds."

As they began to move off to the side, Leonard asked Mabel, "Do you like cheese?"

"Yes, I love it!"

"Do you want a cheese sandwich?"

"Yes, I'd love one!"

"We'd love one too," chimed in Reuben, "Wouldn't we Lorna?" and before she could answer he added, "we'd like ours between two big slices of bread."

Wishing to impress Mabel, Leonard complied with everyone's wishes and told John Blessey's wife Effie what they wanted. They all stood back watching as the store's owner sliced through the great loaf of white bread. Then turning to the chopping block on which lay a large mound of yellow cheese, she began the process of cutting off a large chunk. This chunk was sliced into layers of a quarter inch thickness and the cloth netting and blue mold around the edges was trimmed away and the slices placed on the waiting bread.

Reuben and Lorna went outside carrying their soda and sandwiches, while Mabel waited for Leonard. He pulled the snap-lock coin purse from his pocket and fumbled around in it for the right change and laid forty cents on the counter. Then the two of them went to join the others at the wooden picnic table under a maple tree. Although the sandwiches were delicious to the taste, the thickness caused them to stretch the muscles of the mouth to the very limits. And, they were extremely dry! After each bite, a drink of soda was necessary to swallow but, each pretended not to notice the other's predicament and laughed and enjoyed the time together. More young people joined them and the evening was carefree and pleasant.

Leonard was proud of his date, if Mabel could be called a real date. She stayed close to him and never left his side, showing no interest in any other young man, which pleased him very much indeed, knowing she was by far, the prettiest girl present.

The sun was sinking low in the west and twilight drawing nigh when he decided, with some reluctance, it was time to go home.

After helping Mabel into the buggy, he turned to see Reuben grinning mischievously at him.

"It'll be dark soon, cousin. Don't dally along the way," he called out.

Leonard blushed and climbed up beside Mabel. The setting sun was at their backs until they reached the turn-off that led home. The horse quickened its pace a little, knowing he would soon be home. Trees lined the half-mile of narrow road on both sides, all but obliterating the daylight. The sun settled down into a fiery red mass of magnificence. Darkness came quickly after that.

Trying not to think of what his cousin might be doing now, his mind was in a turmoil. Remembering Reuben's last words, he pushed them from his thoughts. Mabel uttered a weak laugh and moved closer to him on the buggy seat.

"Oh, it's kind of scary out here, isn't it! It gets dark so fast when the sun goes down."

"Yeah, it sure does, but there's nothing here to be afraid of," Leonard responded.

"I know! I'm not really afraid," pausing, she then said, "I had a good time tonight."

"You did, really?"

"Oh yes, it was fun!"

"I'm glad you had a good time. I did too. I was afraid you might not like doing that but, there's not much to do around here."

"Oh, I did like doing what we did. I liked your cousin Reuben and Lorna too. They were so much fun to be with. He's so witty."

He felt a tinge of jealousy, but let it pass! "Yeah, he is witty all right. Kind of forward and impudent some times. I like him though and we get along good together."

Mabel giggled. "Did you notice how they nearly choked, trying to swallow those sandwiches!"

"Yeah! They sure were thick and dry. I don't think any of us could have eaten them without plenty to drink. It's a good thing Blessey's has plenty of soda pop."

They laughed at the thought of trying to eat cheese on thick, dry home made bread, without the help of something liquid.

"Oh, I don't mean to imply that it wasn't good and I didn't like it because I did," she offered in way of apology. "But, I just think it was rather amusing the way we all struggled, thinking no one else noticed."

Leonard decided maybe they should try to eat something different and a little less dry next time, if there was to be a next time! He sincerely hoped there would be!

It was dark by the time they reached home. He wished the journey would last forever and almost resented the horse walking so fast the last quarter mile, when it realized they were getting close to home. Trying to pull back on the lines to check the forward motion without being noticed was to no avail. The stupid animal only seemed to walk faster, but perhaps it did take a little longer than he thought, for they did develop a certain sense of companionship and he felt very comfortable with her. They talked and laughed together, feeling happy and carefree. Each seemed almost disappointed when the buggy stopped in the yard, indicating the evening was over. Reluctantly, Leonard got down and reached up to help Mabel.

He longed to put his arms around her and hold her close but didn't dare. When she seemed to sway against him, as she stepped to the ground, he felt such a sudden rush of pleasure throughout his body that he quickly backed away, fearful that he might make a fool of himself. Worse still, spoil a very pleasant relationship that was only beginning to blossom. He stood there waiting and watching her in the darkness as she entered the house where a lamp was still burning in the kitchen.

Leading the horse to the barn to unharness and be put away for the night, he dreaded going into the house and put it off for as long as he could. His father would already be in bed asleep, that he knew. He always went to bed when the sun went down! His mother now, that was another thing! He envisioned her in his mind's eye, long hair already let down for the night, puttering around in the kitchen pretending to be busy in a nonchalant way. The minute he walked in, she would scrutinize him as only she could, as he knew she had already done with Mabel, poor girl!

She wouldn't say much, other than, "Well, you're back, did you have a good time?" That's all that was needed! From the answer she received and her hawk-like scrutiny, she knew if anything untoward had happened.

But, he was mildly surprised when he entered the lamp lighted kitchen and his mother never said anything. Eyeing her son speculatively, she went about the business of preparing for the night.

Tired as he had been earlier in the day, Leonard lay quietly in the darkness of his room for a long time, remembering the events of the evening. His mind was in a turmoil. He thought about his brash cousin, Reuben and Lorna and wondered if they had really stopped there in woods as he had vowed. Leonard felt a tinge of embarrassment, even in the darkness, knowing that he probably had made good his promise and also Lorna had been a willing participant. In many ways, Leonard almost envied Reuben for his daring and reckless nature, always seeming to be proficient at whatever he undertook and getting what he wanted, even though he had little ambition about his future. Being satisfied with his life made him careful and likeable, much like his father, Uncle Sidney.

Leonard knew he could never be like Reuben and wasn't sure he ever wanted to be. They were two opposites, making them compatible.

He tossed and turned most of the night, with the image of Mabel in his mind, excitement raging in his veins. Realizing he was in love with this wonderful girl, he dared not admit it out loud, even to himself, knowing full well he wanted to marry her. But, he would have to go slow and take his time, so as not to spoil everything by being too impetuous. God, it would be very difficult though.

Things would have moved along much faster had he known that just beyond the thin wall of his bedroom, Mabel was experiencing the same tumultuous feelings. She too, was in love! All the long days that lay ahead had to be endured, waiting for the outcome of this affair, hoping he felt as she did.

The days and weeks that followed were fraught with agony and torment for each of them. They were so close, yet so far part, neither sure just how the other felt. Leonard avoided Reuben as much as possible, to keep from being teased and having to answer a lot of foolish questions about his relationship with his housekeeper.

During the weeks that followed, many evenings were spent at Blessey's Store, where the two ate cheese sandwiches and drank soda pop together. These were glorious times, as they ate the dry substance, choking and laughing. Every effort was made during the days for Leonard to find reasons for entering the house or barn, just to see and speak to Mabel. Lawrence was becoming more and more exasperated with his son as the days went by.

One day Lawrence exploded when Leonard forgot to close the barn yard gate and the mules got out. The next morning they lost precious time rounding them up, before they could go to work.

"If you don't get that young filly out of your mind, I'm going to fire her and send her back home," Lawrence thundered.

Leonard paled, stopping in his tracks. "Oh no, you can't do that Pa," he choked.

"Like thunder, I can't. You been mooning around here for a month now, half doing your work costing me money and time," the older man pointed out. "You either straighten up or by thunder I'll sure as the devil get rid of her. Next time, I'm going to hire an old woman that won't upset you so much."

Leonard realized that his father meant what he said. He never made idle threats, especially if it involved work or money and both were concerned here. Knowing this, he suddenly became desperate, fearing to lose the love of his life. Therefore he was driven to a direct course of action.

That evening after supper was over and the dishes done, Leonard asked Mabel to go for a walk with him. When they were out of sight of the house, he suddenly grabbed her hands in his and turned her to face him.

In the fading light, he blurted out, "Mabel, let's get married!"

She stared at him, flabbergasted.

"Gosh Mabel, I know this isn't the way it's supposed to be done but, I can't help it. I love you and I want to marry you. Will you?" he pleaded. He felt her rough hands, fresh out of dishwater, tighten in his own.

"Oh yes!" she readily assented. "I love you too. I was beginning to think you would never ask me."

Taking her in his arms, they clung together for a long time and he kissed her and nothing else mattered in all the world. They were two young people in love who had just agreed to be each other's life's partners. It all happened in one of the most unlikely places in one of the most unlikely fashions. He still wearing his dirty, soiled work clothes and she, in her house dress with not even powder. But, it didn't matter and they didn't care. Neither thought there was anything unusual about the proposal.

It was fully dark as the two walked back to the house to tell the news. Hurried plans for the future had been made and if they expected to see the rest of the world rejoice with them, they would have been disappointed. His father was already in bed snoring. Bessie, who was busy puttering around in the kitchen, her hair undone for the night, gazed at them as they entered all aglow. There was very little surprise on her face, because she had seen it coming for a long time. In her own way, she was glad for them. She had never known love as most young folks know it. Hers had been a marriage of convenience more than anything else. She had always known that but, she loved her man, just the same, in her own way and knew he loved her, in his way but, not as these two young ones did.

The three of them stayed up later than usual that night, making plans about getting married. They had no desire for a big wedding or to even wait awhile. Neither Leonard nor Mabel considered it as rushing into anything. Their minds were already made up and so that settled it. The one big obstacle that stood in the way was, a couple had to turn in a blood sample and make application for a license and then wait three days before getting married. This all seemed like an eternity and a lot of hog wash to young people in love.

Bessie offered a solution to this problem, "Indiana don't have that waiting period," she said. "All you two have to do is go over to Evansville and get it done."

They were delighted with this suggestion and decided to go there immediately. However, another obstruction arose.

"How are we going to get over there?" Leonard questioned. "That's nearly eighty miles away."

"Take the train, you idiot," his mother responded. "Gawd it's a good thing I'm here to help out, you two never would get married the way you're thinking."

The young couple readily agreed and secretly marveled at the older woman's foresight.

"You know the train runs through Zachery every day, so you wait a couple of days and cool down some, then go," said Bessie.

A little reluctantly, they agreed to wait until Thursday, which was two days off. Then Leonard thought of another deterrent.

"What about Pa?" he exclaimed. "He'll have a fit when I tell him I'm going off to get married. We're awfully busy right now."

"You leave your Pa to me," Bessie said brusquely. "I'll handle him. He can get Sidney to take your place for a couple of days. Or Reuben!"

So, it was settled there in the lamp lighted kitchen.

On Thursday, Reuben drove the young couple in the buggy the four miles to Zachery.

Arriving a good hour and a half early at the depot, which also served as a loading and transfer facility, Reuben wished them good luck. Regretting that he couldn't stay with them, he returned home, as per instructions of Lawrence, who needed him to help with the work while Leonard was off gallivanting around over the country. But, he didn't leave without much good natured kidding and advice, and telling his cousin things would never be the same in life again.

Zachery was a bee-hive of activity in those days. The primary mode of transportation, other than the horse and wagon, for the thriving village being the CS&T railroad which ran through the same area. Daily freight trains carried the larger commodities and produce such as grain and lumber and live stock, east into Indiana. Some of these products were dropped off at the Ohio River, to be transported by boat or barge down river or go on to Evansville and points east. Passenger trains coming through here were known as "locals" because they stopped at every hamlet along the way, picking up and dropping off fresh milk, poultry and various other products, as well as passengers.

After purchasing their tickets, they went into the only restaurant in town, across the street from the depot for a soda and to get out of the summer heat for awhile. After that, there was still a long wait, so Leonard took his bride-to-be on a walking tour of the village, which didn't take long. As they walked along, he pointed out the different businesses and buildings. Beside the depot and restaurant, there were two general stores, much like the ones in Blairsville, one across the street from the other. Entering the larger of the two, it took several seconds for their unaccustomed eyes to adjust to the darkness. A large selection of various types of merchandise and sundry greeted them. Along one side was displayed the dry goods such as material for making clothing, along with the finished products and toilet articles and smaller household goods. The other side was devoted mostly to food products. But, with the placement of these items there was very little organization, as things belonging in one group were intermingled with another. Overalls, men's shirts and galvanized washtubs and buckets and washboards hung from the ceiling. All types of tools and hardware were strewn down the middle.

They were greeted by the store's owner, who knew the Reynolds family, and Leonard felt a little embarrassed, feeling that the man could tell why they were there. He purchased two candy bars and they quickly made their departure. The outer coating of the Baby Ruth bars immediately melted in the bright sunlight and the sticky dark chocolate soon covered their fingers and mouths. The situation only brought laughter to their lips. Mabel tried dabbing at Leonard's plight, with her handkerchief, amid giggles that attracted the attention of the occasional passerby. Taking out a large handkerchief from his hip pocket, he wiped his face and hands as clean as he could, until they reached the pump down the street and stopped there to complete the job.

The religious population worshipped at one or the other of the two churches. The Baptist church stood on one street corner where the two main streets crossed. The community congressional church occupied a lot at the edge of town. Both were wooden structures, in need of fresh paint but, very lively houses of worship on Sundays. The grade school was at the side of town, next to a large field of corn. Perhaps two dozen or so houses lined the two main streets. But, the majority of the commercial trade came from the surrounding region.

When the train's whistle was heard, far to the west, the little town came alive. Children ran down the dusty street to the depot to watch as the giant locomotive pulled into its place along side the wooden structure. The station master emerged from his office and pushed the loaded, four wheeled cart into place on the loading dock, carrying a small package of mail in one hand. Several five and fifteen gallon cans of milk and cream lined the platform for distribution to the creamery at Bedford.

By the time the engine came into view, half the town was out, either on porches, in doorways or in the street, waiting. Everything was in readiness, including the two sole passengers, as the great engine chugged to a stop, belching clouds of black smoke in the air. Horses tied at the hitch-racks strained at their halter ropes to be freed.

Leonard and Mabel sat back on the seat with the window open, smoke blowing through the car. The train picked up speed as it rumbled out past the grain elevator and the animal holding pens.

The few others in the rail car paid little heed to these young lovers. Everyone seemed engrossed in his own thoughts. The ones that did notice only smiled, perhaps in recognition of past days in their own lives.

Eventually, Mabel undid the package that she had been carrying all this time. It contained sandwiches and homemade cookies, prepared by Bessie, specially for the event.

CHAPTER 4

The following years were prosperous ones for the Reynolds family. Prosperous that is, in the sense of accumulative and material wealth.

Leonard immediately had a comfortable home built on the old Muley Seles place just down the road, halfway to the woods and cabin, where his mother first served as mid-wife by delivering Sidney and Lottie's second born, Gertrude. The house was in a pleasant enough setting, surrounded by large oak and maple trees, but a little smaller than that of his parents. There was already one good well and a large fenced cow lot. They now had several out buildings such as barns and sheds. The main barn was patterned after his father's, with a wagon scale down the center and was fully constructed with wooden pegs instead of nails, the same as Lawrence's.

They had their own milk cows and chickens and vegetable garden and life was good, for awhile, at least. Two babies were added to the young Reynolds couple. Both girls, they soon became the center of attention with the grandparents. Helen was the first born. Two years later Mildred, dubbed Millie, came along.

As luck would have it, Bessie was on hand to deliver each baby. By now, she had helped deliver many others. These two were not difficult deliveries, in the normal sense of the word, but Mabel contended after each birth that her mother-in-law acted excessively rough with her.

"She acted as though she were delivering a calf," Mabel told her husband afterwards.

"I reckon you just imagined that," Leonard tried to assuage her. "You being in pain and all, anything would seem excessive."

"No, I'm not imagining it at all," Mabel retorted, "She did things to me that hurt more than they should've. Sometimes I think she's jealous of me."

"Why in the world would she be jealous?"

"For one thing, because I married you and took you away from her."

"That's ridiculous!"

"No, it isn't! You don't live there any more and she can't control you."

"She never did control me. Besides, she's my mother. Why should'nt she control me when I was little!"

"You're not little any more," Mabel protested. "And she does too control you. Your father does too. You jump like a frog every time one of them hollers and run down there to see what they want."

"That's plumb silly, Mabel and you know it. Why shouldn't I go down there when they call, they're my folks and we farm together," he defended.

"I almost feel like an outsider and don't belong. I think she's jealous too, because we have two babies and she doesn't have any. You just wait and see, she'll do something to try and get them away from us," she predicted.

Leonard stared at her, aghast. "You don't know what you're saying."

"I do too know what I'm saying and you know it too, if you'd only admit it," Mabel said vehemently. "Your mother is the cause of trouble between us. She criticizes everything I do. And you know it too, only you won't admit it."

It was an old argument that came up more frequently these past three weeks. Leonard admitted privately to himself that she likely had some basis for her feelings. He had noticed on occasions that his step-mother was very sharp with Mabel and found fault with things she did. His father wasn't much better! He often kept Leonard down at his house,

82

piddling around longer than necessary and made off color remarks about Mabel.

Being of a more quiet nature, perhaps after his real mother, he chose to ignore the storm brewing and tried to go calmly about his business. He wished that everyone could get along together and live in harmony. He had everything that any man should possibly want. He had a good wife that he loved and two adorable little girls, a top notch farm and good health. What more was there! Down deep in his heart he knew where most of his problems lay, and that was just down the road where he had been raised. He seldom complained or argued. When Mabel said his father applied too much pressure, he merely worked harder in an effort to forget it.

With Mabel however, it was different. Loving her two girls, she tried to draw them closer to her when she was despondent.

She also loved her husband, but didn't like the way he catered to his father and mother, leaving her alone to shoulder the brunt of their jibes and everything else they cast at her. Leonard never seemed to realize or notice the little things they did or how difficult it was for her, whether purposely or not. He even tried to ignore her when she complained, by walking away or just not answering.

She had no recourse but to draw closer to her small children or to confide to Lorna. The two shared many secrets and confidences. They had become good friends since Reuben and Lorna were married. That marriage had come about as a result of their little escapades in the woods and he decided to make an honest man of himself and do the right thing by her. They and their small son lived with his family, just temporarily of course, for the past seven years, until he could get on his feet, so to speak.

Sidney and his brood lived in the big house just across the field on the other side of the big drainage ditch. Mabel could see the big silo and barn and the roof of the old ramshackle house from her kitchen window. Although the distance was minor, maybe a quarter mile separating them, it proved very difficult trying to visit back and forth. They each had so many chores to do and so much work ahead of them, they seldom found the time or energy to make the trek. When they did though, they agreed it was well worth the effort. When no one else was around, they would unburden their souls by telling their innermost thoughts and feelings, something they could never do with their spouse.

Lorna's main complaint was living in that big old house with so many people. They had no privacy whatsoever, day or night, not that it stopped them from doing the natural things between a husband and wife. Reuben had never been a shy person. He treated her good, but they never seemed to have anything to rea11y call their own. They never managed to get ahead enough to buy the simple things that young women liked, such as nice clothes, make-up or little doo-dads. He still promised they would soon be out on their own. After seven years, she had just about given up hope of that day ever coming.

Mabel, on the other hand, never really lacked anything she needed. She had her egg and cream money for household items, and Leonard was always agreeable when she wished to buy something not considered to be every day necessities. There always seemed to be money enough so long as she spent it wisely. Many times she gave her friend a lipstick or can of powder or pair of earrings or some other such trinket important to young women.

The day after Mabel's quarrel with Leonard, Lorna came trudging across the field for a visit. Mabel put the coffeepot on the stove and stoked up the fire a little. The day was blustery, with dark clouds hanging low in the sky and Lorna had bundled up good to brace herself against the wind. Being a little surprised to see the figure out across the way, Mabel nevertheless felt very happy at the prospect of a good visit. Leonard happened to be down at his folk's house helping his father on some project or other and likely wouldn't be home for quite a spell.

As Mabel opened the back door for her friend, Lorna said, "I snuck out for a spell. I just have to get away from there once in awhile or I'll go stark raving mad." She stomped the mud off her boots on the back porch before entering the kitchen. "I pretended to go out to the barn and just kept on coming. I hope you don't mind my dropping in this way."

"Heavens no, Lorna! I'm tickled to death. Why I've been thinking about doing the same thing and go see you, but for my two girls. I hated to take them out in this bad weather."

"You know it's been four weeks since we seen each other!" Lorna exclaimed. "Has anything happened since then? I feel like I don't never hear no news."

They spent a very pleasant afternoon as they sat and talked. They both laughed and sometimes almost cried, remembering the old days when they were young and felt carefree. And they told each other secrets and intimate things of their present lives.

The two little girls soon grew weary of grown up talk and went back to playing, oblivious to the women who talked about things that made no sense to them.

Lorna hadn't lost her enthusiasm for life or changed her happy personality, which cheered Mabel up and made her world seem brighter.

Looking around at the neat kitchen as she always did, Lorna said, "I just love your house, Hon. It's always so clean and cozy in here." Gazing long at her friend she went on. "You know Mabel, you're about the best housekeeper I ever saw. I always feel comfortable here with you. You don't know how lucky you are, having a good man and a nice new home and family like this. It must be real nice, living here like this, just you and your own family. I don't reckon I'll ever have a place like this," she said a little sadly. Then, she brightened, exclaiming, "Did I tell you, we've got our own private room now?"

"You have! That's wonderful, Lorna."

"Well, it ain't really that private, not like all by ourselves. Little Willie sleeps in there, too. He has to, because there ain't room no place else for him, but he don't really count. In one way the room is private. When we close the door nobody can see in, but the walls are so thin, you can hear everything that goes on in the next room. And even knowing that somebody else can hear has never stopped Reuben yet when he wants something, if you know what I mean," she said, grinning mischievously over the top of her coffee cup.

Mabel did know what she meant and would have felt embarrassed with anyone else. By now though, she was at ease with Lorna, even about the most intimate things and they laughed together.

"Of course, having our own room ain't all it's cracked up to be, sometimes," Lorna went on. "It's on the northeast upstairs corner of the house and the cold wind blows in around the cracks of the windows. It gets pretty cold and we have to cuddle up to keep warm and you know what that leads to. Of course, I'll bet it'll be plenty hot this summer."

They laughed again!

"What about you though, we've been talking about me all the time?" Lorna asked. "How's your love life going?"

Mabel looked at the girls playing on the floor. They were engaged in their own past time!

"We don't seem to have much of a love life any more," she replied.

"What do you mean, you're not having problems are you?"

"Well, sort of! I think everything would be all right, but for Leonard's folks," Mabel confided. "His mother criticizes me all the time and finds fault with everything I do. And his father is an old tyrant who wants to run everybody." She related some of the problems of the past few weeks. "I can't even take my own eggs over to the store to sell. She insists on doing it for me and I'm not even sure I get back the right amount of money for them. Why, one time she even charged me a quarter for taking them, because I had more than usual."

"Oh, you poor thing," Lorna consoled. "You know what we need?"

"No! What?"

"We need to curl our hair and get all prettied up!"

That brought back the gaiety and Mabel went into the other room for the curling iron, while Lorna lit the coal oil lamp. "I'll do you first. You just sit down there in that chair and relax," she said.

She stuck the curling iron down inside the lamp globe, the metal curling end just above the flame and let the handle rest on top of the globe to heat. Sticking her finger to her tongue and then to the metal curler, she determined it to be about hot enough. Then she took a strand of Mabel's hair and wrapping it around the round end of the iron, she clamped the ends together. After the iron cooled, she pulled it out an let the newly formed curl fall loose. Repeating the process over and over and over, Mabel's head was soon covered with cute curls.

Holding up the mirror to admire her reflection, the two changed places.

"Don't get the curler too hot and burn my hair now," Lorna giggled. "Reuben would run me off if I went home with all my hair burned off."

After the curling was finished, Mabel said, "I think now we need a little make-up to finish the job of getting us pretty. I got some lip-stick the other day. It'll look good on you. It's bright red!"

"Oh, my favorite color!"

Taking turns, they applied lip stick, rouge and powder to the other's face, then held the mirror for the other to see better. Standing before the dresser mirror in the bedroom, they agreed they did indeed look rather fetching.

"Now, that's better," Lorna said.

"You look beautiful," Mabel told her.

"You don't look so bad yourself, just wait 'til our men see us. We'll have to fight them off."

Helen finally broke away from her game and said, "Mama, you look pretty. Why don't you look like that all the time?"

Mabel smiled at her oldest daughter, "Well, it's hard to look pretty all the time when there's so much to do."

They were so engrossed in their cosmetic activities that neither noticed when it began to rain. Leonard came in dripping water and was surprised to see Lorna's boots on the back porch. After emitting the usual amenities, he headed out to the barn to harness up the buggy and take her home. She had decided to wait until it slacked up a bit before starting out and he suggested she spend the night with them. She refrained from such a thought, however, saying Reuben would worry, not knowing where she was. Leonard agreed it was a bad suggestion, therefore he offered to take her home. He didn't want her wading across the field in the dark. Besides, very little rain was needed to flood the Big Ditch and then she couldn't cross. There being no bridge over the ditch, the only way to the opposite side was to go down the steep embankment, wade the water and climb up the other side, behind the barn.

Halfway to the barn, a horseman rode into the yard.

"Hi, Cousin" Reuben called out. "You got a spare wayward woman around here?"

Relieved, Leonard assured him that he did have. It was about a two mile buggy ride around by the road, one that he didn't relish taking in the rain. The two men went inside the house and Reuben stopped dead in his tracks, staring at his wife.

He whistled through his teeth and exclaimed, "God Lorna, you look just like you did before we got married. You too, Mabel! Don't she Cousin?"

"Yes," Leonard agreed, staring at his own wife.

Lorna smiled appreciatively. "Well, it's a good thing you two noticed, that's all I've got to say," she said. "We worked all afternoon getting to look this way, didn't we Hon!"

Standing there in the kitchen bantering back and forth was almost like old times.

"How did you know where I was?" Lorna asked her husband.

"Where else could you be!" Reuben answered. Besides, Ma said she saw you cross the ditch and I figured I better come and get you."

"I'm glad you did, so Leonard won't have to make that long ride around."

Leonard asked them to stay for supper and then if the rain didn't let up, they could stay the night.

"Mabel won't mind the cooking and we'd like to have you stay for a spell, wouldn't we?"

His wife readily agreed that it would be nice, since they had so little company, but Reuben declined the invitation.

"The folks will worry if we don't get home before dark," Reuben explained. "And if the water rises in the ditch, we may have to be here a week or two," he laughed.

"Oh, I hate to go out and get wet," Lorna wailed. My curls will come loose and all this make-up will wash off."

"That's all right," Reuben assured her. "I'll love you anyway, now that I know how nice you can still look. I can solve that part of it. Here, let me put my slicker over your head so it won't get wet. I can't keep the rest of you dry, though."

"You can wear this old coat of mine," Mabel offered. "Reuben, you wear Leonard's jacket."

When they were dressed for the weather, Reuben lifted his spouse up into the saddle. Rubbing the white exposed leg, he said, "We just might stop off for a nightcap, some place before crossing over," and swung his lanky body up behind her and hugged her close.

"Better not take too long," Leonard advised. "You know how fast the water rises."

"Just kidding, Cousin," Reuben laughed.

They rode off, waving and laughing. Mabel and her two girls returned their waves from the porch. She watched wistfully for awhile, until they passed the fence at the turn in the lane.

She envied those two! They seemed so much in love and so much younger than she and Leonard. They had very few earthly possessions and expected little out of life. But being in love seemed to count for everything else. Some day maybe they would have their own place but, until then, they'd make do and be happy.

Reuben had surprised almost every one when he married Lorna. He had settled down and been a good husband. They were still carefree and happy.

As they were leaving, Lorna had hugged Mabel and said, "Hang in there, Hon, it'll all come out in the wash and be all alright for us both. I just know it will."

Neither of them realized that this would be their last visit together.

Mabel said, "Come on in the house, Leonard and get out of them wet overalls. You'll catch your death of cold."

It rained all night, sometimes hard! One of those rare early spring thunderstorms, passed through, knocking down some trees and blowing limbs from others. Toward morning, it slacked up a bit, then started in again.

Leonard went out early, just after daybreak, and did the chores and dragged the downed limbs off to the side out of the way. Then he walked down to see how his folks made out. Things were about the same as at his own home, with a few limbs down and a couple sheets of roofing loose on the barn. After helping his father do what he could, they went into the house to warm up and drink coffee.

"Looks like it might rain all day," Leonard observed.

Law took a sip of coffee and ran his fingers over his big moustache. "I don't like the looks of this weather," he said. "It ain't natural to have a storm like last night, this time of year. I remember once before, having one just like it and it rained for two solid weeks. Them clouds hanging back there in the west, low in the sky like that these past days, just hanging there, look the same as they did the other time."

"I thought that was before a bad storm or cyclone," Leonard said.

"Then too, but they also predict other drastic changes in weather, if you pay attention."

"They don't look that much different to me than a hundred other times."

"That's cause you don't pay attention to things like that. It's different, I tell you. You just look at them clouds and see how they're moving and watch the farm animals. They can tell too, so can the dogs. We're in for a bad time, I tell you. Maybe not a real storm but, a change for the worse."

Leonard knew from past experience that it didn't pay to argue with his father about the weather. He watched and studied it religiously. That's one of the reasons he was a successful farmer. No one else could predict the forecast as well as he. A few of the other farmers watched and planted when he did, while others failed.

"What do you think it's going to do?" Leonard asked.

Law tugged at his moustache again.

"I reckon we'll have lots of rain," he replied.

Leonard walked back home after awhile, with mud and water sloshing around his boots.

The following morning the rain was still coming down. It hadn't rained really hard since the first night. After that it was just a slow relentless out-pouring of water without a let up. Ditches along the road and the pond out beyond the barn lot were already filled and running over and low places in the fields could be pointed out from afar.

Lawrence threw a slicker over his shoulders and went out to the barn to saddle up Prince. He rode the big, white stallion down the road and out across the Bottoms rather than the open fields, where the horse's hoofs would sink knee deep in the soft mud. Even here, the ground was soft and sloppy. Before long the knees of his pants were soaked and water ran down from the brim of the floppy felt hat.

The Big Ditch that ran along the north edge of the farm was his main concern. He rode up the slight incline of the embankment for a close view. It was already nearly bank full. The swirling brown water raced angrily downstream.

"When they dug that ditch, they done a fairly decent job," he mused to himself. "It's doing what it's suppose to, but it's not going to be enough this time."

Watching the tree limbs and debris float past, he thought, "The water runs good now with not much brush or trash blocking the way. That's because it's still new and flows free and hasn't had time to grow down inside. In a few more years though, trees will be in the bottom and along the sides and the brush will dam up the water and slow down the flow. It'd be all right if everybody along the waterway would keep it cleaned out, but they won't. They'll let it grow up and flood and then complain and want the Government to send somebody back and clean it out for them."

Standing on the edge of the raging water made Prince nervous. He began to fidget and prance around. Suddenly, a small portion of the bank gave way. Law jerked abruptly on the reins and swung his head around sharply. Kicking his heels violently into the animals flanks, he yanked back so hard on the reins that Prince squealed in pain as the bit tore his mouth. Pulling hard on the right hand line, he turned the thrashing animal sideways, floundering for a foothold. After several futile attempts, he found solid ground and leaped forward. When Law halted him, some feet from the edge of the embankment, the horse stood quivering, his nostrils flared and wild red.

Law patted him on the shoulder, holding the reins taut, trying to soothe him. "That was a close one, ol' boy." he said. "It was my fault. We shouldn't've been that close. I knew the ground was too weak there. If we had gone down there in that, we'd both be goners. There's no way we could've got out of that."

He was correct in that assumption for it would have been almost impossible for either to climb out unless he was fortunate enough to grab one of the few overhanging branches. The ditch had been dug into a Vshaped flume type canal, more than thirty feet wide at the top, sloping down to perhaps twenty feet wide at the bottom. When full, the water was a good ten feet deep. Having been constructed as straight as possible, with only a few wide sweeping bends, the water flowed freely and swiftly down the channel, allowing little erosion along the way. In dry weather only a trickle ran along the bottom, except for an occasional deep hole.

Further down stream, he noticed a low spot in the embankment where the water was already spilling over and flooding the field.

"Well boy, I reckon we ain't seen the last of this bad weather yet," he said to the horse. "If it keeps on all over like it has been here, the rivers down below will soon be full and backing up. And when it does, we're in for a bad time."

The next day, it hadn't slacked up any. Leonard rode down to his folk's house. His father stood on the back porch, looking out across the fields.

"You think we're going to get flooded?" Leonard asked.

"Of course I do," his father retorted. "Look out there," he waved his hand northward. "The ditch has already got full and is running over. Can't you see that water out there?"

All of the surrounding fields were flooded. They went inside where Bessie was noisily preparing dinner, and sat at the kitchen table.

"What are we going to do?" Leonard wanted to know.

"Looks like we might have to move to higher ground."

"Maybe it will stop!"

"It won't stop! Not for awhile yet at least. Look at them clouds out there. They say it will rain for several more days." He walked over and stood looking out the window. "With the ditch full, that means all the cricks and rivers down below are full and backing up. You ought to know when that happens everything above will overflow. There's no place else for the water to go but out over the Bottoms. With the Ditch running over, that means Beaver Crick, Skillet Fork and the Little Wabash are all full and right on down the line." He tugged at his moustache. "Reckon we're in for a good soaking."

"You mean we have to move out!"

"Sure looks that way, Boy. I always said when we got that ditch, I'd never be flooded again. Reckon I was wrong. Remember the last time we flooded and had to leave, Bess?"

"I remember," his wife replied. "It was no fun, I can tell you that. It was cold and wet and I didn't have half enough food or anything to cook with."

"I remember, too," Leonard said. "I was just a little feller, but I remember."

"If I do decide to leave, it'll be different this time," Law assured them. "I've already been making plans and we'll have everything we need."

"You really think we'll have to leave then?"

"No," his father retorted. "You don't really have to leave. You can stay home with your family and all drown, if you want to! Of course we have to leave, you dang fool."

It was a wound to his pride though, being driven from his home. He always did things his own way, in his own good time and moved over for no one. But, this had been created by God Almighty and he knew even he couldn't go up against God, although he sometimes tried to.

By mid afternoon, one could almost see the water rising in the fields. The house and barns became like islands and it washed up over the road. It seemed not to be moving much however, which only meant there was no run-off and all the water that fell from the sky, stayed where it fell, backing up from the streams below.

He saddled up Prince again and rode down to see his son.

"Start getting your things ready and round up the animals," he instructed Leonard. "Pack up enough food for your family to last three, four days or longer. I'm going up to see Tom Quigley." Pulling on the reins, he turned and rode off.

Law and Tom remained good friends down through the years, helping each other when help was needed. Tom was perhaps the one person who could stand up to a sometimes belligerent Lawrence Reynolds. They often cursed each other in a friendly fashion, without exhibiting any real anger.

As Law rode into his yard, Tom came out and held up a hand in greeting.

"Hi Law, it's good to see you."

"Hi Tom," Law returned. "Reckon you know it's been raining a spell."

"Yes, I noticed. Looks like you got some water down at your place. You better be getting out while you can."

"I aim to. Can I bring my family and belongings up here for a few days?"

"Sure! You don't need to ask that. Me and Kate have been waiting for you to make up your mind and it took you long enough."

"I don't think it's going to let up for awhile, so we may be here a spell."

"That's all right. Me and Kate will be glad of the company. We've got plenty room in the house, by moving things around a bit."

"No, we won't impose on you by staying in the house. We'll make camp outside here someplace."

"I figured as much. You're just as contrary as ever. There's no need for your women folks and little girls to get pneumonia out in the weather just because you're too stubborn to come in out of the rain."

Law ignored the barb. "Where can I pitch camp?"

"I didn't think you'd come in the house, so we cleaned out the smoke house for you. It's plenty big enough to do the cooking in. Kate does her canning there in summer. It's got a cook stove that Kate uses some times to heat wash water on when the weather is bad and to do some heavy cooking and baking. So, the oven works too.

"Oh, I almost forgot," Tom went on. "I cleaned out the long tool shed over there where you can make your camp. As you can see, it's only open on one side, so you'll be in out of the wind and rain and all your things will stay dry. You can have a good roaring fire in it too, where you couldn't in the barn. And it's clean too. But, I still wish you'd stay in the house with us."

"No, this will be fine. Thanks Tom! I appreciate all this. We'll make out fine. You shouldn't've gone to no trouble though."

"Tarnation man, it was no trouble. We been friends and neighbors a long time. You'd do the same for me."

"More'n likely! I see there's others out there in the woods," Law observed.

"Yes, I think there's four families over there now. Come in from the Bottoms yesterday. Smart enough to get out before they drowned, like you should have done. Poor souls, they haven't got much, even in fair weather. But they do know how to pitch a camp and seem to be making out pretty good. I took some hay down for their animals this morning. I hear that Hi-pockets and some others on that side of the Ditch went up to the hill behind Blairsville."

"I've been wondering if he left yet and figured that's where he'd go," Law said, relieved that his brother's family was safe.

Climbing back into the saddle, he said, "Me and the boy will bring the live stock up shortly. Like to get them out before dark. In the morning, I'll bring the family and other belongings."

Riding along behind the various assortment of animals, Law and Leonard herded them through the water and up the long grade leading to the Quigley farm. They fenced them in the extra pasture that was not presently being used by Tom. Law pointed out in jest that he didn't want any of his cows to breed with any of Tom's scrawny bulls.

Tom had his own come-back ready, replying he was glad the animals were not mixed. He didn't want his own to pick up some of the bad habits developed down there in the Bottoms. His were traditionally of a much higher breed, being raised for show and for sale, whereas Law's might be of a sturdier stock, but bred for work. The two were of a very different lineal descent.

Mabel put her two girls to bed extra early that evening to get a full night's sleep. Listening to the rain on the rooftop, Helen dozed off immediately and fell sound asleep. Millie however, being of a more inquisitive nature, remained awake for a long time, knowing there was something in the wind other than the floodwater.

She was right, for soon afterwards, her Mama and Papa had one of their frequent quarrels, only this time it was louder and more vocal than usual. Millie scooched down deeper under the covers for warmth, leaving only the top of her head sticking out, the better to hear all that was said. Although her parents were in the next room, trying to keep their voices low, the sounds carried plainly into the adjoining room and Millie heard nearly every word.

As usual, Mama did most of the talking. "How long do you think we'll have to stay up there on that hill?" she asked tremulously.

"Until the water goes down," Papa answered, shortly. "I don't have any idea when that will be. You know as much about that as I do."

"Well, if it stops raining, how long will it be before we can come home?"

"Lord, I don't know, Mabel. I reckon three or four days maybe. Maybe sooner, maybe longer. It depends on the cricks and rivers down stream from here and how much stopped up they are," he answered.

"That's not much of an answer. I don't know any more than I did. Didn't your father tell you how long it will rain? He always knows everything, he surely knows how long it's going to rain."

"For crying out loud Mabel, what in the world has got into you lately?"

"You know good and well what's got into me," Mama flared. "I'm sick and tired of this place. We never do anything on our own any more. All we do is stay home and work, work, work. Some times I think Lawrence Reynolds invented work. That's all he knows. And your mother is just as bad. All she does is work and find fault with everything I do. Why can't we pack up and go some place else!"

"You know I can't do that!" Papa answered meekly. Millie felt sorry for him because he could never stand up to anyone.

"Your mother never liked me since the day we were married," Mama said.

"You know that's not so," Papa answered. "She always said you did good work and were handy to have around."

"Of course she did, but that was when I was hired help. She liked me all right then, when I had no strings attached to you and she could order me around. Once we were married though, things changed. She wouldn't like any woman that you married. She's a jealous old woman and wants you back there in that house where she can tell you what to do. All those little digs to me are driving me crazy."

"I never heard her make any digs to you!"

"I know you haven't. That's because she's so sneaky about it and when she does, you never pay any attention. She usually waits until you're not around, most of the time."

"I just can't believe any of this."

"Well, it's true, if you'd only believe it. I don't see why we can't leave. If you thought as much of me and the girls as you do them down there, you'd sell out your part of the farm and buy one some place else, away from here. Don't you want us to be together and happy?"

"Of course I do, but I can't sell any of the farm, you know that."

"I don't see why not. You always said it's partly yours and you have a share in everything that comes from it. Do you really own part of it or not?" she demanded.

"In a sense I do but, I can't sell any of it."

"Why not, if it's yours?"

"It's all in Pa's name and I couldn't sell any of it, even if I wanted to."

"That's what I thought. He's going to keep everything in his name too, so you won't ever be able to get away from him. Your mother and him will keep you under their thumbs all your life and we'll never have a real place of our own. I don't think they really even care that much about you, as long as you can work and help him control these Bottoms."

"Let's go to bed Mabel. We got a hard day ahead of us."

"Yes, I don't doubt that a bit. Every day is a hard one. I don't see why we had to wait so long to leave. We're the last ones and by morning the water will be so high, we can't get out and we'll probably all drown. You know how scared I am of water. Oh, I know, your father said to wait, so you did. You can't go against your father. I hate that man!"

Millie was a smart little girl, smarter than most girls her age. She liked to listen to grown-ups talking, especially when they didn't know she was listening. She learned a lot that way, sometimes things she wasn't supposed to know. Like how Earl Lee came to be living with Grandma and Grandpa. It was supposed to be a big secret, but she knew by overhearing Mama and Papa discussing it, when Earl Lee first went down there to live.

It seems that cousin Gertrude, (that's Papa's cousin) went off to town someplace to work for a family, housekeeping, and while she was there she got a little baby. Millie never did learn where the baby came from or how she happened to end up with it, but she brought it home to live with her folks. Uncle Sidney already had a house full of family living with him, with thirteen of his own and didn't have room for any more, since most of them either lived there or close by.

Since Grandpa was Uncle Sidney's older brother as well as close friend, he said the baby could come live with them. They didn't have any small children of their own and they would raise him, which Millie thought was mighty nice of them. Earl Lee was a year younger than Millie, which allowed her and Helen to boss him around, and he spent a lot of time at their house because he had no one else to play with. They tolerated him because he was after all a cousin and besides, he had a certain knack for thinking of things to do and getting them all into mischief. And he was fun too, even Helen had to admit that.

But, back to the problem at hand. Millie couldn't understand why Mama and Papa were always arguing. They didn't use to! That was one thing she didn't understand about grown-ups. She and Helen argued sometimes, but it never meant anything and in a little while all was forgotten.

Usually Mama did most of the arguing while Papa listened. Then, he would get up and go outside to get away from her, which only made her more angry. She then said things she surely didn't mean and then felt bad about it afterwards. She was sure they loved each other and didn't understand why they argued so much.

Millie thought that maybe sometimes Mama exaggerated a little when berating Grandma and Grandpa about things they said or did. Maybe she should take Mama's side more, but she found it difficult, feeling the way she did about them. Knowing that Grandpa often treated Papa like a child made her feel sorry for him, yet there was a love in her heart for her grandfather. He always treated her special, like she and Helen were important to him. He called her his "little pumpkin head" or just plain Pumkin, which she liked. When he went to the store in Blairsville, he brought back a stick of peppermint candy or sucker for each of them. Who could resist such treatment. Earl Lee was special to him too, but being a boy and little besides, he didn't really count for much. Millie felt that she was Grandpa's favorite.

With all this exhausting contemplation, she fell asleep!

It seemed like in only a short time that she heard her mother say, "Come on girls, it's time to get up," almost the same as always. The night certainly went by in a hurry!

She snuggled down deeper under the covers, absorbing all the warmth possible until her mother repeated the call. Then, throwing back the quilts and gathering the nightgown tightly about her young body, she set her bare feet gingerly to the floor. An immediate wail erupted from her mouth.

"Mama," she cried out, the floor is all wet."

"I know, there's water in the house," her mother answered. "Come on and hurry up so we can leave."

The girls got out of bed, cautiously putting their feet down into the thin layer of cold water on the floor. Grabbing up clothes, they ran out of the dark room, into the lamp lit kitchen. The linoleum floor felt spongy and rubbery beneath their feet as water raised it up off the floor. Their mother was already fully dressed, wearing rubber boots. She hurried the girls into warm clothes and a warm breakfast. Papa came in from outside, saying that everything was ready and waiting.

After a lick and a promise in the kitchen, Mama blew out the lamp and they all went out. The wagon stood there, loaded with things they would need and covered over with a tarpaulin, tied down on the sides. The mules stood patiently, waiting in the rain and Papa's riding horse was tied on behind the wagon. Walking through the knee deep water, he carried the girls out, pushing them into the rear of the wagon, under the tarpaulin.

Millie clung to his neck, when he picked her up. "Are we all going to drown, Papa?" she asked.

"No, Baby, none of us are going to drown," he reassured her. "I won't let anything happen to you."

To Mama, he said, "Come on, you'd better get under here with the girls. No sense in you catching pneumonia out here." So the three of them huddled together in the darkness for warmth, their mother's arms around them.

The wagon started up with a jerk and bounced roughly along over the road. They could hear the water splashing around the big wheels. In the darkness they could hear the rain pelting the canvas above them, although they were unable to see the dull gray that was beginning to light up the sky.

In a little while, Millie heard Grandpa talking to Papa, when they stopped for a minute. "It's about time you got here. I was about ready to come down and get you."

Papa responded with something incoherent and Grandpa's wagon pulled in ahead of them.

The half mile or so ride up to Quigley's seemed much further. Grandpa guided his team as much by instinct as anything else, by keeping between the rows of trees and bushes on each side, since the road was covered over by water and couldn't be seen. It could be disastrous if the wagon fell into the deep ditch that was on one side. Millie kept peeking out from under the cover to see what was happening. Papa stayed close behind the lead wagon, letting his team of mules have their own way as much as possible. When the big narrow wheels dropped into a hole or rut, it jarred the wagon and contents relentlessly.

The wheels dug deep into the mud, as the powerful animals strained in the traces pulling the heavily laden wagons up the long sloping grade. Once they surmounted the hill, they quickened the pace over the level roadway leading to the Quigley home. Following the front wagon, Leonard pulled in behind it, alongside the open side of the long equipment shed. Most of the tools had either been moved out completely or down to one end.

Leonard got down and came around to the rear of the wagon to raise the tarpaulin up and help Mabel and the girls out. They all scurried for the protection of the nearby shelter. As soon as the front wagon stopped, Earl Lee peeked out into the daylight and jumped to the ground, following his cousins. Bessie climbed stiffly down from the high seat, pulling her wrap more tightly about her ample body. Underneath her rain gear, she wore a pair of her husband's overalls, which was more appropriate than a housedress at a time like this. Water poured down her face from the big wide brimmed hat on her head and some of the long graying hair had come loose from the pins. All this bothered her not a whit, since she had long ago lost interest in such vain things as fancy or vanity about her looks.

Tom had been waiting for them under the shed and now his wife came out of the house to greet them, even before they were in out of the rain. She too, was wearing her husband's overalls with a dress underneath, as well as one of his old hats.

"Hi Kate, haven't seen you in a coon's age," Bessie greeted, slapping her hat against her leg.

"It's good to see you Bessie. It's a pity it takes a flood to get you to come visiting," Kate returned.

"We've been mighty busy lately. Just ain't had time for socializing," Bessie said.

"I know what you mean all right, but we do need to get together now and then," said Kate. "I've got a big pot of coffee on the stove. It'll be ready before long and that'll warm your body some. How have you been, Mabel? I haven't seen you much lately neither."

Mabel had always liked this friendly, out-going woman, though they were never really close friends, with the age difference and all.

Earl Lee had already stepped in a puddle of water and had both feet wet. Bessie grabbed him by the arm and yanked him back under the shed. "You just can't stay out of any mudhole," she scolded. "If there's a puddle of water any where around you'll find it and fall in."

Tom said, "We'd better get this fire going so the boy can dry out. I think we could all benefit from it."

"I brought my own wood." Law said.

"I figured you might," Tom smiled. "But, I got it all laid out anyway to get things started. He bent and struck a match, lighting the dry straw beneath a well laid out stack of kindling wood. Being situated at the edge of the roof on the high side of the shed, it flared up at once and the smoke drifted up and away from the interior. The rainwater ran down to the rear, allowing the wood to stay dry.

"Now, you women folks come on over here and dry out, while we get these wagons unloaded," Tom commanded.

The wagons were unloaded much faster than they had been loaded. Extra clothing and bedding and such was stored under the shed, towards the rear. Food and cooking utensils were carried to the smokehouse where the meals would be cooked.

After things were properly distributed in the designated places, they stood around the fire, drinking coffee.

"Now Mabel, come night time I aim to take your girls in the house to stay the night," Kate announced.

"Oh no, Miz Kate, I wouldn't want to impose on you," Mabel objected. "They'll be just fine out here with me."

"Nonsense! I've already got a place fixed up for them. They'd catch their death of cold out here. So, I insist they spend the nights inside where it's warm and dry. The boy can come too."

The girls were very pleased and happy at the idea of sleeping in the house. Earl Lee however, balked at not being allowed to "camp out" as he called it. He looked at Bessie pleadingly, "I don't want to sleep in there. I'd rather stay out here with you, Aunt Bessie," he implored.

She looked down at the little boy, at the plea in his eyes and said gruffly, "He'll stay out here with me," and the subject was closed.

Later that day, the three children, Millie, Helen and Earl Lee donned their rain gear, including galoshes and set off to visit friends who were camped in the woods, not far away. The Wilmores were at the first camp. The girls were glad of this because two of the Wilmore girls, Jessy and Pip, were the same ages and in the same grades at school as they, when they went, which was only now and then. The brothers were older and wanted nothing to do with the girls at first, so Earl Lee had to tag along with them or not have anyone.

After awhile though, the boys began following them, teasing the girls and splashing water on them, to hear them squeal. But, they soon tired of this and wandered off to find something more interesting to do.

The girls went to the next camp, less than a hundred yards away. This is where the Sam Hathorn family was. Lizzy Hathorn was another of the girl's school friends. Living so far out in the Bottoms she didn't get to school very often. Lizzy was the only girl in the family of four strapping young boys, besides the baby, that always seemed to be crying, like it had the colic or something.

This camp appeared to be much like the Wilmore's. The big farm wagon, standing under a giant oak tree, had a tarpaulin tied to one side and stretched out, fastened on the other side to poles, forming a sort of lean-to. Apparently, this being their living area, another canvas was stretched over the top of the wagon, protecting their meager belongings and providing a relatively dry sleeping area. It was obvious that the smaller ones slept in the wagon and the others under the tarpaulin. Two horses and a cow were tethered out to graze at the end of long ropes. A fire was burning out in the open, over which hung a large iron kettle on an iron pipe tripod, filled with rabbit stew. Rabbits were still plentiful and these had been driven to the higher ground by the water and hunted down by Lizzy's older brother. When the lid was raised, a delicious aroma emerged along with the steam.

Each of the four camps seemed to be set up much like the other. After all, there are only so many ways to set up a camp! Each had its campfire for cooking and warmth and lean-to for protection against the elements. They each had one thing in common, survival from the flood water in the valley below and from the cold damp weather.

That evening, even before dark, the Reynolds family gathered under the shed for supper. One thing was a little out of the ordinary. Law and Leonard had done the milking! There was no good reason for them not to, since they were on idle time and the women folks were in the smokehouse cooking. The kitchen table, if one could call it that, consisted of boards laid out across wooden barrels that were still packed with canned goods and what not. Each woman hurriedly carried a covered dish from the smokehouse to the shed before it got cold or wet and it tasted little differently than at home. Each person found their own private place to sit and eat, on hand made benches, buckets or as Earl Lee, atop a barrel. He constantly swayed forward on his perch, nearly losing his balance, but never fell off, to the surprise of everyone.

Millie looked at each member of her family, eating their fill of good food and wondered about her friends, not too far distant. Did they have enough food? The rabbits stewing over the open fire in the big iron kettle, was that their entire meal? Did they have potatoes and biscuits or corn bread and other things? She realized they never had plenty, even in good times, knowing this by keeping her inquisitive ears open. She supposed they were considered "Poor" people, what ever that meant. She didn't see them too often because they missed school a lot and lived too far out to go visit. But, she did like those girls and all the families seemed nice and friendly and she felt pity and compassion for them out there in the rain. She wished the night would end so she and Helen could go back and play with them.

She paid no attention to what was going on around her until Grandma exclaimed in an irritated voice, "I-Gawd Almighty, what's wrong with these biscuits? They ain't hardly got no taste to them."

Everyone paused in eating and stared at the biscuit in their hand. Apparently, no one found anything amiss in the big fluffy, golden brown morsel and looked at Grandma for clarification.

"I don't see anything wrong with mine," Grandpa ventured.

"Me either," declared Papa. "Mine tastes the same as always, maybe even better."

"That's because you've got used to them that way," Grandma told him. "Mine tastes like there's not a speck of salt in it. That's why it's so flat and tasteless. I always put a nice big pinch of salt in mine."

Millie and all the others knew that Mama had made them and she lowered her head, before looking at her mother. Everyone else was staring at her also, not knowing what to say or how to take this bit of sarcastic criticism.

Mama just sat still on her bucket stool, her face beet red in embarrassment. "I did put salt in them," she murmured meekly.

"They sure don't taste like it," Grandma said. "I guess I'll just have to make the biscuits too from now on."

Millie felt a great compassion for her mother. As she sat there, it was difficult to tell by the look on her usually cheerful face if she was really mad or about to cry. She remembered the argument she had heard the night before between her mother and father. She went to her mother and putting her arms around her neck, whispered, "Mine is good, Mama. Just the way I like them."

"Mine too," chirped Earl Lee.

The rest of the meal was eaten in silence. Mabel said hardly anything the rest of the night.

When Mabel walked with the girls up to the house later, she hugged them tightly before releasing them for the night and going back to the rest of the family. She was thankful for friends like the Quigleys for letting her girls sleep in a warm, comfortable house out of the damp chilling weather.

The night under the shed left much to be desired in the way of comfort. However, all one had to do was remember those other families out in the open, under a canvas or make-shift lean-to. Rain pelting the tin roof seemed much louder than usual, enough in itself to keep one awake, without the worry of being away from home. That, plus the fact that her mother-in-law seemed to be trying to drive her away. She thought she couldn't bear to hear Bessie say, I-Gawd another time.

Mabel slept very little that night on the pallet of hay, covered over with a heavy blanket, next to a weakling of a husband who hadn't enough gumption to stand up to his parents. But then, not many folks did stand up to either Bessie or Lawrence. The unfamiliar snoring of others besides Leonard didn't help any either.

The next morning, Millie and Helen prolonged their stay in the warm, dry house as long as possible. Missus Quigley insisted they stay and eat a nice hot breakfast before going back outside in the cool, wet weather, for which they were grateful.

Upon reaching the shed, Millie knew at once that all was not well. Papa sat at one end of the structure all alone, whittling on a piece of wood. Mama appeared irritable and cross, which would have been unusual until these past few weeks. She used to be so happy and cheerful and pleasant. Lately, she seemed unhappy most of the time. This morning, she looked like she had been crying, her eyes were so red. She probably didn't sleep well. Listening to the conversation of the adults, Millie was able to draw her own conclusions of what was wrong.

It seemed that Grandma had been at it again, making disparaging remarks and downgrading Mama. Grandma never said anything really bad, just little comments about how Mama cooked or sewed or kept house. She said things like leaving a dirty kettle on the stove from one meal to the next or Papa's overalls not being quite as clean as they used to be when she washed them. She also said the seams on the girls dresses were not perfectly straight. Millie couldn't understand why she even said such things, unless of course, it really was as Mama had claimed and Grandma wanted her to leave. But, it just didn't make sense to her.

Everyone knew that Mama kept the cleanest house of anybody and was a much better cook and seamstress than Grandma, who practiced that old adage, a lick and a promise, which meant she glossed over the surface, with a promise to come back later and do it right. But, once she gave it the lick, she never did come back for the promise.

Millie knew that Mama made the best meatloaf of anyone. Everyone said so. When they attended Sunday dinner on the ground at church, she nearly always took it. Even the other ladies bragged about how good it was and said, "That Mabel Reynolds makes the best meatloaf in the country."

Grandma scoffed at such sayings. She liked some bay leaves in her meat loaf, which Mama never used.

And Mama's cakes were fluffier than most and her bread and biscuits lighter. Another thing, Grandma complained that the girl's dresses were too short and when they ran while playing, their knees showed. Little girls should never wear dresses that short. Millie wished her dresses were even shorter so her legs could have more freedom and she could run faster.

She saw her mother walking toward the Quigley's house. Her face wore a very determined expression and when Millie started to follow, she was told to go back out of the rain. The little girl had no way of knowing that her mother would call her own father from the Quigley's house. They were the only people, to date, to have such a contraption in the neighborhood. It so happened that her own parents also had one, clear over in Mill Town and Mabel Reynolds planned to take advantage of this fact while she could.

Turning the crank of the gadget hanging on the wall, by standing on her tip toes, she waited for what seemed like several minutes before the voice on the other end of the line reached her ear. Feeling a slight tinge of disappointment at not hearing one of her own family, she realized the voice belonged to the operator. After forwarding the desired information, she waited again, listening to the crackling on the wire as the operator, in turn rang the phone on the other end. Her father's voice finally reached her ear, faint and barely audible. It was wonderful, hearing him and in her present state of mind, she broke down in tears. After some seconds, she calmed down enough to explain the reason for her call and asked her father to come and get her and take her home, because she intended to leave Leonard. He, of course, was upset at the idea, but agreed to come.

"Wait three or four days until it stops raining," she said, "If it ever does. There are a few things at home that I want to take with me, but we can't get there now."

He promised to come as soon as he could get through and hung up.

Kate Quigley listened to the conversation in a state of shock and Mabel swore her to secrecy until she was gone. She apologized to the older woman for using her telephone to make such a call and hoped it would not jeopardize her friendship with her mother-in-law. After the first initial shock, Kate admitted that she had seen trouble brewing between Mabel and her family. She also told Mabel not to worry about her friendship with Bessie because they had been friends a long time and she could handle her.

Tragedy even worse than the floodwater struck that morning. Even before Millie and Helen were ready to go over to the camps with the Wilmore girls, Jessy came walking towards them. Seeing her coming through the rain, Millie knew something was wrong. Jessy walked slowly, staring straight ahead, not bothering to step over or around the puddles of water.

Bessie grabbed her by the arm as soon as she reached the shed and pulled her over to the fire.

"Sakes alive girl, what's wrong with you? You're soaked to the skin. Come on over here and dry out before you catch your death." Seeing the tears running down the girls white face, she said more sympathetically, "Now tell me what's wrong. It can't be that bad!"

Jessy stared at her, lower lip trembling, but she couldn't speak.

Bessie took her by both shoulders and shook her, "Now, you tell me what's wrong, so I can help you."

"I think Pip is dead," she quivered.

"I-Gawd girl, what do you mean, you think she's dead?" Grandma demanded.

"I think she's drowned!"

"Drowned!"

"Yes'm."

"What makes you think she drowned?"

"She fell in the water and couldn't get out," Jessy sobbed.

"Papa said for me to come get somebody to go there to help."

Bessie hugged the little girl to her ample bosom and patted her on the back. Mabel clutched her own two girls tightly to her. Earl Lee dropped down from the back of the wagon and went to stand beside Bessie, taking in the "goings on."

Admittedly, Bessie was usually brusque and sharp, but she did have a soft spot in her heart for a grieving child and immediately went into action.

She stuck her head out from the shelter of the shed and called, "Lawrence, yo Lawrence," as though calling up the pigs.

Presently, he came out of the barn, where he and Leonard were passing the time of day with Tom Quigley.

"What's wrong with you, woman? They can hear you clean over in the next county," he called back.

"Come on over here," she hollered. "We got a big problem."

Realizing there definitely was something amiss, Law went to his wife, followed by the other two men.

"What's all the fuss about?" he asked.

"We better get over there to the Wilmore camp," Bessie told him. "This young'un says her sister drowned."

Law looked at the little girl who was crying openly now.

"I reckon we'd better get over there then," he said and started off at a fast pace with Leonard and Tom following him.

Bessie grabbed a jacket and put it on. "You stay here with the kids," she told Mabel. "You'd best stay too, Jessy." She left, sloshing along after the men.

At any other time Mabel would have been resentful at such an order from her mother-in-law, treated like a child! For once, however, she felt grateful for not having to be a part of this ordeal. She just didn't feel up to it. She and the three children sat quietly around the fire, waiting. No one said much and even Earl Lee kept still, which was quite a feat for him, in itself. There were a million questions crowding his young mind, but he dare not voice them now. Being always inquisitive and full of questions about things he didn't understand, he sat and stared at Jessy. Death was only one of the many things he knew nothing of, but he would ask about it later.

They seemed to be gone for ages when Bessie and Leonard returned. Millie listened attentively as they related to her mother what had happened.

The way Millie gathered it, Jessy and Pip had been walking along the edge of the woods. A ditch about two feet deep separated the woods and an open field. It was full of water. Pip carried a stick she used to slash at imaginary foes along the way. Standing on the edge of the ditch, she probed around in it to see how deep it was. Suddenly, the soft earth gave way and Pip slid down into the water and couldn't get out.

"You'd think a child could climb out of two feet of water," Mabel said.

Bessie explained the reasons why she couldn't. The ground was soft mud and with all them heavy clothes on and galoshes, the poor thing didn't have a chance. When the galoshes filled with water, they became dead weight on her feet and she couldn't move them enough to get a foot hold. Then she panicked and began threshing about until she just went under, while Jessy stood on the bank watching, horrified. When Pip stopped moving, Jessy ran to tell her folks and her father and Mr. Hathorn went and pulled her out. She never had a chance at survival, once she fell in. Mrs. Wilmore had been sitting on a stool all this time, holding the girl in her arms, rocking back and forth, sobbing and humming. It's enough to break your heart.

The children sat quietly, not sure how to re-act, since this was their first encounter with death in any form, except of course an animal of some kind. The women folk however knew exactly what to do, the same as had always been done at such times, when a neighbor had a death in the family. It was common practice that they take food to the family to relieve them of that burden. So, they dug around in their larder and began cooking food for the bereaved family. Bessie accepted Kate's invitation to prepare everything in her house rather than work in the smokehouse and the three ladies cooked a meal fit for a king.

Tom Quigley found some boards in his barn and the men laid them atop saw-horses in the tool shed. After the food was ready, the Wilmore family and Hathorns were invited to come eat. Most of what was left over went with the bereaved family back to their camp. It was dry and warm under the shed, compared to what these families had experienced the past few days. They all ate a hearty meal that was warm to the body.

The other two families camped in the woods a short distance from the Wilmores had been included in the invitation to eat, but refrained from coming. No one really knew them that well anyway, they lived so far out in the Bottoms. Law knew them better than anyone else perhaps, but just in passing on the road or meeting at one of the Blairsville stores. Even then, it was barely a "Howdy." He wasn't sure of their names. Many such families were still scattered across the valley, seldom going to town or associating with anyone other than their own kind. There was still enough timber that they could eke out a living by hunting, fishing and working a small acreage. They did not merit the name dirt farmers and were church mouse poor. Most of them were camped around the rim of the valley in the same fashion as all the others.

These Bottoms dwellers were called, not too fondly, Bottoms Men. Mostly, they sired large broods of family offspring that were brought into the world without the assistance of a doctor or a mid-wife. Seldom did any of the children go to school or receive any sort of formal training and only sporadically at best, barely enough to master the three R's. The Bottoms Man's earthly possessions consisted mainly of a piece of land, often not his own, a cabin, one or two mules, a cow, chickens, a litter of pigs, geese, and a goat. And a passel of hound dogs. A weed infested vegetable garden and produce from his livestock and hunting ability, supplied food for his livelihood.

They were a special breed of people left over from the logging era. Living there quietly they bothered no one other than poaching on some farmers cleared land occasionally. When they decided to move on, they would leave without notice to anyone, except a close friend, taking with them, whatever they could carry in wagons or mule pack. Usually, they were not heard from again. After these flood waters subsided, Law guessed, many more would vanish. Good riddance, he said. They did nothing to help improve the land. However, that night, these two men came over to Wilmore's camp to offer condolences, after hearing of the tragedy.

The next morning, as the Reynolds family was doing the few chores that needed to be done, Tom Quigley came over. Going under the roof of the shed, he stood at the fire warming his hands.

"I've been to the Wilmore's," he finally said. "Kate fixed them some breakfast and I took it over."

"How're they holding up?" Bessie asked.

"Not too good. The Hathorn baby died last night and it upset all of them."

"Land o'goshen," exclaimed Bessie. "Well, I ain't really that much surprised though, with all this rain and wet weather. It must have had pneumonia, from the way it coughed and carried on yesterday. If it don't stop this raining pretty soon so we can all get back to our own homes, we'll all die."

"It's a sad thing," Tom commented. "I just don't know what to do about it."

"There's nothing any of us can do except try to stay out of the weather as much as we can," Lawrence said.

"I'm beginning to understand how Noah must have felt," Mabel said. "Just these few days have been dreadful."

Bessie sat pondering for a few minutes. Then brusquely, "Law, why don't you go and see about burying them two little ones!"

"Tarnation woman, I ain't going over there and butt into their business," he exclaimed. "Death is a private affair and up to the family to take care of. Where in sam-hill would they bury them in all the water, any ways!"

"Well, you can go talk to them about it!"

"I ain't going to do no such thing!"

It appeared to be a stalemate for a minute.

"You know, Law, she may be right," Tom said. "Them poor souls may need some help at that."

"I don't think it's any of our business what they do. I wouldn't want some outsiders coming in to tell me what to do."

"That's not the same at all," retorted Bessie. "Them folks need some comfort and help. They won't even be thinking straight for awhile, what with losing a child as well as their home."

"I guess it won't hurt none to talk to them and see what we can do," Tom suggested. "It'll be the Christian thing to do."

"Just suppose they agreed to our helping to bury them, where would anybody dig a grave?" Lawrence reasoned. "They'd probably want to bury them close by, on their own land and we sure as thunder can't do that."

"Maybe you're right," agreed Tom, "But it just don't seem right to leave them young'uns lying there for no telling how long, until the water goes down. That could be weeks and you know as well as I do that that wouldn't work out so good. Them bodies need to be in the ground. Besides, them folks can't start to get over their grieving until they do. If we have to, we can use our burying plot. There's plenty room and it sure won't hurt none to have them there."

"No need for that," Bessie said. "Why not in the cemetery up on the Hill?"

"You can't do that," Law told her. "That's a private cemetery that belongs to the church."

"I know that. It belongs to the people who go there. We're members there and have a right to say who can be buried there. The Hathorns go there too, some times! Not often maybe, like every month, but that's where they go to church. So, that makes it all right for them to use the cemetery. That gives them as much right as anybody."

"She's got a point there," Tom agreed.

The church they referred to was the Pleasant View Primitive Baptist Church, also called the Church on the Hill, where the Reynolds family had attended since moving to the Bottoms. It was a conveniently located church made up of others sharing the same faiths and beliefs. The well kept cemetery was shared by many who were not connected with the church in any way except through family or friends.

"But, we can't just go in there and bury somebody on our own, without some authority," Law protested.

"Huh, that's the first time I recollect you worrying about authority or right or wrong," Bessie scoffed. "You're always one to do things the way you want. Now, you and Tom get on over there and talk to them folks. We can't have no real funeral maybe without a preacher, but come next meeting day, I'll explain it all to Brother Smith and let him conduct a regular service. You might even slip him an extra dollar to make it all right with the Lord."

Reluctantly, Law got to his feet, threw the slicker over his shoulders and started to follow Tom out into the rain.

"And when you do that, ride on over to the church and dig a grave," his wife ordered. "And dig it in a good spot, I-Gawd, where it'll drain good."

"Confounded women, I don't know why God ever put them on this earth," Law muttered half to himself. "Unless it was just to aggravate us men."

Tom smiled at his friend. "Yes, you do! We've both been fortunate enough to have good women to take care of us. Not many would put up with either of us. What would we do without them!"

Law grunted in response.

It took some talking to persuade the bereaved families to have an early burial. The men felt it should be done at once, but had a difficult time convincing the mothers to give up their babies. Mrs. Wilmore had held onto her daughter Pip all night and wouldn't give her up for any reason. After much coaxing, however she finally gave up and turned the girl's body over to others. So, arrangements were made.

"We'll need to have a coffin," Tom said.

"Yeah! You make one and me and the Boy will go dig the grave," Law told him.

It had been agreed upon, by general consensus that the two would be buried together in one coffin after considering the circumstances. If one or the other family wanted to dig them up later for separate burials, they could do so. But, they never did!

Law and Leonard saddled up their horses and rode off, each equipped with a shovel. After riding the mile or so, they turned into the yard of the little white painted church. It was a very pleasant and peaceful place in the spring and summer, when the big oaks and hickory trees were leafed out. Now, the trees were barren and bleak in the dreary rain, being still too early for the buds to form. Walking around through the small grave yard, they found a site that appeared to be just right, though each man knew Bessie would find some fault with its location.

Digging in the soft earth proved to be no great chore and when the grave was finished, Law spread a canvas over the top, hoping to prevent it filling with water before the coffin could be lowered into it.

Tom had the coffin finished when they returned. It sat on the end of a wagon in the tool shed. Kate rummaged around until she found a large piece of material suitable for lining and spread it around the interior of the wooden structure. Tom apologized to Jeb Wilmore for the rough lumber used, but it was the best he had. Smooth, finished boards were hard to come by without going to a lumberyard specifically for that purpose.

Jeb assured him it looked fine.

Pip's and the baby's bodies were brought to the shed in the Wilmore wagon and the coffin was positioned on saw-horses which were much lower than the wagon and could be prepared and viewed more handily. Kate, having had more experience at such things than the others after losing some of her own family through the years, did most of the arranging of the bodies, with the help of Tom and Bessie.

Pip lay full length in the box, with the baby cradled in her arms. Around them was an old, brightly colored quilt, donated by Kate. Tears came to the eyes of all the women. They looked so life like, peaceful and serene. Such tranquility had never touched them in life, but now there was nothing other than contentment on the innocent little faces.

As the small gathering stared down at them, many tears flowed openly. Mabel began crying and turned away to clutch her own daughters to her.

Presently, Tom Quigley broke into the mourning to say, "I hate to break this up, but I think it's time to go if we want to be back by dark."

"You all go on and I'll stay here with the children and cook us something," Kate volunteered. "We'll all need some warm food in our stomachs."

"I'll stay and help and watch the children that don't want to go," Mabel offered, feeling she just couldn't go through such an ordeal as having to help bury two children.

Jessy of course, wanted to go, but the other children chose to stay behind, because of the weather. Helen went along and Millie was undecided until her mother said to stay with her. Earl Lee begged to go, so Bessie motioned him to the wagon.

The lid was nailed in place as the two mothers sobbed and the procession of only two mule drawn wagons rolled off.

Kate went to the house to finish her cooking. Mabel cautioned the children, who were left in her care, to stay in the shed and out of trouble and followed Kate to help cook.

Taking the double loaf pan of bread from the oven, Kate spoke for the first time of Mabel's leaving home. She had never been nosey or one to pry into someone else's business, but felt the need to say something if it could help to resolve a tragic problem.

"I know it's none of my business," she said, "And you can tell me so, if you want to, but have you really thought things through about leaving Leonard?"

"I suppose maybe it is some of your business, since you're so close to the family," Mabel replied. "Yes'm, I have thought it through. That's all I do think about, day and night. I can't even sleep, for thinking about it. I know it's going to be a terrible thing to do, but I just can't take it no more."

"Do you want to tell me the problem?" asked Kate. "Now, you don't have to if you'd rather not, but sometimes it helps to talk to somebody."

"That's just it, I don't have anybody I can talk to and share confidences with. Oh, there's Lorna, she's Reuben's wife and we're good friends and we do talk now and then, but I don't get to see her very often. It wouldn't really help much anyway, though. Nothing will help as long as I stay there, so close to Leonard's folks."

"I guessed as much!"

"It's not that they do anything bad, but Miz Reynolds can do and say things about me when Leonard's not around. Just little things, like criticize me about the way I do things. She didn't used to be like that when I worked for them. It all started after me and Leonard got married."

"You took her boy away from her," Kate said calmly.

"I didn't really take him away. Why, he's still down there nearly as much as he was before. When I try to explain to him what she does, it doesn't sound bad at all and he won't believe she did anything wrong. He just refuses to listen. You surely know how she is, Miz Kate!"

"Yes, I know how she is. I've known Bessie Reynolds for a long time and probably know her better than anyone else on earth, except maybe Lawrence. I consider her a good friend, maybe my best friend." Kate paused, trying to decide what to say next. "She thinks you took her boy and she wants him back, at least that's how it looks to me."

"But, why can't Leonard see that? I don't understand why we can't go away from here and start over some place else. Why can't he at least believe what I tell him!"

Kate gave her that, "you poor thing" look of sympathy and said, "I'm sure he knows. He just can't do anything about it. You see, he's not made of the same stuff as some of us are. From what I've heard over the years, he must take after his real mother. She was patient and gentle and Leonard has all her good traits and that's good, except when it means standing up to such a formidable person as Bessie, or Lawrence either, for that matter. It's easier to choose the path of least resistance and follow it. I'm sure he loves you, but he can't find it in himself to rock the boat, so to speak."

She stirred the great kettle of beans on the stove. "Now, I'm not saying anything against your mother-in-law, because like I said before, she's my best friend. I only want you to understand about her. She's a kind and caring woman, most of the time. Why, she'll do anything for people in need. I know she talks a little loud at times and is a little gruff, but that's her character and the way she is. Underneath that rough exterior is a big heart."

"I know! I used to like her a lot, before we got married," Mabel wailed forlornly, "And even afterwards for awhile. But I've just got to get away, Miz Kate. I can't take it no more."

"Do you plan on taking the girls with you?" Kate asked.

"Oh yes. I couldn't leave without them. When I saw that little girl lying in that coffin today, it just broke my heart. It could have been one of my own."

"You know, of course, he won't let you?"

"What do you mean? Who won't let me do what?"

"I mean Lawrence won't let you take the girls away!"

Mabel was aghast. "I don't understand why not," she exclaimed. "They're my children."

"That's what you think!"

"But, they are! They're my very own."

"Listen to me, young woman. They are Lawrence Reynolds grandchildren. You only gave birth to them. There's a big difference," Kate tried to explain. "He will never let them go. Why he fairly dotes on them. I've seen the way he watches them and I'm telling you, I think he cares more for them than he does any one else in this world, including his wife and son. He don't take kindly to losing something that belongs to him. As far as he's concerned, they're his. He goes after what he wants and don't anyone take it away from him."

"But, I still don't see how he can keep me away from my own flesh and blood." Mabel was horrified at the thought.

113

"Believe me, my dear, you can't win. Between the two of them, you won't have a chance. They are the most strong willed folks I ever met."

"I'll just have to take them when there's no one around."

"And when would that be? Even if you did succeed in getting away, how long do you think it would be before he went and got them?"

"Oh Miz Kate, what am I going to do," Mabel wailed. "I just can't stay there."

"I don't know! Like I said, Bessie is my friend and I won't be a part of anything to spoil that friendship. I'm truly sorry, but that's all I can do."

Mabel felt as though the bottom of the world had dropped out for her. "You won't tell no one about this, will you!" she pleaded.

"No, I won't mention it. After all, I never was one to butt into other people's business."

The families returned from the make-shift funeral just before dark. Bessie explained the proceedings, while the food was brought out. Everyone ate a hearty, but solemn meal, by lantern light.

Earl Lee seemed to be at his best behavior. Being quiet, which was totally unlike him, he hardly spoke a word, deep in thought. When everyone besides his own family had departed, he sat beside Lawrence. There was something on his mind and he was bursting with curiosity. The best source of information was his Uncle Lawrence. The boy had no father that he knew of, or real mother either for that matter. Gertrude never acknowledged him as her own. When Bessie and Lawrence had taken him in, he was taught at an early age to refer to them as aunt and uncle. This was all fine and dandy with him and he never questioned why he never had a real mother or father like all the other kids and accepted things as they were. Uncle Lawrence proved to be the father figure that he went to in time of trouble.

"Uncle Lawrence, will we ever see Pip again?" he asked.

Slightly caught off guard, Law had to think of the implications here.

"No," he answered, looking down at the boy.

With this question, both Millie and Helen perked up, their interest immediately aroused. They knew from past experiences with Earl Lee, that this question would be followed by others. He would never take a simple no for an answer to anything and the next questions were the ones they wanted to hear answered. They were too grown-up to ask themselves.

"Why?" Earl Lee asked.

This was one of the answers they wanted to hear and it would be followed by other questions. If he had asked them first, as he usually did and they didn't know the answer they made up one just to appease him. If that failed to satisfy him, then they walked away with the attitude, "Boys, they don't know anything."

"Because, she's dead," Lawrence said. "You know that. You were there when we buried her!"

Now, Earl Lee was no dummy. He had seen a lot of dead animals and birds, snakes too, but it seemed like it should be different with people. He had heard Brother Smith preach in church about a man named Jesus who died and came back to life. Maybe Pip and that little baby might come back too. So, he had to pursue the matter a little farther, to make sure, just as Millie and Helen knew he would.

"She won't ever come back?" he asked.

"No!"

"What will happen to them?"

"I reckon God will come take them!"

"Take them where?"

"Dad nab it boy, to Heaven I guess!" Lawrence exclaimed.

"How will he get them?"

"I don't know," Lawrence replied, after thinking for a minute. "Go ask your Aunt Bessie, she goes to church all the time. She knows all about such things."

Bessie turned her "thanks for nothing" look at him and waited for Earl Lee to come to her.

"How will God get Pip out of that coffin, Aunt Bessie? I saw Mr. Quigley nail it shut, real tight," he wanted to know. "And then him and Uncle Lawrence shoveled dirt in the grave on top of it, so nobody could get in there."

"Well, God has ways of getting in places and doing things that we just don't know about or understand," she made an effort to explain. "Maybe it's better we don't understand about such things."

"When will He come and get her?" Earl Lee queried.

"He's likely to already have her with Him in Heaven by now."

"Why didn't He take her before they nailed her in the coffin? Seems to me it would be a lot less trouble. Then He wouldn't have to dig her up again." Each time he considered the lame answers given him only tended to confuse him more. But the two girls absorbed them all and for once were grateful for his inquisitiveness, though they didn't understand any better than he.

"I don't know. That's just not His way of doing things," Bessie replied.

"But, if God wants people up in Heaven with Him, why don't He just take them while they're alive and well? Why does He always wait until they die? It seems to me it'd be better that way."

"I guess He wants them to be with their family as long as they can."

"Then how come he let's little babies die," he persisted. "They haven't been with their family hardly any time at all!"

Bessie could take no more, so in response, she said, "My stars, look at the time. We all better get to bed."

Now, Millie knew that Grandma didn't have a pocket watch and she couldn't see the old alarm clock in the wagon. She never did know why they had an alarm on that clock, because it was never used. Grandpa woke up at the same time each morning without an alarm, even before the first rooster crowed. She also knew this to be Grandma's way of getting out of a ticklish situation by not having to answer a delicate question. Somewhat disappointed that she would not learn the answers, she kissed her mother and father good-night and followed Helen up to the house and to bed.

It stopped raining just before dawn. An almost eerie silence followed, after long days of steady pattering on the tin roof.

Law sat up on the pallet and said aloud, "Tarnation, it's stopped raining."

Everyone under the shed was awakened by the quiet, after becoming accustomed to the constant sound of rain. Morning came early that day and Leonard got up to put more wood on the fire.

With the light of day, the clouds drifted slowly away and the sky cleared. By afternoon, the sun came out, brightening the otherwise dismal day. One could tell that the rain had truly ended at last. Folks began to feel better and became cheerful. The ordeal was not yet over, but the future looked brighter, even with the floodwaters spread out over the Bottoms. All this still had to drain off and dry out! Better days were ahead and in sight.

Jeb Wilmore came over and asked to speak to Lawrence, alone. They walked off to one side, away from the others. Seeing that the man was nervous and upset, Law took the plug of tobacco from his pocket, cutting off one corner and offering it to Jeb and then repeating the procedure for himself. They each positioned the chew firmly in their cheeks before speaking.

Not being one to beat around the bush, Jeb took the bull by the horns and came straight to the point. "Mr. Reynolds, I aim to sell out and leave here. Will you buy my place from me?"

He had been expecting the offer from the very outset of the flood and came prepared. Hesitating a minute before answering, he spat a brown stream and asked, "What you aim on doing?"

"Take my family back to Kentucky where we came from."

"Where abouts in Kentucky?"

"Just below Paducah," Jeb replied. "That's where my woman is from and she wants to go back and be among her kin."

It mattered little to Law where the man was going, except to better figure about how much it would cost him to get home.

"Since our Pip died, she's got a hankering to get away from here. She never did want to leave Kentucky in the first place. And now that Pip is gone, she says she just can't stand it here no more," Jeb explained. "I guess I pretty much feel the same way now. With all that water, everything will be ruined. Will you buy me out, Mr. Reynolds? It's good land and about half is cleared."

Law had learned years ago that the best way to get a good deal in a transaction was to let the other man do the talking. By waiting long enough, he usually came down in his estimation of the value of his property. So he waited, as though only mildly interested, rolling the quid of tobacco around in his jaw.

"Some of it is fenced and it drains good; in ordinary times least wise," Jeb went on, trying to increase the value. "The house only has three rooms, but it's in fair to middling condition. I wouldn't try to put one over on you, Mr. Reynolds. The roof leaks a little, but it can be fixed up easy with some tin or tar paper. I just ain't had the money to buy none. You know how it is!   With a little money it can be made into a real nice place. And it's got three sheds and a deep well of good drinking water. There's a spring on the bottom. I dug it myself, me and the missus."

Law let Jeb do the talking.   He already knew all there was to know about his plot of ground. Years ago, most of the acreage in the bottoms had been laid out in forty to eighty acre plots. Jeb happened to have a forty acre one. The house was just a cut above the cabins built by many of the Bottoms men. Made of rough cut clapboard with tarpaper roof, Law guessed that it leaked more than just a little. The fence that

Jeb mentioned was of hand hewn rails and barbed wire and barely good enough to contain any live stock that wished to wander.

Yes, Law knew all about the place, without being told of it's good qualities. The land was good, the same as his own, but would need to be cleared some more before cultivation.

The so-called house and buildings were of no value to him at all and therefore would have to be destroyed, probably burned, which was easier, faster and a better way of clearing.

He had had his eye on this particular piece of ground for some time and had waited patiently. Now, the time arrived, as he knew it would. This was the piece on the northeast side of his own farm that would square off the boundary of his property!

He thought of all this while Jeb was still talking and already knew what he'd pay.

"I'll have to spend a lot of time and money on the place, and I don't really need it," Law reflected. "But, I'll give you four hundred for it."

Jeb's jaw sagged slightly and he spat, "Could you make it four-fifty?" he asked. "I'll need a little to get me started again."

"I'll make it four twenty five," Law offered. "Like I said, it's going to cost me some before I can use it."

"I sure do thank you, Mr. Reynolds. I knew I could count on you. You're a good man," Jeb said. "I'll bring the paper to you, just as soon as the water goes down. It's in a tin box with some more things I hid in the attic where it'll stay dry."

A firm handshake closed the deal.

"The money will be here when you come for it," Law promised him, and Jeb walked away happy, as though a great load had been lifted from his shoulders.

CHAPTER 5

Lawrence stood on the side of the hill, about halfway down, as he had done the past couple of days. Now the sky was clear. No more rain fell and judging from the feel of the atmosphere, he knew it was over. The air, being still chilly and damp from all the water, would change when the sun came out. He could only see as far as the Big Ditch because of the trees. One day he planned to buy the land beyond the Ditch, but for now, he was more concerned about the present state of his property.

Apart from the trees on the far side, the Ditch could be detected by the flow of water. It moved rapidly, whereas in the rest of the Bottoms, it flowed slowly. Weeds and bushes sticking up above the muddy surface wavered slightly, indicating the water was receding.

Gullies had been washed out along the hillsides, washing topsoil down into the valley below. To some, this soil would be welcome, but to Law, he was satisfied with what already lay there. To the farmers on the higher ground, it meant losing much of their best topsoil, though that in the Bottoms was already superior and he would be pleased to leave it that way. But, there was nothing he could do about an act of God, so he accepted it as such. It only meant he'd have to plow a little deeper this year to mix the two types together for a good crop.

On the other hand it could be beneficial, adding nutrients and elements that his own land was low in. Yes, it could be good!

Later, he threw the saddle and bridle on Prince, his big white stallion. Not having heard from anyone other than those at Quigley's since leaving home, he decided it was time to ride down to Blairsville and check on his neighbors from the Bottoms. The road ran along the base of the uplands, just above the receding water. Only a couple of places in the road were still covered, so there was no problem on that score.

Several families from the Bottoms had sought refuge on the higher ground behind Blairsville Store and along the road. No landowner objected to the encroachment of these unfortunate people on his land. The camps were all similar in most respects. Each had at least one or two hastily constructed lean-tos for shelter. These were fabricated by corrugated tin, tarpaulins or boards covered with tarpaper. Primitive perhaps, but effective.

Law was surprised to find the camps were not clustered together. Instead, each had staked out his claim upon arrival, the earlier ones choosing the choice spots. Being scattered about allowed them some privacy, but mainly it provided them space for their animals to roam and graze. There were plenty of these, for everyone had to bring his entire conglomerate or lose them. This was supplemented by the many children of various ages and sizes and now that the rain had stopped, those not under the weather with a cold or flu, took advantage of the respite and were running and playing vigorously with friends to make up for lost time. In a few days, they would all be gone, leaving behind the clutter, trash and debris, the remnants of a difficult ordeal.

Dismounting at the hitching rail of Blessey's store, Law greeted and talked to men he hadn't seen lately. Once the water was gone, they would undoubtedly melt back into the Bottoms and only return again to civilization to sell their wares, whatever they might be, and buy supplies. He liked and respected most of these men and they in turn respected him.

Upon entering the store, Law told John Blessey to cut off a big chunk of chewing tobacco. John laid the slab of solid brown elixir under the sharp edged knife. Before he brought down the blade, Law said, "Move that over a bit, John, I need a piece about three times that size."

"You must've run out a couple days ago, to want that much," John observed, moving the slab over.

"Nope, it's just that I may not get back here for a couple of days and I want plenty on hand," Law replied, wrapping his handkerchief around it before putting it in his hip pocket. "Do you know where Hi-pockets is camped?"

"Sure, just about the third spot down the road, right past them twin oaks."

After discussing the weather situation for a few minutes, Law left the store to find his brother.

Sidney was easy to find. His massive brood occupied a large space of woods and grazing land. Most of his children had left home, but some of the ones that remained had some of their own. Sidney was seated on a stool by the open fire, talking to his wife, Lottie. Seeing his older brother, he stood up and stretched his big body. Over the years, he had put on some weight and the pouch was evident under the faded overalls, fastened by a single strap over his left shoulder. The floppy felt hat that bore the stained tell-tale signs of long wear, lay on the ground at his feet.

"Well, I see you made it, Big Brother," he greeted. "Where you been?"

"We stayed up at Quigley's." Law returned.

"I figured as much. I reckon you made it alright!"

"Yeah, we stayed in Tom's machinery shed."

"You always was lucky! That must be almost like living at home," Sidney laughed.

"It's better than being out in the weather."

"Living like that you don't know what it's like out in the weather. Why, you can't even appreciate this nice spring weather we're having."

Lottie took a tin cup from a wooden box near the wagon and handed it to Law. Taking a big, smoke blackened granite coffee pot from the fire, she filled the cup with the strong, dark liquid.

"Tarnation, Lottie, you must've heated this coffee twice," Law exclaimed, after touching it to his lips. "Nobody could get it this hot with just one heating." The tin cup itself made it all the more hot. "I don't know why they ever made tin cups for drinking coffee anyway!"

"They didn't," Lottie retorted. "They're made for drinking nice cool well water. But, it's the best I can do under the circumstances."

"I didn't mean to offend you. It's just that I burned my tongue on it."

"It wouldn't hurt none if it burned some of that brush pile off your upper lip," she responded, good naturedly.

Lottie was still pleasant to be around for she had retained her good sense of humor. The hard work and long childbearing years had taken their toll on her, though. Her once shapely body was now thin and her shoulders bent forward. She enjoyed trading barbs with her brother-in-law.

"This woman of yours ain't changed one whit," Law said to his brother. "She's still as sassy as ever."

He took the plug from his pocket and cut off a corner to stick in his mouth and handed it to Sidney.

"Gawd Law, looks like you aim to do a lot of chewing, with that plug," Sidney said.

"No more'n usual," Law returned, "Just don't plan to run out again."

Sidney refused the offer, saying, "You know danged well I don't use that stuff. You turned me against it years ago when you kept harping on the bad habit and ill effects and how nasty it was." He pulled the bag of Bull Durham from his shirt pocket and rolled a cigarette.

"I can see you pay attention to what I say. You give up one bad habit and take up another just as bad. Smoking will kill a man quicker'n chewing."

"You two boys are still the same as you were twenty five years ago," Lottie chimed in. "Arguing back and forth in the same way. I wonder if you'll ever grow up!"

"Likely not," her husband said, petting her on the backside. "Long as we each have us a young, good looking woman, we plan on staying just like we are."

Lottie smiled and they sat around for quite some time, reminiscing about the old days when they were young. It turned out to be a good visit, one of the few times over the years that they had the time to really sit down, relax and remember back.

Law told them about the two little girls they had buried, the one that drowned and the other that probably died of pneumonia. Lottie said, "Tsk, tsk, such a pity to lose one that way."

"We'll likely be able to go home in a couple of days," Sidney said.

"That's the way I figure," Law agreed. "Unless the creeks are all damned up down below so the water can't get out."

Lottie enjoyed this afternoon and remembering the days when they were all young and she and Bessie were such close friends.

"I wish you two would build a bridge across the Ditch so me and Bessie could visit together some," she said wistfully. "It's so far around the road and takes too long."

"Maybe we will one day, Lottie," Law halfway promised. "It'd be a big help to all of us."

But, the expanse was too wide for a simple footbridge and they never seemed to find the time for a better one, so it was never built.

The next morning the sky was clear and blue and the sun came out. Everyone felt in a much better mood. Even those living on higher ground, the ones not directly effected by flood waters, seemed to find renewed life because they too had been limited in their activities as a result of the weather.

Law was saddling up Prince when Sam Hathorn strode up.

After the usual amenities, Sam said, "Jeb Wilmore tells me you bought his place yesterday."

"That's right," Law replied.

"Would you buy mine, Mr. Reynolds? After losing our baby, it's going to be real hard staying down there."

"What you figure on doing?"

"Don't rightly know yet. The wife is the one who wants to leave, but don't want to go back to Arkansas. The boys all want to stay. This is the only home they know, they was all born here and like this way of life, all the hunting and fishing and they want to farm. They don't mind the work, at all. I guess we could make it somewhere's else if we had enough for a start."

"How long have you been in these Bottoms, Sam?" Law asked.

"Seems like all my life. I came here when I was a young man, for the logging. When me and my woman got married, I bought my place and we just stayed on."

"Looks to me like you ought to think it over some more, Sam. Moving someplace else won't help much, not if you and your boys are all satisfied. Why don't you talk to your wife and get her to come around!"

"I guess you're right about that Mr. Reynolds. The only thing is, I need me a little money to fix up the place, if I stay. You know, the roof and a couple other things that I been putting off. And now with all the water, I don't know what else will be needed."

Law knew the man to be trustworthy and hard working so, he made him a proposition, but first he needed to know one thing. "How much do you need to pay for these things?"

"Well, I reckon about a hundred dollars would square things away."

Now, Law had been calculating all the time they were talking and decided he could use this man to his advantage. Sam himself, was a man of medium build, strong and wiry and hardened by years of working out in the weather. That in itself would be enough to convince Law to keep him here. Added to this fact were the four strapping sons. Two of them were already nearly big enough to do a man's work, while the younger ones were not far behind in age and size. Law knew it would be worth his while to keep the family close by, in his debt, as all of them could prove useful. The farm was of no value to him. Though mostly cleared, it lay more than a quarter mile from his own boundary line, making it unfeasible for him to farm, and he didn't really need it anyway. Other property that he had his sights set on and adjoining his was more desirable.

"Why don't you go back and talk to your missus, Sam. If you get her to come around, maybe we can make a deal."

"What kind of deal?" Sam showed interest.

"I'll loan you the hundred dollars you said you needed and you stay on. You can pay me back a little at a time, whenever you can. You and the boys work for me when I need help and I'll pay a fair wage. I need somebody I can depend on to take care of that side nearest your place. You and your family can live there the same as now and work your own place the same way. But, when I need help, you come work for me. This way, you'll have a little money coming in and won't have to be dependent on a good crop."

Sam had grown excited as he listened to this very generous offer. It was more than he ever expected to have in life.

"Why don't you go on back and talk to your family, Sam, and see how they feel about it," Law suggested.

"I will," Sam exclaimed. "I know they'll be happy about it. This'll kinda make up a little for losing the baby." He grabbed Law's hand and shook it vigorously. "I sure do thank you, Mr. Reynolds. I'll come back and tell you if we'll take it. We'll all look forward to going home now and start cleaning up, when the water goes down."

He hurried back to his camp to spread the good news.

Law and Leonard rode down to reconoiter and check the damage done by the water. At the bottom of the hill, the horses hesitated briefly before entering the water and as the riders let the reins hang loose, they stepped gingerly into the water. Letting them choose their own way, they quickened the pace, splashing forward while staying in the middle of the road where it was barely knee deep. Law stopped at his own house, while Leonard rode off down the road to his own.

Fearing the very worst for his home in the way of water damage, Law was somewhat relieved when he pushed open the kitchen door. The water had risen only a few inches since he left, which surprised him, for he expected more. This meant there was only minimal damage to most of his furniture because what could be raised had been placed on blocks, which kept it high enough to be only damp from moisture. Even the beds were high enough to escape any real damage, though the feather mattresses would have to be dried out in the sun for a few days.

He decided that he had been fortunate, more so, than many others in the valley. His loss could be determined as minor. Once the water receded from inside the house, he would open all the doors and windows for as long as needed to air it out and to dry it out. The linoleum would lay flat again on the floors and the walls would dry out. The house had been well built and he had no doubt that when the plaster dried it would adhere to the laths and stay firm and solid.

All in all, the house had fared very well and he felt pleased. Wading in water above his knees, he went to the barn. Walking up the scales ramp, he entered through the big door to relatively dry ground and the scales platform. Here, life flourished in the form of chickens and other feathered fowl. They gazed at him ostentatiously and then began to cluck and squawk, letting him know they were out of food. Going to one of the barrels on the raised platform, he dug out great scoops of grain to scatter over the dry surface of the scales. The noise from the grateful birds assured him they were alive and well.

"It won't be long before you'll all be back where you belong," he told them. "Just a couple more days."

From one of the several nests in the hay-loft, he gathered a couple dozen eggs and placed them in an old bucket, nestled in a bed of hay to prevent breakage. Because of the cool weather, he knew the remainder of them would still be all right, without danger of spoiling. After all, they often stayed in that back room in the house for a week or more!

He mounted Prince again and the horse floundered back out to the road where the ground was higher and the water barely knee deep. By the time Leonard arrived, Law was beginning to shake. The wind came up and blowing across the cold water, added an extra chill to the April air. By now, he was in a hurry to get back up on the hill and out of these wet clothes and dry off, before catching pneumonia. This was definitely no time to get down sick.

Arriving back at the machine shed in just a few minutes, Bessie made them shed their garments and after drying off their bodies, put on dry clothes. Then they huddled by the fire, for its warmth, hopefully to ward off the flu or bad cold.

The quick action of the previous day undoubtedly prevented them from any ill effects. The sun was shining and the chill breeze had abated. Warm weather seemed to have arrived at last. A happy Sam Hathorn agreed to stay on his farm, under the agreement set out by Law, and work for him. The family was anxious to return home!

Law and Leonard rode back into the Bottoms. Even before this, evidence of subsiding water was apparent. Weeds and bushes stood up higher than before. The water moved eastward. Law imagined that the streams affected by the flood, such as Beaver Creek, the Skillet Fork and Little Wabash Rivers probably rushed in torrents to the Wabash River that flowed southward and emptied into the Ohio. The streams were large enough not to be dammed up with logs and brush, therefore allowing a free flow, which could drain the bottoms fairly fast.

Though the streams ran swiftly, the water covering this vast acreage moved slowly, which was good. It provided time for silt and sediment to settle out, instead of being carried down stream to no telling where. The brown mud left behind would cover the ground and harden into a layer of crust an inch thick, but when plowed under and mixed with the already rich soil, would make it even richer.

When Law opened the back door this time there was no water inside the house. But, the floor was covered with mud. Walking through the rooms, the raised linoleum creaked under his weight. The water mark had been left on all the walls as a reminder of how high it had been. Wading out to the barn, he returned with a large grain shovel and began scooping the mud out. He soon tired of this tedious task and gave it up for more important chores.

He threw more grain on the scales in the barn and climbed to the loft. Standing in the open doorway in the rear of the loft, he gazed out over the inundated fields, pondering the situation. It would be a while before everything was back to normal! Bessie would insist on him helping get the house cleaned out. He figured he might help enough to get the cook stove back in working condition, so she could cook his meals and help dry out the beds so, he could rest at night, but beyond that it was her job. He had his own work to take care of! She could go hire some woman who hadn't been affected by all the rain. There were surely plenty around that needed the work!

The things that concerned him most at present were the wells of drinking water. He must go see Coy Adams this very day, before some one else hired him. Coy lived up on the high ground and was the best well digger in the country. Law must hire him and his helper to drain and clean out his wells as soon as the water went down, and before he had to use them. Other farmers in the Bottoms would have the same idea, but Law planned on being first on the list. Until then, it meant carrying water from Tom Quigley's, but the well at the house had a good stream in it and should have suitable drinking water in a couple of days.

He stood there for a half an hour, thinking and planning. At the end of that time, everything was clear in his mind and he knew just what lay ahead, unless of course, it began to rain again. It didn't, however and the rest of the season had a normal amount of rainfall. The water kept going down and by tomorrow he could start bringing his family and livestock home.

Remnants of the flood would remain for some time to come. Water marks on the buildings as well as on the trees, served as grim reminders. Mud on bushes and covering the grass must dry out. They would soon begin to sprout green with the warmth of spring and grow for the animals. He would plow deep to reach the soil down under the newly deposited silt and mix them together for extra richness. And he knew his crops would flourish.

Four days after the families returned home, Mabel left Leonard for good. Clean up had been back breaking because, as the mud dried, it had to be scraped off the furniture and walls and floors with putty knives and wire brushes and strong soap and water. But, her house once again bore the signs of her labor.

Leonard had taken Helen with him on the wagon, to haul some things down to his parents. When Mabel saw her father's Dodge touring car coming down the road, she hurriedly gathered all the things she planned to take with her. Realizing the importance to get away at once, before her husband returned, she decided to take Millie now and come back later for Helen. Millie grew excited at the prospect of going to visit her other grandparents. She never saw them very often! When she realized her mother was crying, she knew then that something was not right and this would not be just a regular visit. Her grandfather seemed more stern as he talked to her mother, trying to persuade her to reconsider, which fell on deaf ears. Her mind had already been made up before. She placed a note on the kitchen table and they left.

Now, an automobile passing through the Bottoms in those days was an event in itself, so when the elder Reynolds recognized the big touring car, they stood in the yard and watched and waited for it to return. Law and Bessie were suspicious of its reasons for being here, but Leonard had no idea why his father-in-law should make such a trip at this time. They were all standing there and waved as it went by. Mabel's father honked the horn and waved, as did Millie, but Mabel stared straight ahead, looking neither to the right or left, tears running down her fair cheeks.

"Wonder where they're going!" Leonard muttered.

His parents stared at him, "You poor fool," they thought. "You should know."

Returning home, he was stunned by the note on the kitchen table. He read it over and over. It read, "Papa is here to take me away. I am leaving you for good. I'm taking Mildred with me and will come back for Helen. Don't try to come after me, because I'm not coming back to live with you. Yours truly, Your wife Mabel Reynolds."

For a long time, he sat there, trying to comprehend what had happened and why.

Lawrence was furious when he learned of this. He couldn't understand why Mabel would do such a thing as leave.

"What in tarnation got into that woman anyway. She had everything a woman should want, why wasn't she satisfied! Was you and her having trouble I didn't know about, Boy!"

"Good riddance, I say. You're better off without the likes of her around," Bessie soothed. "She's been getting too uppity lately. I-Gawd, the way she's always fixing up the inside of the house while letting some of the important outside work go begging."

Law swore Mabel would not get Helen or keep Millie. No one had ever taken anything away from him and he certainly wouldn't let some female be the first. Though he never publicly displayed any show of affection for anyone, the two little girls were the apple of his eye, so to speak, and being his granddaughters, they belonged to him.

His mother and father discouraged Leonard from making any attempt at reconciliation.

Mabel never came back for Helen, but she did file for divorce. The judge in the case awarded Mildred to her mother and Helen to her father.

Not at all satisfied with the ruling, Law decided to get both girls. A few days later, he hired a friend with an automobile to take him over to Mill Town. The only ones at home at the time were Millie and Mabel's sister. Law told the girl to get her things, they were going home. Gleefully, yet apprehensively, Millie gathered up her few belongings.

"You tell Mabel, if she wants my granddaughter back, she can see me in court," he told the woman, and taking Millie by the hand, went out to the waiting vehicle.

No one knows for sure just what transpired after that. A court date was set a couple of times but cancelled for some unknown reason. Some folks believed that Law paid off the judge in the case. Others thought Mabel felt it would be useless, because Lawrence Reynolds always got what he wanted. Eventually the matter was dropped and things returned to normal. Mabel decided to wait for awhile and try again later on. She never did though and the girls stayed on the farm. She later re-married. Earl Anderson, who still had relatives living around Mill Town, came for a visit and met Mabel. They fell in love and married and he took her over to Wood River to live, where he had a job at the Standard Oil Refinery. They had two children together, a boy and a girl.

The wheat that year all died from lack of oxygen from the flood-water and mud. Being planted in the fall and at the stool stage in growth, the tiny plants had no chance of survival. He planted more corn than usual and more hay, such as timothy and red top, along with alfalfa and clover, whose roots would grow down deeper into the hard pan of the soil and loosen it and add nitrogen. But he left plenty of acreage for fall planting of wheat and oats. Law and Leonard each used two teams of mules pulling gang plows in order to get the earth prepared and planted as soon as possible after the long delay.

Needing and hiring more men for all this work, Law seemed to enter the season on a large scale, working from sun-up to sun-down. Two of the hired men stayed on full time for two weeks, sleeping either in the hayloft or the barn or on the back porch of the house and taking their meals with the family. Bessie considered hiring a neighbor woman to help with her own share of the duties, cooking, washing, cleaning, milking and working the garden. But, someone else would only be in her way she theorized, so she did all the work herself with a little help from Helen and Millie.

Law had Sam Hathorn and his boys took what they wanted from the Wilmore place and burned the rest of the buildings. After that they were to start clearing the land. There being no great rush, they could do it as they farmed their own places.

Leonard and his girls ate at Bessie's table at first and slept at home, but this soon grew wearisome, running back and forth. His parents finally persuaded him to move in with them. He could keep his own house and maybe one day move back, when things changed. The two milk cows were moved down to Law's, but the rest of the farm animals stayed where they were and Leonard cared for them.

It was a busy time for the girls also. They had to accept new responsibilities in helping their grandmother, which was good for them. They learned many things that would be necessary in their lives.

Earl Lee became exuberant when he found out the girls were going to live with them in the same house. Although they had all played together part of the time before, now they became almost inseparable, much to the chagrin of the girls. To them, he was a pest and nuisance, but they tolerated him because he accounted for another person to play with. When something went amiss, they often blamed it on him, and he did have a certain knack for thinking up mischief and getting into trouble, which made life more interesting.

When the girls came home from school around the long way, Earl Lee and Shep, their shepherd dog, walked almost up to the main road to meet them. But, if they came the short way, he only went as far as the "Other place" as the other house was referred to, where Millie and Helen were born and lived in until recently. He never walked beyond that house alone. Just past the house, there was a small branch of water, over which a bridge lay. And beginning at the bridge was Cox's Woods.

Cox's Woods is where Sidney and Lottie first lived in a ramshackle cabin and where Gertrude was born. Everything was all right in the woods until that time, but after that, things began happening there. The way the girls learned of the legend was a family named Cox moved into the cabin. There were many children in the Cox family, no one besides them knew for sure just how many. They seemed to be a rowdy bunch and very unfriendly towards their neighbors. Since no one got to know them and because of the commotion that seemed to be erupting in the woods, folks began to refer to them as Cox's Army.

After awhile they moved away, no one knew just where they went and cared not at all. And that is when the legend began and grew. Folks passing that way after dark swore they saw and heard very strange and disturbing goings on in the woods. Reports went about of pigs squealing as though being butchered where there were no pigs. Lights from lanterns and bonfires were seen at night. The following day a group of men would go to investigate and find no evidence of such occurrences. This only added fuel to the legend and so it grew and no one dared go there after dark.

Adding more fuel to this, reports came out that a woman could be heard screaming in the middle of the night. At first, this was accepted as being a h'aint and besides all the Cox's in there, the place was haunted. But, some of the more level headed folks suggested it could only be a wampus cat that came up from the Bottoms and decided to make its home there. Now, a wampus cat did sound very much like a woman screaming at night. This theory was at least partly accepted but to the children of the neighborhood, this could be even scarier than the Cox's Army one. None of them had ever really seen a wampus cat, therefore assumed it to be something big and mean and terrible to look at and maybe even worse than all of Cox's Army.

For this reason, Earl Lee never ventured farther down the road in that direction than the "other place". When the girls saw him coming towards them as they returned from school, Millie was always happy, though she'd never admit it to anyone, especially to Earl Lee. She sorta' liked seeing him and Shep running down the road after a long day at school. She did miss him sometimes. As soon as the weather started to warm up, he quit wearing shoes and his feet grew brown and tough as shoe leather, as did all three, when they were home. He seldom wore a cap, but when he did it sat on one side of his head, down a little over one ear. This covered a head of sandy colored hair that was kept short by Grandma's scissors and hair clippers. His patched overalls were worn, fastened by one strap over his left shoulder, to allow his shirt tail to hang out a little. As he drew nearer to the girls, he began to run and wave. Shep ran on ahead to reach them first. Walking home together, the three picked up stones and clods to throw at trees and bushes or just up in the air. The girls could still out throw him, but not by much. He was growing and getting stronger.

He was excited on this day as he told them his news.

"Guess what," he said, "I know where there's mushrooms, all ready to pick."

"No you don't," Helen retorted. "It's too early for mushrooms."

"It is not too early. I saw some today and I'm gonna' go get them."

"I don't believe you saw any," Millie scoffed. "It's too early and besides if you really saw some, why didn't you get them yourself?"

"I've been waiting for you to come home and go help me."

"I still don't believe you."

"Well, you just better. Uncle Lawrence believes me, cuz he saw some too and he said we could get them if we're careful and not get any toadstools."

Now, the girls liked to gather mushrooms, and they loved to eat them too. Grandma knew the best way to fix them, by rolling them in flour and frying them good and brown.

They hurried home to change clothes, and each armed with a small basket, set off for the woods. Earl Lee led them to a place alongside the big ditch among the oak and sycamore trees, where the ground was still damp and moist from the high water. The warm sun had brought life to the earth in the shade of these trees. A layer of flowers bloomed in the underbrush. Wild daffodils and violets and bluebells were scattered about, along with May apples. Grass was green and robins were chirping, flying about for insects.

Sure enough, there were mushrooms! Lots of them! They hadn't grown to full size yet, but were plenty large enough to fry and eat, still young and tender. The kind that they knew about was in the shape of a cone on a white stem, and perforated like a sponge. There was no doubt about them being the right kind, and they began gathering them, careful not to break off the stalk part, because that was just as delectable as the main part. Knowing that mushrooms grow very fast, they could come back again in a couple of days for many more.

Looking into each others baskets to see how many they had, Helen exclaimed, "Er-ly, you've got some toad-stools in your basket! Can't you tell a mushroom from a toadstool!"

Staring down in his basket, the boy agreed that perhaps he did have one or two toadstools, but what difference did it make. There were not enough to matter, all mixed together.

Helen was aghast. "Doesn't matter! You don't know anything Er-ly. Just one or two toadstools could kill our whole family. It's a good thing I saw them. Grandma would skin you alive if you took them home to eat. Let me have your basket so, I can take out the bad ones." Taking out a large toadstool, she held it up close to his face. "Look at this, it don't even look like the rest of them, and here's another one. Boy, you don't know anything. I don't know what you'd do without me and Millie."

Earl Lee was stricken by this out burst, but didn't let it affect him for long. He was not one to be daunted and recovered quickly.

"I know something else we can do," he said.

Naturally, the girls were interested.

"How about some sassafras. I know where there's some young trees."

Now, the girls liked sassafras tea as much as anybody, in the spring of the year. Grandma did too! She always said a body needed sassafras tea to thin out the blood in the spring, because during the cold weather it thickened up and got sluggish and it needed thinning out so a body could move about more freely. But, the girls liked it because it tasted good and the only time you could get it was in the spring. When the sap began to rise in the young trees, it was no good, for it lost it's flavor and turned bitter.

This latest suggestion squared things considerably with the girls as they followed him to the next destination.

Digging up the roots of a tree is no easy task without a shovel, hoe or other tool, but for an innovative little boy, it was soon accomplished. Unable to pull the young tree up by its roots, Earl Lee searched around for a stout stick. Poking it around the tree to loosen the roots from the dirt, he then stuck it under the roots, then began trying to pry it loose. After he was satisfied with his efforts, he told the girls to help pull it up. Straining and heaving, it suddenly broke free and all three tumbled to the ground, but held onto the sapling, and they lay there laughing.

Earl Lee broke the tender roots off the tree as best he could, wiping the dirt off on his overall legs.

A puddle of water at the edge of the woods presented a challenge to him. Rather than walk around it as the girls did, he chose to jump over. It proved to be a mistake on his part. Whether it was wider than he thought or he couldn't jump as far as he thought, it didn't matter. He landed far short of his goal and when his feet touched the ground they slid out from under him and he sat down firmly in muddy water. Sitting there with a stunned look on his face, the girls began teasing him. He got slowly to his feet, water and mud dripping from him. Fortunately, the contents of his basket were intact.

Arriving at the house, he lagged behind while his companions took their baskets in to give to their Grandma. Bessie was pleased at the prospect of having so many mushrooms. Also, with the sassafras roots. She dearly loved her sassafras tea. That is, she was pleased until she saw Earl Lee!

"I-Gawd, boy, what happened to you?" she exclaimed.

"I think I got all wet," he answered meekly.

"I can see that. I'm not blind. How'd you get that way? You look like you been wollering with the pigs."

"I fell in a puddle of water. I couldn't help it."

"Hah, don't tell me that. If there's a mud hole any place around, you'll manage to fall in it."

At first, the girls wanted to giggle, but now they felt sorry for him and wanted to defend him, if they could.

"He's telling the truth, Grandma," Millie said. "It wasn't really his fault."

"I suppose he was just walking along minding his own business and this big mud hole hopped up in front of him and before he could stop, he fell in," Grandma said sarcastically.

"Well, maybe not exactly," Millie defended. "But, he couldn't help it."

Bessie grabbed the boy by the arm. "Just look at you. Get over there and stay behind the stove while I heat some water to give you a hot bath. While I'm waiting on it to heat up, I'll clean these mushrooms before they go bad. Now, you two go on down to the other place and gather your Pa's eggs like you're suppose to. You want he should have to do that too. Now, go on and get."

Gathering the eggs at the "other place" was one of their many daily chores. But this one they didn't mind, because it was for papa's good, and they could go there alone and take their time and not have to hurry. Papa's chickens and guineas and things had been left here and they came down each day to gather the eggs after they quit laying. This way Papa kept his own eggs to sell, in the little room on the back of Grandpa's house. When they had time, they even fed and watered them so Papa wouldn't have to when he come in from the field all worn out and had to take care of the other animals.

Earl Lee had already had his bath and changed clothes by he time they returned and put away the eggs. As soon as he saw them, he started out the door.

Bessie yelled at him before he got out, "Where do you think you're going?"

Stopping immediately, he replied, "Outside with Millie and Helen."

"Oh no, you're not. You know better than that," she scolded.

"Why not, Aunt Bessie, I'm all dry now."

"You know why. I've told you often enough," the woman said. "You only think you're dry. When you have a hot bath in this kind of weather, all that scrubbing opens up the pores of your body. If you go outside too soon, all them pores just suck in the cool air and you'll catch your death of cold. Or maybe even the whooping cough."

"But, Aunt Bessie, it's warm outside."

"Makes no difference, it's still cool to the skin. You stay inside til all your pores close up."

"How can I tell when they close up," he asked, inspecting his skin for any openings.

"You don't have to tell. I'll tell you when they're closed. In about half an hour maybe. Then you won't have to worry about it," she replied.

He let this logic soak in, but wasn't satisfied. Bessie, realizing he would come back with another illogical question, said, "Supper's about ready so you can come set the table while your hands are nice and clean. The menfolks will be in shortly and hungry as bears."

Millie couldn't be sure if she was glad when school was out or not. Of course it meant an end to studying and the routine of going every day, but it also meant she wouldn't see her friends of school for three months. And if she wasn't in school, it meant she had to work at home and that could be no picnic. But, everything considered, it would be nice because one could always find some time to play and just do things. Life could be exciting if one let it be.

During the summer months, water had to be pumped for the cows. This was done in the old fashioned way. The deep limestone lined well in the yard supplied this need, but in order to get the water to the cows, it had to be pumped across the road to them. A tank in the yard would be filled by the girls taking turns at the pump. When the tank was full, the plug in the bottom was pulled and the water ran through a pipe under the road to a big concrete trough on the other side of the fence. The animals always seemed to know when the girls were pumping, for they came up to the trough and waited. As the water gushed in, they fell upon it and drank it dry in one fell swoop and then would low and moo until it was full again. It was a back breaking, arm aching task that the girls detested.

Millie felt that bringing in the cows for milking was a task that fell to her a lot more than to Helen. In the evening it wasn't so bad; they stood at the gate waiting, because the stupid animals always seemed to know when it was time. She assumed it to be instinct or something. But, what she couldn't understand was, why didn't that same instinct work mornings when it was still dark out. Occasionally, they stood out by the gate more often they stayed in the far reaches of the pasture. If the faithful Shep had been the kind of dog to oblige his master, he should have gone forth and drove in the cows on his own or at least after being commanded, but no, he would not go out alone, for some unknown reason.

Millie could never understand this line of reasoning. Shep was as loyal and obedient as any dog could be, except for going out to bring in the cows. Wading through the weeds, wet with dew, just as the sky began to show signs of another day, was not anyone's idea of a cheerful morning. Once Millie entered the pasture gate, Shep would be right beside her, all the way. He even ran on ahead, barking at the cows, wagging his tail joyfully, driving them before him to the far away gate and then across the road and into the barn lot, to await the inevitable. Millie would come along, soaking wet from the dew drenched weeds, with cockle-burrs hanging from the hem of her dress.

Shep always seemed happy that he had done something great and worthwhile. Why then, Millie wondered, didn't he go out without her!

Grandma always did the milking. She drove the cows into their stalls in the barn and they, knowing where to go, lined up in the proper places. Each had it's own feed box, already supplied with feed, and Grandma sat down on the three legged stool with the bucket in hand. Millie never knew why a milk stool only had three legs. Having seen others at different farms, she knew they were all this way. It seemed to her that four legs would be more comfortable and solid. When Grandma sat down, her buttocks more than covered the small seat, with only the lower portion of the three legs visible. Her hands were tough, but firm and strong and when she gripped the two teats, one in each hand, the milk squirted forth in a large, steady stream. She finished each cow by pulling out the very last drops, stripping, as she called it. Millie wondered if she would ever be able to milk as good as Grandma. She tried it many times, but only got a small, weak trickle because her hands were not strong enough. Maybe some day she'd be able to do it right, but Grandma didn't like someone else fooling with her cows. They were used to her and the feel of her hands and gave all they had to her.

That summer Bessie decided she needed a telephone. Some of the neighbors had one, some who could hardly even afford such a luxury. She had to go easy with Lawrence though. When she first brought up the subject, he tried to dismiss it as nonsense. A day or two later, she brought it up again. Realizing now that the woman was determined, he became irate and declared he wouldn't have such a foolish contraption in his home.

A few days later, a woman who lived on the other side of Blairsville died. Folks said it happened because there was no Doctor available. Bessie was known for her medical skills. She often attended to the neighboring sick and many believed her methods of healing to be just as effective as most Doctors. Living so far out from town, Doctors were usually not even called, especially since telephones were scarce and riding horseback into town was time consuming. Bessie's fame as a mid-wife had spread and therefore many believed her to be a god send to the community. There was no real proof however that she ever really saved anyone's life, but her confidence and store bought pills cured many an ache. She mostly prescribed rest and plenty of chicken broth soup and unless it turned out to be something serious, the patient was up and about shortly.

Her argument now being that, had they had a telephone in the house, she might have been able to go there to save that poor woman's life. Even with this suggestion, Law remained reluctant, but after some very serious soul searching he relented, not knowing that the woman in question did not have a telephone herself.

Several of Law's friends jokingly asked why his wife needed a telephone, since she could be heard all the way to the Blairsville store. Undaunted by such jest when she heard of it, Bessie contended that most people just didn't talk up. If they wished to be heard they should speak loud and clear, instead of mumbling as many do.

That same summer, Leonard decided to buy an automobile, which upset his father even more. He could never understand why any-one wanted one of those noisy, new fangled contraptions.

"Some people are never satisfied with what they have," he told his son. "I've heard all about them things and they'll never take the place of a good horse."

"But Pa, they're faster and more comfortable than a horse," Leonard argued.

"Humph, don't tell me that, boy. Why old Nellie out there can run circles around an automobile, any day of the week. If that there Mr. Ford, way up there in Michigan ever owned a good horse and buggy, he'd never have started tinkering around with that thing. I tell you boy, it'll never catch on."

"I'm afraid it already has, Pa," Leonard said. "They say that in the towns and cities all over the country, the streets are full of them.

They even came out with new models every year so folks can keep buying new ones by trading in the old ones."

"I know all that. I read the newspaper too. You ain't the only one in the family that can read. And I've seen all them things running up and down the streets in town," Law pointed out. "You must think I'm just saying they'll never catch on. You mark my words. It won't be no time at all 'til everybody'll be back buying horses."

"I don't think so, Pa. Everybody will have one some day, you just wait and see. They're faster and can go farther and you don't have to feed them all the time when you're not using them."

"You trying to pull my leg, boy," Law thundered. "Of course, you have to feed them things. You think they run on air! You have to feed them gasoline and oil and water and there's always something or other wrong with them."

"Gasoline and oil is no problem. Blessey's already has a pump for gasoline and is selling quite a lot of it."

"I still say they ain't as reliable as a good horse. Just wait for a good rain and see what I mean. I've seen them stuck in little mud holes in the road that a horse wouldn't even notice. Why, I've even pulled out a few, with one horse. So, don't tell me an automobile will ever replace a horse."

His logic had merit. Many times in the spring and winter, automobiles were left sitting along the road, stuck in mud, until a team of horses came to pull them out.

Leonard got Billy Settle to take him into town where he bought a used Model T Ford touring car. He returned home, roaring down the road at nearly thirty miles an hour, his bill cap pulled snugly down on his head, with a cloud of dust fogging out behind. Law often rode in it, but only when necessary and then with the front door open and his right foot on the running board for an easy exit, in case he had to bail out in a hurry. He didn't trust anything he couldn't holler at.

Later on, he did try his hand at driving one day, but the three pedals on the floor confused him. Leonard tried to explain that one was the brake, one for forward and one for back up. Then there was the hand brake on the side. He always stepped on the wrong pedal. And the two levers on the steering column, just under the steering wheel, he didn't even try to master. Leonard told him not to worry about them until he learned about the ones on the floor, because one was to give it gas and make it go faster, like an accelerator. The other was the magneto. This, when pulled down, supplied an electric spark that caused the gasoline and vapor to explode and made the engine start, when cranked. The crank was something else! A man could get his arm broke while trying to spin it around to start the engine, if he wasn't careful. If he was unfortunate enough to get it started, then he must try to guide it down the road.

After the first lesson, Law gave up on learning to drive. He would stick to his horses, something he could talk to and giddy up to or merely flick the lines over the broad rumps and let them have their heads and not worry about keeping them on the road.

Even Law had to admit that perhaps the telephone may have its advantages, after all, when it saved him a trip to Blessey's store.

Preparing to go out to put a saddle on Prince, Bessie asked where he was going.

"Over to Blessey's," he told her. "I ordered a plow share a week ago and I'm going to see if it come in yet."

"Why don't you save yourself a trip?"

"How? I can't find out if I don't go to check on it."

"Why don't you just call the store and ask!"

He hadn't thought of that. He still didn't like the dang thing hanging there on the wall. He had never used it and swore he never would. If he couldn't talk to a man face to face where he could look squarely at him, he'd be danged if he'd try talking to him through a long length of copper wire. But he didn't have much time to be gallivanting around when it wasn't necessary.

"Alright, I'll call," Bessie offered. "I know how you feel about these things."

Going to the telephone just inside the back door, she removed the receiver end from its hook and listened.

"Get off the telephone, Pansy," she ordered.

Pansy Settle was the neighborhood gossip. Since the advent of the telephone, she became one of the first in the area to get one. As other households got theirs, she became friends with each owner, spending most of her waking hours on the party line, learning and spreading gossip and rumors about everyone. It was said that if one needed to know anything about anybody, just call Pansy Settle.

When Pansy heard that voice on the wire, she knew immediately who it was. "Oh, is that you, Bessie?" she said.

"Of course it's me! Now get off the telephone. I got a important call to make."

"Is somebody sick or get hurt or something maybe?" Pansy asked hopefully.

"No, nobody's sick or nothing. Now get off the telephone so I can make my call, and don't listen in."

Pansy's hopes were somewhat dashed as she hung up, but the other women on the line quietly waited to hear the call and would repeat it to her.

Standing on her tiptoes, Bessie vigorously turned the crank on the side of the box. Why they ever installed these things so high up on the wall, she'd never know, unless the installer happened to be a very tall man.

"Central, hello central," she yelled into the mouth piece. She knew she needed to talk loud, which came natural to her, or how else could sound carry so far through them tiny little copper wires. After repeating this a number of times, a woman's voice answered.

"What number do you want?" the voice asked.

"I ain't got no number," Bessie answered. "I just want to talk to Blessey's store."

"I need to have a number so I can connect you."

"I told you, I ain't got no number. All I want is to talk to Blessey's store."

"But, they surely have a telephone number. That's the way people get connected with them."

"I-Gawd operator, don't you know I ain't got no number. If I had a number, I'd be glad to give it to you," shouted Bessie.

"All right now, let's see if we can straighten this out. Where is Blessey's Store located?"

"Where it's always been! Right here in Blairsville."

"Oh, I see. Why didn't you say so?"

"Because you never asked! All you asked for was a number."

"Well, let me give you their number so you'll have it next time," the operator said. "You write it down now and I'll connect you."

"But, I don't have a pencil here handy to write it down with," Bessie retorted. "And no paper neither. Just connect me with Blessey's and I'll get their number the next time I go there."

"I guess that would be best," the operator said, relieved.

The telephone was answered on the first ring at the store.

"Hello, Effie, this here is Bessie Reynolds," Bessie greeted. "I-Gawd, I had me some time getting hold of you."

The other silent, women on the line had long ago held hands over the mouth piece of their own telephone to smother the giggles and snickering. This was priceless to them and well-worth repeating. All would agree that a telephone was not really needed in this case; Bessie's voice could probably be heard anyway, as it was less than a mile distant, as the crow flies.

"Effie, I want to know, did Law's plow share that he ordered come in yet," Bessie inquired.

"I don't think so, Bessie," Effie returned. "It won't be here until tomorrow, that's when the tool supplies come in."

Bessie hung up and turned to her husband, triumphantly, "There now, it ain't in yet and that call saved you a long ride to find out."

Blackberries were especially nice and plentiful that year, thanks largely to the earlier heavy rainfall followed by the warm spring. Bessie had been watching their progress and knew when the time was right. At the supper table one night she announced that she and the children would go up on the hill behind the church to pick the first of the crop.

The next morning, Leonard hitched up Nellie to the buggy and after breakfast, Bessie, the two girls and Earl Lee set out. Arriving at the appointed destination, they dismounted from the buggy just before the sun came up. It was very quiet and chilly. Each person was armed with a half gallon Karo syrup bucket and a stick. The stick was to be used to help raise up briars and supposedly to ward off any snakes or other varmints lurking in the underbrush. Bessie carried a gallon bucket to pick in, because she planned to pick lots of berries, whereas the others would do well to fill the smaller buckets only once. They would be emptied into larger buckets on the buggy. Each one wore long sleeved jackets or shirts with the cuffs tied tightly around the wrists. Coal oil had been rubbed on the cuffs and around the ankles and at various spots over the bodies. This, being the only defense against the tiny, blood sucking chigger, which invaded every known blackberry patch. Even this often proved useless.

Millie stared at the formidable thorny bushes and tried skirting the outer fringes. The only way to reach the best berries was to tackle the foe head-on, which she did. Soon, her clothes were drenching wet from the heavy, early morning dew. Her hands were scratched from the thorns and stickers and leaves and weeds filled her shoes.

Earl Lee did surprisingly well. His bucket was half full when the wire bail came loose and fell, spilling all his berries. Picking them up from out of the weeds proved useless, and he never had so many again.

Helen picked more than Millie, being older and bigger, by emptying her bucket twice, to Millie's once and a half. Bessie repeatedly filled and emptied her bucket. She had a strap tied through the bucket bail and around her neck, leaving both hands free for picking. As she reached for a cane, the berries just seemed to fall into her container.

About mid morning the larger buckets were full and they loaded them on the buggy. Going home, Millie and Earl Lee sat on the back, letting their legs dangle out. Helen sat on the seat with Grandma. The sun had become very hot now and the dampness of earlier was forgotten.

Bessie spent the rest of the day cleaning and canning and making jelly. Working around the hot stove all day affected her very little, or so it seemed, but by the middle of the afternoon sweat began running down her rosy cheeks and her hair was straggling about her face.

By supper time there were several jars of whole canned black berries, both quart and half gallons, and several smaller jars of jelly lined up on the table.

They would go out again for another picking in about a week. This time they'd go back across the big ditch. The berries there should be ripe by then and be even nicer than the ones picked today. Law and Leonard would go out one day too. They picked for making wine and for just plain juice the whole family could drink.

One day Millie realized that the 4th of July was just around the corner. She mentioned this feat to Helen and they reminded Earl Lee. All remembered last year when neighbors came.

Law decided to have a little celebration on the 4th of July. After all, the crops were all planted, but not yet big enough to be cultivated. It had been a difficult spring for them all and they deserved some relaxation. He told Bessie to call his sister, Lucille in Mt. Hebron and ask her to come visit for a few days. He hadn't seen her for quite some time now and felt he had neglected her. They had been very close at one time and she was the only one of his siblings that he really cared about or even wanted to be around much, and a short visit with her went a long way. Sidney was all right, but he tried to avoid being with him whenever he could.

Bessie was not too happy with the prospect of spending time with her sister-in-law, but she complied with Law's wishes and made the call. To her dismay, Lucille accepted the invitation and agreed to come on the second of July and stay the rest of the week, since she had nothing better to do.

Because they seldom had time to visit with Tom and Kate Quigley and they really did owe them a debt of gratitude for the inconvenience caused by the flood, Law had Bessie call and invite them for ice cream on that evening.

On the appointed day, Leonard drove to Zachery to meet his favorite Aunt. As soon as the three children found out he was going, they began clamoring to accompany him. He had this other Ford automobile now and it always was a real treat to ride in it. Most of the time it just sat in the barn gathering dust and only occasionally did he get it out to drive into town. The children deemed it a luxury to ride in such a vehicle, a Model A, closed in with windows all around that cranked up and down to let fresh air in or keep cold air out, as the conditions warranted.

Helen sat up front with her father, and Millie and Earl Lee rode in back, with the windows rolled down (they only went halfway), letting the hot air blow through and watching the countryside fly past. They laughed joyously each time they hit a bump or chuck-hole in the road.

As usual, the train was late in reaching Zachery. They never minded the delay too much however, because they spent the time enjoying the activity of the community. Compared to the farm and Blairsville, it was a very lively place. Papa escorted them into one of the stores where he purchased each one a bottle of pop, much to their delight.

Aunt Lucille was the only passenger to disembark from the train when it arrived. Papa hurried forward to greet her and take her single valise. After the customary comments about how much the children had grown, they went to the Model A for the hot ride home.

Helen now rode in the back seat, so Aunt Lucille could sit up front and talk with Papa. Millie sat on the far side of the back seat and could only catch bits and pieces of the conversation, but it was enough for her to realize that Aunt Lucille thought that Papa and the girls would be better off in the long run now that he and Mama were divorced. Papa never commented about this and fell silent until asked about the rest of the family, the crops and things of that sort.

Millie watched Aunt Lucille, trying to remember all the things she had heard about her, by eavesdropping on various conversations between Papa and Grandma and Grandpa. Millie decided that she wasn't really her true Aunt. Being Grandpa's sister made her Papa's aunt, which in turn made her Millie's great aunt, not quite the same. It was all rather confusing but not enough to cause a great deal of thought trying to analyze it. She was a rather nice looking woman who kept a wave in her beginning to turn gray hair, and she always wore a pretty, large brimmed hat with flowers on the top of the brim. Her nose was a little too large, perhaps, kind of like Grandpa's and they favored each other in many ways, which was quite natural. She sometimes seemed very stern and though she often did not seem overly friendly at times, Millie found that she liked her. Not that she hadn't liked her before, but she just hadn't thought about it until now.

She tried to remember some of the things she had learned by listening quietly when others were talking and not paying attention to her. She knew that Papa had lived with Aunt Lucille for some time, when he was little. There had been a hotel some place and Papa was sent there to live, for reasons she never learned.

She also learned that later, after Papa came back home, that a certain drummer, or salesman staying at the hotel, got Aunt Lucille in a family way, whatever that meant. Anyway she got married to this salesman and they later had a baby. It was born dead though. Right after that, they got divorced, because the salesman was already married to somebody else in another state. In order to stay out of trouble with the law, he gave Aunt Lucille a lot of money to get rid of her and keep her quiet.

She gave up the hotel and bought a nice house in Mr. Hebron, which was only ten or twelve miles away. It was in a good, middle class neighborhood on a maple tree lined street paved with bricks. Millie and Helen went there to visit a few times. It was a nice house with nice furniture. Aunt Lucille always kept it spotlessly clean. The big easy chairs and sofa in the living room were not meant to be sat on though, because although they had slip covers on, they also were covered with bed-spreads to keep the dust off and stay clean. One just knew right off not to sit down in there. Going there was like going to another world almost. Millie wondered what it would be like to live in a place like that. It was difficult to imagine having running water right in the kitchen at the sink and not even have a well. And to think that there was not an out-house in anyone's back yard on that street. Instead, each house had it's own indoor bathroom with a white wash basin and a big white tub to bathe in. And there was not even a stove to heat the house in the wintertime. A big furnace downstairs in the basement heated the whole house by burning coal.

Millie decided she probably wouldn't like living there very much! It was no place for an energetic little girl. She loved the farm and the outdoors and all it represented. But, it was a nice place to visit!

That night after the supper dishes were done, and they were all sitting in the dining room, Aunt Lucille opened up her valise and brought forth three neatly wrapped packages. Handing one to each of the girls and Earl Lee, they eagerly tore off the paper. Millie stared down at the gift in her hands, a book of poems! She could hardly contain her delight. Reading was one of her favorite pastimes, especially poetry. Glancing hastily through the pages, she recognized only a few and all the others were brand new to her. She felt happy that so many were new, because now she would be able to read them for the very first time and savor their meaning. Being too young to understand them now, she knew that one day she surely would and this was something to treasure always.

Helen had a book of poems also, and Millie knew that she felt the same way about hers. The books were different, so they could share with each other.

Earl Lee's eyes were wide with excitement as he held up his gift. It was a Jews Harp! Though he knew basically the procedure for playing the instrument, he had never before held one in his hands. A man who lived back in the Bottoms came by now and then and often walked along the road while strumming a Jews Harp. Another man sometimes sat outside the Blairsville store on the porch and played. The boy always marveled at the unusual sounds that came from it. Placing the tuning fork against the front of his teeth, he held the round part with thumb and forefinger. With the other hand, he stroked the flat spring or loller. After several futile attempts and no sound, he grew discouraged.

Leonard reached over and took it from his hands. "Let me see that a minute, Boy," he said. Putting it up to his mouth, he began strumming against the spring with the side of his left hand and strange sounds erupted from it. Sitting there playing for a few minutes, the others watched, fascinated. Earl Lee studied how he held it and played.

"I used to have one of these when I was a boy," Leonard told him.

"I remembered that you did," Aunt Lucille said. "You used to play it a lot when you were staying with us at the hotel. That's the reason I bought it for Earl Lee. I knew the boy would like it, the same as you did."

Leonard held out the small instrument. "Here, you try it again."

Earl Lee tried again, without any success. Hardly any sound came forth. "I see your problem. You're holding it right, but keep your

145

mouth open a little so the tuning fork will only touch your teeth. Don't let it touch your tongue or lips," Leonard instructed. "That deadens the sound. Now keep hitting that spring with your other hand and at the same time, blow your breath in and out and change the shape of your cheeks as you blow. There, that's the way. You can make up your own tune that way as you go along."

Elated, Earl Lee walked around the yard, strumming vigorously. It remained his constant companion for many days to come.

With Aunt Lucille in the house, it changed the sleeping arrangement somewhat. Earl Lee already slept with Grandpa in the front room so it didn't affect them any. Papa slept alone in the little room just off the back porch, so he was alright too. But Millie and Helen slept in the extra bed in Grandma's bedroom! That meant they had to relinquish their bed to Aunt Lucille. They didn't really mind that much though, because now they got to sleep on a pallet on the dining room floor. They always enjoyed doing this although it didn't happen often. It was cooler sleeping on the floor and somewhat like an adventure.

The girls were last to fall asleep, for they lay awake quite some time, giggling at the sounds of the night. All sounds seemed even louder in the otherwise still, dark house. Grandpa, in the front room, snored just as loudly as ever. Grandma in the bed room offered up her brand of harsh, deep breathing, with Aunt Lucille joining in, as though trying to outdo her sister-in-law. Helen quoted a line from a poem in her new book, "the stars and moonlight filtered through the window, down upon them in the still of the night." They giggled at this analogy until finally falling asleep. The reference "in the still of the night," certainly couldn't be applied in this house.

Millie always liked having company. It seemed exciting with someone besides family in the house, though Aunt Lucille wasn't supposed to be company, being Grandpa's sister and all. But, Grandma did consider her as such, since her presence meant extra work. Grandpa had said that this 4th of July would be a time for them all to relax and enjoy the holiday. Millie could tell, however that Grandma felt differently about it. There was no less work for anyone, except maybe Grandpa and Papa, but even they spent much of the day working. Grandma still had all her regular chores to do, such as taking care of the chickens, with the assistance of the girls, of course. And she still had the milking to do, along with separating the milk and cooking and cleaning. The girls could help, to a certain degree with some things, but it was very little help.

Grandpa never figured that one more mouth to feed made any significant difference in cooking. Just add a few more beans to the pot! That shouldn't be any problem, anybody could do that! Aunt Lucille was an excellent cook and housekeeper from her years of experience in the hotel.

She looked around the kitchen. The big cook stove with the warming oven on top and the reservoir on one side was just the kind needed on a working farm of this size where food could be kept warm for the next meal or water could be heated any time the fire burned. Her own stove at home was white and clean, with no ashes, now that gas had been installed. The cabinets here were badly in need of a new coat of paint, but she guessed they would go wanting. The work counter top could certainly use a new sheet of oil cloth. And the galvanized water bucket with the community dipper that everyone used was deplorable, leaking at the bottom seam. She had gotten away from such things long ago, with running water in her home and indoor plumbing.

Aunt Lucille never offered to help clean up the house, since she had left such chores of other peoples doing behind her, years ago. Her own home was spotless, but she did have to admit this one was something else, in her eyes. The linoleum floors were rarely scrubbed, but she did have to admit they were litter free, up to a point, if one didn't count shoes or boots just inside the door as litter. And the beds went for days on end without the benefit of being made up. She had no desire to become a house maid again.

Now, cooking was a different matter. Being an excellent cook in her own right, helping out in the big kitchen would give her ample opportunity to display her culinary skills and be useful at the same time.

Grandma disagreed with her wholeheartedly on this score. Without really saying anything to her directly, she let it be known from the outset that the kitchen was her own private domain and no one better try to interfere with her preparation of a meal for her family. It wasn't that she couldn't use the help so long as she felt in control. It boiled down to the changing of recipes and snide criticism that she couldn't abide.

Millie observed the little rift between the two older women and could only partly understand the reasoning. They were very much alike in many ways, both very stern and formidable and accustomed to having their own way in most things, especially cooking. Each felt their way of cooking and seasoning to be best and wanted no advice from anyone.

If Grandpa or Papa noticed anything amiss, which they probably didn't, they showed no signs of it.

July Fourth was a joyous day. Bessie made a big cake the day before. Not the kind that Lucille would have made! Hers would be round with two layers and rich, thick icing between them and on top and the sides. Bessie's was the type that hungry farm hands liked, baked in a large rectangle shaped bread pan, with powdered sugar icing on top.

In the middle of the afternoon, the three children rode into McCleansboro to buy ice and rock salt for making ice cream. The ice house being the only business in town open, there was no reason to extend the excursion. After Leonard bundled the chunk of ice in a gunny sack and wrapped it in an old bed comforter, they hurried home before it melted.

Bessie already had the formula ready and waiting in a stone crock. While she prepared it in the gallon freezer, Leonard began breaking up a portion of the ice. Wrapped in a gunny sack to avoid loosing any of the precious commodity, he broke it into small pieces with the flat side of an axe. Lemons had been purchased the day before at the store in Blairsville. Lemonade was always a rare treat on the farm, so the few times that ice was available, Bessie made sure they had lemonade.

She instructed Millie and Helen to stay in the house and cut the lemons in quarters for the drink. After cutting the first one, Millie touched the juicy side to her tongue to savor the sour flavor.

"You better not let Grandma catch you doing that," Helen scolded, "She'll skin you alive."

"I won't let her see me," Millie said, holding one out to her sister. "Here, why don't you do it! They taste good."

Helen hesitated, but then cut one and touched it to her tongue. After that, the girls licked each piece of lemon they cut, giggling with each lick. When Earl Lee came in and witnessed what was going on, Helen knew she must get him involved or get into trouble. Handing him a piece, she made him lick it. He drew back and made a face as his lips puckered up. She made him lick another before he realized what had happened.

"I'm going to tell Aunt Bessie on you," he declared.

"You cant, Er-ly," Millie said

"Yes I can too. I'm going to tell her that you and Helen licked all the lemons."

"You better not," Helen told him, "You're just as guilty as we are."

"No, I'm not either. I only licked one and you made me do it."

148

"You licked two pieces, Er-ly," Millie said. "Besides, licking one is just as bad as licking a whole lot."

"It is not! One is not near as bad as a whole lot."

"Oh yes, it is. If you ran that dirty ol' tongue of yours over just one little bitty corner of one piece of lemon, it would ruin the whole jar of lemonade, if any body knew it. So, you better keep still about it cause you'll be in just as much trouble as me and Helen."

The boy tried to come up with a positive rebuttal and failed, so he went out leaving the girls to their own devious devices and no one was the wiser.

No one ever suspected what had happened with the lemons. Alas, all present bragged about how the cool lemonade hit the spot on such a warm day and they should have it more often.

Papa, Grandpa and Tom Quigly took turns churning the ice cream freezer, and when it would turn no longer, Papa packed more ice and salt around and over the freezer and let it set to freeze even harder.

The family and friends were all gathered in the yard under the big maple trees. No breeze stirred the leaves and birds fluttered about among the branches. The adults lounged in straight back chairs and cane bottom rocking chairs. The three children scampered about on blankets on the ground, waiting for the magical moment when it was time to uncover the freezer and dish out its contents.

Sitting on the blankets with a dish of the frozen vanilla cream in one hand and a plate of Grandma's cake in the other, they devoured it in short order and were ready for more. It was the coldest they had ever eaten and the very best.

In a little while, Grandma complained that all that cold stuff made her teeth and head hurt, but that didn't hinder her consumption of it.

Earl Lee seemed to be playing with his, by chopping it up with his spoon and mashing it out.

Noticing his actions, Millie asked why he would do such a thing that ruined the ice cream.

"No, it don't either," be replied. "It makes it better, 'cause there's more of it this way and I can eat it faster."

"You know you're disgusting," Millie said.

He grinned happily without answering.

The afternoon passed on and everyone began to grow weary and nod and doze where they sat. It wasn't natural for any one of them to sit quietly on an afternoon without being surrounded with work.

Grandpa took a knife from his pocket and ran the blade back and forth across a whet stone that he carried for that purpose. Cutting off a sizeable chunk of tobacco, he offered it to Tom who declined the invitation.

The women began to talk again in undertones and Millie, sensing an interesting conversation, rolled over closer to them to hear better, without attracting attention to herself. Though the women tried to lower their voices, Millie was able to make out enough to catch the general gist of it. Kate Quigley spoke low, barely above a whisper, but grandma's voice was still a couple octaves above the others, therefore carrying plainly to a small girl's big ears.

When Millie heard Kate say, "I heard that the Sanders girl drowned in the well," she knew this would be well worth listening to.

"Tch, tch," Grandma muttered. "Such a pity to be taken that way. But, then again, I'm not at all surprised. The way these young things traipse around over the country, doing no telling what. If I had one like that, I'd give her what for."

"I feel sorry for her poor family," Kate said. "Imagine having to live with a thing like that. Why every body knows why she did it. The humiliation of it all. They'll never be able to live it down."

Now, Aunt Lucille loved a bit of good juicy gossip as well as the next one and not averse to passing it on, but not knowing the family in question, she had to be content to merely sit back and listen.

"And it wasn't even her own well," Grandma went on. "It seems like she could at least have jumped in the well at home instead of going to the neighbors."

"I agree with you wholeheartedly, Bessie," Kate said. "But these young people nowadays don't have any consideration for others at all. I surely don't know what this world is coming to."

"Sometimes I think judgment day is almost upon us."

"I-Gawd, all these new fangled ideas and gadgets they keep coming up with just ain't good for the country. They'll be the ruination of us yet," agreed Grandma. "Even Law says that before you know it, all our work will be done for us and common folks won't have nothing to do but sit around and wait til somebody else does things for us." She grew reflective, looking at her brown callused hands and thinking of her aching back. "Of course, some darn things might be all right. And then, there's the telephone! If I didn't have a telephone in the house, I might not have even heard about this Sanders girl."

"I don't use mine often, but it surely does come in handy at times," Kate said.

"I don't use mine much either, I don't have the time."

"I picked mine up one day to call Blessey's Store, and as usual, Pansy Settle had the line tied up talking to that missus Ferguson down the road. I listened in for a minute before I cut in and that's when I heard. Pansy was telling all about how it happened and everything."

"Tell us what you heard," coaxed Kate.

Grandma glanced around to make sure no one else was listening. Millie quickly closed her eyes and pretended to be sleeping.

Grandma leaned forward to speak directly to the women, trying to lower her voice a little, unsuccessfully. Aunt Lucille and Kate began fanning themselves briskly with the cardboard fans taken from the funeral home in McCleansboro.

"Well," Grandma began, "Pansy said that this girl, Polly Sanders, had been going out with a young man from Fairfield and they think he's the one that got her in trouble. But, I blame her just as much as him, riding around all alone on these back roads in a buggy. Anything can happen. A buggy is no place for a young decent girl if you ask me. There's just too much temptation!"

The others agreed, though such temptations had left them long ago.

Grandma warmed to her task, "Anyway, as soon as this young scoundrel found out the girl was in trouble, he left the country, to no telling where. They think he either went over to St. Louis or clear up to Chicago. It don't matter now anyways."

Grandma went on to relate what happened after that. Millie, being too young to fully understand the implications, did grasp enough to analyze what happened. It seems that poor Polly Sanders had ordered a baby and she wasn't even married yet. She must have thought that her friend planned on marrying her, so she went ahead and ordered the baby ahead of time, without telling him. When he found out about the baby, he became very upset with her and ran away without telling any one where he was going. This left poor Polly Sanders to face the situation all alone. With a brand new baby coming and Polly without a husband of her own or a father for the baby, it presented a delicate situation. Even Millie knew that she shouldn't have ordered it without at least telling him to see if he really wanted to marry her and if it was alright to order it. She put herself in an awkward predicament. Unable to face the embarrassment it would cause her and her family, she jumped into the well. Not the well at her own house, but at a neighbor's house and drowned herself. They thought she chose this particular well because it was deeper than the one at home and she was less likely to be saved. The neighbor man discovered her down there when he went to draw some water. Being very shocked and surprised to find a dead girl in his well, he ran for help to pull her out.

Maybe that's not exactly the way Grandma told it, but that's how Millie heard it. After a story is repeated a few times, especially on the party line, it often undergoes a few changes.

Millie could hardly wait for a chance to recount this story to Helen. Seeming to awaken from her nap, she motioned for Helen to meet behind the smokehouse where she reiterated what she had heard. Earl Lee had followed and heard everything.

"Well, what's so 'portant about a baby," he said. "All grown-ups have them."

"Not if they're not married."

"That's what I mean. If you're married you have lots of them," Earl Lee said. "I don't know why anybody would want so many, though."

"I bet sometimes they order them by mistake," said Helen. "Or maybe the orders get mixed up."

"Well, any way, I don't see why that girl jumped in the well. Even if she couldn't send it back, it looks like somebody else would take it."

"Maybe some people just don't want a baby."

"Yeah, 'specially if they already had some of their own," Earl Lee said.

"I don't understand why anybody wouldn't want one. I'd certainly like to have one," Millie said. "I'd play with it and take good care of it."

"Aw, you couldn't take care of a baby," Earl Lee doubted. "You're not much more than one yourself."

"I am too," Millie told him. "What do you know about such things anyway, you're just a boy!"

"Well boys know things too!"

"What I don't understand is, how could she get a baby if she didn't order it?" questioned Helen.

"Somebody has to keep it," Millie reasoned. "I don't think they can send them back."

"Couldn't they give it to somebody else?"

"Don't be silly, Er-ly, who'd want a baby that somebody else ordered!"

"What difference does it make who ordered it," said the boy, "A baby's a baby."

The girls were a little perplexed by such logic that only Earl Lee could produce, but not completely without an answer, as only they could come back with.

"Isn't that just like a boy," Helen retorted. "They don't know anything about such things."

"Yeah," Millie said, completely ignoring Earl Lee, "They don't realize that they have to find some body first that's married and they probably already have enough of their own."

"He doesn't even know that a person has to be married before they can even order a baby. That's how dumb boys are."

"But, Polly Sanders wasn't married," Earl Lee said. "If you're so smart, how come she was allowed to even order one!"

This piece of logic completely stunned the girls for a moment.

"Oh, you make me tired, Er-ly," Helen returned haughtily as the girls turned and walked away. "You just don't understand anything."

Meanwhile, during this conversation, the men folks were having their problems in the front yard. Apparently, all three were on the verge of being drunk. It seems that the day before, Law rode Prince back into the Bottoms for the purpose of buying a jug of whiskey for this occasion, from a certain Bottoms man that he knew. Clem Dolittle wasn't your typical moonshiner by any means, because he did own a piece of ground which he farmed. Whiskey making was just a side effort to add a little extra cash to his pockets.

Clem's whiskey was made from corn mash, with malt added. Very simple! (Real moonshiners used various grains for a base.) Yeast was then added to the mash, causing it to ferment. Now, newly distilled whiskey is colorless and (green), meaning it has a raw taste. It mellows and gets its color from the wooden barrel in which it's stored.

Clem happened to be out of the mellowed brew. But he did have a new batch that was still green and bitter. Since July Fourth was the next day, he bought a jug of the new batch.

The effects of the drink proved to be more potent than the cured whiskey. After passing the brown stone jug around the third time, each man began to feel the powerful effects of the brew.

By the next day, no one was quite sure how the whole thing started. The three men would have agreed that it went something like this. Leonard took too long with his turn on the jug and Law grew impatient with him.

153

He reached over saying, "Come on, Boy, pass that jug around."

Leonard resented being called Boy and flared up, "Don't call me a boy. I'm not a boy no more. I'm a man and my name's Leonard. Why don't you call me that?"

Surprised by this outburst, Law replied, "Not to me you ain't no man. You're still the boy you always been."

"I won't give up this jug unless you call me by my real name."

"It'll be a cold day in hell when that happens. Give me that jug."

The potency of the raw drink gave Leonard a false sense of courage and all the resentment that had been building up inside of him over the years rushed forth. He said things to his father that he would not have said otherwise. Law, in return became indignant at being talked back to in this fashion. One word led to another until finally, Law raked the back of his hand across his moustache, grabbed the jug from Leonard's hand, and said, "I ain't give you a whipping in a long time. You've had this coming for a long time, now I'm going to clean your plow for you."

Before Tom Quigley realized what had happened, the two men, father and son were rolling about on the ground, cursing and pounding each other with their fists. He tried to separate the two and fell, some how ending up in the middle of the fight. He was the only one that showed signs of any injury with a mouse over his right eye, caused by an accidental blow from one of the combatants.

The fray was short lived, however, lasting only as long it took for Bessie and Kate to reach them. Bessie grabbed a foot and pulled on it only to have it kick free. Getting a better hold on it next time, she yanked hard and Leonard was dragged free. Kate managed to pull Tom out and away easier, being an unwilling participant.

The men were subjected to scathing remarks by the women; such things as acting like little boys and can't be left alone without supervision.

It was the first such confrontation between Law and Leonard, but would not be the last.

Everything considered, it turned out to be a pretty good Fourth of July. The company left early, they each had chores to do at home. Law and Leonard stretched out on the blankets in the yard for a nap, while Bessie and the girls did the milking and feeding. At dark they lit the sparklers.

Aunt Lucille never stayed to the weekend as planned. She left the next day, longing for the peace and quiet of her own, cool home.

She didn't relish the hot weather or being away more than one night as she once had.

CHAPTER 6

One morning, Lawrence hitched up his team of horses to the wide bed hay wagon and left the house at daybreak. The afternoon before, he had nailed boards all around the outside edges of the wagon to keep his load from falling off. The barrels he ordered some weeks earlier should be ready by now. He was not in dire need of them at present but, having lost a couple in the flood and knowing the stave factory would likely go out of business before long, he wanted enough to carry him over, he knew not for how long. The barrel business was in a decline, due largely to metal drums being manufactured for certain commodities, as well as cloth and burlap bags for others. There would always be a slight demand for the wooden ones, but they'd be made in the larger plants around the country instead of in the back woods of rural areas.

He ordered ten, not because he needed that many, he really only needed two at present, and the rest would be stored in the hay-loft of the barn, after coating the inside with a thin layer of tar. This would prevent insects from eating at the wood and also keep rot from destroying them. They should last for years if treated properly. Barrels were used mainly for storing ground corn and other grains as well as being used to catch rainwater from the roof of the house.

Riding by the Jeb Wilmore place, he wanted to see if any progress had been made in clearing it off.

Very little had been done, but that was to be expected since Sam Hathorn had his own place to take care of. The understanding between them being, that Sam take care of his own crops first.

In this case Law was in no great hurry, since he didn't have time to plant more ground this year anyway. But next year he expected to put most of these forty acres in corn.

He noticed that some of the fence had been transferred over to Sam's place as well as parts of the house and sheds. Feeling satisfied that Sam would live up to his end of the agreement, he drove on until he reached Sam's place.

Even though it was still early in the day and had not yet reached the peak of the summers heat, all the family was out working, as they would be later in the day. Pulling up in the yard, Law got down from the wagon and drew the big red handkerchief from his back pocket. Wiping the inside brim of his straw hat, he mopped the sweat from his forehead.

After a drink of cool well water from the communal dipper and a brief discussion with Sam, he drove on. He liked Sam and felt he had a good man watching over this part of his property.

The narrow road wound around through the trees, with deep ruts in some places, until it reached the railroad tracks. Then it ran along beside the tracks for less than half a mile and the road was better out in the open. The brush grew tall and dense, as a result of the past flood waters. Many signs were still visible along the right-of-way, the most noticeable being the tall weeds strewn along the roadway, deposited there after being left by the receding water. One section, showing recent repairs to the rails and ties, was further evidence of the flood, probably due to a washout and likely not the only one on the line.

This railroad was not like many others. It ran only through the Bottoms. The Egyptian Lumber Co. had bought up the remaining timber in the valley and built a large sawmill over near Mill Town. The tracks were laid through the valley, reaching from Mill Town all the way beyond Blairsville, yet no where near that village, a total distance of about thirty miles. The rails were smaller than most others, though the tracks were of standard width. A number of spurs, switches and camps strung out at intervals, provided lodging and loading facilities for workers. Provisions were brought in by a wood-burning locomotive, as it hauled out the cut logs for the sawmills.

The loggers now were of a different breed from the old days. The early men made their living strictly by following the logging from camp to camp, from one territory to another, with allegiance to no one. The new logger had roots here. They were from the area and lived on surrounding farms and in the villages, in at least three counties. They worked hard and lived in the camps a week at a time, going home on weekends to their families.

Some of the larger camps that the men lived in during the work week had eight to ten crudely built cabins, with more than one occupant living together. Some had cook stoves inside for heat as well as to cook on. Much of the cooking was done over open fires outside. Most of the beds were merely cots of sorts, made of rough planks covered with straw ticks as mattresses, not very comfortable to an outsider, but served it's purpose very well to the man who labored all day in the forest.

There was one man who lived in a box car parked on one of the switches. His wife cooked meals for some of the loggers for extra money.

If one is fond of nature and is able to see beauty in it, the Bottoms, at least through here, is a beautiful place to be, with its peace and quiet. Many types of birds find refuge in the various variety of trees. At night, the calls of the whippoorwill and the owl are a comfort to a tired man's ears. Even the cry of the lynx or call of the wolf add to the solitude.

It was said that a giant oak tree once stood near here that was more than eight feet in diameter. When they cut it down, they cut it into four pieces to transport it to the saw mill, one piece at a time, only to discover they couldn't use it. It was too big to cut with their saws! The remaining three pieces were left to rot where they lay, deeming it unworthy of the time or effort to pursue it further.

A hand car, with a two man sexton repair crew went by. Each man waved between strokes as they pumped the man-powered vehicle forward.

It was along here on this day that Law caught his first sight of the "Bottoms Tramper," as he would become known, and only a glimpse at that. It would be remembered later.

A figure emerged from a thicket. Beside it, a big red dog trotted. As soon as Law and the wagon were seen, the figure paused in mid stride for an instant, then dashed forward and disappeared in the undergrowth.

Surprised, Law stared after the vanishing figure. With hardly more than a fleeting glance, he determined that it was a man, perhaps middle-aged, tall and with a lanky build. He had a heavy beard, tinted with gray, but not as long as might be expected. More of the kind a man would grow over a period of three or four months maybe. His faded and patched overalls had been cut or torn off halfway up to his knees. A bill cap sat on the man's head, pulled down just above the ears. He also wore a blue work shirt, the kind most farmers wore. Law couldn't tell about his shoes or even if he wore any at all. Carrying something in one hand what appeared to be a stick soon belied the fact that it was a small caliber rifle, as the sun glistened from it. The big red-bone hound stayed beside his master, just as anxious to be away, but staying right beside him, instead of going ahead.

Law was surprised at himself for observing so much in such a short period of time, although he was known for this peculiarity. There appeared to be something strange about the man besides not wanting to be seen. But Law had other things to think about and soon dismissed the incident from his mind, at least for the present.

Driving down the only street, if you could call it a street, he noticed that some changes had been made even though it hadn't been that long since he was last here. Only three or four clapboard houses seemed to be occupied. Dense weeds had grown up and the unoccupied houses had windows broken and doors hung loosely on their rusted hinges and were in a bad state of repair and neglect. At one time, it had been a thriving community of more than twenty dwellings. The barber shop had closed long ago, as well as the grocery store and blacksmith shop. The old two story boarding house, or hotel as some called it, was the only business in town that remained open, other than the stave mill. The only reason the boarding house was still open was because the owner had no place to go.

The name of this once bustling village was Slapout. No one is quite sure how this name came about but, like do many other places one is not sure about, some at least have a theory. You see, back then before the turn of the twentieth century and well into it, drummers traveled the country roads, calling on stores. Even after an order for merchandise was placed, it often may be from two to four weeks before the goods arrived at its destination. Therefore, most stores ran out of things. One day, when a man came into the grocery store and ask for something they didn't have, the merchant said, "I'm just slap out of that today but I should have it next week." This phrase, after being used a number of times, became a joke among the customers and the name stuck, making it the only Slapout in the state.

Law stopped near the office and went inside. It was a one room building, about twelve by twenty feet made of clap-boards, much like many of the cabins in the Bottoms, with a roof made of cull barrel staves. Two windows provided light and ventilation, one in front and one in the rear, with no glass or screens, merely a wooden enclosure that opened and shut as weather dictated. A single door in front provided the only entrance or exit. An attached wood shed on the side was used for firewood, extra tools and junk. The outhouse sat to the rear at the end of a well worn path.

When Law entered the office, a man sitting behind the desk rose to his feet and extended a hand to the newcomer. Joe Hyten, owner and operator of the stave mill, was a man much the same size as Law, but at least ten years his senior. A scraggly gray beard covered a thin face but his eyes were still sharp. His baggy trousers were supported by suspenders.

No one else was in the office at the time. Not too long ago, Joe Hyten's clerk would have been sitting at the other, now dilapidated desk. And other men probably would have been sitting around on the straight back extra chairs, telling tales or receiving orders. In the wintertime, the old wood stove would have been hot with fire. Now, there was only Joe Hyten here, his desk and wooden file cabinet, which was full of orders that had been filled long ago.

"Howdy, Mr. Reynolds," Joe greeted. "It's good to see you."

"You too, Joe," Law replied. "I come after my barrels. I reckon they're ready?"

"Yes, have been for some time. Come sit down and take a load off your feet. If you're like me, you need to set down every chance you get," he laughed.

"I'm getting that way," Law returned.

"How about a cup of mud," he offered, using a common phrase for coffee. "I know it's hot out, but coffee always hits the spot. It might be a little strong though, at this time of day."

Law sat on a chair opposite the desk, watching the other man take a chipped blue granite cup from a shelf and fill it with black, strong coffee from an equally black granite pot from the stove.

160

"Why you got a fire in the stove on a day as hot as this?" He couldn't resist asking.

"How else could I keep my coffee hot," Joe grinned.

Law took the extended cup and sipped from it. "You're right about one thing, Joe. It is strong." Although it was strong, the fire in the stove did little to heat it, being only lukewarm.

"I know it's not very hot, but after all, the weather is too hot for much fire," Joe observed. "I boil it in the morning on a hot stove and then just keep it warm for the rest of the day."

"It's all right, just the way I like it," Law said and they both grinned.

They talked casually while drinking the coffee, about the weather, crops and business. Law took the plug of tobacco from his pocket, ran the pocket knife back and forth across his whet stone and cut off a chaw. Sticking it into his jaw, he handed the plug and knife to Joe Hyten, who did likewise. Working the cud around in his mouth a few times, he spit into the bucket of wood ashes, next to the stove.

"Did you get much damage from the flood?" Law asked.

"Not a whole lot. You see, the ground is a little bit higher right through here," Joe said. "We had water all right, but not near as deep as most places in the Bottoms. Likely you had more than we did. Oh, we had water and had to let the fire go out in the furnace, else it would've busted it. And we had to string fence around the east side to hold in our lumber or it'd washed out all over the Bottoms and ended up down around Cairo some place. We came through all right though. How about you?"

"Can't complain much," Law answered. "Fared better'n most. A lot of folks lost just about everything they had."

"Yeah, I know several that did."

"Funny thing, Joe, the ones that lived on high ground hardly even knew there was a flood. That is, unless they lived close enough to see down in the Bottoms. Even then, it didn't bother them much. They knew it rained a lot, but it didn't bother them, except for the inconvenience of having to put off plowing for a while."

A whistle sounded outside and Joe took a watch from his pocket. "It's noon," he remarked.

"Thunderation," exclaimed Law, "I must've stayed at Sam Hathorn's longer than I thought. I guess I've been here longer than I thought too. It ain't often that I feel comfortable about just setting around talking, don't have the time. I'd better get loaded and head back home."

"What's your hurry, Mr. Reynolds! Why don't you come eat with us at the hotel!" Joe offered. "There's only five of us left here at the mill now and Mr. Bond's wife cooks dinner for us. I'm sure there'll be plenty of food. She sets a good table. You see, we all take our noon meals there. Two of the men live in shacks alone and to save money, they do their own cooking mornings and nights. The rest of us take all our meals at the hotel, but go home Friday evenings and come back here Sundays."

"I don't want to impose on anybody," Law objected.

"I can assure you, it won't be an imposition to Mrs. Bond. They stay here all the time now and she don't get to see many folks, other than the ones that work here. Come on, it'll be a welcome treat for both of them," he persisted.

Put that way, Law wasn't hard to persuade.

The once fairly respectable looking hotel had seen much better days, but was still an adequate living quarters for an aging couple. At one time, in the village's hey-day, a full time cook had been employed, along with two girls who worked as servers and house cleaners. All the rooms were occupied then, most of the time by workers from the mill and loggers. Now, Mrs. Bond did all the cooking and cleaning herself, with the help of her husband. She had once been a rather attractive woman, but with age come wrinkles, gray hair and stooped shoulders. Mr. Bond was a small man, who tended the garden and two cows and chickens and helped with some of the housework.

Joe was right! The Bonds were delighted to have company and they asked many questions and kept up a line of chatter, a vast difference from their normal disposition.

The four other workers came in and they all gathered around the long table that used to seat more than four times as many in the large dinning room.

One man was minus his left hand, thanks to the shearing blade in the factory, when he became careless. Another was short two fingers, for the same reason.

One man was a negro who fired the furnace at the mill and he lived in a room at the rear of the hotel. His name was Isaac. If he had a surname, no one knew it.

The Bonds did most of the talking, while Law and Joe added an occasional comment about the food. The other four men hardly spoke at all, but ate with great gusto.

After the meal, Law thanked them for their hospitality, offering to pay for the meal. They would accept nothing and invited him back another day.

Walking back to the office, Law asked Joe what the Bonds would do after the mill shut down completely.

"Don't really know for sure," Joe replied. "Stay on here, more than likely, 'til they die. They don't have any family and no place else to go. This has been home to them for most of their lives."

"It's a pity," Law mumbled. "Don't they have any money saved?"

"I would imagine so, they never went anyplace where they'd spend much. If they do, it's probably in a bank someplace. The one that survives, the other may use it some time, but who knows."

"What about you, Joe. You figure on staying around here?"

"Nope, nothing here for me with the mill closed. I'm going to stay at home with my wife in Fairfield. I live there, you know. I'm here most of the time and go home most weekends. She says it'll be nice having me there every night. My daughter and her family live there too. I'm going to work at the Gueyden Lumber Co. They've been after me for a spell. Said I'd be good for the business, with my connections in the lumber industry."

"Guess you'll be an asset to their company!"

"I hope so! We've been friends a long time."

They went back to the office where Law paid for the barrels.

"How long you going to be here?" Law asked.

"I figure it'll take about three more weeks to clear things up."

"I sure hate to see you go. This mill has been here supporting a good many men for a lot of years."

"Yes, I bought it from the John Springer family after he died. I don't know exactly when he started it, but it was way back there," Joe replied. "But with the choice timber being used up by the logging company and the metal drums they make now-a-days, the wooden barrel is eventually going to fade from the market."

"I doubt that! There'll always be a demand for them."

"Maybe, but not enough to keep a man like me in business. The bigger factory can make what's needed a lot cheaper, along with other products and not have to rely solely on one item. I can't produce anything else here without spending a lot of money for new equipment. At my age it's not worth it. So, I say let the bigger companies have it. That's what they call progress."

"Progress be dammed," Law said emphatically. "I hate progress and I hate change. All these new ideas that come along! Who needs them. We got along all right all these years without the automobile and telephone and such. Why can't these do-gooders mind their own business and leave us working folks alone. Such things surely won't last but they disrupt things while they're here."

"I agree with you Mr. Reynolds, at least in theory," Joe smiled. "We might as well accept it though, I think most of these things are here to stay."

After the business transaction, Joe said, "Mind if I ask what you plan on doing with all these barrels? I know you must already have all you need!"

Law grinned sardonically, "I may have, but if I need more some time, I'll have them. I won't have to go pay twice what they're worth to some man out to make a big profit off me."

"But won't they rot before you need them?" Joe queried.

"Maybe! I'll treat the inside and store them in the hay loft. They'll last for years."

Law stood looking at the crude mill for several minutes, remembering being here in the past, when things were going full blast. A few years before, the saw mill boiler exploded, killing the operator. Yes, it was then and still is a dangerous occupation for a careless man. Much hard work went into making a barrel, but these men were craftsmen and were proud of their professional skills.

They cut their own logs and brought them into the mill to be made into stave bolts. A stave bolt is a length of log cut to size for making the staves. The bolt was steamed for twelve to fourteen hours in a hot box so that it could be bent and processed.

The hot box was built much like the icehouse of that day. Thick walls filled with sawdust to hold the steam until the bolts were softened enough that they might be cut to proper thickness for the staves.

There is more than one way to trim the staves. One being a large knife was fastened to a table and the stave bolt moved along against it, to accomplish the cutting operation in some cases. Another, the bolt itself was fastened down and the knife moved along against it.

Yet another operation was trimming the raw edges off the staves. This was done by putting the raw edge of the stave under another knife and tripping it so that it cut off the edge of the stave.

In either of these operations, if the operator grew careless and got his hand or fingers under the knives, they were cut off, as were the staves. Quite often the man doing this work had his fingers or even a hand missing.

Law turned back to Joe. "I appreciate you putting these things together for me," he said as they went to load the wagon.

"Glad to do it, Mr. Reynolds."

This had once been a large operation with many employees. Although the wood was cut nearby and made into various shapes and sizes and the entire product was fashioned here, the barrels were not normally put together. The sides, bottoms and heads and even the wooden hoops, before metal hoops came into to being, were fastened together in bundles and shipped out to other places where they were made into barrels. Joe Hyten had a few "Preferred" customers, like Lawrence Reynolds, that he catered to by making the complete product as a favor.

After the barrels were loaded on the wagon, Law climbed aboard and secured them with binder twine. Putting three of them together, he wound the twine around them tightly several times before tying it. After the three groups of three were secure, he placed the single remaining barrel in the center of the groups and tied them all together. Space-wise the ten barrels made a fairly good load. With the boards he had nailed around the sides, they could hardly slip off the wagon without the entire load going, which was not likely to happen. Satisfied with this endeavor, he got back to the ground.

The two men shook hands!

"Goodbye and good luck, Mr. Reynolds," Joe said.

"And good luck to you, Joe Hyten," Law returned, climbing back on the wagon, giddy-upped his team and departed.

Just down the back road from the Reynolds farm and on past the "other" house and Cox's Woods, lived the Kincaids. Black walnut and wild cherry trees and blackberry bushes grew in the fence-row along the lane to the house. If there had ever been a coat of paint on the house or big barn, it vanished long ago, leaving a weather beaten appearance. They owned several acres that Alva and his half-grown sons farmed. It was good land, but poorly tended. Alva wasn't the most ambitious man in the world, though he did manage to earn a living for his family.

The house sat on concrete blocks, two high, which made it usually above floodwaters that overflowed the big Ditch during the spring rains. Sitting this high off the ground, it provided good ventilation as well as cool shelter in the summer and warmth and protection in winters for various small livestock and feathered fowl. It also provided a good hiding place for children. Between the children and animals, the cobwebs had little chance to form, though an occasional snake did find refuge in the darkness.

There were no screens on the windows or doorways, thus leaving everything open during hot weather. Dogs, cats, goats and even a pig now and then, were free to wander in and out at will. Flies, mosquitoes and gnats might have been a problem in most homes, but this was merely noticeable, as being a way of life. However this fact was not too unusual at this time period. Screen wire, not being in vogue, very few homes supported that industry. As far as an animal straying into the house now and then, perhaps the Kincaids were not too much different. Many of the so called lower class farms left doors open and a special animal went in. Of course, they were usually shooed out.

The Kincaids had many children, being "blessed" with a new one every ten to twelve months, since the day Alva and Vesta were married. Some lived and some died! In one productive year, two were born. One the latter part of January and the other, the following Christmas day. Still being very prolific, she hadn't reached the age in life that babies were forbidden her. She did appear to be much older than her actual years, a trait not uncommon among the women of the time and region, who lived their lives amid hard work and bearing children. Alva and Vesta were each tall thin people, with stooped shoulders and a hesitant stride in their walk. Vesta's hair turned prematurely gray and her breasts sagged loosely under her soiled cotton dress, except of course, just before and after childbirth when they were full with milk.

When a baby died, there was little sorrow or genuine grief displayed. Alas, it could be taken as a blessing, of sorts. But even so, Vesta made sure it received a Christian burial. Alva always built a small wooden coffin and placed the infant inside it wrapped in a piece of quilt. The babies were all buried in the family plot in Springdale cemetery, about four miles down the road at the outskirts of the village. Not having owned a hat other than one to work in outside, in nearly twenty years, Vesta always went to see her good friend and neighbor Bessie Reynolds.

Bessie had two hats, besides the everyday work hats. Both had large brims. One was adorned with black ribbons. The other Sunday hat had flowers around the base of the crown. They were kept wrapped in tissue paper on the top shelf of her bedroom closet. Because Vesta was her friend and out of sympathy for the baby, Bessie always lent her the good Sunday hat. Usually, Vesta and Alva were the only mourners for the funeral, traveling with their newborn, in the wagon. There was no preacher and no graveside service, other than the few awkward, uneducated words of the father. He would report the birth, death and burial of the infant at the courthouse the next time he went in to Mcleansboro, which may be three or four months.

One day a slight mishap occurred at Bessie's back door. Just finishing up the dinner dishes, she carried the dishpan of dirty water to the back door, as always. Without looking either way, she slung the water out into the yard. Vesta, who happened to walk around the corner of the house at the same time, caught the full force of the sudsy water in her face.

"Whoo-ee," the startled Vesta exclaimed.

Bessie, being equally surprised, dropped the dish pan and began wiping her wet hands on the apron that she wore.

The first thing she could think of was, "I-Gawd, Vesta, why don't you make a noise when you come around a body's house!"

"I never had no reason to before," Vesta replied, trying to wipe her face with her hands.

Bessie grabbed a dish towel and went to Vesta. Together, they began brushing her face, hair and front of her dress, in an effort to dry her off. Tiny bits of food clung to her hair and Bessie picked them out.

"Come on in the kitchen Vesta and have a cup of coffee," Bessie offered.

"It's kind of warm for coffee, ain't it?"

"It's not very hot."

"Guess I might as well. Sounds pretty good after that dunking you give me."

"I'm sorry about that," Bessie said in the way of apology. "You know I wouldn't do nothing like that on purpose. I-Gawd, Vesta, you sure gave me a scare."

"You gave me one too, don't you know. That's the first time I had dish water throwed in my face."

Bessie handed her guest a cup of black coffee. "What are you doing coming around here, this time of day. It can't be just a visit with all the work I know you have to do."

"I came to see can I borry your hat again," Vesta answered.

"Don't tell me you lost your baby."

"Yes! It was only three weeks old," Vesta said, without rancor or regret. "Don't you know, he just died this morning. He was ailing for the past few days and just died. I don't know what was wrong with him."

Bessie looked at her with pity in her heart. "Of. course you can borrow my hat," she told her.

"When will you bury it?"

"Tomorrow morning, when Alvy gets the box ready."

Bessie said, "Maybe I'll go with you, if you don't mind my company,"

The offer seemed to please Vesta. "I'd like for you to, if you've got the time."

"I'll make the time. You just stop by and pick me up. Here let me get that hat."

"You're a good friend, Bessie. I don't know what we'd do without you. And Mr. Reynolds too! I'll take real good care of your hat. Maybe it ain't necessary to dress up for a burial, but I feel it wouldn't be right not too. After all, it's about the only thing I can do for my own flesh and blood, after bringing it into the world and all, don't you know."

She walked down the road towards home, holding the hat almost tenderly in her hands so as not to bend or soil it.

Bessie thought that more of Vesta's babies would live and be healthy if only she had some help in their delivery. Bessie had helped with two of them and they turned out all right, but other than that she went through it alone. Her husband tried to help out, but was about as proficient as teats on a boar. Though Bessie had often told her to send one of the kids down to get her when the time came, she always waited until it was too late.

The next morning when the Model T Ford stopped at the house, Bessie was ready, wearing her other hat. Vesta sat proudly beside her husband wearing the hat with the colorful flowers and a clean dress. When she reached the Ford, Bessie noticed that Vesta was not wearing shoes. Realizing that the woman probably didn't have any, she went back in the house and returned with a pair of her own. She hoped they would be big enough. Vesta never wore shoes in the summer and her feet spread out to at least two sizes larger than normal. Luckily, Vesta got them on and laced up.

Bessie said, "A mother needs shoes for her baby's funeral."

"Yes, respect, don't you know! After all, the good Lord did bless us with another one."

"I'd just as leave he didn't bless us so much that way," Alva mumbled.

Bessie climbed in the back of the dilapidated vehicle to share the seat with the small, crudely built, wooden box. At the cemetery, Alva dug a hole in the plot of earth alongside other graves. It was a small hole, not much bigger than the wooden casket, but deep enough to sufficiently ward off any scavenger dogs or wild life in search of sustenance. After the little casket had been placed in the grave, Alva and Vesta stood beside it and he muttered a few incoherent words over it. Standing a little off to the side, Bessie was unable to understand them, so didn't know if it was meant to be a prayer for the child or one of thanksgiving for having one less mouth to feed. Bessie also noticed the tears on Vesta's hollow, brown cheeks and knew that the mother felt some remorse at losing such a small portion of herself.

After that, Alva covered it over with the dirt he'd taken out and without further ado, they returned home. Maybe one day he'd fashion a grave marker and place it here, when he had the time!

Law kept his promise to Tom Quigley through the years. The pasture that had once been encircled with a hand-split rail fence when he purchased the original farm, now had barbed wire around it. The big stump that was credited for Tom's father's death, still rested where it had been in those days. As though nature understood the significance of the stump that sat on a slight hummock of land, it seemed to ignore the rotting process. It now lay in a petrified state, hard and firm. A woven hog wire fence had been strung around the nearly obscured monument. Grass and weeds grew prolifically around it.

Three adventurous children found their way there one day, though they were often cautioned about going so far from the house.

There was almost a feeling of reverence here, though not many knew of it. Being so peaceful and quiet gave it a sacred atmosphere. Over the years, even legends grew up about it, by those who knew the story and why Lawrence Reynolds had preserved it. Leonard explained it to the girls one day, just as his father told him.

Now, they stood in awe, a little short of the fence, gazing at the big stump. Earl Lee went forward to climb over the fence for a better look. Both girls grabbed the inquisitive boy before he got through and pulled him back.

"Hey, what did you do that for?" he demanded, trying to pull loose.

"Well, it can't keep me out," whereupon he climbed on top of the fence and jumped down on the other side, before they could stop him this time. He climbed gleefully up the stump and stood on top waving his arms. "Look," he shouted, "I've conquered the old stump and it's mine. Nobody can take it away from me."

"You'd better get out of there Er-ly before something terrible happens to you," Helen told him.

"What can happen to me, it's just an ol' tree stump?"

"That's not just an ordinary tree stump," Millie said. "You better get out of there!"

The girls were afraid that lightening or something even worse might strike him dead.

"Look at it real close and you'll see that it's different than other stumps," Helen said.

"How do you mean, different?" Earl Lee asked. I don't see anything different about it."

"That's because you're a boy. Boys don't know anything."

"They do too. We know more than girls."

"You're not supposed to go in there," Helen said.

"Why not, it's just a big old stump."

"Why do you think they've got a fence around it! That's to let people know to keep out," Helen told him.

"I don't see what difference that makes. We always climb through fences. They're supposed to keep cows and horses in pastures, not to keep kids like us out!"

"This fence is. It's there to keep everybody out, not just animals."

"Hah, then why do you think that stump isn't rotten?"

"Because it's not old enough. Everybody knows stumps rot when they get old. It just takes a while."

"That's with other stumps," Millie said. "Why I'll bet that one's nearly a hundred years old."

"Not this one," he kicked it gingerly with his toe. "Look, it's hard as a rock. It can't be very old."

"That's because it is a rock. Papa told us all about it one day," Helen said. "He said that it is petrified."

"Petrified! What does that mean?"

"It means that it turned to stone. Papa said that some times certain trees turn to stone," Helen explained.

"How could a tree turn to stone? They're made out of wood. Tell me that, why don't you!"

"I don't know how they do it, they just do."

Earl Lee stood on the stump, laughing. "Who ever heard of a stump turning to a big rock!"

"You better be careful what you say Er-ly. It might kill you like it did that man along time ago," Millie cautioned him.

"What man?"

"Mr. Quigley's father. It killed him a long time ago, even before papa was born. That's why Grandpa put the fence around it, so it couldn't kill anybody else," Helen told him. "So you'd better get down from there."

He got down and turned to kick it once more, but not quite so gingerly this time.

"Where did it come from?" Earl Lee asked.

"Over there someplace," Helen pointed to the open expanse of pasture.

"If it was way over there, how did it get over here?"

"I'm not sure, but I think Grandpa and Mr. Quigley dragged it, after it killed Mr. Quigley's father. They wanted to drag it out of the way so it couldn't hurt anybody else," Helen explained. "That's why they put the fence around it."

"Why didn't they just burn it up and get rid of it?"

"Grandpa promised he'd never move it again. He said he'd leave it here as a monument to Mr. Quigley's father."

"Well, couldn't they break it up now and get rid of it? Then it wouldn't be any problem!"

"You just don't understand anything, Er-ly," the perplexed Helen retorted. "I just told you Grandpa promised to preserve it. It's kinda' like a sacred place where real people aren't even supposed to be. Why I'll bet at night time it's even haunted with Mr. Quigley's father's ghost sailing around."

"Don't say things like that, Helen," Millie pleaded. "It's too spooky."

"Yeah, besides Aunt Bessie said there ain't any such things as ghosts, anyway," Earl Lee added. "She said ghosts are only in some people's minds."

"Maybe so, but I'll bet Mr. Quigley's father's ghost comes out here at night when it gets dark," Helen told them. "You know that when somebody gets killed, their ghost comes out to get even with who killed them. When the killer is a big petrified tree stump, it takes a long time, maybe forever."

Earl Lee had lost some of his bluster by now, as he looked furtively around. But, his curiosity returned, almost immediately. To a small boy eager to learn, inquisitiveness often proved to be a virtue. He discovered at an even earlier age that the best way to learn something was to ask questions and he seldom hesitated in that respect, often to the chagrin of a companion.

"Well, Miss Smarty, if that ol' stump did kill Mr. Quigley's father, how did it do it?" he demanded.

Papa hadn't exactly told her how it happened, he just said it killed him, so she didn't have a ready answer.

"What difference does it make how it happened? It just did!"

"I don't see how it could! It don't have any hands or arms or anything and it can't even move. So, how could it kill some body! If you know so much, tell me that!"

"Er-ly, you know you're a pain, asking all them questions all the time. Papa said it killed him and I believe him, so there," Helen retorted.

Earl Lee felt he had the advantage and he pressed it. "I'll bet I know how it did it. I bet that ol' stump just raised up its roots and grabbed him and wrapped around him and choked him to death. How do you like that? I bet that's the way it happened." He began laughing at his joke.

"Boys sure are dumb," Helen said to her sister. "To think that a stump could raise up and grab somebody. You'd better watch out Er-ly, it might grab you."

He looked around quickly to make sure it hadn't moved. It hadn't! It lay dormant. But they all three saw something even scarier. At the very edge of the woods, not too far distant, stood the figure of a man. A gasp of alarm came from their mouths at the same time, as they stared, too frightened to move. Later, when they tried to describe his looks, they disagreed on most aspects, but all agreed they had never seen anyone exactly like him before and hoped never to again. What they actually saw and thought they saw were two different things, which was not unusual for already terrified children in an eerie place.

Regardless of the three separate descriptions that each was convinced of, the man wasn't nearly as formidable as one might believe. It so happened that he was the same man that Grandpa had seen some weeks earlier. He was tall and thin with a partly gray beard and hair. His overalls were much too short for the long, scarred, hairy legs; making him appear even taller. The eyes staring at the children from under the cap seemed to be intense and boring. The big red dog stood silently beside its master.

As soon as they were physically able, the girls turned and began to run. They reasoned that surely this must be Mr. Quigley's father's ghost come back because Earl Lee had desecrated this hallowed stump. Earl Lee, still inside the fence, screamed at them to wait for him. In an effort to get over the fence, he became entangled in the wire and tore off a portion of his shirt sleeve. Kicking, yelling and scrambling, he finally managed to tear free. Wiyhout a backward glance, he ran after the girls as fast as his legs would move, screaming all the while.

Recounting the episode at supper that night, they were still unnerved and excited, as each related what had happened. After awhile, Grandpa held up a hand for silence. This was too much rigmarole for a man to digest along with his food!

"Helen, you're the oldest, so you tell us what happened," he said.

So, Helen related her version of the incident, leaving out the part about Earl Lee climbing over the fence and standing on the fence and standing on the stump.

"What were you doing back there?" Papa asked.

"We just wanted to show Er-ly that big stump. We didn't see anything wrong with showing him. He never saw it before," Helen answered, with averted eyes staring down at the table.

"I told you girls never to go back there alone, didn't I?" Papa scolded.

"Yes Papa!"

"That's what happens when you disobey."

"I'm not interested right now in whether they obeyed or disobeyed," Grandpa interrupted. "I want to know what this creature looks like. Was he big, tall or short?"

Millie and Helen claimed him to be at least ten feet tall, while Earl Lee guessed him to be big as a giant and real mean looking.

All three began talking again, at the same time.

"He was the biggest monster they ever saw. He's so big his overalls only reached down to his knees. His feet were great big and he wore heavy shoes; he didn't wear shoes, he was barefoot. He had little beady eyes that glared at them from under a bill cap, like Papa's with a broken visor. And he carried a gun, like a rifle."

"Did he say anything or try to bother you?" Grandpa wanted to know.

"Not really," Helen told him, "But, he acted like he wanted to."

"Yeah, he stood there and glared at us, like he would pounce on us if we didn't run away in a hurry," Earl Lee said. "And that was the meanest looking dog I ever saw."

"You say he had a dog?" queried Grandpa. "What color was it?"

"Red!" Earl Lee said. "The biggest, meanest red dog I ever saw."

"Hah, that's the same man I saw over around Slapout," Grandpa said.

Grandma spoke for the first time. "I-Gawd Law, you got to do something about him. Go tell the sheriff or go out and run him down or something."

"Why? Because a man tramps around in the Bottoms by himself! There's no law against that, so long as he don't bother nobody," Law said. "He didn't really try to do anything, did he?"

"No!" Helen replied. "He just stood there looking at us."

"Fiddlesticks, Law, you plan on leaving him run loose out there so he can come kill us all in our beds," Bessie said. "I've heard about things like that happening and they don't know what happened. I-Gawd man, you better do something."

"I tell you, there's nothing to worry about," Law said. "You kids stay away from that place out there and don't any of you wonder off alone, understand?"

"It ain't natural for a wild man to go tramping around in them Bottoms like that," Bessie argued.

"All right, I'll go see if I can find him when I get time and see what he's up to."

He never seemed to have the spare time though and the matter was more or less dropped. The children remembered and spread the word around among their friends. Because he tramped about in the Bottoms, he became known as the Bottoms Tramper. He was not seen again for some time, which allowed for his legend to grow. It soon rivaled that of Cox's Army and the legendary Wampus Cat of Cox's Woods. These legends were more prominent with the young, the older folks still remembering their concern in past years and, so often added tidbits of their own to keep the stories alive.

The children were always happy when Bessie went to the store for trading and allowed them to go along. As the men would be out working, she harnessed up Nellie herself. After loading the eggs she wanted to trade in the back of the buggy, she and the three children climbed in. Usually, she and Helen sat on the seat, Millie and Earl Lee rode in back, facing the way they had come. With their feet dangling out, they laughed merrily as they bounced along, holding on dearly to the sides of the buggy.

On this day, Grandma traded at the Blairsville Store, which was just across the road from Blessey's Store. She liked to divide up her business between the two, since both stores were honest and the owners being friends of long standing.

Millie marveled at all the activity as they approached the store. Though perhaps not as exciting as in the years before her time, it still was far more lively than at home. She waved at a couple of men driving big work wagons and at an occasional buggy. Grandma of course knew everyone and greeted them with a wave of her hand and a hearty howdy.

She knew that the village wasn't nearly as big as it used to be, because she often heard Grandpa and Papa talk about the old days when there had been one house for every forty acres. When hard times came along, the small land owners borrowed money from the more prominent neighbors, who often foreclosed on them when payment became delinquent, just like Grandpa did some times. The smaller farms began to disappear and eventually, a few of the more prosperous land owners remained, just like Grandpa. Soon after a foreclosure, usually all signs of the once existing farm disappeared, as the buildings gave way to cultivation. And along with that, there were fewer people to patronize the businesses.

Not that all the remaining farms were big or even prosperous, for that matter, because they were not! To some extent, they were larger than before, which made fewer of them. Many were far from thriving, where owners lacked the ability or resources to become successful. To some people, failure is inevitable and try as they may, they barely eke out a living.

They waved to Mr. Dawson, the blacksmith. He and his son were the only such men left in Blairsville. Two shops used to stay busy all the time, but now that so many farmers were gone and with the automobile coming on the scene and being used for much of the transportation, only enough work remained for one smithy shop. He did have all the work he could handle though, since a good blacksmith could do so much more than shoe horses.

Millie had learned a lot about the history of Blairsville by listening to Papa and her grandparents talking. She even new how the store they were going to today came about.

It seems that the store building itself was bought at another location and transported from about three and a half miles away. Two huge gray horses were used to pull the building along. It was set on logs and pulled with a windlass, whatever that was. It moved as far as possible, stopped, and the driver unwound the ropes and pulled again. Needless to say, it was a very slow process, but proved to be effective.

175

The original owner was an elderly lady who opened the store with ten dollars cash money. She could neither read nor write or count above twelve. Very often, as was the custom in those days, she would be paid with eggs or other produce rather than cash, because money was scarce.

When selling or buying eggs, she laid out the eggs on the counter top, one dozen per lot to arrive at the price. Sugar, beans, flour, etc. figured two cups per pound. Although it may not have been so accurate as modern scales, it worked out

Grandma would laugh when recalling the story. "I came out many an egg ahead on her, over the years," she laughed. "I-Gawd, it was easy to slip an egg or two my way when the old woman was counting and she never knowed the difference. It wasn't my fault she never learned to count." She didn't feel that she ever cheated or took advantage of the woman, since it was only a couple of eggs now and then.

Grandma guided Nellie in between two other buggies and Helen jumped to the ground and tied the line to the hitch rack by the store.

After leaving the glaring sunlight outside, one had to pause for a few seconds just inside the door, to let their eyes become accustomed to the darkness. Once the initial shock wore off, you could see very well.

The store boasted of having the first electricity in the area. A battery powered, one piston unit had been rigged up to provide enough electricity to light the store. Since there were only four, twenty-five watt bulbs in the main building, it used very little power. Nothing else was electric at the time. Although the power unit was loud, it served its purpose in fine style, by eliminating the coal oil lamps, even if a person must squint a little to see clearly. Neighbors would often come in and look at it in wonder.

Like Blessey's Store across the road, the Blairsville Store carried just about everything a farmer could want. The general merchandise consisted of all kinds of groceries, hardware, drygoods and notions as well as tobacco, roofing, stove pipe, nails, bolts and a brand new item, motor oil for automobiles. They bought eggs, poultry and butter all the time and in winter, quail, rabbits, squirrels and other wild life, preferably dead of course, and animal hides.

Grandma took the coin purse from her apron pocket and extracted three nickels, one for each of the children and smiled as they scurried about trying to decide the best way to spend them. Earl Lee could get the most for his money. After much deliberation and soul searching, he always settled for the same thing. Licorice sticks were a penny each, jaw breakers, two for a penny and suckers, a penny each, so

176

a nickel went a long way and he had candy for two or three days. The girls however usually chose a big bottle of orange soda pop. The store proprietor suggested they try a new drink that just came on the market. He said that everyone liked it and it would likely outsell all the other soft drinks, in time. It was called Coca Cola! Helen was dubious about spending her nickel on something she knew nothing about. Millie on the other hand, being more daring than her sister, paid her nickel for the new drink. One swallow was enough to tell her she had made a mistake. The bitter flavor remained in her memory for years and she never acquired the taste for a cola drink, mainly due to the fact she had squandered her precious money on something that tasted so awful. She tried to trade drinks with Helen to no avail and had to settle for merely watching her sister savoring her orange.

Bessie was busy conducting her business in the room that had been added on the east side of the main store. This room was about half the size of the store. Here is where chickens, eggs, milk and other forms of produce were bought and stored until it could be transferred to town. Also in the east room were coal oil, vinegar and molasses, in wooden barrels. Coal oil was a very popular product in those days, as all homes were lighted by coal oil lamps and many cooked on coal oil stoves, especially during the hot summer months.

Law kept coal oil in a fifty gallon steel drum in the shed, but when it got low, Bessie bought a gallon at the store to tide them over until he had a chance to refill it. Today she had her can filled and placed a new potato on the spout to replace the missing cap. With the trading done and the groceries loaded on the buggy, they started home.

Once they turned off the main road onto the side road, the children began to clamor for the next best thing about going to the store. Buying soda pop being the best, but running along behind the buggy was next best. They usually did this unless Grandma was in a bad humor.

She stopped the horse and the children jumped to the ground. Hanging onto the back of the buggy they began to move forward, slowly at first. Grandma flicked the lines over Nellie's back and she gained momentum. Laughing and shouting faster, faster, Nellie's gait turned into a gallop and they ran as fast as they could to keep up. Dust flew from the wheels of the buggy. The three children yelled and laughed, running breathlessly behind it, three inches of hot dust spiraling up around the bare feet.

By the time they reached the corner in the road, they were hot and out of breath, but the sweaty, dusty faces beamed with joy.

177

Bessie recognized the automobile in the yard as belonging to the sheriff of the county. Billy Tate and Law had become good friends over the years. Part of the reason being that they could be helpful to each other and partly because they were alike in many ways. The sheriff was probably a couple years older than Law, about the same size, but he sported the same big moustache. They were also similar in the fact that each was inclined to go after what he wanted and usually got it, even at the expense of others. Bessie rather liked the man, for he was always polite and friendly to her and the children.

The two men sat in the shade of the maple trees in the front yard. When the buggy stopped, Billy Tate walked forward and spoke tipping his big hat, smiling.

"Howdy, missus Bessie," he said. "You too, young ladies. And you too, young man."

As Law remained seated, he watched his friend help unload the groceries and carry them in the house.

The sheriff had come out on another business deal. Some might call it an underhanded deal, but it didn't worry either of them. When the sheriff had a few prisoners locked up, he liked to think it was his duty to see they received a normal amount of exercise, while at the same time helping to pay for their keep. So, he hired them out to Lawrence Reynolds on the sly and Law could use them for any work he had. He paid the sheriff fifty cents per day, per prisoner. The sheriff figured they owed the county something for their keep, though he pocketed the money he received. Not many people were aware of this arrangement, because they were delivered to the farm before daylight and picked up after dark.

The prisoners presented very little worry or problems, being mostly transients or vagrants or merely arrested for some minor offense. No real criminal would be taken out, so if one of these decided to sneak off before pick up time, little was said or done about it. Never more than three or four men were brought out at one time.

When extra men were there for dinner, besides the two normally working, Bessie simply increased the size of each pot. Instead of cooking more variety, she added to. The children ate in the kitchen when this occurred, to make room for the extra help at the long dining room table.

No one knows for sure just when Mondays became "wash day" for women. As near as can be determined, it has always been that way. There has been much speculation on the subject, but very few learned men agree on the matter as to when and why it came about. Some say it's because Monday is the first day after Sunday, for whatever reason that proves. These people reason that the women want to wash on that day to clean the Sunday go-to-meeting clothes and have them ready for the following day of worship. Others contend it's because the women are more rested after Sunday which is considered a day of rest. But, that couldn't be the reason, because most women in the olden times cooked bigger meals on Sundays and then had to clean up afterwards, so that theory didn't hold water. If they wanted to be assured of having clean clothes for Sunday, why not wait until Friday or Saturday! But by then they may be tired from working all week or be wrapped up in some other project and not have time to wash. And one must remember that Sunday clothes must be ironed after washing to get the wrinkles out, which proved to be another major project.

The flat iron that most women used, must be heated on the kitchen cook stove, meaning hot fire was required, winter or summer. It was made of solid iron, with a handle sitting upright of the same material, which got just as hot as the base and must be picked up with a heavy hot-pad or cloth to keep from burning the users fingers. In order to test the iron for the right amount of heat, one wet her finger to her tongue and touched the bottom of the iron. If it sizzled, it was hot enough. Ironing took a certain amount of skill because, if left in one place too long an instant too long could very well be disastrous, leaving a scorched hole in the material. Some of the newer models of irons had removable handles that could be detached and the same handle used for more than one iron.

Bessie Reynolds had never been one to follow tradition or even think about it, but she did wash her clothes on Monday. But, she did try to iron what little she did iron, on Tuesday, sometimes. Like most women, she sprinkled her clothes down the night before. Everyone knows that a hot, dry iron will never smooth the wrinkles out unless it's dampened first.

When the weather permitted, she heated her wash water outside on an open fire in the back yard, in a blackened copper boiler that had been made for that purpose. It sat up on bricks, well above the burning wood fire. The water, she carried from the rain barrels at the sides of the house. They had been placed there for the sole purpose of catching rainwater. When the barrels were nearly empty, she had the girls take turns pumping water from the cistern on the back porch and carry it out, a half bucket at a time. Plenty of hot water and good strong lye soap that she made herself would clean the dirt out of any work clothes.

One day while washing, disaster struck. Bessie scrubbed on the board two pairs of grimy overalls, clean and after wringing them out by hand, put them in the other tub of clean rinse water. Just as she bent over the board again, she was bumped from behind. Earl Lee had been chasing Shep across the yard and the big dog accidentally ran into Bessie, knocking her off balance. Before she could recover, she had turned over the bench on which the two tubs of wash water sat. Water and clothes sloshed out across the ground.

Needless to say, Bessie was infuriated. She grabbed Earl Lee by the arm before he could get away and boxed him up beside the head with wet, open hands. When she let him go, after scolding him severely and calling him all kinds of a little fool, he ran crying out to hide in the barn.

"I-Gawd boy, I've a mind to tan your hide good for you," she shouted. "Look what you've done now. Now I got to heat more water and start all over again."

The two girls had witnessed the incident, but dared not display any sort of verbal emotion, for two reasons. One, they did feel sorry for the boy who hadn't meant to cause the accident. The other reason being, they didn't want to bring down Grandma's wrath on them. They hurriedly went about helping pick up the clothes.

Lawrence was on his way out to the barn when he first spotted the mule rider coming down the road. At first he didn't recognize him, but as the mule drew closer under the easy gait, he noticed the man's floppy hat and the saddelless animal, without a bridle, it being controlled by a mere rope halter. Law stopped and stood gazing at the new arrival, for he knew he was coming here. He wondered why and his curiosity was deeply aroused and he walked forward to greet him. It surely must be important for Sam Hathorn to ride all the way from his own place to see him. It couldn't be a neighborly visit!

The mule turned in the yard and walked up to Lawrence, where he stopped automatically. Sam slid to the ground. After the usual greetings, the two men went back towards the barn to take advantage of its shade. Law extracted the tobacco plug and knife from his pocket and each cut off a wad. Squatting down on their haunches, Law finally asked, "What brings you way over here, Sam?" Sam made sure the wad was settled right in his jaw before answering. "I had a visitor yesterday, Mr. Reynolds.

Puzzled, Law asked, "What kind of visitor?" He couldn't figure out why it should affect him, even if it was a person. Maybe the visitor had been the man he'd seen that day in the Bottoms, and the one the girls had seen and named the Bottoms Tramper! Yet, Sam wasn't the kind to be concerned about such likes, and he did seem worried.

"A man!" Sam said. "He said his name is Reynolds."

"Reynolds!" Law said. "What did this man look like?"

"Well, he kind of favored you in some ways, 'cept he didn't have no moustache. 'Bout the same size though, but maybe a little younger."

"Hah! I don't know of any other Reynolds around here, except family," Law replied, very interested by now.

"That's just it, Mr. Reynolds. He is family! Said he's a brother of yours."

Law's body stiffened! "Did he give you a first name?" he asked quietly.

"Said his name was Arthur!"

"What?" Law exploded.

"Yes sir, that's what he said, Arthur Reynolds," the surprised man told him.

Before Law could make another comment, they were interrupted by loud screaming from over near the house. Their attention was immediately drawn to Millie running wildly around in the yard, yet from that distance, they could see blood streaming down her head and covering her face. Running around in circles at first, she then straightened out and went around and around the house.

Bessie emerged from the house with a wet dishrag in her hand. "What's going on out here?" she demanded, wiping her hands on her apron. Helen and Earl Lee stood farther out in the yard watching tearfully, neither offering any assistance.

Millie continued to run. Bessie yelled, "Stop you little fool," as she ran by. "How do you expect me to help you, if you don't stop that running!" Starting to follow the girl, she changed her mind, knowing she'd never catch her. So, she stood and waited for the next round.

When Millie came by this time, her Grandma lunged forward and grabbed her, clasping her granddaughter tightly. She pressed her tenderly but firmly to her bosom as though she shared the pain, trying to absorb a portion of it. In that instant, she felt great tenderness for her, but out of constraint and ostentation, it passed quickly. Looking down at the little head, she saw the deep gash across the crown that laid back the hair. Blood ran from it and down her face and onto her dress.

Bessie picked up the frightened girl and holding her under one arm, carried her to the corner of the house. The old wooden rain barrel was two thirds full of rain water from the roof of he house. It had grown stagnant and yellow, full of mosquitoes and wiggle tails.

"This is the best thing in the world for cuts," Bessie prophesied. "It'll cure anything."

So saying, she turned Millie upside down and doused her head into the water. She repeated the dunking three more times, holding her down a little longer each time.

The girl continued to kick and scream but, was no match for her captor.

"If you don't stop that kicking, girl you're liable to slide right out of my arms and go head first into that barrel and drown," Bessie reproved.

After the last dunking, Millie quieted down somewhat and was set back on her feet, her head, face and dress soaked with blood, tears and stagnant water. Her Grandma slapped the wet dishrag that she still carried over the cut and told her to hold it.

"That's another good thing for cuts of any kind, dirty dish water," she said.

Miraculously, the bleeding stopped in a short while and the wound healed eventually, though it did leave a tiny scar for the rest of Millie's life.

"Now, you two tell me what happened!" Bessie demanded of the other two.

"We were just playing," Helen said. "Millie climbed up the ladder and fell off and hit her head on the wheelbarrow."

The two men, still in the shade of the barn, had witnessed the spectacle and for the moment, lost their train of thought, but recovered quickly.

"Maw, what's all that caterwauling about anyway?" he shouted.

"Nothing much," Bessie called back. "Millie just cut a little place on her head."

"Well, it can't be too bad. Nobody that can run that fast and carry on the way she did can't be hurt too much. Keep her quiet. A man can't even think with that much racket."

Law forgot the incident immediately as he turned his attention back to Sam Hathorn.

"Is this Arthur Reynolds really your brother?" Sam asked.

"I'm sorry to say, he is," Law answered.

It wasn't a pleasant acknowledgment. He hadn't heard of his younger brother in years, not since that trouble he got into and skipped the country. Being so much younger than he, they had little in common and Arthur had always been on the wild side. He never liked to work and Law had turned him down for a job once because of this. Being unpredictable and not dependable, Law had no use for him on his farm where every man was expected to carry his load. In and out of trouble

182

seemed to be a way of life for him. If he had been to see Sam Hathorn and Sam was worried about him, then that meant he was up to no good, but Law couldn't figure out, for the life of him, what Arthur could be up to.

"What does he want?" he said.

"Well, for one thing, he wants my farm," Sam said. "Said it weren't mine anyway and he's going to get it."

"What!" Law exclaimed. "What's got into that hot-head anyways?"

"He said he went to the courthouse in McCleansboro and there ain't no record of me buying it," Sam said. "He's going to make a down payment on it and get the deed and I'll have to move out. Can he do that, Mr. Reynolds?"

"Of course not! You've got papers showing your claim, haven't you?"

"I've got that paper from the logging company, that they gave to all the men that worked for them and bought land. It says on it that I paid two hundred dollars cash money and it tells where the land is, the boundary and everything," Sam told him. "I got it hid in the attic in a tin can since the flood so it won't get wet and ruin."

"That's all you need, Sam," Law said. "Most land here in the Bottoms that belonged to the big lumber companies hasn't been registered yet at the courthouse. It should've been, but it ain't. Your claim will hold up in court. I can't figure what's got into that boy."

"He knows about that money you gave me, too," Sam said. "I don't know how he found out about it and I don't think he knows about our deal of me and the boys working for you. I told him the farm belongs to you because you gave me some money and we shook hands on it."

"I wonder how the Sam Hill he found out about all that! I reckon it don't matter none though."

"He said you don't have no proof that you gave me any money and I don't ever have to pay it back, if I don't want to. I told him we shook hands on it, and that's the same as a written agreement," Sam went on. "He laughed and told me a hand shake don't mean nothing."

Law cut in, "A hand shake is more binding than any piece of paper."

"That's what I told him, but he only laughed and said I was stupid to believe such things."

Law was seething inside with anger by now. "I wonder what that fool is up to. What else did he say?"

"He said he'd come back in a few days and for me to start getting ready to move out."

"He's trying to get back at me," Law blurted out, remembering a past incident. "He threatened to get even with me one day a long time ago and have a bigger and better place than me. That boy ain't got the gumption to settle down and work at anything worth while, though."

"What can I do, Mr. Reynolds? I can't afford to lose my farm. It would just about kill my missus. She plans on living there til she dies of old age" Sam said. "I don't see how he can do such a thing, me and my boys has worked hard to build it up and keep it going."

"You don't have to do anything, Sam. You just stay there and protect your property same as if anybody else tried to take it. It's yours and there's no way he can take it."

"What if the sheriff comes with him? I can't go up agin' the law."

"You won't have to. I'll talk to the sheriff and tell him all about it," Law promised. "He's a good friend of mine and he'll let me know if anything comes of it. If Arthur does come back, you just stay right there, and send one of your boys to come tell me. We'll straighten this thing out."

The two talked on for awhile, until Sam was satisfied, up to a point at least, that he had nothing to worry about from Arthur.

Before Law had an opportunity to talk to the sheriff, however, he had a visitor. Working in the hay loft, dragging bales of hay over close to the opening, the automobile had turned into his yard before he became aware of its existence. Standing in the opening, he watched as it stopped and the man got out. Emerging slowly it seemed a little reluctantly, the man stood up, stretching his arms over his head, his eyes searching about, until he saw Lawrence in the top of the barn. He attempted a smile but gave it up and waved a hand half-heartedly.

Law examined the newcomer carefully from his loft and didn't return the salutation. Although he hadn't seen his brother Arthur in several years, there was no mistaking him. Many similarities about the younger man could be applied to himself. The wide brim, slouch hat for one thing and each wore suspenders this day, to support their baggy trousers. And like Law, Arthur wore his shirt open at the throat, minus the collar. Arthur had light stubble of beard, just beginning to turn gray, but lacked the large moustache. They were about the same in stature and mannerisms.

Law tried to remember him as a little boy, so lively and carefree, but it was difficult after what had happened since. His feelings for his little brother of by gone years had vanished long ago. It's a pity, he thought, that little boys have to grow up to become men. There would be much fewer problems in the world if they could remain as little boys.

He went over to the ladder and climbed down from the loft, still holding the hay hook in his hand. Anyone not familiar with a hay hook, it's exactly what its called; a hay hook. Made from a length of round steel rod any where from ten to eighteen inches long, it was fashioned into a pointed hook on one end with a cross piece of wood six to eight inches long on the other for a handle hand grip. It is used for picking up or moving bales of hay. It can be a handy or dangerous tool or weapon, depending on it's use.

"What do you want?" he demanded.

"Is that any way to greet your long lost little brother?" Arthur asked, good naturedly.

"How else would you expect to be greeted?"

"I thought maybe you'd be happy to see me after all these years," Arthur said. "After all, we're still blood brothers."

"I'd just as soon not have you in the family."

"You ain't changed a bit, big brother. Still have to have things your way, don't you!"

"I'll ask you again. Why did you come back, I thought you was gone for good," Law said.

"Why shouldn't I come back? I was born here. This is home," Arthur pointed out.

"I plan to settle down and farm here in these Bottoms. Why, between the two of us, we could own this whole valley someday."

"You plan on owning this whole valley which is forty acres?"

"That's just the beginning. A man has to start some place."

"Why'd you pick that particular farm?"

"Oh, so Sam Hathorn's been to see you? Well, to be honest, that's the only place available right now. I aim to own lots more as time goes by."

"Maybe you didn't understand, Sam owns that place. He's got papers to prove it."

For an instant Arthur was taken aback by this revelation about papers.

"That's a good try Law, but I been to the Court House and looked things over pretty good. His place was never recorded, so it is open to whoever buys it and I aim to do just that."

"Why that farm, Arthur," Law asked. "Is it because I had something to do with it?"

"Maybe it is," the other man grinned, "I remember the time I asked for a job and you turned me down, your own brother. I always looked up to you, but you made me feel like dirt, when you said I wasn't worth anything. I promised myself I'd come back and show you up. Well, here I am and I aim to prove I can do it."

"Where did you get all your money?" Law asked.

"It's none of your business, but I don't mind telling you," Arthur replied. "Me and a couple friends been working over in Missouri on a deal for a long time and it finally paid off. We made a killing."

"I'll wager it wasn't honest," Law ventured.

Arthur laughed. "What difference does it make if it paid off. I'll wager you've done a few things in your life that wouldn't stand up to close scrutiny. Don't forget, I'm your brother, so I know you pretty well."

Just then Bessie come outside. She liked having company and recognizing her brother-in-law, exclaimed, "I-Gawd, if it ain't Arthur Reynolds. Where in the world have you been all this time?"

She rushed out to greet him, and he received an invitation to dinner that he couldn't turn down. However, Law had a different notion.

"He can't stay for dinner," he told his wife. "He has to get back to town."

"I can't refuse an invitation to one of Bessie's meals," Arthur responded. "I ain't in no hurry. It's been a long time, Bessie and I hope I'll be invited back again, because we'll be neighbors before long."

"Good," Bessie said. "It'll be nice having more of the family around. I hope you have a good wife so we can visit."

"I'm not married," Arthur replied, "At least, not any more."

"That's a pity. Everybody needs to be married. What happened to her? Did she die?"

"No, she ran off with a business partner," Arthur said.

Bessie clucked tsk, tsk a few times, "That's a shame."

"I may look around and find another woman here," he added. "It'll be nice to have one around. A man needs a good woman."

"You're right there," Bessie agreed. "It ain't natural for folks to live alone. I think I know just the woman for you. There's a widow lives up by Needmore that just happens to be looking for a good man."

"Whoa there, Bessie, not so fast. I just now got here," Arthur laughed. "Give me a little time and I'll look around on my own."

Bessie walked over to the pole stationed in the yard, and jerked vigorously on the bell rope hanging down. The peal of the dinner bell rang loud and clear across the Bottoms. Presently Leonard and the two hired hands came in from the field for dinner. After scrubbing their hands at the pump, they all went inside for the noon day meal.

Leonard remembered very little about his uncle, except what he'd heard from his father. There was nothing exemplary about any comments having to do mostly with Arthur being a no-good and shiftless.

Nine people sat around the long dinner table. The three children developed a case of shyness around strangers. Leonard spoke only in response to a question or comment directed at him.

The two hired hands talked not at all, concentrating strictly on nourishment. Law, who normally tried to direct a conversation his way, was unusually quiet, listening to his wife and brother carry on a constant line of chatter. He would like to have blotted out everything his brother said and ask him to leave, but knew that would never do, so he sat, trying to eat and ignore him at the same time.

"So, these young-uns must be yours, huh Leonard?" he heard Arthur ask.

"Just the two girls," Leonard answered.

"Oh yes, I forgot that you only had the two. He looked at Earl Lee. "Then this must be the bastard grandson of Sidney!"

"Don't say that," Law snapped. "How'd you find out about that anyway?"

"Why, it's common knowledge," Arthur replied calmly. "Every body knows about it."

"Not clear over there in Missouri where you been," Law said vehemently. "How'd you know so much about what goes on here and how'd you find out about Leonard's girls?"

Millie had perked up when the strange man made that remark about them and Earl Lee. Not being sure just what he meant, she did know that it must not be very good or Grandpa wouldn't be so mad. She watched him at the end of the table. It was easy to see that he didn't like his brother very much, because he hardly spoke to him at all, except now. The way he kept pushing his food around on his plate and not eating it certainly wasn't him. Grandma seemed to like Uncle Arthur all right, but Millie couldn't be sure if she herself did or not.

The man acted overly friendly and seemed to be trying to upset Grandpa even more than he already was. Being brothers, they should get along together! She didn't know where he had been all these years, but Grandpa surely wasn't happy that he came home. He must be up to something and Millie was determined to find out what. The best way to learn things was to listen and she decided to do just that!

"I know about a lot of things," Arthur said. "You surely don't think you own everything and everyone in these Bottoms do you? I've got ways of finding out things that interest me, and right now I'm interested in going into farming and buying up land. You'll soon see just what I mean."

"I still want to know how you found out about my family," Law demanded. "You don't know anybody around here good enough for them to tell you anything, besides Sidney. He wouldn't confide in you any more than me. Sid don't like you any better than I do, since you borrowed that money from him and ran off without paying him back, along with his only saddle horse. In the old days you'd be strung up for a horse thief."

"I intended to pay him back," Arthur replied, "Circumstances just didn't work out that way."

"They never did with you. Why don't you pay him now? He could use the money!"

"I might do that! I want to start off right, because I aim to be around for quite a spell."

Bessie saw her husband almost sputter over his food at this last remark. She could tell by the smirk on Arthur's face that he was trying to antagonize his brother and was succeeding. She decided she'd better get them talking about something else or hurry the meal before the fireworks began, for Law was about ready to explode. She wished Arthur hadn't come back! Even when young, he meant trouble.

The others at the table seemed intent on the food before them and unaware of any undercurrent or animosity, but Bessie knew better. They listened to every word and wondered what was going on.

Bessie made a big display by pushing her chair back noisily and leaving the table. Returning from the kitchen a moment later with a dish of vegetables, she realized she had failed in her attempt to divert the conversation.

"Yep, I plan on settling down, right here in these Bottoms and make a name for myself," Arthur was saying. "I might even find me a good woman, like you got, big brother. Only thing, I won't work mine as hard as you do yours, though. I'll bet you work Bessie about the same way you do your mules. You need to hire her some help. I notice you got hired men working out in the field. You oughta' hire her some help around the house. Have you looked at her lately, Brother? She's still a fine figure of a woman, don't you agree?"

Bessie sat down and felt a blush spread over her face. She realized she wasn't pretty in any fashion, but she also knew that some men were attracted by her rather rugged features.

"Don't you agree, Law?" he repeated.

Law's face was red too, but with anger, not accustomed to being put down, especially in his own house by his own brother.

He harrumphed again and furiously pushed back his chair, and rising, went outside. No one raised their eyes from the plate before them.

In a few moments, Leonard and the two hired hands also left the house and settled down for a brief rest under the maple trees in the yard before returning back to work.

When Arthur finished eating, he thanked Bessie and went outside. Immediately, Millie jumped up and followed, careful not to be too close, so as not to draw attention to herself. Knowing that something may happen, she wanted to be in on it at the very beginning.

Before she even slammed the screen door on the porch, she saw Uncle Arthur walking towards his automobile and saying, "Thanks for the dinner and hospitality, Big Brother. I'll pay you back after I get settled in, over on the Hathorn place." To Millie, it sounded more like a sneer rather than a grateful thanks.

Then Grandpa snarled at him, "You stay away from that place, you hear me!"

Uncle Arthur laughed at him and Grandpa got really mad. Not being close enough to hear what he said, Millie could only guess at what he meant. There was some profanity from both men now. The next thing she knew, Grandpa had that hay-hook in his hand and ran at Uncle Arthur. Before he could defend himself, the pointed hook caught the front of his shirt and ripped it down the middle, tearing it off his body. Grandpa swung the hook again and tore a deep gash along the side of Uncle Arthur's head. He stumbled backwards, in an effort to get away from the deadly weapon. In so doing, he fell to the ground and rolled over on his hands and knees. When Grandpa went at him again, he began crawling across the yard as fast as he could. There was no defense for an unarmed man against such an outraged individual, and his only thought and hope was to get away from him. Uncle Arthur managed to get to his feet and started to run and stagger towards his automobile. But, Grandpa closed in on him from behind. The next swinging arc caught him on the left shoulder and opened the arm down to the elbow.

Uncle Arthur was covered with blood now and yelling, "You're crazy, you're crazy," over and over as he turned and ran to his automobile. Frantically twisting the key in the ignition, he pumped the starter and choke. Fortunately for him the engine turned over and started on the first try. He had no desire to stay around and try to defend himself or fight back. His main concern being, to get away from his brother. He had somehow lost all the bravado displayed earlier.

Grandpa yelled at him, "If you ever come back around here again, by Gawd I'll kill you."

Uncle Arthur roared off down the road in a cloud of dust. Millie stood there, bewildered at what she had witnessed, at the violence in her Grandpa. He surely must hate his brother!

Papa and the hired men were on their feet watching, but making no effort to intervene on anyone's behalf. Helen and Earl Lee were also in the yard now and stood spell bound by the exhibition. Grandma came out, wiping her hands on her apron.

A worried look creased her forehead as she went to her man and took the hay hook from his hand. He walked slowly out to the barn, somewhat subdued and his anger spent.

The next day, as expected, the sheriff came out. Only Law and Bessie were at the house at the time. Bessie invited him in for a cup of coffee and he accepted, as always. The two men sat at the kitchen table, while she filled two granite cups with the black liquid; coffee at this time of day was a word used loosely for the drink. The big granite pot had sat on the stove since daylight that morning and the grounds had settled firmly in the bottom. None of them poured out into the cups. At the Reynolds, dinner was the main meal, the same as most farms. Supper was usually leftovers from dinner, was kept warm in the warming-oven of the stove. The fire being allowed to die down after dinner, except of course during winter months, the coffee was only lukewarm, but tar black strong after having absorbed every particle of strength from the grinds.

The sheriff sipped from his cup and grimaced inwardly, not wanting to hurt his hostess' feelings.

"What brings you out this way, Billy?" Law asked, to begin the conversation.

"I reckon you know," the sheriff replied.

"Yep, reckon I do!"

"It's about your brother, Arthur!"

190

"I figured as much. What about it?"

"Well, he filed an assault charge against you!"

"You mean over that little ruckus! Why that didn't amount to nothing at all."

"You could of danged nigh killed him, Law," the sheriff said.

"It wouldn't've been no great loss!"

"You should never have used a hay hook on him, they're dangerous. If he had been a little bit smarter, he could've charged you with assault with a deadly weapon. Or even attempted murder! The way it stands now, it's only simple assault and battery."

"What's going to come of it?" Law asked.

"Well, I had to write out a warrant, there's no way around it, since Arthur preferred charges," the sheriff informed him. "But, there's no law says I have to take you in. We better get it over with as soon as possible. You can go to town tomorrow and see Judge Cox and see what he says."

"I'll get Leonard to drive me in, in a couple of days," Law said. "I'm too busy now."

"Confound it Law, you get your big butt in there tomorrow."

"Excuse me, Miz Bessie," he apologized, "But this man of yours can be aggravating some times."

"I know what you mean," agreed Bessie.

"You get in there tomorrow Law, or I'll have to come get you and lock you up. We'll go together to see the judge and get it straightened out without any problem. But you know Judge Cox, he is a stickler to the letter of the law, and you better be there."

"All right, I'll go in the morning," Law promised. "Whatever happens though, it'll be worth it. That brother of mine is about as worthless as tits on a boar. I'm not sorry I beat him up."

"Beat him up!" the sheriff exclaimed. "That's putting it pretty mild. You cut him up bad. Why it took old Doc Sawyer two hours to sew him up. He's got stitches all down the side of his head and down his arm, from shoulder to elbow. He'll carry them scars the rest of his life."

"Good. He had it coming!"

"What the devil did he do?"

So Law explained to him about Arthur's scheme to take over Sam Hathorn's place and then going on to others.

"Sounds to me like that runs in the family," the sheriff grinned.

"I never beat nobody out of anything, Billy, and you know it. I always treat folks square and pay a fair price for what I get."

"Don't get all riled up at me, Law. I was only kidding. I'd as soon deal with you as any man I know of. Maybe Arthur won't follow up on his plans, now. I'll look into the matter though and see if there's some way I can block it."

He finished his coffee, that had cooled down to room temperature, and left.

Leonard was a fast and somewhat reckless driver, which did little to soothe his father's nerves and endear him to the new mode of transportation. With his cap cocked jauntily on the side of his head, he pulled back on the throttle and held onto the steering wheel with both hands. The ruts in the road had long ago been filled in and flattened out allowing good running speed.

They made the hard road in almost nothing flat. Great clouds of dust rolled up behind them. To an observer it would appear that Leonard was racing to keep ahead of it, with the cloud staying dead even with the rear bumper. Only twice during the three mile ride did they meet another automobile. Instead of slowing down out of sheer courtesy for the other and letting the dust settle, both drivers speeded up, all but blinding each other.

After passing the first one, Law slapped his son on the shoulder, coughing and choking. "Slow down, you danged fool," he shouted. "What're you trying to do, drown me in road dust."

The highway had only been paved for three or four years. It had always been there, but was a gravel road before that. When the automobile came on the scene and appeared to become a permanent part of American life, the road was paved with concrete all the way from McCleansboro to Wayne City and beyond. As with all such roadways, it had a number to identify it. Officially it became State Highway 242, but for years it was simply referred to as the hard road or the slab. Needless to say, it also became a speedway for some of the younger generation with automobiles that were manufactured to go as fast as sixty miles per hour. Because of all the slower moving horse drawn vehicles, speed limits were installed and strictly enforced by police.

McCleansboro was a thriving, pleasant town of some three thousand souls and had maple trees lining the quiet streets. As with many of the smaller farming towns in the state, McCleansboro was proud of its red brick courthouse in the center of the public square. The streets were wide around the Square. On the south side, three lanes were used for parking the various types of vehicles; one lane on the inside and one on the outside, leaving enough space for a row in the center. The main source of income was derived from the surrounding farmland. But there were other businesses as well that supplied additional revenue, such as the Mark Twain Shirt Factory, down next to the railroad. Also a dress factory on the east side of the Square employed a number of ladies. Then of course there were the grain elevators and lumberyards and farm supply stores. Around the Square, a variety of stores and businesses occupied the two story brick buildings. Two banks and a Gothic style library, along with all types of offices and small restaurants helped supply the needs of the citizenry.

Leonard parked between two wagons on the west side of the Square, and the two men emerged.

The men who occupied the wooden benches around the court house lawn were tolerated, whether affectionately or not, and allowed to gather there each day. They were known as the McCleansboro Board of Trade. On a normal day they numbered fifteen to twenty strong and appeared to be out in full force on this day, despite the hot weather, while taking advantage of the shade beneath the large maple trees. This group was made up of men mostly past the prime of life, with a few younger ones infiltrating their ranks in hopes of acquiring a good trade. The status of these men had almost reached that of professional loafers. They were skilled at their trade, though many of the watches, pocket knives, etc. had very little real value. Occasionally, one came across a bargain if he really knew the ropes and could outwit the holder, especially if the object was new to the Board. But, many articles were traded back and forth among the members and a man may own the same piece a number of times. Requirements for membership on the Board were simple. One merely had to come and join in discussions of some object offered by one of the men or present an object of his own. A new piece was always greeted with interest and speculation, and if the new arrival came back a number of times, he automatically became one of them. The main object of the Board was the skill and fun of trading and swapping jokes and tales and often lies about ones past achievements. But, one must always have something to trade. They were mostly retired farmers, professionals and retailers with time on their hands, and this gave them something to do.

In foul weather most stayed home, but the ones that did show up were allowed to go inside the Court House and use the benches along the main hall, provided by the sheriff's office. If they became noisy or blocked the hallway or caused any commotion, the sheriff moved them out.

Walking up the sidewalk, Law in the lead of course, Leonard heard his name called. Even before turning he recognized the voice as that of Lenny Huffstutler, an old school chum. Lenny lived on the higher land, out of the Bottoms. The two boys had been good friends all through school. Seven or eight years ago, a horse kicked Lenny on the side of the head, as he stooped down behind it to pick up a stick. The blow seriously damaged his way of thinking, leaving him a little addled in the head. Being of limited use around the farm, his father or a brother brought him into town some mornings when the weather was right and came back to pick him up in the mid-afternoon. Lenny always brought a couple of sandwiches for lunch, which he often shared with one of the other men. Whiling away the time, trading and talking, he seemed to be happy.

Turning to greet his friend, Leonard saw Lenny walking toward him, grinning.

"I ain't seen you lately, Leonard," Lenny said.

"I've been busy and haven't been to town much," Leonard replied. "What's new with you?"

"Nothing much. The same old seven and six. I work hard around the farm for a few days, and then come into town to spend some time with my friends here," he waved his hand at the men occupying the benches. "Paw brought me in this morning." He took off his cap and wiped his forehead with a big red handkerchief. "I heard your wife left you, Leonard. That's too bad! And now you're stuck with raising two little girls."

"I wouldn't say I'm stuck with two girls, Lenny. I want them and had a hard time getting to keep them."

Lenny noticed the agitated tone in Leonard's voice and tried to make amends. "I'm sorry! I didn't mean nothing by it. I guess I'd want to keep them too, if I had two girls."

"That's all right, Lenny, I know you didn't mean nothing by it."

"I'll tell you what, Leonard, just to show I didn't mean nothing by it, I'll give you my good pocket knife. Here take it. You can have it for nothing."

"No, I can't do that, Lenny. You need it."

"Well, how about making a trade then! I'll trade you my knife for your watch. I know you got a watch because I can see it in your pocket there. I'll make you a good trade since we're friends. Look at this knife! It's got three blades in it. They're sharp too."

"Look at this, I'll prove it to you."

He wiped some spittle on his arm and shaved the hair off, leaving a bare spot.

"See that!" he boasted. "This here blade is just as sharp. And this other one has only half of it gone. I broke it prying open a tin, but it's still a good knife. I'll trade you even for your watch, sight unseen. What kind is it, Leonard?"

Leonard pulled the watch from the watch pocket of his overalls. It was tied by a braided leather shoe lace chain.

"It's a Klicker," he said.

"A Klicker! Gosh that must be a good one or you wouldn't have it. Don't see many Klickers around here."

"My wife gave it to me for my birthday one year. I don't think I'd trade it off."

Lenny was sincere in his efforts to make a good trade with his long time friend, not realizing that the broken bladed knife was al1 but worthless to anyone but himself or another member of the Board. He could trade it up or down and maybe finally acquire a piece of some value. Leonard, however, had nothing on his person to trade, though he wished he did have, for Lenny's sake.

Law yelled from the doorway of the Court House, "Hey, Boy!"

Leonard looked at his father and then back at Lenny. "I have to go, Lenny," he said. "Pa's in a hurry. It's good to see you."

"Yeah, you too Leonard. You go ahead."

"I'll see you around, Lenny."

"O.K!"

When Leonard climbed the steps to where his father stood, Law said, "What are you wasting your time on that dumb-head for?"

"He's not a dumb-head!" Leonard retorted.

"Sure he is. He's even dumber than you."

"He's not a dumb-head. Before he got kicked by that horse he was as smart as anybody."

"Well, he's not anymore and I don't see why you waste your time talking to him. I've got more important things to do."

"He used to be my friend and I like him."

"That figures," Law growled. "Two of a kind."

The door to the Court House was propped open and one could see the day-light at the far end of the hallway where the door was also open. Naked light bulbs hanging down from the high ceiling did little to brighten the hall against the glare of the outside sunlight. Windows and doors of the various offices were open to let fresh outside air circulate through the building. This did not alleviate, to any great extent however, the odors that had permeated the walls over the years. The smell of oily sweeping compounds used on the floors to keep down dust while sweeping, the smell of tobacco, both chewing and smoking, and the foul air trapped inside during the months of closure, had all penetrated the walls to the extent they would never lose the aroma within.

They walked halfway the length of the building to where the north to south hallway crossed, before their eyes became accustomed to the darkness. Turning right, they entered the open doorway of the sheriff's office. The sheriff looked up from his desk in the rear office, then continued to write on a yellow tablet for a full minute before speaking. Rising slowly to his feet, he came out to greet them.

"Well, I see you made it, Law," he said, and nodded at Leonard.

"Where's Judge Cox," Law asked, "In his chambers here in the Court House or his law office?"

"He's over in his office," the sheriff replied. "I think I'll walk over with you. I better be in on this."

"Good," Law said. "I'd rather you was there."

The three men went back outside, into the bright, hot sunlight and crossed the street. They climbed the dark, narrow stairway up to the second floor, over the hardware store. Three other offices occupied this floor. Judge Cox's office consisted of two rooms, the outer one where clients entered, little more than a cubicle, containing a small desk with a swivel chair and two additional chairs for waiting clients. The swivel chair was occupied by an elderly, spinster type, but very efficient secretary.

"Morning, Sadie," the sheriff greeted her as they entered.

Looking at the new arrivals over the top as her spectacles, she greeted each man by his first name.

"Come on in, gentlemen," the judge called through the open door of his office. "I saw you coming across the street."

This room was somewhat larger than the other one. The two windows were wide open, allowing air to drift through the rooms from the stairway. It also provided the Judge with a certain amount of entertainment during his slack hours, with the sounds and sights of the street below and across the Square. The small oscillating fan in the corner blew hot air across the feet of the men when they sat down. Later in the day, it would not be able to dispel the heat and only serve to circulate the hot air around the room.

The Judge was a big man with a big belly that he seemed rather proud of. Red suspenders supported the wrinkled seersucker trousers. The black ribbon tie already hung loose at the open collar of his shirt. If he came out from behind the big oak desk, one could see that he already had kicked off both shoes to ease the pain of corns on the middle toe of each foot. His eyebrows were almost as bushy as the gray side-burns growing over his ears and the shaggy hair on his collar.

He didn't waste the effort to rise to his feet, but motioned them to seats around the room. Law sat on the straight back chair against the wall, to be on an equal, if not higher level with the Judge. Leonard and the sheriff sat down on the leather couch that sank almost to the floor with the weight of a man, from years of supporting clients.

They discussed the weather, crops and families for a few minutes, since they were friends and the Judge seldom had the opportunity to just sit and visit. Then the Judge got down to business.

"Well, Law, Billy here tells me you dang near killed your brother," he said. "I've got no reason to believe that ain't so."

"He had it coming," Law replied.

"Billy told me what you said. Suppose you tell me why."

To anyone else, Law very likely would have said it was none of his business, friend or no friend. But, in this case he felt he couldn't afford to rile the Judge as it might cost him a lot of money, so he related to him the reason for his action.

"You better learn to control your temper Law before it gets you in a heap of trouble," the Judge told him after he finished. "You always have been a little quick on the trigger."

"You mean to tell me you wouldn't've done likewise under the same circumstances?" Law asked.

"That's beside the point and you know it," the Judge said. "What I'd do is not relevant in this case. It's you we're discussing here. Suppose you had killed your brother! It wouldn't even be self-defense and there's nothing I could do about it. You'd be up for murder and no lawyer in the county could save you. With a little luck you might get life in Menard instead of the electric chair. How does that sound to you?"

"It would have been good riddance!" Law said, but not so force-full this time. The Judge was trying to make a point about his temper that Law knew sometimes went out of control, and he probably wanted to make his decision about punishment a little easier to swallow.

"Confound it Lawrence Reynolds, you better pay attention to what I'm saying," the Judge said.

"I am paying attention. I just won't stand for the likes of him to run over me."

"I think you mean you don't want nobody to cross you," corrected the Judge.

"Have it your way then. By the way, how is he? He must be in pretty bad shape for all the trouble he's causing."

"I understand he stayed in the hospital one night, but now he's with a friend here in town until he heals."

"I didn't know he had a friend here! Who is it?"

"That's none of your business and don't try to find out who it is or I may have to issue a restraining order against you."

"You don't need to worry. I don't even want to see him again."

"Good! Now let's get down to the penalty for this little fracas." He became a Judge now, stern and about to mete out punishment.

All the while Leonard had sat quietly. The sheriff only spoke once, when Law looked to him for some kind of support. He shrugged his shoulders and said, "Don't look at me, I only came along for the ride."

"You know, I have to do this, Law," the Judge said apologetically. "It's the law and you admitted dang near killing him, provoked or not makes no difference. Since he filed assault charges against you, I have to act on it." He stopped and considered for a moment, while the other three waited.

"I think under the circumstances, you had just cause," he continued. "I'm going to fine you fifty dollars. That's mostly for mine and Billy's time on the matter. Since you didn't spend no time in jail, I can't charge you for no meals." Law breathed a sigh of relief, for he thought it would be much more.

"And you can pay for your brother's Doctor and hospital bill," Judge Cox added.

"How much will that be?" Law asked, seeing dollars slipping through his fingers.

"I have no idea," the Judge answered, "You'll have to go find out and pay it."

Law felt deflated and tugged at his moustache, trying to figure a way around this last part. The Judge recognized the signs and said, "Do it today Law and it will be over and done with and you can forget the whole mess, but do it!"

He sputtered and fumed a few seconds more before agreeing. Finally, he reluctantly paid the fifty dollars to the Judge and even more reluctantly, searched out the Doctor and paid him.

Back at home, he continued to rant about the injustice of things until Bessie pointed out a couple of facts he would rather not admit.

"I-Gawd Lawrence, you better be glad you got off as lucky as you did," she told him.

"How in thunder do you figure I got off lucky, woman," he demanded. "Look how much it cost me!"

"It could have been a lot worse. What if you'd have killed Arthur! You would either spend the rest of your life in prison or been hung by your neck," she pointed out.

"But, I didn't kill him," Law sputtered. "He's still alive and I still had to pay his Doctor bill."

"You was lucky there too. What if you had gone up against old Judge Portridge instead of Cox! You know how that money grabbing reprobate is! He probably would take the farm and divided it amongst him and Arthur and still sent you to jail for trespassing. So just be thankful for the way it turned out."

He stormed out of the house and to the barn, grumbling, "Confounded woman, you amaze me with your logic about my money and what's good for me."

The two brothers never saw each other again. A few days later, Law heard that Arthur had recovered sufficiently enough to leave town. He went back to Missouri and so far as anyone knew stayed there until his death. Law did discover one thing that nagged at him. How did his brother know so much about him and his affairs and life here! It turned out to be a simple fact. The information came from his sister Lucille.

Lucille and Arthur had been corresponding with each other over the years, not regularly, but occasionally. She supplied him with news of the family, as a matter of course, since he often grew home sick and she felt it her duty as a Christian to keep him informed. Law of course, looked at it differently and demanded to know why she would even give him the time of day.

"I've been writing to him ever since he left home," she said, "And I'll continue to do so. After all, he is my brother the same as you are and I love him."

"But, he's no account!"

"That's what you say. I think you did wrong for what you did, I don't care what you say. He needs to keep up with his family."

And so it went. When Arthur died some years later, a friend sent Lucille a copy of the death notice from the local newspaper where he lived. Following is an almost exact copy of that obituary as it appeared in the paper:

Obituary written by a gentleman from the newspaper for the family:

On February 13, 1931 the death angel spread its wings and hovered over the bed of our friend Mr. Arthur Reynolds and took him to the sweet beyond to join those gone on before him.

James Arthur Reynolds was the son of John P. Reynolds and Frances Reynolds.

He was born near Belle Prairie, Ill. on Dec. 9, 1877 and died February 13, 1931, being 53 years, 2 months and 4 days old.

At the age of 28 he left the family circle and went to Charleston, Mo. where he married his wife who passed away June 1, 1923.

Mr. Reynolds was loved by all who knew him. He was always cheerful and tried to make life pleasant for all with whom he came in contact.

We feel sure that God did not call him unprepared. The minister called to see him and offered prayer. While he was sick he prayed a lot and talked of God's mercies. A smile came over his face and then he waved his hand goodbye and passed into a deep sleep from which he will wake no more on earth, but will wake in the presence of his creator. He bore his illness patiently, never murmuring, though he suffered intense pain.

God in His wisdom foresees all things.

It was his time to go for even the best medicinal aid and all that willing hands could do, he passed away.

His father, mother, brother, sister and wife have preceded him to the great beyond.

He leaves to mourn his departure, three brothers, Charlie, Mill Town, Lawrence and Sidney of near McCleansboro, and three sisters Lucille, Virda and Katherine, and a host of other relatives and friends.

Weep not, dear ones, his sufferings are ended and he will always rest in the paradise above. And so, let us so live that we will join him. Friends and relatives weep not, Earth's losses, Heaven's gain.

Written by his friend at the Baltimore Hotel, Poplar Bluff, Mo.

The obituary was sent to Lucille and was in her possession until her death. At that time it was passed on to Millie, who's grown up.

CHAPTER 7

As Millie and Helen grew in size and age, so did their chores and work around the farm. This is not to imply that they were over burdened, but small things were added to what they already did. Bessie always worked the garden, did the cooking, cleaning and canning and the girls learned by helping out in small ways. Besides having small chores inside the house, they also gathered eggs, fed chickens, slopped the hogs and brought in firewood. Earl Lee, still being too little to handle any major size job, simply tagged along for something to do.

Millie liked Sundays better than any other day of the week, at least, some of them! On many Sundays when most farmers were relaxing, Law and Leonard worked. They repaired and mended fences and checked over harness and equipment. This was not a day set aside to relax to any great extent.

In the late summer, the girls and Earl Lee had their own minor chores. Beating sunflowers happened to be the one they liked least of all. Sunflowers were planted each year, and cultivated and harvested like most other crops. When the flowers ripened, they were cut and piled in stacks. The young children had the task of pounding the flowers with sticks, knocking the seeds loose to fall on pieces of canvas. It was then mixed with corn and other grains, ground up into feed for chickens and other feathered fowl. No matter how much fun it was in the beginning, the girls came to despise it more than any other chore, except perhaps, pumping water for the livestock.

On the third Sunday of each month, they went to church. Following the meeting, they always had "dinner on the grounds." Everyone took food, meats, vegetables and lots of desserts. Each lady tried to out-do the other by cooking her own favorite dish, using her very own secret recipe. Each lady bragged about the others dish, whether she liked it or not, so as not to hurt anyone's feelings and also to encourage good remarks about her own dish. On these occasions Millie could eat all the sweets she wanted without being scolded and she took full advantage of the situation.

Grandpa seldom went to church, though he did visit with friends, who were also inclined as he to remain on the outside while services were going on. This small select group of men did manage to be there for dinner however.

Brother Josh Smith came over from Wayne City on these weekends to preach the sermons.

Millie always enjoyed these meetings and sat very attentive watching and listening to everything that went on. Earl Lee, on the other hand, grew restless after a few minutes.

Each family of the church had its own special pew each Sunday, meaning, when they arrived, their bench had better be vacant. The pews were not designated to any particular family, it was just where they always sat and they almost felt offended if someone else dared to sit there. After awhile, one grew so accustomed to a certain bench, they began to believe it belonged to them.

The Reynolds family always sat about halfway down on the right side. Being a small church, it had remained the same size in membership for many years and was referred to as The Church on the Hill, because it overlooked the vast valley below. The church had no belfry or bell to summon its members that it was time to come worship. They believed that God would let His flock know it was Sunday. They also believed in predestination, so did not go out into the highways and byways as some churches did, searching for lost souls. God had decreed before hand that some souls would be saved and others lost, therefore He already had those saved souls written in the Book of Life.

They would come to the church of their own accord. They were called Primitive Baptists.

The preacher was not an ordained minister, as other, larger churches boasted. He felt he was simply called by God to preach and he answered that call. He received no salary! Members handed him, on the sly, a fifty cent piece or a quarter and sometimes a dollar bill when they could afford it, since there was no offering taken up. The building and grounds were kept spic and span by members whenever they had time. Any major repairs, such as painting or roof repair were taken care of on special "work days." Even the two privies, one for women and one for men, situated well away from the church, were kept in tip-top condition, with lime sprinkled around the inside to eliminate odor and flies.

When they went in, Grandma made Earl Lee scoot down the bench first, then she sat down and Millie and Helen sat on the other side of her. This seating arrangement kept Earl Lee at a safe distance from the girls to cut down on any mischief he could get into. Papa being an Elder in the church, liked to arrive a little early, to greet folks as they came in. In winter time he also helped Brother Smith get a fire going in the big heating stove. And in warm weather, he helped open the windows all around and pass out the fans that the funeral parlor in town had donated.

Usually, Brother Smith led the singing. He began with a song of his choice and thereafter, different members of the congregation called out a number in the song book. In the rare cases that he did not know the tune, the caller started singing and the others joined in. It was not their belief that music was necessary, so all singing was a cappela. When a song started, all verses were sung, regardless of the number.

An elderly woman named Cassie Taylor sat behind Earl Lee. She had a very high pitched voice that carried above all others, even though it was always off key. During the singing was the boy's most difficult time and he wondered if that high screeching as he called it, might surely burst his tender ear-drums. He scooched down in the seat to get away from it, to no avail. Then he got tickled and tried to look around past Grandma to the girls, but they knew better than even glance his way.

The tall skinny woman sitting in front of him only added to his problem of being still. Her head was almost without hair and the little she did have, being coarse and fuzzy looking, reminded him of a pig they had, with a little imagination, of course. Low on the back of her head, a big wrinkle stood out very prominently. To a young active mind, this suggested a big smile and by adding two beady little eyes above a make-believe nose, he had a grinning pig. He held up his finger and traced it through the air, not six inches from the wrinkle. Bessie quickly slapped his hand down, but not before the girls saw and understood what he meant. Of course, they too became tickled and Grandma threatened to slap them.

Earl Lee settled down for a few minutes. That is, until he saw a tiny white feather floating around the room. Sitting anxiously watching, he seemed to will it in his mind to come his way. And it did! Before it was quite within reach, he stood up and grabbed it. All eyes turned to him. Bessie boxed him up beside the head, causing him to sit back down heavily. Other children there all snickered and Brother Smith, frowning as only he could, went back to preaching.

The part that Millie liked best was the foot washing. At the end of the meeting all the adults went down to the front, men on one side and women on the other. There, they took off their shoes and stockings and the men rolled up their pants legs. Taking turns, they dipped the wash cloth in the white granite wash pan and washed each others feet. Then they dried the feet with the big terry-cloth towel. This was all done very solemnly and religiously in recognition of Jesus, who gave His disciples His charge, that if He could wash their feet, so should they wash each others. Therefore, the Primitive Baptists felt it was their duty to carry out His command to them.

The women were careful not to wear corsets with straps to hold up their stockings on these days. Millie watched carefully to learn how this was done. The women ran a hand just under the hem of the dress and hooked a thumb under the garter where it was rolled in the stocking, just above or below the knee. With one quick, deft movement the stocking fell down around the ankle. Millie was fascinated by the dexterity of these women, especially the older ones. But, she supposed one got used to doing that, with years of practice. She only hoped she would do as well when her time came. The only thing though, she wouldn't get to rehearse ahead of time because she only wore stockings during the winter and the elastic didn't stretch very much over the legs of long underwear.

After "foot washing", there was communion.

Papa always helped in this rite. There was a pitcher of grape juice (called wine) and a water glass at the front on each side of the room on a white table cloth covered table. The glasses were passed up and down the pews of worshippers. When empty, they were taken back to be re-filled at the front.

Millie liked this part too, watching each person as they turned the glass ever so slightly, so as not to put their lips on the same spot as the previous person. She always smiled at this gesture. Each one thought no one else noticed, but after the second or third person, all lips over-lapped, leaving no new spot on the glass that hadn't been touched. Sometimes, a man would casually let his thumb slide over where he would drink, which may have helped somewhat. Only the adults participated in this ritual, as children were too young to understand it's meaning.

At the end of the meeting, everyone sang a song, shook hands and hugged each other. This was a very profound and meaningful gesture, done to say good-by in case I don't see you again in this life, I'll meet you in Heaven. One never knew if they would be alive on the next meeting day.

Each autumn, the Associational Meeting of the churches took place, usually in October. All the Primitive Baptists in that district met, alternating between the churches each year, to discuss policies and get together for good preaching and fellowshipping. It turned out to be a memorable year that Law invited the Association to meet at his home for the meeting and dinner.

Millie grew very excited that so many people were coming. She heard Grandma and friends discussing the things that must be done. Grandma began planning what to cook for the dinner. but of course not much could actually be done ahead of time. However, the day before, she did bake a large cake and prepared the meat.

Grandma decided now would be a good time to dispose of the two Rhode Island Red roosters that were eating more than their worth. So she kept the chicken house door closed until she was ready. Then, going out she cornered the two beasts, one at a time. The first one, she carried outside, where she held it by the head. Giving the body two twists of the wrist, she jerked off its head with a flick of the wrist. The headless bird fell to the ground, where it twisted and flopped. Going back inside, she brought forth the other hapless bird and repeated the procedure as the remaining chickens walked around watching in wonder.

After many years of practice, she could kill, clean and quarter a chicken in a very few minutes. She had her own way of cleaning one. Perhaps it wasn't very orthodox, but it proved to be effective for her. Of course, one must know when the scalding water reached the right temperature and how to dip it in the water. If left in the hot water too long, the meat became tender and pulled off with the feathers.

When the first one stopped flopping around, Grandma took it by it's feet and dipped it in a tub of near boiling water to scald it. By scalding a rooster in this fashion, it makes plucking the feathers much easier. Tail and wing feathers being the most difficult to get off, it's best to do them first while the water is still very hot.

The tiny short pin feathers or hairs left on the body are virtually impossible to pull out with one's fingers. So, they must be singed off over an open fire. The scorched flesh cancelled out the moldy smell of hot, wet feathers and lingered in the air.

With this done, the bird was ready to be dressed and cut up for frying or left whole for roasting or baking.

Breaking the joint between the leg and foot with a snap, she cut off the foot and tossed it to the waiting dog. She broke back the legs from the body and using a sharp knife, cut down to the hip joint between the thigh and body. With the hip joint exposed, she broke and cut through the flesh, severing the leg and thigh from the body. She repeated this process on the other side. Flipping the body over on its back, she pointed her knife to the top front of the breast. Pushing the knife in, she cut downward through the breast bone and cut the pulley bones loose.

Separating the breast, she was careful not to cut too deep for fear of going into the gall which was still inside. If this was punctured, it could give the meat a bitter taste. The liver, heart and gizzard are the only parts of the entrails that one kept. Law often kidded her by saying the only part of the chicken she didn't keep was the squawk.

The only difference in cleaning a chicken for baking is that it's left whole and the entrails removed differently.

About twenty new converts from all the churches were baptized that day, making it a very special day. This ordinance took place in Johnson's pond, just down the road from the Blairsville store, since it had good, clean water, whereas most ponds muddied up at the slightest disturbance. Each preacher immersed his own members.

Millie watched, enthralled as they waded out from the bank of the pond, holding on tightly to the deacons hand who led them out into the water and to their pastor. He stood, almost waist deep, waiting patiently until the deacon handed over the next convert to him. The ones to be baptized seemed happy with the new experience, yet a little hesitant about being dunked under water. Many of them were still considered to be children, but were much older than Millie and Helen. The men were more anxious to get it over with, while the women had a tendency to hold back, though they emerged just as happy. In some churches of different denominations, the baptized person came up shouting and waving their arms in glory. But, these saved souls were entered into the Book of Life quietly, knowing they had been the Chosen people and one day would be with God.

Millie looked forward to the day when she too could be baptized, but Grandma said she was too young to know what it was all about and God would let her know when the time came. She didn't relish the idea of being dunked all the way under water however, since she always held a fear of water because of her friend Pip drowning in it. But Jesus would protect her and she knew Brother Smith wouldn't let her go.

After this, everyone went to the Reynolds farm. It turned out to be a larger gathering than usual. Automobiles of all kinds lined up along the road and into the yard, even a couple that Millie had never seen before. Mostly, they were Model-T Fords, with a couple of Dodge touring cars and one or two Chevrolets, with one thing in common, all were black. Of course, some local families came in buggies and wagons. It was a joyous day, with many children of all ages who scarcely knew each other, but they soon became friends. It was a joyous day to for the adults who met only once a year. The long table was made of boards mounted on saw horses and covered with white table-clothes. It stretched across the yard under the maple trees, and was loaded with enough food to entice anyone to be friendly.

Everything went along fine for awhile. Then Millie saw Grandpa come out of the pantry with a jar of blackberry juice. This instantly caught her attention and she watched him as she played. He also carried some water glasses that he handed to Brother Smith and the other preachers. Grandpa poured some of the liquid into their glasses. Paying close attention, Millie guessed that this was really the good blackberry juice and not the other. Knowing her Grandfather as she did, she also surmised that this was merely to get the preachers to taste the real juice to throw them off guard. Then the other would be brought out, surprising them. They'd never know the difference!

Presently, he went back into the house pantry, to return only seconds later, carrying a half gallon fruit jar.

During blackberry season, when Grandma had time, she liked to pick lots of extra berries. She canned some whole for cobblers and made jelly and jam and then put up many jars of plain juice. All the family enjoyed a glass of cold blackberry juice during the winter! Besides drinking, it was also used to make additional jelly when needed. Everything was canned and put up in glass jars of various sizes; pints, quarts and half gallons and stored along with other fruits and vegetables on shelves in the pantry.

Grandpa had learned long ago that occasionally a jar would go bad if the lid didn't fit tightly and the contents spoiled. But, with blackberry juice, it fermented and turned sour so that the children were not permitted to drink it. To Grandpa, however it turned into wine, which made it an intoxicating beverage. Millie had witnessed him sneaking into the pantry on the pretext of searching for something on more than one occasion. As always, she pretended not to notice him, as he picked up a jar of juice. By pulling on the ear of the rubber ring that fitted around the mouth of the jar under the lid to seal it, he broke the seal and this allowed a minimum amount of air in. Tiny bubbles pushed their way out around the lid. He then pushed the jar back behind the other jars to hide his handiwork. When Grandma noticed it later, it had fermented. Before she could destroy the contents, Grandpa said he'd take care of it. It was a long time, after too many jars had gone bad before she became suspicious of what was happening. Only Millie knew for sure and would never tell anyone.

Now, Grandpa was about to serve this fermented juice to the unsuspecting preaching Association. Millie decided it would be interesting to see how it turned out.

Not one of the preachers would knowingly allow a drop of alcoholic beverage to pass his lips. But, no one could find anything scriptural against a glass of good, plain old blackberry juice. Now, that was a different matter altogether! Grandpa received many complimentary comments as time went by. Millie observed that all of Grandpa's drinking friends were either preachers or deacons in their church. Younger men and older boys were pitching horseshoes or playing baseball. Children played various types of games or wandered about in the field or in the woods. A few of the young men and women paired up in couples and strolled down the road or walked back to the Big Ditch where they sat on the bank, tossing stones into the nearly dried up stream below.

Brother Barnhart, the preacher from over around Mt.Carmel, drained his glass and held it out for a re-fill. "That's mighty fine blackberry juice, Brother Reynolds," he said, smacking his lips. "Just a little bit tart perhaps but mighty tasty. Just the way I like it".

No one seemed to be aware of the fact that they were now drinking very potent wine. It affected each man a little bit differently. Most became jovial and friendly towards one another, praising the Lord for all His blessings and for their own earthly brothers and sisters. There was much laughter and good-hearted joshing. Not one turned down an offer for a re-f ill. One man found a quiet spot in the shade and fell asleep.

Zeke Bledsoe from down below Harrisburg insulted his wife, not intentionally, of course, but in such a way that it got him in trouble. For some unknown reason, he began to criticize the way his wife cooked. Now, any man alive knows he should never, ever speak negatively before others about his wife's cooking.

That's one positive way of getting in the dog-house and staying there for some time to come. She did have the good sense though to keep quiet about it. She merely glared at him for a long time, surprised and wondering what had come over him. Then she found a spot off to herself, where she sat and sulked for the rest of the day, deciding how to get even once they were alone.

Not realizing the men were drinking wine, most felt happy and carefree, thankful that the meeting this year turned out to be such a great success.

Admittedly, it was a very good assembly. Even most of the wives agreed on that. Nearly all the husbands were happy and showed signs of affection towards them, even to the point of being foolish at times, but who were they to complain! The preachers themselves never guessed that they were on the verge of being intoxicated and for the moment, didn't care.

After all the others had gone, three families remained behind to help with cleaning up. The Quigleys and Kincaids were members of the Church on the Hill, but Law's brother Sidney never went to church anyplace. Law invited him and his wife Lottie by his own choice to attend the meeting and dinner so they stayed also. The men folks sat around, talking and laughing about different things that happened during the day. Sidney especially enjoyed the part about getting the preachers drunk, as he looked on it as a sneaky thing to do and deserving some sort of recognition.

Eventually, the men felt relaxed enough to fall asleep.

As the women carried the left over food and dirty dishes in and cleaned up, they discussed the preceding afternoon. Actually, it turned into a hen party rather than discussion as they went back and forth from yard to kitchen. Being the first real opportunity to be together where they could talk and visit, they took advantage of it. Most of the good ladies who had come and gone were included in the gossip fest. No one was completely immune from their scrutiny.

"I'll bet that Zeke Bledsoe got what for by now," Bessie said. "I-Gawd, I don't know what ever got into that man, insulting his poor wife that way!"

"Tsk, tsk, it's a pity, that's what it is, but I'll wager she can hold her own with him," said Kate, setting a load of dishes on the table. "She looked like she could bite nails. I'm sure she'll tell him how the cow ate the cabbage."

"It seemed to me that all them preachers acted mighty strange. If I didn't know better, I'd almost say they was drunk. Or at least a little tipsy," Lottie said. "And I'm one who knows the signs."

The ladies finished cleaning and sat around the kitchen table with a cup of stale, strong coffee or a glass of weak tea or warm lemonade and got down to their discussion in earnest.

Eadie Izack was the first to come under fire.

"Did you notice Eadie Izack?" Kate asked. "She must have put on twenty pounds since last year."

"Yes, it hard not to notice," Vesta Kincaid agreed. "That dress was the same one she wore last year, don't you know. Without that tight corset, she never would've got into it."

"I'll bet her husband had a time lacing her into it."

They all laughed at the thought!

"They say that somebody has come out with a new type of corset. I think they call it a girdle. It don't have to be laced up. It just stretches out over the body parts and fits like a corset. The only thing is though, with a shape like mine, I'd never get it stretched over all the parts."

"I never wear a corset, myself."

"You don't have to Vesta. With a shape like yours, you don't need to. I don't see how you stay so thin."

"Well, I can tell you in a nut shell. Have a baby every year and work from sunup to way past sundown every day."

"Yes, I know just what you mean. I have my share of both, too," Lottie agreed.

"Well, I ain't saying too much about weight," Bessie laughed, patting her stomach. "I think I musta' put on a couple pounds myself. I-

Gawd, for the life of me, I don't see how though, with all the work around here."

"I think that young Molly Crouch is in the family way," Vesta said.

"That young girl, why she ain't even married yet. Besides, she's too young," Bessie exclaimed.

"I don't know her, but I do know for a fact a girl don't have to be married to have a baby," Lottie said thinking of her own Gertie. "And I'll wager she ain't too young."

The other ladies agreed wholeheartedly. "You know what they say, young girls are like new potatoes, if they're big enough, they're old enough."

Of course, this drew a laugh!

"Well, I ain't too surprised, by the way that girl prances around. That little poke bonnet hat she wears and all that powder and rouge."

"Yes and looking sideways at the boys, giving them the come on. She's just asking for it, if you ask me."

"If I was her mother, I'd give her a good spanking. That's just what she needs and she ain't too big for it neither."

"I wouldn't be a bit surprised if it wasn't that Redman boy, by the way he's always strutting his stuff, trying to show off! He needs a good hickory taken to him too. His pa oughta' whip him 'til the cows come home. That'll take him down a notch or two."

"Then there's that other boy. You know, the one that's always bragging and showing off! It could've been him. He'll never amount to a hill of beans, for all the schooling his folks are giving him."

"He's just got enough education to show his ignorance, don't you know!"

"Too much education just ain't good for a body. You can only learn so much and all the rest, goes in one ear and out the other."

"I think he'd be better off to learn a little bit about farming, since that's all he'll ever do. His pa needs some lessons there too, from what I hear."

"Oh, he's learning all about farming in school. He studied all about cows and talked his pa into buying all then high bred cows. He then told his pa to buy a expensive high bred bull to go along with them and they'd breed and have the finest herd of cows in the whole state. Well, he bought this big expensive bull and kept it in a separate pasture. He figured he'd turn it in with the cows when they got ready for him. Well, a scrawny bull of one of his neighbors would get out and service all

212

them fine cows, one at a time before they knew anything about it, don't you know!"

"I- Gawd, I seen it happen many a time, cows choose a skinny old rogue over a fancy bull."

"You're right there, Bessie. Cows ain't no different from dogs when they come in heat. Along comes a mangy cur dog and wham, you got yourself a litter of mongrel puppies."

"I agree! They ain't waiting for no fancy pedigree."

They paused for only seconds before continuing.

"Did you hear how Harla's man broke his arm?"

There had only been conflicting rumors so, no one seemed to be sure.

"You know how he's always experimenting with something or trying to invent something! It's mostly some silly thing or other to keep out of work. That lazy cuss always did say he could fly if he had some wings. He went out and laid under a tree for two days after putting a dead cat out in the field. He killed a great big buzzard that landed to get the cat. So, he cut off its wings and had Harla tie them to his back. Then he climbed up on the barn and was going to fly away. Of course, she believed he could do it. She said, "fly low honey so the kids can see." He stood on the edge flapping his wings a few times to make sure they stayed on and worked right. The whole family stood in the yard watching their pa fly off. He flapped real hard and jumped off. He fell straight down. The only reason he didn't break his fool neck was because he jumped off the low side of the barn and landed on the pile of manure and hay where he cleans out the cow stalls and throws it out the window."

The ladies all laughed uproariously!

"Did you hear about Elphege and Ernest Pierce going to Mt. Hebron awhile back?" Kate asked.

The others answered that they hadn't but were ready to listen.

"Well, Ernest had to go there for some kind of business, and it took longer than expected," Kate said. "They decided to go eat in one of them fancy restaurants, Kerleys, I think it was. Elphege ordered a hamburger and a bottle of Cleo Cola. Ernest decided to have a plate lunch for a quarter, but then asked for a bottle of Cleo Cola along with it, making the price of the meal come to forty cents. He didn't know that coffee or ice-tea went with the meal, but soda was extra. It liked to've killed poor Elphege. She ain't got over it yet. She'll likely grieve over that forty cents for the rest of her life."

"If she'd knowed they would be so long, she should've packed a couple sandwiches like the rest of us do".

They talked on for quite some time, enjoying every episode of the conversation, at the expense of friends and neighbors, of course. When the men woke from their naps and got ready to leave, there was almost a feeling of melancholy among them.

"This little visit has done me a world of good, don't you know," Vesta said wistfully.

"Me too," Lottie added. "I don't know when I laughed so much."

"Maybe we should get together now and then and just sit and talk and visit. I guess you might call it gossip," Kate offered. "I think it might do us all a lot of good."

They agreed it was a good idea and they surely would do that, but they never seemed to find the time. Millie, Helen and Earl Lee called to Bessie that they were going to walk part way home with the Kincaid children.

"While you're down that way, take the basket and gather your Pa's eggs at the other place," Bessie told them. "And go ahead and lock the chickens up for the night. And don't dally along the way too much. And get on back here and do your chores. Don't forget to slop the pigs either. There's plenty left over garbage here from the dinner."

Passing Cox's Woods in a group, there was no thought of what might be lurking in its depths, so they went all the way to the Kincaid's house. But, on the return journey, with the sun sinking low in the west, the trees cast long shadows across the road. With trees on each side of the road, darkness fell quicker here than farther down.

Whippoorwills began their night calls, indicating that twilight was not far off. A hoot owl sounded off and received its answer from another owl in the woods across the field. For some reason, the hoot of an owl is enough to cause alarm in small children, especially when close at hand.

"It's just an ol' hoot owl," Earl Lee said, glancing at the girls and then looking at the woods.

"I think I heard something else," Millie said, "and it wasn't no owl."

"There's nothing to be afraid of," Helen scoffed. "That's just your imagination."

Just then, a loud crackling sound, like a stick being broken startled them. In the quiet of the day and in their young minds, the sound was magnified many times over. Looking at each other fearfully, they began to run. In his fright, Earl Lee had no trouble keeping up with the girls. Out of breath, they stopped running only after reaching the "other" house and then walked slowly out to the chicken house where the chickens had already gone to roost.

"What do you think it was?" the boy asked. "Cox's Army?"

"I don't know, but I thought I saw something moving around in the woods," Helen replied.

"Maybe it was that big wampus cat," Millie speculated. Earl Lee's eyes were wide as he considered this possibility. "I'll bet that's what it was all right," he said. "That ol' wampus cat could take on all of Cox's Army."

"Maybe it wasn't either one of them," Millie suggested.

"What do you mean?" Helen asked. "It had to be one or the other, because I just know that wasn't any ordinary sound I heard."

" What about the Bottoms Tramper!" Millie breathed, hardly able to voice the name. "It could have been him."

They all shuddered. That was even worse than the other suggestions, because they had actually seen the Tramper up close and knew him to be real. In their minds and dreams he had gained several inches in stature and became the most formidable creature alive since the actual encounter. And that big, red dog had become mean and ferocious, three times its original size. Yes, that's undoubtedly what they heard. No one else would dare go into that woods so close to dark.

"Yeah, I'll bet that's what we heard," Earl Lee said, trembling. "That ol' Bottoms Tramper could wipe out the whole Cox's Army all by hisself. And that big, mean dog of his could whip the wampus cat while he's doing it. I wish I had stayed at home and not come along."

"Well, you did come along, Er-ly so you have to stay with us now."

They each had worked out in their own imagination what might be lurking in the darkness of the woods, perhaps even watching them at this very minute, trying to decide whether to come after them or not. Earl Lee considered going on home without waiting for the girls to gather the eggs and lock up. But, that meant he would be all alone on that open stretch of the road. He doubted if he could out- run whatever decided to chase him. The best thing to do was stay with the girls. At least he'd have company and there always seemed to be comfort in company.

They scurried about, gathering up eggs, putting out feed and locking the chicken house door, so as to get home as quickly as possible. One thing they agreed on, not to mention this experience around Grandma. If she thought there was any danger in Cox's Woods, she wouldn't let them go to Kincaid's to play. So, the incident ended there, but remained in three active minds for a long time!

Autumn came early that year, as the old-timers had predicted. Caterpillars were very prolific during the summer months and their body hair grew long and black, indicating a cold winter. Adding fuel to this theory, the husks of the hickory nuts were much thicker than normal. Horses hair grew long and shaggy, making it difficult to curry and comb, if one was so inclined.

Ducks and geese came down weeks early from Canada on their way south. They could be heard almost every night, flying low in the darkness to keep their bearings. Even in the day-light hours, one could spot large flocks high in the sky, beyond the range of hunters guns, on the way to Horse Shoe Lake, down near Cairo or to Reelfoot Lake in Tennessee. There, they would rest and feed for a few days prior to joining other flocks on the long journey south to Texas, Louisiana and Mexico.

Late apples and peaches had been put up in glass fruit jars and stored along with the earlier canning and the pantry was full. Apple butter had been made in the big black kettle, over an open fire in the back yard.

The pigs were no longer pigs, having reached the status of hogs, weighing nearly three hundred pounds. A couple of them would be butchered for meat a little later on, and the choice ones saved for breeding purposes in the spring. The rest would be sold for cash money.

The children gathered walnuts from the trees along the fence row after school. Several hours were spent removing the oily, outer husks from the nuts. The yellowish brown stain would remain on their hands for days; even coal oil had little effect on its removal. Then, more time would be spent cracking the nuts on the anvil with a hammer and picking out the meat. All this was worthwhile when they considered the prospects of Grandma putting some in a cake or candy. Nothing else could possibly add a more distinct flavor.

The leaves had changed their color, displaying all the bright hues of autumn. Up close, the colors were gorgeous, but on the higher ground looking out across the valley, the view was spectacular. The brilliant red of the maple, gold and brown of the oak and hickory and the bright yellow of the ash, offered an unforgettable array of splendor.

Many farmers in the Bottoms had meager crop yields that year, due to the spring flooding and late planting. Much of it could be blamed on their own eagerness to get the seed in the ground without first preparing the soil properly. The Reynolds had hurried but, not to the extent of jeopardizing the results of their labors. Besides plowing deep into the soil and disking it into tiny particles, there was another very important factor. Law kept back the best corn, oats, wheat, etc. for seed, to be planted the following spring, thereby helping to ensure a good crop. During the spring flood, he safeguarded his precious seed by taking some with him and storing some in barrels in the barn loft.

Lawrence sat astride the big, white horse Prince, riding out to survey his land and his crops. The jacket was pulled tight around his upper body to ward off the chill air. But, the brisk wind caused the animal to step a little more lively, putting vigor in its body. The hair had already grown long for the winter months ahead. Walking down a long lane between two fields, Law gently pulled back the reins and when the horse stopped, he dismounted. Prince stood hip-shod, waiting for his master to resume their inspection.

Looking out across the big field of green wheat, Law absent-mindedly pulled the tobacco plug from his pocket and cut off a corner. Poking it in his mouth, he rolled it around with his tongue until it was settled properly between jaw and teeth. Then, spitting out a stream of the dark juice, he wiped his moustache with the back of his hand.

Bending down, he felt the long blades of a plant with his fingers. They were soft and pliable, yet firm to the touch. He went out into the field, inspecting other plants. Since they had been planted at the right time, they had stooled out nicely and many shoots emerged from each plant and the deep green color was good. This all indicated that the plants should fair well during the cold months ahead, lying dormant and be ready for good fast growth in the early spring.

Satisfied with his observations here, he mounted Prince again and rode on down to the first field of corn. Tops of many stalks were broken over and the leaves brown, but still pliable. Riding out into the field, he stopped and from the saddle, leaned over and pulled back the husks from a large ear. The heavy silks were brown and dry. The golden kernels, hard solid, ready to shuck. Checking other ears in different sections of the field, he determined it to be time to pick.

Back at the house Law told Leonard to saddle up and ride out to Sam Hathorn's place across the Bottoms.

Leonard hadn't seen Sam in a couple of months and was surprised at the improvements done on his place. Although Sam and his boys planted a few acres of corn and did some work for Law, they still had time to make repairs on the small house and out-buildings and fences. Leonard reluctantly, privately praised his father's good judgment in the man. It was a wise decision on his part! But, of course, Lawrence Reynolds was noted for his understanding of men!

As Leonard rode into the yard, both Sam and his wife stopped their chores and came to greet him. Being so far off the beaten path, they were always happy to have company and enjoyed any news that he might have. Just having someone different to talk to for a change was a treat, but Leonard proved a poor substitute for a news bearer or a conversationalist. He felt ill at ease around folks he barely knew and therefore anxious to take his leave.

After delivering the message sent by his father, he rode off, after only a brief visit. Sam promised to be in the field with his son and wagon the following morning.

Arriving back home, Law yelled at him from the machine shed, "Go on down and tell Sid," he called.

Without dismounting, Leonard turned his horse and rode on. Passing his own place and then the Kincaid's, he stopped at the Big Ditch. There, he tied the reins to a sapling and went down the steep embankment. Very little water remained in the stream, but it was enough to wet one foot when he failed to jump all the way across.

By now it was late in the day and most of Sidney's family was scattered about doing various chores. Asking one of the small boys the whereabouts of his grandpa, he was told, "In the house."

Unlike Sam Hathorn's house that had undergone some improvements, Leonard's uncle's house had fallen into even further decline. The two-story structure still needed a coat of paint, another window had been broken and covered over with corrugated tin, and the back porch had another board missing. Two small children in the yard, he didn't recognize at all, and wondered if they belonged here or were neighbors. But they were a happy lot and looked healthy.

Going up on the porch, he looked in the open doorway, holding his cap in his hands. Aunt Lottie stood at the stove, stirring something in a big iron pot. Lorna, setting plates on the table, saw him first and called out his name, as she went towards him. Uncle Sidney came in from another room, stretching a strap of his overalls over one shoulder.

Leonard had almost forgotten how much he liked this family. Even with their apparent lack of ambition and the other faults they might have, they were a loving, carefree and happy clan. He always felt comfortable and at ease with them. It was one place he never hurried to leave. When Reuben came in, much talking, laughing and kidding went on among them. Leonard hadn't been here since back before the time Mabel left, though it was only a half mile from home. Work all summer had kept him too busy for even minor social contact with anyone. He enjoyed this little visit tremendously, in fact, so much that he forgot his real purpose for coming, until it was time to leave.

"Oh, I almost forgot, Uncle Sidney, Pa wants to know if you can come help pick corn tomorrow," he said.

"I reckon so," the older man replied.

"What about me?" Reuben wanted to know. "Can he use me too?"

"I don't know, Reuben, he just said tell Uncle Sidney."

"I could sure use the money," Reuben said.

"Who all has he got?" Sid asked.

"Besides me and you and him, he's got Sam Hathorn and his boy," Leonard said. "And I guess Clint Wheeler and Bert Schultz."

That makes six wagons, Sidney figured. "That's probably all he needs. You and the boys stay here and start getting in our own corn, Reuben. We ain't got as much as he does, but we have to pick it anyways before the weather turns bad. Likely I'll only be helping out down there two, three days and then I'll be back to help finish up here."

"Well, I better be getting back," Leonard said. "I sure did enjoy being here for a spell."

"You know you're always welcome here, Leonard. Why don't you just sit and eat with us," Aunt Lottie offered. "It'll be ready in a few minutes and they's plenty of it."

"I sure would like to Aunt Lottie, but I better get on home. I have to help get the wagons ready for tomorrow," Leonard replied.

Reuben walked with his cousin out to the Ditch where he'd left his horse.

"How's everything going with you, Leonard? I ain't seen you around in a long time," Reuben asked.

"I've been pretty busy, this summer. You know how it is with all the work," answered Leonard.

"Yeah, I know, but you don't even go to the store to loaf with the boys, no more."

"Like I said, I've been busy and I just haven't felt like being around anybody much."

"You really miss Mabel, don't you?"

"Yeah!"

"She was a great girl. You shoulda' taken the bull by the horns and moved out. You had a good little wife and family and you shoulda' gone some place else and started over. She woulda' still been with you, if you had done that."

"I know! She begged me to do just that. I considered doing it many times Reuben."

"Well, why in God's name didn't you do it then?" Reuben demanded.

"I honestly don't know. Scared, I guess! I've always been afraid of leaving home. I don't think I could make it on my own. Pa's always planned everything and told me what to do and how to do it and I depend on him. It would be hard to try it alone."

"I don't see why," Reuben exclaimed. "You ain't stupid. I think you're smarter than he is in lots of ways. You could do real good if you'd get away from him."

"I can't ever do that. Sometimes I think he don't really like me much at all, but he is my Pa and we do work well together."

It was the first time Leonard had talked to anyone about Mabel or his father.

"I sure don't understand it. If you're going to stay around, why don't you get another wife?"

Leonard was surprised at the mere thought of such a thing.

"Why would I want another wife?"

"Well, for one thing, you need a woman and them girls of yours need a mother. There's lots of good women out there who would jump at the chance to become Mrs. Leonard Reynolds, whether you believe it or not."

Leonard considered this a moment, aghast!

"In fact, I know two or three myself," Reuben said. "I tell you cousin, it's something to think about. You've got that good house and farm over there, just waiting for the good loving care of some warm, caring family. It ain't natural for a man to go through life without a woman."

"For gosh sakes Reuben, she's only been gone a few months," Leonard exclaimed. "You make it sound like years, and I'll never marry again."

"With you, it might as well be years. I doubt if you'll ever get over her."

"So do I, Reuben. I don't think I'll ever want to marry anybody else. Sometimes, I really miss her a lot," Leonard said pensively.

"Lorna misses her, too. They didn't have a chance to get together very often, but it was something for her to look forward to and remember afterwards. She always seemed happiest after a visit with Mabel. She was Lorna's best friend. Actually, she was the only real friend she's had since we got married."

They stood silently for a few minutes, each man immersed in his own thoughts. Then, Leonard said, "I have to get home, Reuben. I've got work to do."

"So long Cousin. Take care of yourself and remember what I said about another girl. You deserve a good one."

The sky broke red in the east and the day dawned clear and the air was still and crisp. Frost had come early this year! The six wagons were already in the field, facing the sun when it arose above the horizon. They lined up at one end of the first field as they arrived and picked their way down the long rows of corn. Sam Hathorn and his boy Jesse with their wagon; Sidney, Law and Leonard each with a wagon and Clint Wheeler and Bert Schultz with their own. It was a formidable force of men, teams and wagons that extended out across the cornfield.

The teams moved along slowly, so that the walking men could keep up. From years of experience each man used his shucking-peg deftly, to peel back the thick husks on the corn and snap the ears off at the base and toss them at his moving wagon. The wagons filled up slowly as the ears thudded against the higher side boards on the far opposite sides. It was no contest and each man worked at his own pace, letting his team determine how fast he moved, for they too were experienced in this endeavor. Because the ground was dry and hard, the were able to work a little more steadily, not being hampered by mud and water that sometimes stood in the fields.

By mid-morning the first two of the six wagons were loaded to the top and they went back to the grain shed to unload. Entering the long structure two at a time, Sidney drove the lead wagon the length of the enclosure, while Sam came in behind him and stopped. One shoveled off to the left, into the latticed bin, the other to the right.

The other men came in one or two at a time and went to the well for a drink of water and rest while awaiting their turns to unload. After Sam had finished unloading, he followed Sidney out to the well at the back of the barn lot for a brief rest and smoke before returning to the field. The bucket had already been filled by the others, and they took turns drinking from the communal dipper. Each man drank long and deep of the cool, sweet water. Many wells went dry during the hot summer months, but not this one. It was dug deep and spring fed in the bottom and never fell below a certain level on the sandstone lined walls. The water was considered to be "hard water," not good for doing laundry, because of the minerals that interfere with the action of soap. But, it was sweet and pleasant to the taste. Law boasted that this well was worth a fortune to him and no one disputed his claim. Sitting on the end of the wagon, Sidney pulled the "makings" from his overalls watch pocket and rolled a smoke. It was almost a thing of art, the way he rolled the tobacco into the tiny piece of thin paper. Jesse watched him admiringly. It was customary to pass the sack around and Sidney certainly wasn't a man to break a custom. He handed the sack and papers to Sam. Jesse's eyes never left the older man as Sidney made the cigarette by holding the makings between thumb and forefinger and rolling it over and together, with a tiny edge of paper sticking up. Wetting this edge with his tongue, he creased it together and had a well packed smoke. Sidney raked a match along his overalls leg producing a brilliant flame that he touched to the end. Blowing a large ring of smoke skyward, he seemed contented.

Sam handed the sack back to him and proceeded to make his own smoke. Sidney held it out to Jesse. The boy looked at it longingly, aware that his father was glaring sternly at him. He turned his head away and looked out across the field. Sidney grinned and stuck it back into his pocket, letting the tag dangle loosely.

"Well, Sam, do you have a crop of corn this year?" Sidney asked.

"I reckon so! Fair to middling."

"Lots of farmers in the bottoms don't have much, considering the flood and late planting."

"Some of it is their own fault."

"Yeah, I reckon so!"

"They're not bona-fide farmers, not in the true sense of the word. They're mostly a class of misplaced men out of their element, trying to eke out a living with little effort and failing," Sam said, taking a deep drag on his cigarette. "Most of them use what ever seed is available and it just won't produce a good crop. I've been trying to pattern my work after Mr. Lawrence. He's showed me how to plan ahead and save the best grain for seed, keep enough for my live stock and sell the rest for profit. Course I won't have much to sell for a couple years, but I know how to do it."

"You could do worse than follow his example," Sidney agreed, perhaps wishing he had done so all these years. He never had any bumper crops of his own.

"So many men won't take the time to figure and plan things ahead and just end up working their tails off and never make a success of farming. They just seem to work their whole lives without ever getting ahead," Sam expounded. By nature he was a quiet man, not given to much in the way of conversation, especially to someone he knew only slightly and seldom had a chance to talk to. Maybe he spoke freely because he felt grateful to Lawrence, his benefactor! Without Lawrence Reynolds, Sam Hathorn would not have his farm and very likely be working for someone else and never have anything of his own. "I've stopped doing that. I plan ahead like Mr. Reynolds does and it pays off. Course I've still got a long ways to go yet, but I can already see a little difference in my crop. He says, even on my little piece of ground, if I plant right and do some outside work for him, I can make a pretty good living."

He talked on for awhile, proudly telling Sidney of his plans about his place and Sidney listened, interrupting now and then to clear up a point in his own mind. He figured maybe he needed to make some changes in his own life style, but he was not ambitious enough to carry out any long range plans. Having said what he had to say, Sam slid off the back of the wagon and replaced the tailgate.

"Reckon we better be getting back in the field," he said. "Climb on Jesse."

The boy took the tail gate back out and pushed it into the wagon and then he sat on the back, with his feet dangling.

On the first round, halfway across the field, Sam noticed the hub nut on a front wheel had worked loose. Stopping the team, he examined the wheel and determined that all it needed was to be tightened. He stepped between the wheels to retrieve a wrench from the toolbox on the side of the wagon. Jesse, who was a couple steps ahead of his father and obviously engrossed in his own thoughts, didn't realize the wagon had stopped. He continued picking corn and tossing the ears to his left, without looking, as he had been all morning. The ears should have landed in the wagon had it been moving. Instead, they hit the near horse in the flank, causing it to jump forward.

The sudden movement of the wagon caught Sam by surprise, knocking him to the ground. By falling forward, he was clear of the wagon, except for his right leg. As the vehicle jerked forward, the rear wheel rolled over the outstretched leg, just above the ankle. Sam cried out in pain as he felt the bone snap under the weight of the narrow, iron rimmed wheel.

The horses moved only a few feet and stopped, but the damage was done. Jesse heard his father cry out and immediately ran over to him.

"What happened Pa," he wanted to know.

"You spooked the horses and they run over my leg," Sam told him, grimacing in shock. The real pain hadn't set in yet, but it would only be a matter of a few minutes, then he would be hard to hold. "You better go get Sid over here to help, cause my leg is broke."

"How'd it happen, Pa? What made the horses get scared? How'd you get run over anyways?" the boy wanted to know. Then looking down at his father's leg, he exclaimed, "My God, Pa look at your leg, I can see the bone sticking out of it." He stared at the leg for several seconds in an effort to comprehend. Finally, gathering his wits about him, he ran towards the other wagon in the field, yelling, "Mr. Sidney, Mr. Sidney!"

Sidney stopped and watched the boy running and waving his arms wildly, as he jumped over the corn rows. He was nearly out of breath by the time he reached the big man.

"Whoa there now boy, slow down and tell me what happened," Sidney said, looking across the field to the other wagon. He couldn't see Sam lying on the ground, since he happened to be on the opposite side of the wagon. "It must be something serious, to cause you to move that fast. Why I ain't seen anybody run like that since that old sow got after Reuben when he was a boy."

"It's Pa, Mr. Sidney. You better come quick, cause he's hurt," Jesse blurted out.

"Calm down now, boy," Sidney encouraged. "It can't be that bad, they ain't nothing out here for a man to hurt hisself on. Stand still a minute and tell me what happened."

"I can't stand still," the boy answered, jumping up and down. "You best come quick. Pa's hurt awful bad."

Realizing he wouldn't get much more out of the boy and that it probably really was serious, Sidney left his team and wagon standing where they were and followed Jesse, who kept running ahead and then having to wait for the other to catch up. Stepping over the corn rows made it difficult to walk fast, and he wasn't as light afoot as the boy.

"What happened to your pa anyway?" Sidney asked.

"The wagon ran over his leg," Jesse answered, while waiting for the other to catch up. "Wait'l you see his leg. It's all broke and the bone's sticking out of it."

This bit of information enabled the big man to hurry a little faster.

By the time the two reached Sam, the real pain was beginning to set in and he was thrashing about on the ground, talking incoherently. However, many of the words were recognizable as the choicest expletives which were normally used in dealing with cantankerous farm animals and words that Sam never used under any other circumstances.

Sidney bent and pulled up the overall leg to get a better view of the wound.

Whistling through his teeth, he muttered, "good gawd almighty, Sam, what happened?"

"The dang wagon wheel ran over me," Sam answered, through clinched teeth.

"Does it hurt much, Pa?" Jesse asked.

"Hell yes, it hurts," came the reply. "But don't you worry now Boy, it wasn't your fault."

"What are we going to do Mr. Sidney," Jesse wanted to know. "We have to do something for him."

"I reckon we better try to get him home," Sidney replied, staring down at the crooked, distorted leg.

At the sound of wagons, they turned their attention to Law and Leonard coming across the field.

After the two newcomers had been apprised of the situation, Law squatted down beside the stricken man to examine the wound.

"That was a mighty careless thing you done Sam, letting yourself get caught 'tween the wagon wheels that way," he observed.

Sam could only stare at the face above him, without answering.

Law touched the foot and wiggled it back and forth. The pain brought a scream from Sam.

"Let's get him up in his wagon and take him home," Law decided, straightening up. He stood looking down at the deformed leg a moment, then said, "No, we can't take him home like that. We have to get them bones back in place first. Sid, grab his foot and see if you can jerk it back in place."

Sidney looked at the leg and then at his older brother. Taking off his cap, he fingered the broken visor, considering the pain it would cause Sam. Being a softhearted, compassionate man, he just couldn't bring himself to do it.

"I can't do it, Law," he said, placing the cap back on his head.

"Why not?" demanded Law. "There nothing to it. Just one hard yank should put them bones back where they belong."

There was pleading in Sam's eyes, looking up at the man. "I just can't do it," Sidney answered.

"If them bones ain't snapped back in place now, he may never walk again. How about you Boy, you do it," he said turning to his own son.

"I can't do it either, Pa," Leonard told him. "My hands don't have the feel for doing it right."

They all knew that Law was right. Now was the time to set the leg if it was ever to be done. Sam had no voice in the matter. It was out of his hands. He was only the victim.

Law looked at his brother and son in contempt. "All right," he said scornfully, "I'll do it myself."

Sam's normally brown skin had turned to a pasty white under his face whiskers and large beads of sweat covered his forehead.

"You sure you know how to set a broke leg, Mr. Lawrence?" he asked.

"Course I do. I set broke bones on dogs and animals lots of times," Law answered him. "A man's leg ain't no different. Come here Sid and help turn him around a little."

Sidney grasped Sam under the arms and dragged him around so that his head was against the rear wheel of the wagon.

"All right now, Sam you just reach up there over your head and grab holt of a couple wheel spokes," Law ordered. "This might hurt a mite so you just hold on to them spokes real tight."

With the victim stretched out flat on his back, Law cut the overall leg with his pocket knife, to just above the knee and pulled the flap aside.

Blood ran down his leg from the wound made by the protruding bone. Picking up the foot, he held it in his hands as Sam grimaced in pain.

"Sid, get down here and hold him down. Sit on his chest if you have to," Law told him. "Leonard, you hold his other leg so he can't kick me."

When they were positioned in place, Law worked the foot back and forth. Sam yelled out in pain and the two men were hard put to hold him down. When Law was satisfied on how he wanted the leg to re-act, he jerked downward on the foot, and feeling the bones snap, he twisted slightly and forced the foot upward, so the bones went back in place.

In the second that the operation took, Sam's hands tightened on the wagon wheel, his body stiffened and his back arched, raising Sidney off the ground. He screamed loud enough to be heard across the bottoms, before passing out cold.

Jesse, who had been watching the proceedings fearfully, suddenly came to life. Lunging at Law, he screamed, "You killed him, you killed my Pa."

The sudden unexpected onslaught sent Law sprawling. The boy landed on top of him, with arms flailing.

"Sid, git this crazy young-un off me," Law called out.

Sidney picked up Jesse by the seat of his pants and the nape of the neck and held on to him while he explained what happened.

"Calm down Boy, your Pa ain't dead, he just passed out is all. He'll be all right," Sidney assured him. "Law had to do what he did or your Pa's leg wouldn't never get well. It's best that he passed out, 'cause now he can't feel anything."

After the boy calmed down, Sidney turned him loose. Law was back fingering the damaged leg, feeling and pressing where necessary. Sam lay quietly, his body twitching slightly when a nerve was touched.

Satisfied that he had done all he could here, Law stood up.

"Reckon we had better get him home," he said.

"Want me to take him?" Leonard asked.

"No! Help put him on my wagon. I'll take him," Law answered. "I'll explain to his wife what happened."

Sidney removed the tailgate from the wagon and placed Sam inside.

"You come along Boy and bring your Pa's wagon," Law said, climbing up on his own. "I'll need you to help get him into the house."

It was just as well that Sam remained unconscious on the trip home. The rough ride would only have aggravated his pain as the wagon bounced over the hard, uneven ground.

The two wagons caused some commotion as they came down the lane and entered the yard. Compared to most farm yards, where litter was the norm, this one appeared to be exceptionally orderly and neat. There was the usual amount of farm tools, but they were in the barn lot or beyond. The three older boys and little girl all seemed busy with chores that had been assigned to them. While most children closer to civilization were in school, these worked at home, learning the three R's from their mother when she found the time to teach them. They stared at the approaching wagons, then one by one came forward to greet them. Sam's wife came out on the porch, wiping her hands on the soiled apron she wore, looking from one wagon to the other, knowing something was amiss. Wives and mothers have a sixth sense about such things. Strands of hair that had fallen down about her face, were pushed back by a callused hand, in order to see more clearly.

Recognizing her son and Lawrence Reynolds, she knew it had to do with her husband. By the time Law had stopped his mules, she was already on the ground, going to the rear of the wagon to look in. Seeing her husband lying there, she anxiously leaned over and grasped his hand.

Sam was regaining consciousness and groaning as he tried to move his body to a more comfortable position.

Law stood in the wagon, looking down at Sam and at his wife on the ground.

"What happened to him, Mr. Reynolds?" she asked.

"His wagon ran over him!" Law answered.

"His wagon ran over him," she repeated. "How could that happen? Is he hurt bad?"

"Reckon he will be laid up a while, ma'am," Law replied, pulling on his moustache. "It run over his leg. It's a bad break, but clean."

"I don't see how he could let a wagon run over him!"

"It was a freak accident. He was getting a wrench out of the tool box on the side of the wagon. The horses got spooked and knocked him down before he could get out of the way."

She stroked her husband's forehead tenderly and Sam smiled at her, "It'll be all right."

"Well, we better get him in the house," said Mrs. Hathorn. "Jesse, you come over here and help Mr. Reynolds with your Pa," she ordered briskly. "The rest of you get back out of the way. Go on, now scoot."

Jesse was almost a full grown man, and he and Law managed to get Sam inside the house. The house was sparsely furnished, with a few newly made pieces here and there, thanks to the devastating water a few months earlier. But, it was clean and cheerful looking. In the bedroom, Mrs. Hathorn pulled back the heavy, handmade comforter and fluffed up a pillow. They placed Sam as gently as they could on the bed.

"Will his leg be all right?" Sam's wife wanted to know.

"Yes ma'am, I reckon so," Law told her.

"Is it set yet?"

"I done the best I could with it. I think it will grow back straight if he keeps off it until it heals."

"That'll be a problem with Sam. He ain't one to set around idle. But, I'll see that he does."

"He set it good," Sam said to his wife. "I felt the bone snap when the wheel ran over it and felt it snap back in place when Mr. Lawrence pulled on it. It sure did hurt like hell, though! But, I could tell it went back right."

The woman looked at their embarrassed benefactor with grateful eyes. Law immediately began soul searching for something to say or do.

"Jessie, go out and find me three, four little pieces of wood about yea wide and so long. We got to make some splints for your Pa's leg," he said and turned to Jessie's mother. "Have you got any old rags I can use?"

"That's what I have the most of," she replied with a slight smile. "What kind of rags do you want?"

"I want something strong that I can rip apart to hold the splints in place."

After rummaging about, she handed him what appeared to be a piece of an old flannel nightgown. "Will this do?"

"It'll do fine," he replied. But after trying to rip it into pieces, he handed it back to her. "You got any scissors? Cut me some long strips. This don't tear worth a dang."

She took the piece of cloth into the other room and got a pair of scissors from the sewing basket.

Jessie came back in the house with four sticks of various sizes. Law grunted at sight of them and walked out to the shed himself. Finding suitable wood for splints, he returned to see Sam's wife tenderly washing his foot and ankle. A pile of cloth strips lay on the bed! Then she wiped his foot dry and spread salve liberally over his ankle

"We use this salve for everything from cuts to the croup to snake bites to poison ivy," she explained. "I don' think it'll hurt him none."

Law had to agree that the salve would probably keep the skin soft and pliable, even if there was no medicinal value in this particular case.

One layer of cloth was wrapped around the leg, from the ankle bone almost to the knee, to keep the splints from rubbing and chaffing the skin. With Mrs. Hathorn holding the splints in place, Law began wrapping the strips of cloth around the leg. Each time around the leg, he pulled tight to hold the splints and bone in place. Each time Sam winced, and sweat beaded on his face.

The ordeal lasted only a few minutes and Sam relaxed and closed his eyes.

"We sure do thank you Mr. Reynolds," Mrs. Hathorn said. "I don't know what we'd have done without your help. I know I couldn't have set his leg right. Do you think it'll be all right?"

"It should be, if he stays off it and gives it a chance to heal."

"You're a good man, Mr. Reynolds and a good friend too.

Law grunted and tugged at his moustache. I'll get him a crutch out here, in a day or two. He'll need it to get around. He won't need it before then. You tell him not to worry about his corn crop, I'll see it's got in."

"Oh, you don't need to do that, Mr. Reynolds, they ain't that much and the boys can do it," she exclaimed.

Being tender or soft hearted didn't happen to be one of the things he was noted for and this bothered him some.

"They'll need a man to help out. You tell him," Law said. "Well, I better be getting back."

"You want some coffee before you go?"

He hesitated before replying, "Thank you ma'am, no. I best be getting back. You tell Sam!"

The woman turned to her son, who had been watching helplessly. "You go back with Mr. Reynolds and help him out so's he won't be short handed," she ordered.

The gangling boy grinned and hurried out to his wagon, proud to be working alongside the men, with his own outfit.

Law left hurriedly after that, before he could yield to another display of benevolence! Soon as they finished his own corn, he'd send Clint and Bert over to pick Sam's. And he'd send Leonard into town for a crutch for Sam. Surely the doctor or hospital would have one to loan or sell. That would take care of his obligation to the Hathorns. If he really had any obligation to them! He'd send Leonard back with the crutch instead of coming himself. The family had already cost him enough time and money, but he figured they were worth it. He needed someone dependable to take care of things over this way, so it was all in his best interest to keep Sam healthy and his wife happy.

CHAPTER 8

Millie remembered vividly the night the men came out from town to see Grandpa. With supper being over, Grandma was in the kitchen putting things in order for breakfast the next morning. The supper dishes had already been done. This had been Helen's turn to dry as Grandma washed. The girls hated this chore as they did most chores, but there was no way out of it. It was etched in stone, so to speak. However, it could have been worse, if they also had to wash as well as dry, as some of their friends did. Grandma said they were still too young to handle the heavy pots and pans that she liked to cook with.

Helen spread the big dish towel over the work table to dry over-night and went into the dining room to join Millie at the long dining room table. The lamp cast a circle of light on the table and only diffused dimly through the gray room. Indeed, the walls seemed to suck up the light and destroy it. As usual, Earl Lee began pestering the girls to play. Trying to ignore him, they soon realized it was hopeless. Papa came in from out side and the draft from the open door caused the flame to flicker in the lamp. Casting dancing shadows on the walls, it gave the boy ideas. He immediately began making figures of his own on the wall with his hands, imploring the girls to look.

Exasperated, Helen said, "Er-ly, leave us alone. How do you expect us to learn to read or anything with you bothering us!"

"Hah, I'll bet you can't make a dog as good as this," he demonstrated with a good likeness on the wall, moving his fingers to imitate a barking dog.

"I can make a horse better than that," Millie said, as she pushed her reader aside and proceeded to prove her boast.

Helen joined in and they were soon laughing and making various shapes and forms, each trying to outdo the others.

Papa stood by the window, looking out. "There's a car coming," he muttered.

They all crowded around him at the window. Sure enough, they could see the headlights of a car that had just turned off the main road and was heading towards their house. A car coming down their road at night was an event that happened very seldom and caused some excitement and speculation as to who it could be. Why would anyone drive way out here at night?

Papa took his cap and jacket down from the nail on the back of the door. He went back outside as the car turned into the yard. The children watched through the window, excited at the prospect of visitors, arguing about who it might be and what they wanted.

The driver got out and walked forward to meet Papa. They shook hands and stood talking. Of course, nothing could be heard from inside the house. Grandma joined the children at the window, but only for a minute. It being too dark to recognize the visitor, even with the headlights beyond him, she turned away and scolded brusquely, "Come on away from that window."

"But, Aunt Bessie, we want to see who that is," Earl Lee protested.

"We'll find out soon enough. Come on away from there now," she ordered. "It ain't polite to stare at folks that way."

When Grandma spoke in that tone, they knew it was useless to argue, even though she was just as curious as they. One by one they went back to the table, but kept their eyes glued on the door and ears tuned to any outside sounds that would indicate Papa and the man were coming in.

Presently, footsteps sounded on the porch and the door opened. Papa came and everyone watched him anxiously, waiting for him to speak. Ignoring their inquiring eyes, he went over to Grandpa's bedroom door. Tapping on the closed door, he called out, "Pa, get up, there's somebody here to see you."

"Who is it?" came Grandpa's muffled voice.

"Earl Shipley."

"What in thunder does he want, this time of night?"

"He wants to talk to you!"

"Tell him to come back tomorrow. Tell him I'm in bed."

"I already told him. He said he has to talk to you tonight."

"I don't see why it can't wait 'til morning when folks are already up and about," Grandpa grumbled.

"He's not alone!"

" What do you mean, he's not alone? Who else is crazy enough to be out gallivanting around in the middle of the night!"

"It's only six-thirty!"

"That don't matter none. I already had my supper and it's dark out and I'm in bed. Tell that fool that."

"I think you ought to talk to them, Pa."

"Who else is with him?"

"Otis Crouch and Banker Endicott."

There was a brief pause. Them Grandpa exclaimed in a harsh voice, "Why in tarnation didn't you say so, Boy. Go on and bring them in the house. Don't leave them standing outside in the cold."

Millie could hear her grandpa stumbling around in the dark room trying to get dressed, still grumbling.

He emerged from his room, wearing his trousers, stretching a suspender over one shoulder, letting the other hang down around his waist. Figuring a shirt wasn't necessary since the long under wear covered the upper part of his body, he felt comfortably dressed for the occasion. In his stocking feet, he appeared shorter than he actually was among the other men.

Millie knew none of the men, but could tell Grandpa did as he called them by name. They were cordial to Grandma too, calling her either Aunt Bessie or Miz Reynolds, so she must know them too.

Staring up at the visitors, Millie soon learned that the spokesman was Earl Shipley, who was some kind of businessman from town. The well dressed man who was soft-spoken and obviously better educated than the others, appeared to be the Banker Endicott that Papa had mentioned. She never learned who the big, loud voiced man was until several months later when this whole affair became public.

233

"I apologize for this inconvenience, Mrs. Reynolds," the banker said to Grandma.

"Land o' goshen, it's no trouble," Grandma replied.

"We could talk outside, just as well," Mr. Shipley said.

"It's too cold to be standing outside gabbing," Grandpa said. "Whatever you have to say, can be said in here where it's warm."

Millie watched the expression on each man's face when he spoke and could tell that Mr. Shipley was embarrassed when he said, "Well, uh, Law, this is kind of private, what we want to talk about," glancing around the room.

"Well, I don't know what this is all about, but we can fix that private part in a hurry," Grandpa said. "Here, you kids go on in the other room and light a lamp. And be quiet too."

As they went to the front room where Grandpa and Earl Lee slept, Papa went back to his own room and Grandma continued her work in the kitchen.

Most locks in the house were made for skeleton keys which opened most doors everywhere, leaving a large key hole, thus making it very convenient for little prying eyes. Earl Lee and Helen soon lost interest in the other room, giving up their turns at peeking to Millie. Her curiosity having been aroused, she intended to hear and learn all she could about what was going on.

At first, the men talked in normal tones and Millie could hear and understand what was being said.

"We waited until after dark, so as not to be seen coming out here and arousing all sorts of speculation about what we're up to." That was Mr. Endicott's voice.

The men sat down at the table, Grandpa at one end and the big man at the other, with his back to the bedroom door, so Millie never saw his face again during the visit. The other two men sat on each side of the table, doing most of the talking. All were facing Grandpa.

"We couldn't call on the telephone for the same reason, not even to let you know we were coming," said Mr. Shipley. "Everybody listens in on the party line and the whole county would soon know we're here and wonder what we're up to. And we certainly don't want any of this to get out. You understand that don't you, Law?"

"No, I don't understand," Grandpa retorted. "I don't even know why you're here or what's going on."

"We must apologize for that," said Mr. Endicott calmly. "We'll explain it to you and then you'll understand why it must be kept quiet."

Through the keyhole Millie could see that her grandpa was about to become irritable. He didn't like people who beat around the bush this way. He preferred things out in the open where he could grasp and deal with them.

The voices were lowered after that so no one outside that room could hear. With an ear pressed against the keyhole, very little of the conversation was distinguishable. Picking up a word or phrase now and then, however, she was able to piece together some of the conversation, though not much of its meaning.

Little by little, she learned that these men wanted Grandpa to go in with them on some sort of big business deal. It seemed that the Federal Government wished to spend a lot of money in the county on some sort of project that Millie never learned fully about. It was a very big deal that must remain quiet for the time being; in other words, very hush, hush. When completed, the project could benefit this county and even neighboring counties tremendously.

Millie could barely hear her grandpa speaking, but by watching his lips, even so far away, was able to determine what he said.

"If it's all so hush, hush as you say, how did you all find out about it?" she read.

The big man sitting with his back to her, said distinctly, "Marvin found out first. Being in the bank the way he is, he hears about everything concerning money before anyone else in town."

This seemed to satisfy Grandpa for the time being until he learned more, but he still didn't know what they wanted from him.

Gradually, Millie began to realize that what they wanted from him was money. In order for the county to get this project, a lot of local, private money must be put up to insure something called good faith. That's where these men and Grandpa came in. By investing a lot of their own money, they were reasonably sure of getting a substantial amount of the government money in return. If word got out about the project ahead of time, everyone would want to invest in it and no one would make any real money. That's why these men were getting together a small group of influential men that had money and could be discreet about the matter. Millie never did learn what the project was.

Once, she heard Grandpa ask, "Isn't that illegal?"

The big man replied loudly, "Hell no, it ain't illegal. If it was, do you think we'd have anything to do with it! It's just good business, that's all."

Apparently Mr. Endicott said something, meant to pacify Grandpa's concern. Now, Grandpa was a shrewd businessman and nobody's fool when it came to money, or he never would have gotten where he was. But, he also was honest! Nevertheless, Millie could tell that he was interested in this endeavor, especially if there happened to be a big profit in it. Who wouldn't be!

Then Mr. Endicott was talking again. Millie wished he would speak louder, so she could understand him better because he seemed to be the one that said anything really important. By pressing her ear as tightly as possible against the keyhole she was able to distinguish two entire sentences.

"You understand, of course, Lawrence, that very little money has to be put up now, don't you? It's just that we must have ready cash for collateral, so to speak, in case something goes amiss. Of course, I happen to know how much you have in the bank. I checked!"

Millie assumed that going amiss meant the same as something going wrong and she wondered about that. If it was such a sure thing, why would anything go amiss!"

"Actually, all we're doing is guaranteeing the government that our share is available," explained Mr. Shipley. "It's called earnest money."

They continued to talk for quite some time. After awhile Millie became bored, which was highly unusual for her. Besides, her ear became numb from being pressed so long and hard against the cold door. Realizing that it had become quiet in the room, she looked around to discover her sister and little cousin were sound asleep on Grandpa's bed.

Two days later, Papa drove Grandpa into town. Apparently Grandpa had considered everything and decided it was a worthwhile investment, so he went in and signed the necessary papers. Very little was said about it at home, but Millie could tell Grandpa felt happy about it. She never heard it discussed again for several months. He seldom talked about business dealings to anyone, not even Papa or Grandma.

Geese often played an important part in the lives of many farmers. They sometimes served as watchdogs during the daylight hours. Few men dared to go up against a big goose that came at him with the long neck out-stretched and hissing as he came. The safest strategy and maneuver being, retreat as quickly as possible beyond the reach of the big bird. Many an ill-fated soul had blundered into a farm yard, only to leave hurriedly with a nipped buttock or wounded leg after being flogged with the strong wings. They were also important for their feathers or down, which was picked periodically for mattresses and pillows, making very soft and warm bedding during the winter months.

When at last a goose was killed, it provided an excellent main course for Sunday dinner. At such times, great quantities of grease came forth. This was used for medicinal purposes, treating symptoms of cold, croup, whooping cough and various other maladies. The grease might be used alone or combined with coal or turpentine and rubbed on one's chest. If goose grease was not available, skunk grease was substituted. It's not known for sure if the treatment cured the patient because of its medicinal qualities or because of the odor just under his nose. Be that as it may, most patients did survive the ordeal.

Earl Lee was subjected to this treatment after catching a cold that seemed to hang on longer than it should. After two days of coughing and moping about the house, the family began to speculate on how the boy caught it. Being a normally healthy and exuberant child, it caused Grandma some concern, for he seldom came down with anything more serious than the sniffles. As far as she knew, he hadn't been wading in any water without his overshoes or hadn't gotten wet at any time. She finally came up with what she thought was a plausible answer.

"I'll bet he caught it Saturday after he had his bath," she said. "He ran outside right afterwards before his pores closed up good. You know you have to wait awhile so the cold air can't get in. Yes siree, that's likely how he got it. I've known many folks that got bad colds and even pneumony the very same way."

"That's all nonsense," Grandpa told her. "That's just old wives tales. There's no truth in it at all. A feller can catch a cold for no reason at all. He can sit behind the warm stove all day and still catch one."

Grandma almost had to agree. She knew plenty of folks who caught colds for no apparent reason, other than sitting in a draft or being too close to someone who sneezed. In fact, she herself had one not too long ago, right after going to the store where Sadie Bates was coughing up a storm. She knew she shouldn't have stood so close to her as they talked! Nevertheless, she took the bull by the horns, so to speak and made up a batch of her goose grease remedy.

Millie felt sorry for her little cousin and missed his annoying antics. He sat quietly around all day, which wasn't natural for him, at all. He showed no interest in the animal she and Helen made on the wall, or even in the stories they offered to read out loud from their schoolbooks.

Bessie always put up a fresh jar of grease each winter. After selecting the goose that gave the children the most problems, it was roasted for Sunday dinner, after plucking it's feathers, of course. Taking the jar down from its shelf, she took out several spoonfuls and emptied it into a tin cup. Adding a liberal amount of coal, she mixed it thoroughly. Earl Lee felt too bad to object to having it rubbed on his chest. The girls watched, half in amusement and half in sympathy as Grandma put a large quantity on the white chest and then rubbed briskly. She had never been known for tenderness and the boy groaned at the rough massage.

But, when the hot towel was placed on his chest, he howled that he was being roasted alive. Grandma had put the towel in the oven ahead of time to insure it's being warm enough to do some good. You see, her theory was that in order for any salve or ointment to perform properly, it must have a heating element applied so the unguent will become pliable enough to penetrate the skin. The only thing, it was left in the oven too long, until it became scorching hot. With this, Earl Lee tried to roll over and get out of bed.

The bewildered girls watched, fascinated at his sudden antics and return to life. He soon settled down, however amid the odor of hot goose grease and scorched cloth.

As Grandma predicted, he improved greatly over night and was up and about some of his old tricks by the next morning. Being convinced of the healing powers of goose grease and coal oil, she spread the word over the party line.

One thing that possibly speeded up Earl Lee's recovery was the prospect of "butchering day." Millie broke the news to him first. Scarcely remembering it from the previous year, the girls enlightened him of the proceedings, telling of all the neighbors who were coming to help and how much fun it would be. So he became as excited about it as they.

As usual, Grandpa was the first to awaken. The sky was still pitch black, indicating that dawn was not far away. He roused himself by throwing back the covers from both he and Earl Lee, who grabbed hold of a comforter and pulled it back over his body. Without rising up, Grandpa called out to his wife in the next room.

"Maw, Maw, how's the weather outside?"

She returned, a little incoherently in her present state, that she thought it was fine.

"It ain't raining, is it?" he asked loudly, probably to make sure everyone in the house was awake.

"No, it ain't rained in four months," she replied.

"Good! Well, we better get up then."

Now, she was an extremely healthy and strong woman, who seldom, if ever, complained about the amount of work she had to do. Her life seemed to be fully dedicated to her husband and the farm. If he was strong willed, she was almost as strong willed in her own way. Being one of the few people able to stand up to him, they never really locked horns over anything. Not that she ever openly opposed him, she usually did things her own way without being antagonistic, letting him believe it was his idea. Not being an educated woman, she could read and write, to a degree. She seemed content with her life, the hard work and drudgery, as though it were her calling. Her skin was brown, coarse and leathery from the years in all kinds of weather and it had made her robust and hearty.

Rising slowly to a sitting position, she looked at the two little granddaughters in the other bed and let her feet touch the cold floor. She quickly pulled the flannel nightgown down over her knees to hold in the warmth of her body as long as possible. In the kitchen, she bent over the wash-pan by the pump and sloshed a few drops of cold water in her face. Reaching back with both hands, she grasped her long hair and began twisting. In a matter of a few seconds, the waist length strands were in a tight bun on top of her head, held in place with large hairpins. As the day wore on, the strands would come free of the pins and blow loosely about her face. This bothered her very little, as she would merely push them aside, and go on with her work.

On this day there was no problem of rousing the girls from bed. With the first sounds from the kitchen, Millie became wide awake. She nudged her sister, saying, "Wake up Helen, it's almost daylight."

Helen slowly turned over under the warm covers, digging knuckles into her sleep filled eyes. "Do I have to get up?" she muttered.

"Of course you do. Don't you know what day this is?" Millie asked.

Helen's eyes widened and she lay perfectly still for several seconds as her mind grasped the importance of the day. Then, as the realization struck her, she sat upright in bed, pushing the covers away from her. "Butchering day," she exclaimed.

The girls jumped out of bed and quickly dressed. It was a day when a few neighbors came to gather to butcher hogs for the family winter meat supply. Always, the first day was here at Grandpa's. He liked to be first! The next day, they would all go to another home and the following day to another and so on, until each family in the group had its day. Often, two or three men brought their animals to one place to save time, which meant butchering several in one day.

The women made sandwiches and plenty of hot coffee, which they ate around the fire. And, everyone brought their children, which made it a very festive occasion, as they were allowed to run wild, so to speak, playing in the woods and barn.

The three children, especially Earl Lee, were cautioned to wear galoshes and scarves and stay bundled up good so as not to catch a cold.

The day dawned bright and clear, but cold. Later, the wind came up, though no one seemed to notice. The snow of two days earlier was soon trampled down to slush.

The unmistakable smell of wood smoke hung in the air as flames licked up around the two large cast iron kettles. Men and boys dressed in overalls and heavy jackets gathered around the fire, holding out their hands to the heat. They moved as the wind shifted directions, trying to escape the gray smoke given off by the burning wood, joshing that smoke followed good looks.

The sharp crack of a .22 caliber Stevens Crack Shot Rifle shattered the crisp morning air and three hundred pounds of Yorkshire hog hit the ground.

This shot came from Leonard's rifle. It was his job each year to deliver the fatal blow. He knew just where to place the shot so the animal died instantly.

Those standing close by backed away as the body convulsed spasmodically and it's heavy short legs kicked wildly. Someone pointed to where the cut should be made to bleed the hog.

"Oh no, I'm not going to touch him yet," said Sidney with the knife. "I had a deer kick a knife right out of my hand one time. Dang nigh broke my arm."

The Reynolds family had four hogs to kill. That may seem like a lot of meat for three adults and three children, but considering the two hired hands and company that dropped in at meal time, and giving an occasional slab of bacon to a needy neighbor, they probably would run out before spring. Alva Kincaid brought one hog and they figured that five was enough for one day. After the first day, they'd likely be able to do more.

After the animal lay perfectly still, Sidney stuck the knife in behind the hog's ear. He twisted the blade until the jugular vein and carotid artery were torn open. Gurgling hollowly, blood gushed out of the cut and onto the ground. The blood foamed and thickened quickly in the cold air. All of the men and women were used to the sight of blood and butchering and watched matter of factly. The younger men were designated to keep the fire going and water in the kettles and help with the cleanup. The older, experienced men and women did the actual butchering.

Tom Quigley and Alva Kincaid sliced down the back of each hind leg to expose the tendons. Using a hay hook to pull the tendons away from the leg, they inserted a gambrel stick.

The gambrel stick, a branch six or seven inches in diameter and two feet long had the ends whittled to a blunt point and a notch cut near each end.

"You turn that notch up so it won't slide off the end," Tom said.

It took four men to lift a dead hog onto a raised platform that rested on logs about two feet high. Leaning against one end of the four by eight foot platform was a large steel drum, held at an angle by a chain and boomer.

Law stepped towards the big kettles and touched the finger tips of one hand into the steaming water. Without speaking, the others did the same.

"She's hot enough," Law proclaimed. The others nodded in agreement, that indeed the water was hot enough. Scooping the hot water up in buckets, they poured it into the metal drum.

Tom and Sidney firmly grasped the gambrel stick and let the hog slide into the hot, water filled drum. After dunking the carcass several times, they removed it from the water and turned it around.

Using the hay hook for another purpose, they pushed it through the hog's nostrils and secured it in the tough cartilage of it's snout. Then, they scalded the other half of the animal.

When they finally removed the hog from the water, they laid it on the platform. Alva scattered a pan of ashes from the wood fire over the carcass.

"Well, that just helps the hair to come off easier," he observed. " I reckon it's the acid in it that causes it."

As soon as the first hog was scalded, more water was poured into the kettles and wood added to the fire. Shortly thereafter, when the water became hot enough, the next hog met its fate.

The women joined the men in scraping the bristly hair off the first hog, using dull butcher knives and scrapers. One of the boys tried using a sharpened cowbell, but to no avail. Clumps of the stiff, wet hair fell between the planking of the platform and collected in piles below.

In some areas where the hair didn't come off easily, someone placed a piece of burlap and poured more hot water.

After the hair was scraped from the right side, they flipped it over and scraped the other side.

Hung by a gambrel stick on a four by six inch board, the feet dangled a few feet above the ground. Atop the eight foot post were crisscrossed boards, so that as many as four animals could be hung for gutting.

Sidney knelt down on the ground, near the head, and used a razor sharp butcher knife to cut through the head, just behind the ears.

"You got to hit just right, between the vertebrae, to get it off," he remarked to nobody in particular, calmly feeling for the correct spot to chop.

His hands were hidden inside the practically severed head. He twisted and pulled on the head until it cracked loudly and snapped off in his hands. The blood left inside slowly dripped onto the ground.

"It's all yours," he said, handing the head to two of his sons.

Using the hog's ears for handles, they carried it over to one side and placed it in a tub of cold water.

These proceedings held a certain fascination for the children as they stared at the bucket staring up at them and watched for some time before wandering off to new adventures.

The hog was left to cool for awhile. As it hung there, Vesta scraped off the remaining hair.

After awhile, they prepared to gut the hog. Experience is important in gutting a hog properly. Usually, Sidney was selected for this job, along with Reuben.

With his razor sharp knife, he started at the top of the under side of the hog and cut all the way down it's belly and cleanly sliced the layers of flesh and muscle to expose the innards. Cutting a circle around the anus, he freed the large intestine and then tied it off with a piece of string.

The front of the rib cage was hacked in two, to allow easier access to the viscera, (the heart, liver, etc.). Using his fingers as a guide, he carefully cut the entrails and avoided slicing into the intestine. This was very important, because the intestine was full.

He cut free all the organs and the elastic like entrails rolled out of the body into a bucket, making a loud plopping sound as they fell.

Steam rose up from the bucket and from the clean looking cavity of the gutted hog.

"I like to save everything on a hog but the squeal," he said, tossing a handful of fresh guts to the anxious dogs that had been hard to keep away since the first cut was made on the hog.

The Reynolds dog Shep had been locked in the shed, because of the problems he might cause. But, the three Kincaid hounds had followed the family and caused considerable trouble from the very beginning. At the first smell of blood, they had to be run off with a stick, only to keep coming back, growling and fighting and getting under foot. After a lengthy battle with them, Vesta finally called one of her boys to take them home.

The boy began to argue that it was too far and he didn't have time.

She grabbed him by the ear and jerked him around. "Don't you argue with me, boy," she said.

"But, Maw," was all he was able to say before she slapped him on the other side of his face, leaving a big red splotch of hog blood.

"You heard me, Boy" she rasped. "Now you take them hounds home, don't you know. And tie them up real good, so they don't come back. Petey, you go help him."

When they caught the dogs and started down the road, Millie, Helen, and Earl Lee joined them, as well as two of Sidney's offspring. The bevy of other children, of all ages, chose to stay and play.

Bessie said to Sidney, "You be sure to save that sweetbread for me, you hear!" The sweetbread is the gland-like body near the throat.

With the gutting completed, Sidney sifted through the bucket full of bloody entrails and removed the heart and the sweetbread and put them into a bucket of water.

Tom Quigley used a hacksaw to saw down through the middle of the backbone, splitting the carcass in half.

After the hog had been hanging for about half an hour, the two halves were laid out on the platform. The men took turns cutting the meat and handing the pieces to the women folks. They removed the tenderloins from next to the backbone, cut apart the spare ribs, removed the hams and shoulders from the sides, thus leaving very little of the body.

No one paid much attention to the children as they came running down the road, across the open space and up to where the butchering took place. Because of the snow on the ground and being bundled up with extra clothes, they were unable to run very fast, but they did move as quickly as possible, with Earl Lee and Petey bringing up the rear, since they were the smallest of the group.

Bessie was the first to take notice, as Helen ran up to her, out of breath.

"Grandma, we seen him," Helen blurted out.

"You seen who?" Bessie asked. "Land o'goshen, you young'uns act like you seen a ghost or something, the way you come runnin' in here."

"I think he chased us, Grandma," Millie chimed in, breathlessly.

Then the other children gathered around, all talking at once.

Grandma held up a hand and spoke loudly, "Hold on a minute. Now, one at a time. Who you talking about that you think chased you?"

"The Bottoms Tramper," they exclaimed in unison.

"The Bottoms Tramper," Grandma replied. "I Gawd! What's he doing, chasing little kids."

"I don't know, but he did," Helen said

Lorna joined the group and grabbed Willie by the arm. "Where did this happen?" she asked her son.

"Down by Cox's Woods," the boy said. "We went down to Kincaid's and when we came back by the woods, we saw him. He had that big dog with him. You should've seen them. They was really scary looking."

Lorna looked at her husband, who was busy sharpening a butcher knife on a whetstone.

"Reuben, you better come over here," she said. "We might have a problem"

Leonard and Reuben went over to talk and see what the trouble was, and soon the other men joined them. Some discussion followed. The younger ones wanted to go out and run down the Bottoms Tramper, once and for all, ridding the area of a menace before he really did hurt somebody.

With such talk, the children's account grew with each telling.

"You should have seen him, Papa," Millie said. "I bet he's ten feet tall, at least."

"Yeah, and that dog must be part wolf," another added. "He's the meanest looking ol' dog I ever saw. He came running after us with them big fangs showing and foam coming out of his mouth."

One by one they added their bit and the event soon became one of monumental proportions. Realizing that the whole thing was about to get out of hand and becoming highly exaggerated, Law spoke up for the first time. Looking at his two grand-daughters, he began questioning them.

"Now, tell me where was this Tramper when you saw him?" he asked.

"He was in Cox's Woods," Helen replied.

"And you was all out on the road?"

"Yes Sir!

"How far away was he?"

Millie pointed to a hickory tree, "About that far."

"What was he doing?"

"He just stood there looking at us, at first. Then he started moving," Millie told him.

"How did he move? Which way? Did he move towards you?"

"I don't know," Millie answered, becoming confused.

"He just started moving towards us and watching us at the same time."

"What do you think?" he asked Helen. "Did he come towards the road or go the other way?"

"I'm not sure," Helen replied after a moment. "He might have tried to hide behind a tree. He acted surprised to see so many of us so close."

"Then he didn't chase you?"

"I don't know. We started running and I never looked back," said Helen meekly.

"So, the man never really bothered anybody!" Law said. "Let's leave the matter drop."

"You mean we're not going after him to teach him a lesson?" exclaimed Sidney's son, Roy.

"Teach him a lesson for what, living?" Law said in disgust. "He never hurt anybody."

"It seems to me we ought to do something for scaring these kids like that!"

"He didn't scare them," Law retorted. "Their over active imagination scared them. He was likely just as scared as they was. I don't think anybody chased them. Why, if he had he'd be sure of catching them. Bundled up the way they are and trying to run in the snow, they couldn't out run a turtle."

"But what was he doing in the woods?" Roy insisted. "He's got no business there."

245

"I own them woods and I don't care what he done there so long as he don't hurt me or mine," Law declared, turning back to the job at hand.

The chunks of fat for the cracklings and lard were thrown into a separate cast iron kettle over a separate fire and cooked down, with intermittent stirring of the mixture with a long wooden lard ladle. Then the chunks were put out into a lard press and squeezed together, with the lard draining into a waiting can.

All that remained after the lard was rendered was the cracklings. Everyone gathered around for a few bites of the crisp, crunchy hot pork rinds.

Tom Quigley used an axe to cut the hog's head in two, splitting it right between the eyes. The brains were saved to be fried and the head and tongue used to make hog's head cheese. The women and young men carried the hams, shoulders and sides to the smoke house to be cured. Some folks liked their meat salted down, while others preferred smoke cured. Whatever their preference, the procedure must be started at once. The same was true in making sausage. That's why this year they had decided to have a day in between each butchering day, to give them time to process the meat before it spoiled, though it was not likely to do so in cold weather. They would be working well into the might and beginning again early next morning. Law and Leonard always helped in the curing and sausage making, as it was too much for Bessie to do alone.

The men were well on the way with the second hog long before the clean-up was finished from the first. There was no time in between for resting. At this rate, the butchering should be finished in good time.

"Lord, I never seen so much meat in all my life," Vesta remarked towards the end of the day as they stacked meat in the smoke-house.

"We'll likely run out before spring," Bessie said, "What with cooking for the hired men and all. How come Alva is only killing one hog, Vesta? That won't last no time at all, with your family."

"I know!"

"I-Gawd ain't he got more than one. I'd of swore I saw more than one at your house."

"Oh, Alva has plenty, don't you know, but he likes to kill one at a time," Vesta answered. "He'll kill another one when we need it. He says it's less trouble that way and besides we always have fresh meat."

"Seems to me it'd be easier to butcher two or three at a time while he's got help and get it over with," Bessie said, a little sarcastically.

Then they carried two big pans to the house to be kept in the kitchen until the next day when the contents could be taken care of. Vesta sat her pan on the table and looked down at the two halves of a big head lying there.

"You going to make hog-head cheese out of these?" she asked wistfully.

"Of course! What else do you think I'd do with hogs heads!"

"I thought that's what you'd do," Vesta said. "I sure do like hog-head cheese, don't you know."

"Well, you'll have plenty of your own, when you make yours."

"Oh, I don't reckon I'll be making any."

"Why in the world not?" Bessie asked.

"I don't know how."

Bessie looked at her incredulously!

"I-Gawd, Vesta, I thought everybody knew how to make cheese!"

"I don't! I never learned how."

"You sure surprise me, Vesta. Why, that's the easiest thing there is. Nothing to it at all."

"Maybe you'll give me your recipe?"

"I-Gawd, I just can't believe it," Bessie said. "I'll tell you right now how to make it. It's so simple I won't have to write it down."

"I sure wish you would."

"Now listen and I'll tell you. You take a hog's head and scrape it and wash it real good, so's you get all the bristles and stuff off. Then you take the tongue and trim it and wash it and put it all in a big kettle and add some salt to it. Pour in enough water to cover it and let it simmer on the stove until the meat falls off the bone. Then drain all the water off and shred and season with pepper and chili powder or sage. Either one will do. Then pack it in a crock and weight it down real tight. Then let it set in a cold spot for about three days. After that, you can slice and eat it."

"That sure does sound good alright," the other woman said. "But, would you mind writing it down on paper for me?"

"For land sakes, there's not much to write down."

"I know, but I want to do it right."

"I-Gawd, Vesta, I ain't much on writing," Bessie swore.

"Well, I ain't much on reading either, but I'll make it out. I'd sure hate to ruin a good hog's head, don't you know."

"Oh, all right. Let me see if I can find a piece of paper and pencil."

She went into the bedroom and rummaged around in the dresser drawer and returned with pencil and paper. They sat at the kitchen table and she began to scribble down the recipe. After awhile, she handed it to Vesta.

Vesta stared down at the paper and finally said, "I'll get one of my kids to read it to me. Most of them can read pretty good."

Law later sent Leonard out to Sam Hathorn's with a couple chunks of pork and a promise to go help him butcher before long. Sam was now able to get around some on his crutches but not able to butcher on his own yet without help.

That winter, Leonard and Reuben hunted and trapped, as they did most winters. They kept their families in fresh meat, to replace the otherwise steady diet of pork and beef. A young calf was always butchered later in the winter, so they could alternate between beef and pork at the Reynold's home. Wild game still being plentiful in the bottoms, the two took advantage of it, not so much as a source of meat perhaps, but for the joy of tramping around and hunting together. Many rabbits, squirrels, quails, ducks or turkey adorned the Reynolds dinner table during the hunting season.

Steel traps were scattered along the banks of streams in a mile radius and produced many hides of fur bearing animals. These hides were stretched, dried and sold to the produce house in Mill Town or McCleansboro. They brought in a substantial amount of extra cash for the two men. Leonard often splurged by spending some of the extra money on his two daughters, buying hair ribbons and bonnets and other things they didn't normally receive. It did him good to see the joy on their faces. Of course, Earl Lee had to be included in everything that pertained to the girls.

It was late winter when the Kincaid boy disappeared. The Reynolds had finished supper and Law was getting ready for bed. Being dark made it bedtime for him. Bessie and Millie were finishing with the dishes when they heard Shep barking at the horse and rider coming in the yard. The children ran to the window and looked out. The rider, being unrecognizable in the dark, dismounted and came up on the porch, standing in the lamp light from inside before the children said, "It's Mr. Kincaid."

Before he had time to knock, Leonard opened the door. "What are you doing out at night, Alva?" he asked. "Is anything wrong? Come on inside."

Alva Kincaid entered the room, holding his cap in his hands.

"Land sakes Alvy, what's wrong? You ain't here at night without a reason," Bessie said.

"It's Max! He's gone," Alva replied.

"What do you mean, he's gone? A boy can't just be gone without a reason," Leonard said.

"Max is. He's just disappeared and we can't find him."

"He's your young'un about the same age as Helen here, ain't he?" Bessie asked.

He was indeed the same age as Helen, but one grade behind her in school, having failed one year. "Tell us what happened Alvy and we'll see what we can do about it," Leonard suggested.

Alva related that the boy had taken his .410 gauge shot gun and gone hunting. One of the hound dogs had accompanied him and he never returned. The dog came back before dark, however, about suppertime. He never liked to miss a meal!

"When did the boy leave home?" Leonard asked.

"I don't know for sure, I wasn't home, but Vesta says it was early this morning. She started worrying when he didn't come home for dinner. He ain't one to miss a meal either. But she didn't get too upset until the dog came in alone. That's when she made me and the boys go out and look for him. We searched all over for him, but didn't find any sign of him at all. I can't understand how that boy got lost. He's awful young maybe, but he knows these Bottoms as good as anybody, at least, around here close. He wouldn't go too far."

Millie and Helen looked at each other. Maybe he didn't get lost and they shuddered at the thought they each had. The Bottoms Tramper! What if the Bottoms Tramper caught him! Poor Max! That would be the last of him for sure.

Law heard the conversation and came out of his room fully dressed.

They searched until midnight, with lanterns, yelling his name, to no avail. After breakfast the next morning, they set out again at dawn. Others hearing of the tragedy via the party line, came to join the hunt. Some came on horse-back while others came afoot, with hound dogs. Vesta said if only their dog could talk, he could tell them exactly what happened. But of course he couldn't talk, and he wouldn't take them to where he last saw Max.

They found no trace whatsoever of him. The big concern now was, had he survived the night and if they didn't find him soon, could he survive another one. The temperature dropped down below freezing the night before and surely would again tonight. Even if he managed to make it through one night, which was extremely unlikely, another one would be impossible. The boy had no particular skills or knowledge of even the basic survival methods, but he had been raised in these parts and knew a little bit about staying alive, so it mostly amounted to instinct. Everyone knew that instinct didn't count for very much with a young boy. And if he was still alive, why didn't he return home with his dog!

Each man had his own theory in the matter. The most prevalent now, in most minds, was the fact that two or three brown bears had been seen in the vicinity. If Max tried to shoot one with his .410 shotgun, he had little or no hope of being alive. The small gauge gun would only anger the beast, causing it to attack the aggressor. The wolves too were a matter of concern. Many still roamed the Bottoms and might attack the boy, especially in the winter time, when food was scarce and they ran in packs.

After three days of scouring the Bottoms without even a trace of the boy, most of the men abandoned the hunt. They reasoned, there was no way a small boy could possibly exist in cold weather this long. By now, he either had to be dead or the wolves got him. In either case the search was a waste of time. Maybe some day his clothing or some of his remains would be found. Some folks like Law and Leonard never gave up hope. They still continued to look, with Alva and a few others, but only a few hours each day. You see, they too had young children that may be lost one day!

Then Max returned. Four days after his disappearance, he came home. There was much joyous shouting when the Kincaids looked out the window and saw him coming down the road from over the Big Ditch way. Along with Vesta, they all ran out to meet him. Being surprised at the concern for his absence, he could only grin sheepishly, afraid he might be in trouble after being gone so long.

Alva, Law, Leonard and Reuben rode into the yard a short time later, the only remaining members of the so called posse.

Needless to say, they were all happy and surprised to see the boy safe and sound and also anxious to hear his story. They found it hard to believe that a boy managed to escape so many men and dogs for so long and survive the cold nights in the woods.

At first Max was reluctant to talk about his ordeal, being naturally bashful and now embarrassed by so much attention. After much persistent questioning, they were able, little by little, to piece together the accounts of these past few days.

The following is Max's story about what happened, not exactly in his own words, but yet pretty much as it actually occurred.

He left home that morning, armed with his father's shot gun and a pocket full of shells. Trotting along beside him, Fred, his favorite hunting dog was anxious to get started. They often hunted together. Sometimes they shot a rabbit or other wild animal and sometimes they returned home empty handed. It never really mattered that much any way, because they enjoyed tramping the woods together.

Though he was still very young, he knew the land as well as anybody, up to a certain distance. His folks knew this and felt no cause to worry. Besides, with so many children in the family and with so much work around the place they seldom noticed one missing until either bed time or meal time.

Max shot a rabbit right off and put it in his pack that he carried over his shoulder. Going on through the underbrush as quietly as possible, he hoped to kill another one. Two would make a fine dinner!

Fred jumped a young deer, driving it within a few yards of Max. Becoming very excited at the animal being so close, he raised his gun and fired without thinking. The buckshot hit the deer, going away, in the rump and it never slowed down. Immediately he felt regret, for he had broken a cardinal rule of his father, as well as most fathers who were hunters. He had shot a deer with a gun that was not meant for larger animals, leaving no chance for a kill. At best, the deer would only suffer and be a cripple. It was an unwritten law that when such a thing happened, the hunter should follow and kill it. Though the deer had no life threatening injuries from the small caliber gun, it ran off swiftly and disappeared in the brush, leaving Fred far behind.

Max, not knowing the extent of the deer's injuries, began to follow in the hopes of putting it out of its misery. Finding it difficult to keep up with the baying dog, he soon realized that he had ventured farther into the bottom land than ever before. The baying of the hound faded away and Max was alone.

He began walking, often hearing Fred, who kept up the chase, then all became quiet, except for his own breathing. He knew he was lost for the first time in his life and looked around for something familiar and found nothing. He kept walking and calling Fred for what seemed like hours, hoping he was going in the right direction.

Coming to a small stream, he started to cross it by walking along on a fallen log. Almost to the end, he slipped on the loose, slippery bark and fell. Luckily he landed on the opposite bank instead of in the stream below. He must have struck his head on something hard and solid, because he didn't remember anything after falling.

Somewhat painfully, Max opened his eyes, staring at a lantern hanging in a dimly lighted cabin. Assuming it to be dark outside, he had been unconscious for many hours. A man stood with his back to Max, bent over a small stove, apparently cooking meat. The red-bone hound dog, lying on the floor, whined in it's throat as Max stirred on the cot. The man turned around and looked at the boy. He appeared to be a big man, looking up at him from the cot, but later Max saw that he was of average size. His face was gaunt looking under the long beard and hair. The eyes were sharp and penetrating.

When Max asked where he was, the man grunted something that he didn't understand.

Suffering from a slight concussion and on the verge of pneumonia from lying on the ground for so long, he was unable to travel. Therefore, he must remain as a guest in this cabin until able to walk home.

The strange man took care of Max, feeding and nursing him. He had his own ideas of doctoring and used his own concoctions of medicines of herbs and roots. They were as primitive as everything else about the man. His methods were crude and rough, but proved effective.

Max slept fitfully that first night, with aching head and fever. The man lay on a pallet near the stove, next to his dog, when not attending to the boy.

By the next morning, he felt better and became curious. The man talked very little at first, his voice strange and difficult to understand, this probably due to the fact that he had no one to talk to other than himself and his dog, Riker. The vocal cords seem to shrink when not being used frequently, causing one to lose his voice. Usually though, it comes back very quickly when exercised.

As time went by, he began to talk more and was understandable. As a boy, Max was naturally inquisitive and asked many questions. The man answered slowly as one who seldom conversed with anyone.

Over the course of his stay at the cabin, Max learned many things about wild life and the bottom land that few men know. But, he learned very little about the man himself. He did learn however, that the man's name was Cain and the dog, Riker. Cain had lived here most of his life. Other than that, Max knew nothing about him. His only gun was an old rifle that he carried all the time. Being an excellent marksman, he felt no reason for another gun, for he seldom missed his target, whether moving or stationary.

Cain hunted and fished for a living, if one could call it a living. Most folks would call it existence. He seemed satisfied with his way of life, killing game only when necessary, feeling that random killing was wasteful. He killed animals only for the fur and the meat they provided for himself and Riker and never for sport. There was no sport in shooting a defenseless creature! Those killed in the winter months usually were of the fur bearing variety. These were skinned and stretched for the hides, which he sold to the feed store in Mill Town. With the money he received, he purchased the few necessary things he needed such as flour, coffee, sugar, salt and of course, rifle shells.

Little else was necessary and money had no other value to him. To kill more animals than needed would be sinful!

He carried a long, razor sharp hunting knife in a sheath on his belt. Years of practice had made him an expert at knife throwing, a necessary skill in his life. With this knife, he kept the long black and gray beard hacked off to just below the chin. Otherwise, it might have grown to a great length and hindered his close up activities. The same held true for the hair on his head, that he cut by simply reaching over his shoulders and trimming it off.

The pocketknife that he carried provided him with many hours of pleasant past time, whittling animal figures, which lined a shelf of the cabin.

Max soon became accustomed to the foul smells in the cabin, the odors of dried animal hides and stale air, the close quarters with little ventilation. The red, powerfully built dog, Riker never became really friendly with him, but did accept his presence.

When Cain talked, the boy listened carefully to learn all he could about this primitive man. A half a dozen chickens roosted in a lean to out back and each night Cain closed a make-shift door across the opening to keep out animals. It was difficult keeping chickens here, as most wild animals had a knack for finding ways through or around the smallest opening, especially opossums and raccoons. A big black and white goat, wearing long curled horns, ran loose during the day time, but slept in a shelter attached to the cabin. During the warm months of summer, there would be a vegetable garden of sorts, dug with a shovel and shared with various animals that wandered in from the woods. Five or six fruit trees, long past their prime of life, produced gnarled apples, peaches and plums, also shared with the wildlife. Wild berries and nuts were always plentiful to supplement one's diet.

He ate badger meat for the first time and found it to be delicious. Cain had killed the animal only the day before and skinned it, tacking the hide over a board to dry. Although most folks never bothered to hunt the animal because of it's habit of burrowing underground and the commonly false belief that it hibernated during winter months, it thrived in the Bottoms. Cain sought one out only now and then. Its hair, used for making fine brushes, brought a good price. He had a taste for the small rich hams they produced.

There were still a few beaver left in the Bottoms, but Cain seldom went after them, preferring meat of other animals. The soft, silky like fur could be a good source of income, but taking too many good hides into town would bring out a horde of hunters. Soon the Bottoms would become barren of fur bearing animals. Too many people coming into the Bottoms would ultimately destroy his life style.

After three days of doctoring and nursing the boy with his own potions of herbs and remedies, Cain declared him to be physically able to walk the four or so miles home.

On the fourth day, they started out. The distance was greater than the four miles, as the crow flies. They walked in circles some of the time and even back-tracked a time or two, so that there was no way Max could find his way back to Cain's cabin.

Max was exhausted and weak by the time they reached the Big Ditch. Cain gazed across the ditch towards the grove that surrounded the Kincaid house. Patting the boy on the shoulder, he said simply, "Your folks will be worried." Turning, he walked away, before Max could reply.

Crossing over the ditch, he walked down the lane to see his brothers and sisters running out to greet him.

Law and Alva queried the boy at great length to get so much out of him. When Law became satisfied there was no more to tell, he said, "Well, I'll be danged. That's the darndest tale I've heard in a long time. Are you sure he didn't mention a last name?"

"No sir, just Cain. That's all he said and I didn't care about no other name," Max replied.

One of Sidney's sons, Roy came up while Max related the story and showed an immediate interest in it.

"I think we should go out and find this man, Cain," he suggested.

Being always wary of this headstrong son of his brother, Law demanded, "What the devil for?"

"Well, maybe Mr. Kincaid ought to thank him for what he did."

"Don't be an idiot," Law retorted. "If he wanted any thanks, he wouldn't have run off. He'd've stayed right here."

"Maybe he's a little backward, living all alone like he does."

"Of course he's a little backward," Law exclaimed. "He's a hermit! He likes being alone and don't want people pestering him. That's why he lives that way."

"But Uncle Lawrence, I'll bet if we could find his cabin, he could maybe show us where the best hunting is. He must know where all the good animals are and how to catch them," Roy argued. "He sounds to me like that Bottoms Tramper. Maybe we ought to go in there and burn him out, before he does something bad. Maybe he just saved Max so we'll let our guard down and then come back when we don't expect it and hurt a lot of kids."

"You listen to me, Boy, and listen good," Law roared, suddenly becoming very provoked at his nephew. "That man saved this boy's life. And he took care of him and nursed him back to health and then brought him back home to his family, safe and sound. If he hadn't done that, this boy would likely be dead. It appears to me he's a peaceful man and deserves to be left alone. Maybe he don't live like we do, but that's his business, not ours. He surely has his own reasons. If a man wants to be a hermit, so be it. He ain't never done no harm to anybody that I know of. So you leave him be, you hear me, boy!" Law took a deep breath. "If I ever hear of you or any of your no account friends even going in that part of the Bottoms, by thunder I'll take a bullwhip to you. If anything ever happens to him, I'll figure you had a hand in it some way so, you better hope nobody bothers him. Reuben, you tell your pa, he better keep a tight rein on this brother of yours, before he gets hisself in a heap of trouble."

Millie and Helen thought of the Bottoms Tramper the first thing when the story was related at home. Max suddenly became a hero to them, for having survived four days in his clutches. They wanted to talk to him and ask all kinds of questions. However, he had already told everything he knew about the man and almost all that had happened. He did elaborate now and then. Max became a big man at school and was the center of attention for a long time thereafter.

CHAPTER 9

Millie was cleaning the lamp globes one day when Grandma came in looking puzzled and perplexed and mumbling to herself. Looking up, she asked, "What's wrong, Grandma? You look like something happened!"

"I-Gawd, I must be getting old," the woman answered. "I could of swore I had more hams than that. I seem to be missing one."

"Maybe you counted wrong," Millie suggested.

"I guess maybe I did. There's so much meat in that smokehouse, it's hard to keep track of," Grandma agreed. "Still, I ain't likely to miscount a whole ham."

Going on about her work, she more or less forgot the incident. That is, until a week later. She went out to the smokehouse again for a slab of bacon. She came storming back in the house a moment later.

"I-Gawd, I knowed it," she said. "There's another ham missing. Somebody's been in my smokehouse. I'd sure like to get my hands on that culprit, I'd skin him alive."

"It could have been an animal of some kind, Grandma," Helen said.

"Hah, there ain't no animal that can reach up and unlatch a door and then go in and pick out my two best hams and make off with them, without leaving a trace," Grandma told her. "This had to be a two legged animal that knew what he was after."

The girls and Earl Lee watched as she fumed and raved about in the kitchen, banging pans and stove lids. They silently agreed that she would indeed skin the culprit alive if she caught up with him.

"Who do you think it was, Aunt Bessie?" Earl Lee asked.

"How do I know who it was!" she returned angrily. "I don't know, but I got my suspicions, alright."

"Who you got suspicions about, Aunt Bessie?" Earl Lee persisted.

"That's none of your affair and I ain't saying, but I still got my suspicions."

The three children looked at each other with the same thought in mind. The Bottoms Tramper!

No one else had nerve enough to do such a thing. But, why would he do such a thing!

He never had before and he obviously had all the meat he could eat, unless he wished to try something different. At least, he was the most likely suspect and their first choice.

When Grandpa and Papa came in, they were concerned that a prowler and thief wandered about loose like that. There had never been a problem before. They never locked a door on the house or any shed or barn and hadn't missed anything. It made Grandpa angry and he swore a little.

Papa was first to mention the Bottoms Tramper.

"I'm surprised at this, Mr. Cain," he observed. "After what he did for the Kincaid boy, I thought he could be trusted."

"We don't know for sure that he done it," Grandpa said.

"Well, who else could it be? He's the only man we don't know and he seems to be mighty familiar with the lay of the land," Papa asserted.

257

"I don't buy that," Grandpa declared. "I never met the man, but my common sense tells me that it had to be somebody else. He just don't strike me as being a sneak thief."

Grandpa seldom made a mistake about a man's character so, if he thought the thief was someone else, she did also.

"We know everybody in these parts pretty well and I can't think of anybody I'd even suspect," Papa said.

"That's just it," reasoned Grandpa thoughtfully, tugging at his moustache. "It has to be somebody we know. A neighbor probably, otherwise how would he know about the meat in the smokehouse!"

"I-Gawd," Grandma said, "we'll all be murdered in our beds, next thing we know."

"Don't be silly, woman," Grandpa said scornfully. "A petty thief like that don't go around killing people."

"If the snow hadn't melted, we could track him," said Papa. "It's strange though that ol' Shep didn't bark."

"That's another reason it has to be a neighbor. The dog knows him. The next time I go into town, I'll buy me a bear trap and set it inside the door. That'll fix him up for good, with a broke ankle."

Grandpa told Tom Quigley about it the next day and he agreed that it appeared to be someone who knew the Reynolds farm pretty good. He also said that if it happened again, maybe the two of them should ride out and try to find the man called Cain. After all, he was wise enough to spot a trap, even in the dark and by-pass it, where another man would step in it.

Before the thief was caught in the trap though, Grandpa solved the mystery. While at Blessy's store in Blairsville, a man came in. Being a stranger here, he began talking to Tom Snider, asking questions. The questions was what caught Grandpa's attention.

The man asked about a young feller named Roy Reynolds, who supposedly lived around this part of the country. Tom pointed to Grandpa and told the man, that's his Grandpa, so the man talked to him instead of the grocer. He lived over around Carmi way. He never told his name though, not that it mattered anyway. He said this Roy Reynolds and another young feller had come by one day and sold him a smoked ham. A week later, he bought another one. The man said they were the best smoked hams he and his wife ever ate. Since the two young men hadn't been back for a couple of weeks now, he thought he'd look them up and see if they had any more.

Grandpa swore at the man, ranting and raving and told him he didn't need to expect any more smoked meat, because there wouldn't be any more. The poor man hurriedly left the store. He stood outside for a minute or two, looking at the building in bewilderment, shaking his head.

Grandpa went straight down to Uncle Sidney's house. Luckily, Roy wasn't home. Had he been, the outcome would likely be different. When he told Uncle Sidney about it, he became just as upset and told Grandpa not to worry about it. None of his boys had ever stolen anything before that he knew of and they never would again. He said to leave it to him and he'd take care of it.

When Grandma asked why Roy stole the hams, Grandpa said the reason was likely two-fold.

"One," he explained, "Is that the boy probably needed some money for his tomcatting around and since the first time was so easy, he tried it again. The other reason being, he figured we'd blame it on Cain and go hunt him down. He'd get to go along and be in on the fun. He could have been right maybe but, he's not smart enough. Why, that young fool ain't got good horse sense, selling it and leaving his name with folks. Sid will give him what for, though. He'll take him down a notch or two, you can bet your bottom dollar on that."

A day or two later, Roy knocked on the back door. Grandma yelled, come on in and he entered the kitchen, holding his cap in his hands. He looked very sheepish.

"Hi, Aunt Bessie, is Uncle Lawrence around?" he asked.

"I guess he's around somewhere," Grandma replied. "Is anything I can do for you?'

"No ma'am, Paw said I should come talk to Uncle Lawrence personal."

"Well, go look in the barn then. He's likely out there," Grandma told him.

After he left the house, Earl Lee spoke first. "What happened to Roy? Did he fall off a horse or something?"

"Don't be silly, Er-ly, of course he didn't," answered Millie.

"Well, what happened then? He must've fell off the barn or something then! Maybe he got in a fight then," he said hopefully. "I bet if he did, he won, because I bet ol' Roy is a good fighter."

Roy did look like he might have fallen from a horse or been in a fight. Walking toward the barn, the limp was very noticeable and the knot on the side of his head was still a dark blue. But, what they didn't know, he had trouble sitting down because of the bruise on his rump.

"No, he didn't get in a fight, neither, Er-ly," Helen said scornfully.

"Well, what happened, then?" the boy persisted. "He sure looks like he fell off a horse or something. Did you see that big knot on his head! I bet he fell off the barn, because when you fall off the barn, sometimes you hurt your leg and that makes you limp like that. If he didn't fall, then what happened to him?"

"Some little boys ask too many questions," Grandma said.

When Grandma went in the other room, Millie whispered to Earl Lee. "I'll tell you what happened if you promise not to let on you know."

"I promise," he promised.

"Uncle Sidney did it," Millie whispered.

"Uncle Sidney! Tarnation," Earl Lee exclaimed, imitating Grandpa. "Why'd he do that?"

"Sh-h-h, not so loud, Er-ly, Grandma will hear," Millie shushed.

"Why would his own Paw beat him up?"

"Because Roy is the one that stole Grandma's hams," Millie said. "And I think Uncle Sidney gave him a good whipping,"

"Gosh, but Roy is too big to be whipped!"

"I know! That's probably why he's got that knot on his head and sore muscles, because he tried to fight back."

"Gosh, I sure would like to have seen that. That must have been a good fight."

"It wasn't really a fight."

"Sounds like a fight to me."

Millie saw Roy go in the barn where Grandpa was working and he stayed a long time. After a while though, he came out and went home. She continued to watch, waiting for Grandpa to come out, so as not to miss anything. Being anxious to find out why Roy had to see him, made her even more curious than usual and she hated to miss anything pertaining to Roy or the stolen hams. Grandpa stayed in the barn for an unusually long time, she thought, but he had to come out sometime. When he did, Grandma would make him tell all about Roy.

Grandpa finally came in. Grinning a little to himself, he went about the business of nonchalantly taking off his cap and jacket and hanging them on the nail on the back of the door. Then he washed his hands in the washpan by the pump, going at the task, methodically, but irritatingly slow, as though enjoying making Grandma wait. Millie looked at her and could tell she was likely to burst pretty soon if he didn't tell what happened. He took his favorite cup over to the stove and picked up the old blackened granite coffeepot. Swearing, almost under his breath, he sat it back down quickly. He should have known to use a hot pad with a hot coffeepot!

Realizing that he wouldn't tell Grandma anything really important in front of them, the three went in the other room. Millie, however, stayed just inside the doorway, to hear everything being said.

When Grandma spoke at last, she said, "What did Roy want? He didn't look too chipper to me."

Grandpa took a dollar bill from his pocket and waved it in front of her. "He gave me this," he said.

"A dollar for two big hams!" she exclaimed. "That won't even pay for the wood we used to smoke them."

"There'll be more!"

"I should hope so. That must have been mighty hard on him, having to come and face you that way. It took a lot of gumption to do that."

"Maybe not! Sid made him do it. Said it would teach him a lesson. Made him give me this dollar too. It's all he had."

"How's he going to get the rest of it?" she asked.

"Work! Him and that Dolittle boy."

"Who's he, the one that helped him?"

"Yes, Clem's boy! Sid knows Clem pretty well, buying his bootleg all the time. He went and told Clem about it and he give the boy a good whipping, just like Sid did to Roy. Sid hasn't always kept a tight enough rein on his kids maybe, but he's kept them honest. I don't reckon Roy will steal again. They're coming to work for me for two weeks, until they work out the price of them hams."

"You got that much work to do, this time of year?" asked Grandma.

"I'll find something. I'm going to teach that boy a lesson he won't forget for awhile. He'll wish he had never been born."

Millie was convinced that he would too. He could find things to do when no one else could. Grandma had often said that she thought hard work had been invented right here on this farm.

Now, Roy was a big, strapping young man of about twenty years of age, not as big as his older brother Rueben perhaps, but strong and a good worker when pushed. He had always been a rebel and headstrong, but never in any real trouble. He learned a good lesson in the two weeks that followed, just like Grandpa said.

The two young men arrived early in the morning and stayed until after dark, with very little time for relaxation in between. During that period, the barns were cleaned, thoroughly, fences mended, post holes dug and new posts set in place. New gates were mounted, fence rows cleaned of brush and wood cut. Law took the opportunity to get sprouts grubbed out along the north boundary of the farm. They never complained, not openly at least, about getting the raw end of the deal and working much longer than necessary to pay for two hams. If it was discussed at all, it had to be done privately, where no one else heard it. Roy knew his uncle well enough to know that he very well could have had them both thrown in jail for the offense. So, he considered himself fortunate. It was a lesson he wouldn't likely forget.

Millie pitied Roy each day when they came in to dinner. Even though he was big and strong, he had never worked like this before. Uncle Sidney expected a day's work out of all his kids, but he didn't stay behind them urging them on like Grandpa did. So, Roy ate a big, hearty meal and sat in a corner on the floor for a short nap. Then Grandpa kicked their feet and said, "Come on boys, it's time to go." Then they rose with an effort, as though every bone in their body ached and cried for relief.

Yes, Millie felt sorry for Roy, but he came through the ordeal in one piece and probably all the better for it. Grandpa remarked later that it made a man out of him. As far as anyone knew, Roy never stole so much as a farthing again, whatever that was.

That spring was pretty normal on the Reynolds farm. Perhaps the most significant thing about it being the fact there was no floodwater to contend with as in the previous year. The rainfall was average, allowing time to plow and plant. The winter wheat got off to a good start early on.

The baby chickens arrived as usual, from the Eldorado Hatchery. Just as usual, about a dozen of the chicks were dead on arrival. This could be expected though being shipped in a large, flat cardboard box with small air holes all around. Yet, this was the best way to ship overnight. That same night, a cold snap arrived and the temperature dropped to below freezing. The chicks spent the night in a big box in the kitchen behind the cookstove, where they chirped loudly all night causing Bessie to get up frequently to put more wood on the fire. It just wouldn't do for them to get cold and catch the "pip." That malady often killed baby chicks.

This was not their only source of chickens, however. Bessie encouraged her setting hens all through the spring and summer, adding many additional ones to her flock. These fowl added much meat to her dinner table. The young roosters, being otherwise worthless except to fertilize the eggs for hatching, were fried and eaten or sold. A few choicest ones stayed with the hens for mating purposes. The older hens were culled from the flock and baked or roasted. So, there was a constant turnover with the chickens to keep them healthy and productive. The smaller bantam variety were left pretty much alone. They had their own lifestyle, causing no trouble and not bothering the main flock. The little rooster had brightly colored feathers and could be very aggressive when attacked. The guinea hens were another type of fowl that helped make up the domestic barnyard menagerie. They were a black and white speckled bird with a small, red combed head on a rather long skinny neck. The sounds emitted from their throats were unique and sharp, serving as a warning when strangers approached. Their eggs were stronger tasting and much darker in color than that of the hen, as a reason for most folks to prefer the hen's.

The cold snap that came at the same time as the baby chickens was also at "blackberry winter," a phenomenon which occurred every spring when the blackberry bushes began to bloom. At this time, other berry and fruit trees were undergoing the same process. Apple, peach, cherry, plum and other varieties were all in the early stages of production, thus being affected. This was not at all unusual, but it did hinder the development of the fruit. A freeze coming before or after the blossoms came on hurt the fruit very little, but being in full bloom, it killed the germination. Since this was not unusual, Bessie found no reason to be concern herself. There would still be more than the family could eat.

With the warm weather, the children acquired new life and energy. Other than going to school and doing chores, they had remained indoors most of the winter and were now fit to be tied, so to speak. With the first warm days, the three were outside exploring anew the things they abandoned or forgot a few months before.

The Rawleigh Man began coming by again in his old Ford truck with the roof over the back and curtains on the sides. It always was a wonderful time when he came. They were never quite sure what day it would be, but one of them saw the truck as it turned the corner down on the main road and called the others. Then, standing and waiting impatiently in the yard, they watched as he turned the other corner and came towards them. They gathered around the truck even before it stopped.

Grandma was just as anxious to see him and came out, wiping her hands on the soiled apron. When the man rolled up the curtains, they marveled at the elaborate display of wonderful things. He carried many items that most of the other Rawleigh men didn't carry, figuring that going out so far from a town of any size, he was doing folks a great service, which he was.

Among his wares were spices of all kinds, coffee, tea, salt, lotions, salves, patent medicines, and notions & sundries such as soap and powder and perfume. He also carried a supply of lice powder, flea powder, sheep dip and fly spray, along with root beer and vanilla extract and hard candy, suckers and peppermint sticks. He could've carried more with a larger truck, but reckoned the other salesman touring the countryside could handle such things as sewing material and household items.

The Rawleigh Man did carry something of great importance to many farm women. That was advice and gossip, being a virtual encyclopedia of information, which he passed on to any customer willing to listen.

Grandma learned things from him that never even reached the "party line." She did love a bit of good gossip! Sorting through the articles on the truck, she listened to every word he said, pausing now and then to ask a question about something she may have missed. The children were allowed one piece of candy of their choice and spent some time deciding, as they always did with such an opportunity. Earl Lee picked a Holloway sucker, sometimes called an All Day Sucker, because after licking it several times, he wrapped the paper back around it to save for later.

After buying several items that she needed and placing an order for some he was out of, they carried them into the house. The Rawleigh Man gave each child a stick of peppermint candy free.

One of the first things they did was make a big pitcher of root beer, a favorite drink of all. Grandma had bought the large size bottle of root beer concentrate which would make many pitchers of the finished product if used sparingly, a few drops at a time. She always went out to the deep well for water for this, because it was colder and the cistern water in the house spoiled the taste of the root beer. They spent much time savoring the delicious taste of candy and cold root beer.

Getting their hair cut was a ritual they must endure, every so often. Because of the cold weather Grandma had put it off as long as she could. Now, the time had arrived and she decided to do it while in the notion. She always cut everyone's hair, including Papa and Grandpa. Tenderness not being one of her good points, the men dodged the ordeal until their hair grew down over their collars. With the children though, the time came when she was ready.

Sitting on a chair on the back porch or in the yard under a tree, Grandma pinned a towel around the victim's neck. With the girls, it wasn't so bad. In fact, they rather enjoyed having their hair bobbed. Earl Lee was a different story. The boy begged the girls to go first. The clippers were not needed on them! Grandma went all around the girls heads with the scissors, cutting hair straight around to the length she desired. She went up higher in back, allowing air to get to the neck, thus making it cooler. And the bangs were trimmed in front. All in all, the girls were satisfied.

When it came Earl lee's turn, he could not be found until Grandma and the girls searched the barn. Grandma dragged him by one arm across the yard pleading and yelling. All during the ordeal, he complained and tried to pull away from the clippers. After the hair was cut all around, she used the clippers on the back of his neck. Her hands, not being too steady pressing the grips, she would move and pull them away before the hair was released. Now, there are few things worse than having one's hair cut with a dull set of hand clippers, which made it almost impossible to sit still and not try to jerk away. Grandma became agitated and slapped the boy on the side of the head demanding, "sit still you little devil, this can't hurt that much."

Getting your hair cut by Bessie was a good way to determine the mettle of a man. Hand clippers in her hands was the main reason Papa and Grandpa put off haircuts for as long as possible. They always ended with harsh words.

"Tarnation, woman," Grandpa complained, "What are you trying to do, trying to pull my hair out by the roots? If you are, let me get the pliers and you can pull it all out at once. That'll save a heap of time."

"What's the matter, can't you take a little pain?" Grandma rebuked. "You two are cutting up worse than Er-ly. A little hair pulling never killed nobody."

Grandpa swore and complained, then jerked the towel loose and stormed off across the yard berating all females.

The warm days of spring brought new life and energy to all living things, especially the very young. They searched for ways of using up that extra energy in various ways, except through work, of course. They were quite naturally inclined to lean towards new adventures or, as Grandma described it, mischief.

The three children were seldom left alone, but on occasion it became necessary. Not that they couldn't be trusted to stay out of trouble! They were old enough to take care of themselves, still one never can be sure that something might not happen to them. One of those very rare days, Grandma rode into town with Papa on some sort of business, after instructing the girls on what to do and what not to. Grandpa was out working in the field, leaving the three alone in the house.

The car had hardly turned the first corner when Earl Lee suggested making some candy. It seemed like a good idea to the girls, despite Grandma's orders. Millie felt confident that Helen knew how, since she was older and had helped Grandma make some one time. They would be alone for quite some time and were sure they'd get it made and everything cleaned up before anyone returned. No one would ever know.

Knowing they needed a hot fire, Millie put more wood in the stove while Helen got out the utensils and ingredients needed. Millie soon discovered that her sister didn't really know how to make candy after all. She wasn't sure what kind of ingredients to use or how much. She did, though have a unique mixture of sorts. Millie stirred as Helen added to the kettle.

The fire grew very hot and the candy boiled. Helen liked maple flavoring so, she used that instead of traditional vanilla. Pouring nearly half a bottle of the maple extract into the kettle, it immediately boiled over onto the stove. The stove was so hot, the candy caught fire, spreading over the entire surface. Jumping back out of the way, they could only watch helplessly as it burned itself out. The kitchen filled with smoke and the maple extract smell would linger in the house for many days to come. Even emptying the candy out and opening all the doors and windows and washing everything connected with the project, didn't help. Nothing they did could possibly prevent grandma or anyone else entering the house, or from finding out about it. And, as expected she was furious.

Another day they were left alone with threats of severe punishment if they tried to make candy again, or cook or bake anything at all. They solemnly promised!

After awhile they thought it might be nice to do something for Grandma, to make up for all the trouble they caused before. Earl Lee suggested painting the kitchen and the girls readily agreed it was a good idea. But, they only had time for the doors and window frames.

266

Searching around in the shed they found just what they wanted. With very little to choose from, they selected a can of bright green enamel, not knowing that enamel didn't dry in damp weather.

Armed with a can of enamel and the good brushes, they went to work.

Some time later, Grandma came home. She stood aghast, in the doorway. "My stars and garters," she exclaimed, staring at her kitchen. The once white doors and window frames were now a bright, streaked green. Splotches of green dripping all but covered the floor beneath the doors and the window panes had green reaching an inch or more out over the glass. "What on earth happened here?"

"We painted the kitchen for you, Aunt Bessie," Earl Lee told her proudly.

Neither girl spoke, knowing by her tone of voice that they were in trouble again.

"I thought I told you to stay out of trouble," Grandma said.

"You only told us not to cook anything, Grandma," Helen said meekly.

"I-Gawd, do I have to tell you everything, don't cook, don't paint, don't burn the house down, don't fall out of a tree, don't do this, don't do that," she scolded. "What won't you young-uns do next."

"We only did it to help you, Grandma. We thought you'd be pleased," offered Millie.

"Well, maybe it won't be too bad, once we get used to it," she relented.

When Papa came in, he just shook his head and went over to the pump and washed his hands. Grandpa was more concerned about his three good paint brushes that were ruined because they were laid back on the shelf without cleaning and of course dried and hardened, never to be used again.

The most significant thing about the project though, the enamel never dried. Staying sticky for weeks thereafter, it attracted flies, mosquitoes and other types of flying insects that landed, never to be released again. It was much like the strips of sticky flypaper hanging from the ceiling. The bad part being, fly paper could be taken down and discarded, where the enamel stayed and continued to build up. Of course, as time went by, the enamel became less adhesive and flies were able to land and fly off again. The dead insects, when dried were able to be wiped off, to a certain extent, but left their telltale signs of having been there.

Shortly after the painting incident, one of much greater proportions occurred. The big Government Deal that should have made Grandpa rich, fell apart and ended in disaster.

The same men came out to see Grandpa. They came after dark of course to avoid being seen. They were not as concerned though, as before. Last autumn, these same men were jubilant and felicitous towards each other. Now, they appeared to be in an argumentative and worried mood.

Entering the kitchen, Mr. Endicott, the banker, looked at everyone as though seeing them for the first time in his life. Millie knew that the men wanted to talk to Grandpa alone, so she went into the other room as before, followed by Helen and Earl Lee. As before, she positioned herself next to the door, leaving it cracked ever so slightly, the better to hear.

They all sat at the table not speaking at first. Then Mr. Endicott got up and began pacing back and forth.

Finally Grandpa said, "Thunderation Marvin, sit down and tell me what's wrong. You're making me nervous. Nothing can be as bad as you look."

Millie could tell that he stopped pacing back and forth, but she didn't know if he sat down or not. When he spoke his voice sounded miserable and hagridden.

"Yes, it is Law," he said, "It's much worse. We're all in deep trouble."

"How do you mean? Is it that big deal you fellers said was a sure thing and would make us a lot of money?" Grandpa wanted to know.

"That's the one." That gruff voice belonged to Olis Crouch, the man who owned the grain elevator. "Some busy body found out about it and reported it to the Federal Government."

"I thought you told me there wasn't anything illegal about it," Grandpa said.

"There wasn't, not really," the banker said quietly. "It's just a matter of miscalculation, that's all."

"Well it seems to me, that it was illegal then," Grandpa rejoined loudly.

"Let's not go off half-cocked, now," Olis Crouch said. "Maybe we can worm our way out of it."

"There's not a chance of that. They've got us cold," Mr. Endicott informed them.

"You're the one got us into this mess Marvin," Earl Shipley blamed him. "You and your schemes to make more money the easy way. I've been doing all right on my own."

"I know," Mr. Endicott admitted. "I'm really sorry, gentlemen. After looking into the matter carefully, I thought it would work out well for all of us."

"I stand to lose everything I have, including my reputation," Mr. Shipley said dismally.

They argued for awhile, blaming each other, then began talking more quietly, so Millie couldn't make out what was being said.

The next morning, grandpa went into town and drew out all of his money from the bank. He took it home and by removing some bricks from the fireplace in the room where he slept, that wasn't being used anyway, found a safe haven for his money by replacing the bricks solidly back. It remained hidden there until autumn when he deposited what was left in the other bank. But, he always kept a substantial amount at home. Millie never learned what the "deal" was, but she did hear what happened to the men involved, including Grandpa.

A couple weeks later, it all came out in the open. Millie was too young at the time to understand fully what happened. Very little news came over the battery powered radio and Grandpa kept listening time to a minimum because most of what came over the contraption was lies. They seldom received a newspaper way out there, because there was nothing in it that they were interested in. Most of their news came by way of mouth, usually over the party line. By the time she was old enough to understand things better, it was all over and done with and mostly forgotten.

She did hear however, that Marvin Endicott, the banker, shot himself. Earl Shipley, the businessman, committed suicide. Earl had lost everything they had and couldn't face the ridicule. Two other men were involved, but she never learned what happened to them. Otis Crouch, the big, gruff man who ran the grain elevator, went to prison for five years. Millie saw him on the street one day after he got out, but didn't recognize him until Grandma pointed him out. He was just a shell of the man he once was with stooped shoulders and thin. The most distinctive feature being his snow white hair. It must have been real bad in prison!

At supper that night, Grandma said, "It's a downright pity, that's what it is. But decent folks oughtn't try to swindle the Federal

Government. They just aren't smart enough. Everybody should stick with what they was learned to do, I always say."

Grandpa went on eating and didn't respond. He appeared to be the only one to come through the ordeal unscathed. It remains unclear, even today, how he came through without a scratch. That is to say, he came through much better than the others at least.

Somehow his name never reached the newspapers or wasn't even connected to the scandal along with the others. Millie theorized, later in life, that the reason must have been because he didn't have access to any of the information or have his name on any of the legal papers. Therefore, as far as the Government was concerned, he wasn't important enough to prosecute. She did learn though, by listening to Grandma and Grandpa talking privately, that he must have paid somebody quite a lot of money to keep him out of it.

The incident was never mentioned again in Millie's presence, so it was forgotten for a long time.

Very little rain fell that summer, a great contrast to the year before, when the Bottoms flooded. The spring rains were far below normal, but substantial enough to get the crops off to a good start. Winter wheat in the low lands was exceptionally good as it came through the winter and started growing early in the spring. Having plenty of moisture then, it grew and developed and by the time the rains slacked off, it had already reached maturity. The drier days and nights helped it to ripen.

Law always used the best seeds, as he did with the other cash crops. And he always planted winter wheat instead of spring or summer. In the old days the seeds were broadcast over the freshly plowed ground, but in these modern times it was put in with a drill to about one and a half or two inches deep. This allowed for more even coverage and better germination. He needed this crop after last year's loss due to high water, when all his wheat was ruined. There had been enough snow the past winter to protect the young tender plants from the cold.

Winter wheat was best for him also, to get the best price. Another reason he preferred it over the other varieties, he could get his oats and corn planted and then have the corn laid by and growing while the wheat was being harvested.

Only a few of the larger farmers planted wheat and oats. Mostly, they raised corn, being a good cash and livestock crop. Frank Bledsoe, who lived over near Piopolis, owned the only threshing machine in the area and threshed for all the farmers who raised wheat. In order to be as efficient as possible, he lined up the schedule well ahead of time, starting with the nearest farm and working on down the road.

Checking ahead of time with the farmers that raised wheat to determine just when it would be ready, he planned his schedule accordingly and notified the farmers what day he planned to be there. He kept to his schedule as closely as possible, but after the first couple of dates he often fell behind by a day or two, due to thresher breakdown, weather problems or something else unforeseeable. Nevertheless, once the word went out, one had to be ready or lose his place in the schedule. Then he had to wait until the end of the season after all the others were finished and be serviced on the return trip. There could be no waiting around for a delinquent farmer, putting the others at risk.

Once word arrived when the thresher would be there, there was much hustle and bustle as preparations were made.

For Millie and Helen, this was another of their favorite times of the year. The air filled with such excitement that only a child could imagine. Because there had been no wheat harvest the previous year, Earl Lee could barely remember two years ago. He asked lots of questions about the event and most of the answers he received from the girls were highly exaggerated, partly because their memories were dimmed or because their imaginations had grown. Whatever the reasons, he soon became as excited as they.

As the big day approached, the excitement grew, at least for the children. For the grown-ups, it meant more work! After supper, the family sat and talked about what had been done and what still needed to be done. Millie listened attentively, not so much out of interest or curiosity as just being aware of things going on around her.

Grandpa seemed to be mad at Papa over something not done right. Papa sat quietly, not answering. When Grandpa kept calling him Boy, she could see it upset him. Why did he call him Boy all the time, when he had a name, she wondered!

Poor Papa! He always looked so sad, especially when he took his watch out to see the time, as he did now. He'd stare at it a long time with a far away look in his eyes. She knew he was thinking of Mama. She had given him that watch a long time ago. It was the only Klicker watch she'd ever seen and it kept real good time. He made a shoelace chain for it and kept it in his overalls pocket. He always looked at it when he felt blue. He must miss her terribly.

Millie missed her mother too, but not like Papa did. She had Papa and Grandma and Grandpa and Helen and of course Earl Lee.

Papa seemed to have no one. He hadn't been happy since Mama left. Maybe he should get another wife! No! Millie wouldn't like that. Maybe they could all move back down to the other house, just she and Helen and Papa! But, of course they were to young to cook and handle all the chores and take care of Papa. Maybe she could talk him into moving back there and hire a housekeeper and then she and Helen could help her. She'd miss Earl Lee, but he'd probably be there all the time anyway pestering them. And she'd miss Grandma and Grandpa too!

She would just have to think of something else. Why did life have to be so complicated!

Looking at Papa now, she realized she hadn't really noticed him for a long time. As he sat there in the fading light, he seemed much older than before. His head was nearly bald. That was nothing new though, he had been that way for as long as she could remember. She just hadn't paid much attention to his baldness before. But, that's the main reason he always wore a cap. He hated bald people! He said it made them look old. He had never been vain about his looks, not really, but when he went to town or someplace, he always wore clean clothes and carried sen-sen's in his pocket. If he thought someone might come close, he put three or four of the little black things in his mouth to cover up bad breath.

Suddenly feeling a surge of pity for him, she went over and stood beside him. Laying her head on his shoulder and he put an arm around her waist. He was never one to display any sort of emotion, but she knew that he loved his two girls.

Millie watched as he got up and went to his room. He hated that room, she could tell! It was hot there in the summer, with very little ventilation or cool air blowing through the open window. She guessed there were plenty of mosquitoes too, since the window had no screen on it. It was just as uncomfortable there in the winter as in the summer, because the room had no stove or heat. So, it had to be terribly cold, because the water bucket froze over in the kitchen, and it was much warmer there. He left his socks on and slept under a mound of cover.

Her thoughts were interrupted by Grandma's voice. "All right girls, it's time to get to bed."

At last the big day arrived. According to Grandpa they were ready for Frank Bledsoe and his big machine. The wheat had been cut, tied in bundles and stacked in shocks all over the field. It presented a pretty sight, like Indian wigwams in rows as far as the eye could see, all brown and golden in colors. Only the short stubble remained where the tall wheat heads blew, only a few days earlier, like waves of water in a gentle breeze. There were barrels of water near, where the threshing machine would be parked, just in case of a fire. Wagons had been checked over to make sure they were ready and the wheels removed and greased. New linch pins were put in two wheels to replace old ones that were worn, to keep the wheels from coming off. They couldn't afford a break-down in the middle of the day. Then the wagons were backed into the pond so the spokes could expand in the water and not come apart.

Grandma was just as busy with her work as the men were with theirs. Though she couldn't cook up much ahead, there was still plenty to do. It would be nice to do a lot of cooking ahead of time, but it would spoil. Cooked food just didn't keep long in this hot weather. Sometimes, even beans spoiled between meals! But, she did bake bread. Even this would only last through the first day. The next day, she would make cornbread and biscuits.

It became Millie's and Helen's lot to make the butter. Grandma had been saving cream from the milk for days and hanging it in the well to stay fresh. Since the dasher in the big churn was broken and hadn't been replaced yet, the girls made butter in half gallon fruit jars. Filling the jars half full of cream and screwing the lids on tight, they began shaking it back and forth. It was great fun at first as they laughed and lifted the jars over their heads and danced around, displaying different ways to shake them.

Grandma scolded, "Stop that prancing around, before you drop them jars and break them. I've got enough to do besides cleaning up a mess of broken glass and butter."

It soon became a tedious chore as little arms grew tired. Earl Lee tried it once, but soon handed the jar back to its owner.

As butter began to form, they kept asking Grandma if it was ready yet, only to be advised that it required much more churning.

When the first batch was completed, grandma pressed it into a butter mold and refilled each jar, until all the cream was used. After each batch, the finished product was placed into a covered bucket and lowered into the deep well, via a long rope, where it would stay fresh. After each meal, the balance went back into the well, otherwise it soon became rancid and spoiled.

CHAPTER 10

The thresher arrived late in the afternoon. He finished up threshing at the Gaines farm and moved on to the next job, which happened to be the Reynolds farm, immediately so as to be ready to start early the next morning.

It could be heard over on the main road and smoke rose up over the treetops, in the distance. The three children and the dog ran excitedly over to the corner crossroad to watch as it made the turn and headed straight in their direction. Moving ever so slowly, it had to slow even more to get around the corner and make the turn onto the long lane. The gathering of young boys and dogs, who had been running along beside it, since Blairsville, turned here and walked back home.

It seemed to take an eternity, chugging along, but always closer and closer to its destination. It kicked up a heavy blanket of road dust in its wake and thick, black smoke billowed forth from the tall smokestack. The monstrous machine reminded Millie of the passenger train arriving at the depot in Zachery.

As it drew nearer, they began shouting and the dog barking. Mr. Bledsoe waved to them from his perch on the side of the machine and they had no trouble keeping up as it lumbered along.

Driving just beyond the nearly dry pond, he stopped, letting the engine idle. The children walked around it, staring in awe. Earl Lee's eyes widened and he began asking questions concerning what made it run and how it separated the wheat from the stalks and how everything worked. After the initial acknowledgements, Frank Bledsoe tried to ignore them, being accustomed to children asking the same questions at every stop. He did warn them about getting too close to moving parts and then went about the business of checking over the thresher to insure everything being in working order the next morning.

Grandpa and Papa came out to greet him and discuss the operation for tomorrow.

Mr. Bledsoe came in, just as it began getting dark, to eat his supper, feeling satisfied that everything was in order. First, he stopped at the pump, the one just inside the barn lot and stripped off his shirt. His skin was a dark, deep brown where it had been exposed to the sun. The part of his upper torso covered by his shirt, remained very white in contrast. The children stood by, watching as he sloshed the cool water up over his head and body with one hand, stopping now and then to apply the bar of strong soap and work up a good lather. Then he sloshed more water from the tub over his long, lean body to rinse off the soap and accumulated grime. The children stared at the procedure, fascinated by what they saw. What amazed them most perhaps, was the fact he did all of this with only one hand. His left hand and part of the arm had been pulled off several years earlier in a freak machinery accident. His hand had become caught between two rollers and in order to prevent his entire body from following, two fellow workers grabbed him and held on, pulling against the rollers. When he was at last freed, his arm had come off at the elbow. But, he was grateful his life had been sparred. He had stopped mourning the loss long ago. He could still do the work of most men with two hands, and he gave little thought to the stub and how it might affect some people.

The children sat watching, enthralled as he ate his supper, talking all the while. There were many interesting stories to tell, mostly about the old days when threshing machines were transported from place to place by teams of horses. Back even before his time, wheat was cut by men with hand scythes and the fuel used to run the machines was the straw from the harvest.

Presently, another man came in and sat down at the table and Grandma brought him a plate of food. He was Mr. Bledsoe's oldest boy who drove the somewhat dilapidated truck for his father during the harvest season. In the truck they carried supplies and extra parts and tools and of course, coal for the threshing machine. After finishing the last job he had gone back home for a fresh supply of coal, where they had a large amount stored.

Father and son slept near the machine under a lean-to tarpaulin, out of the falling dew. Taking turns at waking during the night and stoking the fire, they kept up a good head of steam for the following morning. If the fire was permitted to go out, precious time could be lost before they could start up, waiting on the boiler.

They were all so excited that Millie felt sure that she wouldn't sleep a wink that night, in anticipation of actually watching them thresh the next morning. After talking for a while in bed, Helen went to sleep, leaving Millie with her own thoughts. The alarm clock ticked loudly on the dresser. Intermittent chirping sounds of crickets filled the night air along with the shrill noise of the katy-did. A whippoorwill called to its mate somewhere off in the distance. The big owl that stayed close to the other house at night could be heard making its plaintive cry and was soon answered from Cox's Woods, farther down the road. Added to these familiar sounds came Grandpa's snoring in the other room. Above all the friendly sounds she had known all her life, another had made its presence felt. That of the threshing machine, chugging along in its idle position could be heard above all the other sounds. They were all nice pleasant, soothing noises, all except the mosquitoes that came in through the open window, causing her some consternation. But, even this didn't spoil the drowsiness that soon overcame her and she fell asleep, dreaming dreams of the young and innocent.

Noises in the kitchen woke her the next morning. Punching Helen, they quickly rolled out of bed and dressed. Grandma was taking a big pan of biscuits out of the oven, and the men seated around the table were already beginning to eat the hearty meal set before them. Mr. Bledsoe and his boy ate all their meals with the people they threshed for. Millie was surprised that even Earl Lee sat there with the men. He never got up without being prodded!

As soon as the men finished eating, they went outside, with the children following. Grandma called them back.

"Here, you two girls get back here and eat your breakfast," she ordered.

"We're not hungry," Helen said.

"Makes no difference. You sit right down and eat."

"But, we want to watch them thresh," Millie said.

"You'll have plenty time for that, that contraption will be here all day. And tomorrow too," Grandma told them. "I-Gawd, if I didn't keep an eye on you two, you wouldn't eat a bite. Now, sit right down here and eat." Setting a plate of food before each of them, they began cramming it into their mouths. "Don't eat so fast, you'll end up with the belly-ache," she scolded.

Outside, it was a bee-hive of activity. About half a dozen men, along with their teams and wagons came to work in the field, besides the two regular hired men. Three of these men were ones who raised wheat themselves and who Law and Leonard had helped with their threshing. Now, they were returning the favor by helping them. The other three were hired by Law.

By the time the girls were outside, Earl Lee was already next to the thresher watching the operator's every move. Wagons rolled out across the field among the shocks of wheat, stopping at each one. They had been tied into small bundles previously with a binder, making it easier to pick up and handle.

They watched in amazement when the first wagon load came in and stopped beside the machine. Cousin Reuben was there waiting. It became his job to unload the wagons and feed the stalks into the hopper. With a single stroke, he cut the binder twine around each bundle with a razor sharp knife as he picked it up and tossed it into the big container, all in one motion. Each time a bundle entered, there came a slight surge of power from the engine as it was caught up. The black machine belched up even blacker smoke through the tall smokestack.

The one thing everyone was warned to stay completely away from was the main belt. About six inches in width, it wrapped around the big wheel on the side of the thresher and ran the entire length to the smaller fly-wheel on the other end. Being too long to draw up tight, it flopped erratically. This is what turned the gears and made the machine work. The gears forced the grain from the ear and separated it from the chaff, removing weed seeds and thistle and trash, while holding up the grain with screens.

Sitting on his perch on the side of the machine, Mr. Bledsoe controlled the entire operation through the hand levers beside him.

A long pipe, much like the stovepipe in the house, extended out of one side, through which flowed the harvested grain and into a waiting truck. On the opposite side, in a similar pipe, the straw was blown out, forming a stack that continued to grow with each load.

Papa's truck had been converted into a high stake body vehicle, lined on the inside with tin and canvas to prevent the small grain from seeping through. Millie didn't know the men driving the other truck. As soon as a truck was loaded, it left for the grain elevator in Springhill, since it was the closest one around.

Growing weary of this activity after awhile, the three wandered back to the house. Four other women had arrived to help Grandma with the cooking and cleaning up after meals. Three were wives of men working in the harvest. The other woman caught Millie's attention. Recognizing her as Earl Lee's mother, she stopped and stared at her. She appeared to be about the same size as Mama, rather buxom, wearing rouge on her cheeks. Grandma would say, too much rouge, it made her look like a hussy, but Millie thought that she was rather pretty and looked nice. Her brown hair was in little curls and her skin seemed too pale for this time of year, as though she hadn't been outside a whole lot. The print dress she wore seemed too tight, even to Millie, accentuating the outline of her well developed body. But, it was too short, just about knee length and she wore no shoes. Millie had only seen her once or twice before and she liked her. She always seemed so friendly and happy, exuberant, some said.

Onetime, Grandma said that Gertrude, or Gertie, as most called her, was born in an old cabin down in Cox's woods. Uncle Sidney and Aunt Lottie lived there a long time ago. That was even before Cox's lived there, so it couldn't have been Cox's Woods then. Millie wondered what it was called before that. She shuddered just thinking about living in such a place.

Staring at her cousin Gertie, Millie remembered something that might be the reason she was pale looking.

Grandma believed in an old adage that little boys and girls should be seen and not heard. Another one that certainly applied to Millie said that some little girls have big ears. She did have inquiring ears and listened to everything of interest to her.

One day, she overheard Papa and Reuben talking in the barn. Reuben told Papa a dark secret about his sister that puzzled Millie, but also interested her tremendously. She scrunched down as low as possible among the barrels to avoid being seen.

Reuben told Papa that Gertrude had been working as a housekeeper for a family over around St. Louis for the past year. She planned to come home before long though and stay for awhile.

When Papa asked if something was wrong, Reuben hesitated and then told him, because they always confided in each other.

"She got herself in a family way again," Reuben said.

Papa whistled softly through his teeth, "What's going to happen now?"

"It's already happened," Reuben told him. "She had a baby boy."

"Will she keep it?" Papa asked.

"No, she already gave it up, I don't know who to."

"Who was the father?"

"In the letter that Ma got from her, she said she thought it was the man of the family she worked for."

"That's too bad," Papa said.

The two walked outside still talking and Millie heard no more, but it was enough to really arouse her interest and she thought about it a lot. She never told anyone about what she had overheard, not even Helen, whom she shared most things with. It stayed her very own private secret.

That took place about two months ago but she had only been home a few days, so that's probably the reason Gertrude wasn't as brown as everyone else.

Earl Lee came running up beside Millie, but stopped in his tracks when he saw his mother. He turned around and would have run away. She saw him and squealed, coming towards him with out-stretched arms.

Gathering him up in her arms, she hugged him tightly for a moment then pushed him out to arms length.

"My, how you've growed," she exclaimed. "I wouldn't've knowed you if you was somewhere's else. You've done a real good job on my boy, Aunt Bessie," she exhorted loudly, half turning to see her aunt.

Grandma grunted something in reply.

Earl Lee, embarrassed, tried to pull free of her grasp.

"Wait a minute hon, look I brought you something, all the way from St. Louie," she said, and digging down in her apron pocket, she brought forth a jack-knife. "Look, it has all these little things on it that boys like. I knew you'd be pleased."

He took it as she watched him anxiously smiling. He walked away, looking at the knife and feeling it in his hands, without thanking her. Millie almost felt sorry for Gertrude, at the pained look on her face, but knew she shouldn't. She was not Earl Lee's mother and never would be. She only gave birth to him! Grandma was the only mother he would ever know. He didn't even know his real mother, not any more than the two girls did. They always saw her at the same time as he so, they meant more to him than Gertrude did! Millie had never heard him call her Mama, or anything else for that matter. He simply ignored her completely when she came around.

Just before noon, Grandma told Helen to go out and ring the dinner bell. It could be heard clear out as far as the men were working and beyond. Each man finished loading his wagon and came in. The teams were fed a little hay and watered and left standing in the shade of a tree in the nearby grove.

Each man stopped at the big stock watering tank that the girls and Earl Lee had cleaned out and filled with clean water the day before.

Dinner was never served, not in the finer sense of the word. Bessie and the other ladies cooked mounds of food and sat it on the table and the hungry men devoured it in quick fashion.

Very little breeze flowed through the big dining room, though all the windows and doors in the house were open. Heat from the cook stove in the adjoining kitchen only added to the discomfort of all present. New fly paper had been hung from the ceiling that very morning and dozens of the little black pests already had discovered the sticky substance.

Most of the conversation, what little there was, centered around the heat, the weather and crops, with some bantering back and forth between the younger men.

Men folk always ate first, filling all the spaces around the long table, while the women kept the dishes full of food. They, and the three children would eat afterwards and then clean up.

Millie kept a watchful eye on Gertrude. She proved to be a good worker, fast and very proficient, while waiting on the table. She picked up two empty dishes at the same time and hurrying into the kitchen, returned almost immediately with them filled. She was not averse to rubbing up against a man's shoulder or bending low over the table when setting down a dish or plate of meat, however. Grandpa noticed this too and scowled at her, but she paid no heed and laughed a lot, working joyously. The men seemed to enjoy her presence.

She paid special attention to a man named Carl Mathews. He was one of the men Grandpa hired to help out. Millie noticed him as he came in the house, How he hesitated and grinned when he first saw Gertrude. Also, the way she grinned at him, like they knew each other. Right away, Millie became interested, thinking they would bear watching.

After dinner, the men went outside to lay in the shade for a chew of tobacco or smoke or just to rest a bit before going back to work.

Before long, Gertrude wandered out, with the pretext of getting some fresh air. She walked around to the side of the house, after letting herself be seen, fanning her face with her apron. Every now and then, she raised up her dress a little, fluffing it around her legs and blowing down the front of her dress to cool her ample bosom. The display proved to be quite effective, if it was done for a reason and Millie felt that it had been.

Carl Mathews, who had been lying on the ground watching the back porch, got to his feet and sauntered over that way. Millie, who was watching through the window, quickly ran into a room on the other side of the house. Getting down on her hands and knees, she waited by the open window. Hearing them come alongside the house, she exercised caution so as not to be seen or heard.

"You sure look good, Gertie," she heard Carl say. "You ain't changed a bit."

Gertrude giggled. "Yes, I have. I've changed a lot. You just haven't looked close enough to see it. I'm older!"

"We all are," Carl said. "But, I mean it, I think you're even prettier than you were before. I couldn't believe my eyes when I saw you in the house awhile ago. I didn't even know you were back. How long you been back?"

"Only a few days. I hoped I'd see you."

"I'm glad you did. I heard you was in St. Louis or someplace over there. How long are you going to be here? Are you back home to stay?"

"For a little while, I guess," Gertrude replied. "I'm sorta between jobs and thought I'd come visit the folks. I don't know how long I'll stay. Are you married?"

"Yeah, I married Molly Pierce. You remember her! She's the one you had that big fight with that time."

"You don't say! Yeah, I remember her. She's the girl I used to call Skinny Bones all the time. I think that's why we had that fight. How could you ever marry somebody like her!"

"She's not so bad once you get to know her," Carl defended. "We get along pretty good."

"Well, to each his own."

"Hey Gertie, remember the things we used to do together?"

"Yeah, we did have fun, didn't we!"

"Remember the time we went skinny-dipping in that deep hole down there in the Big Ditch? We heard Reuben coming and we grabbed our clothes and hid in the bushes. And we both got covered in poison ivy!"

"Yeah, that was some fun, wasn't it," Gertrude agreed. They laughed heartily.

"What about the time we got lost in the woods and had to spend the night under a makeshift shelter!"

"I don't think you was really lost. I think you just acted like you was so we could spend the night out there together. I don't think our folks even missed us."

"It was worth it though, wasn't it?"

She conceded that it was.

When grandpa called that it was time to get back to work, Millie wished he had waited a while longer. She enjoyed this interesting conversation.

Then she heard Carl say, "I'll tell you what Gertie, after a while how about meeting me in the barn-loft, so we can 'frolic in the hay' like we used to. I'll find a good reason to go get something from the barn."

Gertrude giggled. "Maybe," she said.

As they left, Millie decided to keep an eye on her cousin that afternoon. She didn't hear Grandpa and Uncle Sidney talking before going back to work.

"I'm telling you Sid, you better keep an eye on that oldest girl of yours," Grandpa warned. "She's fixing to get herself knocked up again."

"I know that Law, but you know how she is. Did you ever lock up a dog in heat! There's nothing you can do to keep other dogs away from her," Sidney answered. "Gert seems to stay in heat all the time."

Millie saw Gertrude looking out at the barn occasionally that afternoon, but Carl never came near. It seems that Grandpa had ideas of his own. Each time Carl made out like he wanted something from the barn, Grandpa yelled at him to do something else. He hired him and figured he had a right to give orders. Millie thought it was just as well. After all, why in the world would two grown up people want to play in the hayloft in this hot weather! It was enough to give a person a heat stroke.

The men worked in the field until dark and then went home to sleep and rest for a few hours. All that is except Frank Bledsoe and his boy, who slept by the threshing machine to keep the steam up.

Work resumed just after daylight the following morning. One of the women failed to show up to help Grandma, sending word by her husband that she felt poorly and wouldn't be much help. About mid-morning Vesta Kincaid came down to help out, not knowing they were short handed. Being a welcome sight, Grandma greeted her with some enthusiasm.

"I-Gawd Vesta, but you're a sight for sore eyes," she exclaimed.

"I didn't have nothing else to do so, I thought I'd come down and give you a hand don't you know," Vesta said, wiping her forehead with her apron.

Millie knew that she wanted to get away from her own home and be around company, more than plain helping out. She had more work to do at her house than she could ever get done if she worked steady day and night. That didn't bother her though. She'd just let that work go, she did any way. Her main concern was to be with other women and talking and hearing gossip, because there was seldom any visitors at her house. She was a willing worker and she and Grandma got along well together. She'd take orders from Grandma and do whatever she was told.

Shortly before noon a commotion occurred out by the threshing machine. Men were yelling and then the thresher stopped, for the first time since arriving two nights ago. The sudden quiet was very noticeable and the women gathered on the back porch and then out in the yard to see what had happened. Of course the three children ran to the gathering of men by the black machine.

Grandpa told them to stay back out of the way but, they could see the man rolling on the ground, yelling in pain. They moved back only as far as they had to, watching the man and his antics.

"What happened?" Earl Lee kept asking, trying to press closer.

"For crying out loud, Er-ly, how do I know. We just got here the same time as you," Helen told him. "But, it looks like that man got hurt."

Millie recognized 'that man' as Carl Mathews, the one who she overheard talking to Gertrude yesterday. She saw the blood all over his head and his shirt half torn off. He must be hurt pretty bad because he kept yelling. The five men who were present gathered around, looking down at him in sympathy.

Grandpa straightened up and looking around said, "Where's Leonard? We'd best get this feller to a doctor."

"He just left with a load," Reuben told him. "He won't be back for quite a spell."

"That boy is never around when you need him," Grandpa grumbled. "Well we can't leave Carl lay here and die. Reuben, go to the house and get Leonard's car and take him to town to the doctor."

Reuben hurried away and came back in a few minutes driving Papa's car. He also had a large piece of a blanket, which he wrapped around Carl's head. Reuben and the Bledsoe boy picked him up and loaded him into the back of the car stretched out on the back seat groaning and carrying on. Once he reached the crossroads, Reuben pulled back the throttle and drove to town as fast as the car would go. Grandpa watched the car fogging up the dust on the road, probably traveling faster than it ever had before. Then he turned to face Frank Bledsoe.

"Now that's out of the way, what in Tarnation happened?" he demanded.

"The belt broke," Frank answered.

"I can see that! But why did it break?"

"I'm not sure yet. It shouldn't have though because it's fairly new." He laid the belt out on the ground and looked it over carefully. "Look, it didn't break, the belt connections came loose." He held it up for Law to see. "He was standing too close. I told him not to get too close. I always tell people not to stand so close but, sometimes they just don't listen. When that long belt comes off the drums or breaks, it lashes out like a bullwhip and tears up anything in its path. It wasn't my fault he stood too close."

"I know that Frank," Grandpa said. "How long will it take to fix it and get back running again?"

"Only a few minutes. We wasn't shut down long enough for the boiler to cool down. We'll start up and be building up steam again while we repair it."

Telling his son to start up again, he began digging around in the big toolbox for the right tools and the alligator belt lacing.

Other wagons came in one by one with their loads and each driver had to be told what happened. The three children were kept at a distance but, remained close enough to see all that transpired.

The big belt was long enough that it had sufficient slack in it to allow Frank Bledsoe to cut off an inch or so from each end. Then he placed a piece of the sharp toothed metal lacing over the end and clamped it shut with a special tool made for that purpose. While he held the two ends together, one end tucked under his arm stub, with the lacing interlocked, his son inserted the small steel rod through it binding it together thus making a long endless belt again.

Placing the belt around the small, flat-faced wheel first, they then proceeded to wrap it on the big wheel. Starting it over the top and holding it firm, the boy began turning the wheel by hand until it went all the way around. He continued turning the wheel slowly, making sure it stayed on. With everyone back out of reach, the thresher pulled back on the gear lever and the wheels lurched into gear, churning the big belt round and round. It was much tighter than before, having lost a couple inches of its length. Black smoke bellowed from the tall stack, the boiler had a full head of steam and they were ready to go.

When Gertrude heard who got hurt, she said, "Oh, that poor man. I hope he ain't hurt bad."

At the dinner table, not much was said about the accident except to wonder how bad he was hurt. Such things were more commonplace or less accepted on the farm!

Mr. Collins, who raised a lot of wheat up on the high ground, remarked, "Law, I was over at Mill Town one day and heard about that Cain feller you folks in the bottoms are concerned about,"

This caught the attention of everyone.

"Yeah, what did you hear?" Grandpa asked.

"Well I guess not a whole lot, I reckon," Mr. Collins answered, "Except the folks at the feed store there seem to know him. They say he comes in about three or four times a year with hides and things to sell. He always has that dog with him, calls it Riker! They say he could be mean if anything crossed him. None of the other dogs will go near him. Just growl and keep their distance. This Cain always carries that rifle with him, like an old time backwoodsman. Probably one of the best rifle shots around. He's not real friendly but, never bothers anybody and minds his own business. He trades his hides and buys what he needs and leaves.

"One old timer says he remembers Cain's old man. He used to go to town there and bring the boy with him. Lived pretty much the same way. He reckons the old man must've died several years ago because, he just quit coming in. Too bad about people like that, never having any friends or any thing else they can call their own."

"Oh, I don't know about that," Grandpa reflected. "He's got his dog and his cabin and rifle and the whole bottoms is his to hunt and fish in, if he's left alone. He may have it all over us civilized folks who work all our danged lives trying to get more. When we die, we don't have a piddling thing more than he does we can take with us."

"I didn't know you to be a philosopher, Law," said Mr. Collins. "But, you may be right at that. No need to feel sorry for that man.

Though I do like having a little more than he does. A man grows accustomed to some of the better things in life."

When Reuben returned from town, he went straight to Law and made his report.

"I took Carl home, Uncle Lawrence," he told him.

"How bad was he hurt?"

"Pretty bad, the Doc says. He won't be working for awhile," Reuben said. "That belt really banged him up some. The Doc said that one laceration alone on the side of his head could've killed him. Laid the hide open all the way down the side of the head. Took twenty-seven stitches to sew him up. And it dislocated his shoulder. He's bound up tighter than a drum now, won't be able to move that arm for quite a spell. There's bruises all over the top half of his body. Lord, Uncle Lawrence, who'd have thought that old belt could do that to a man!"

That night at supper, left-overs from dinner were eaten, as usual. Sitting around the table, with full stomachs, the men talked for awhile before retiring to their respective beds. Frank Bledsoe pulled the blackened corn-cob pipe from his pocket and held it up, to ask Bessie if smoking was permitted. She nodded her approval so, he filled the pipe with Bull Durham from the pouch. The three children watched him, fascinated at the way he went about this task. Holding the pipe in his hand, he filled it with the same hand holding the tobacco sack. Very little being spilled, he placed the pipe on the table while drawing the string of the sack tight with his teeth and stuck it back in his pocket. Picking up the pipe, he tamped the tobacco down with a fore-finger and struck a match along the side of his leg. Puffing vigorously, clouds of flame smoke and the smell of sulfur filled the air. Settling back as a contented man sometimes does, he sucked a great amount of smoke into his mouth and slowly blew it towards the ceiling with smoke ring following smoke ring.

"You know, that young feller is a lucky man," he observed.

"Do you mean Carl Mathews?" Leonard asked.

"Yep! He's mighty lucky!"

"I don't see how you could call him lucky," Leonard disagreed. "He could've got killed."

"That's what I mean. Could've but didn't. Now, I call that plain lucky. Why, I've seen lots worse than that lots of times. I recollect one time over in White County when one of them belts came off and caught hold of a man standing too close. It came off with such force, it wrapped around him and flopped him up and down like a chicken when you wring its neck. It flopped him all over that field before it finally wound down. Broke every bone in his body. Now, he wasn't so lucky!"

He eyed the three children sitting entranced around the table, obviously taking in every word he said and enjoying it. His usually sober eyes twinkled as he blew smoke across the table at Earl Lee. The boy coughed.

He warmed up to his subject and his young audience and after looking at the ceiling and reflecting for a moment, he began talking again. Realizing he was the center of attention, he paused effectively every now and then, to keep the interest up.

"I recollect another time the feller wasn't so lucky. Or maybe he was, depending on how you look at it," he said. "I was out in Nebraska at the time, just a lad of a boy I was. They raise lots of wheat out there you know and have bigger machines than we do around here."

"Bigger than yours?" Earl Lee asked wide-eyed.

"Lots bigger," said Mr. Bledsoe. "Why some of them threshers are as big as a locomotive. They'd make two of that little one of mine."

"Gosh, I never saw a threshing machine bigger than yours," Earl Lee said. "They must really be something."

"Yep, they are that, boy."

"Tell us about that man, Mr. Bledsoe," urged Earl Lee. "You know, the one you said wasn't so lucky maybe!"

"Well it happened like this," Mr. Bledsoe said as everyone listened quietly. "There was this big field of wheat. You could see it blowing in the wind, for miles, rippling out across the plains like a sea of water. It made a pretty sight, them golden stalks swaying gently to and fro. They had two of these big threshers, one on the east side of the field and one on the west side, so the wagons could go to either machine without having to travel so far. I was working as a helper, on the east side, learning the trade.

"Our machine was sitting on the side of a little hill and we could see all over. Well, they didn't have any of them fancy mowing machines and binders like we have now. Instead, there was a long row of men stretched out clear across the field with old-fashioned scythes cutting a swath as they walked along. Behind them came another row of men with old-fashioned hand rakes. They raked up the grain, tied it in bundles and stacked them in shocks."

He paused here a moment to stoke his pipe, mostly for effect.

"A little bit later, they went back with wagons and gathered up the shocks and took it all over to the threshing machine," he continued.

287

"They moved the machines each day so's to keep close to the shocks, so the wagons wouldn't have to travel so far. Just like we do now. Well, the young feller, they called him Jeffy, he kept messing around the machine, trying to get it to running faster. The man who owned it kept telling him to stay away before he caused it to explode or something. You know, they're only made to run so fast! He didn't pay any attention, though.

"They never did find out for sure just how it happened but, somehow that big belt jumped off the drums. Jeffy just happened to be standing there when it flew off.

"Well, you see, if they'd had enough belt dressing on that belt like they should've had, it likely wouldn't come off that way. Being sticky, it helps give the belt traction to pull better, as well as helping to hold it on them shiny, slick drums. They figured that Jeffy had the machine running just a little bit faster than it should and that's what made it come off. It hit poor Jeffy sideways and cut his head clean off. Clean as a whistle!"

The girls and Earl Lee drew deep breaths of awe, waiting for what would come next. He paused again, for an agonizingly long time before continuing.

"Well sir, that head rolled right down the hill there. Strangest sight you ever did see, bouncing along, not attached to any body." He paused again, "Just as strange though, was ol Jeffy jumping around, minus his head. If you ever seen a man dancing around without his head, you'd know what I mean. Yes sir, I never seen anything like it before or since."

Earl Lee closed his mouth and asked anxiously, "What happened to him Mr. Bledsoe? Did he die?"

"No sir, that's another strange thing about it," Mr. Bledsoe said. "While he was dancing around, the man who owned the thresher had presence of mind enough to run down the hill and retrieve that head. He brought it back and two of the men held Jeffy as tight as they could. With him jumping around the way he was though, they couldn't see what they was doing. The main thing they wanted was to get his head back on as fast as possible.

"Now the owner of the thresher always carried a bucket of glue along with him. You never knew when something might break and if you didn't have a bolt to fix it, you just put this glue on it. It was really better than a bolt anyway because, once it dried, nothing could break it loose.

"They spread a lot of this glue on his neck stub and slapped his head back on. Then they put a gunnysack over his head to hold it in place until it dried. After awhile they took the sack off and saw they had put his head on backwards. Now, that was one of the strangest sights I ever seen."

The children sat in wonder.

"What did they do?" Earl Lee asked. "Did they turn it back around?"

"Nope! That's the sad part," Mr. Bledsoe said sympathetically. "You see, that glue had already dried and once it dries it don't come loose. He was stuck with it."

"What happened to him?" Earl Lee wanted to know.

"Well sir, he just had to get used to it," Mr. Bledsoe lamented. "He learned to walk backwards. Of course, he couldn't walk very fast that way, not at first that is. After awhile though, he got around pretty good. Oh, he could walk forward, the way he used to walk but, kept stumbling over things because he couldn't see, going that direction.

"Some of the men said maybe he ought to go to a hospital to see about getting his head turned around, after the harvesting was over. But, by then he got used to having it that way and kinda' liked it. He said he liked seeing where he'd been because he already knew where he was going. Besides, nobody could sneak up on him from behind this way, either. He learned to walk pretty fast going backwards."

When he stopped talking, Earl Lee asked, "What happened to him?"

"Last I heard, he had his own machine and was going around threshing for people. Doing pretty good, I hear. All the wheat farmers wanted to hire him because he had become a real oddity and was famous all over Nebraska."

Law loudly went harumph! "Dangest lie I ever heard," he mumbled.

Leonard grinned broadly at the expression on the children's faces.

Bessie said, "Frank Bledsoe, that's the biggest whopper I heard in a coon's age. I-Gawd, you nearly had me believing you."

The thresher got to his feet and started to the door, smiling. "Come on, boy," he said to his son, "It's time we hit the hay."

The threshing ended about noon the next day. Frank Bledsoe and his machine moved away, to the next farm, leaving behind many pleasant memories with three wide eyed, impressionable children. They stayed around close while the machine was prepared for moving, regretting its departure for another whole year. They followed along behind as far as the crossroads, then watched it chugging along, puffing up smoke and dust between the trees on each side, until it reached the main road and made the turn east.

During the following day, much of the straw from the big stack was used. It found its way into the garden, around plants as mulch and scattered over the floors of sheds and chicken houses, making excellent litter. And it served as bedding in the barns for cows and horses. Mixed with the manure, it provided some of the very best fertilizer, high in protein and nutrients, which was spread over the gardens and fields. This would be used all through the year, until the next harvest.

Perhaps the most significant and important aspect of this commodity was the fact that the entire family received new mattresses for their beds. This was another thing that Millie and Helen looked forward to.

One morning, Grandma had the girls to help her take the mattresses off all the beds. They emptied the old straw into a pile, out beyond the barnyard, to be burned later or spread over the garden as desired. The covers were as large cloth bags and once filled, called straw ticks. The origin of the name has been lost in folklore but believed to have come about because ticks were sometimes found in the straw, which certainly is possible.

The ticks were stuffed with straw as tightly as possible and the opening sewn shut with string, laced back and forth. The result was a very thick, pliable mattress that one sank down into. The first few nights were not always pleasant ones, due to the stiff stems sticking through the covering. Also, the inevitable briars that dogmatically found their way to the tender parts of one's body. After all, items were broken, bent over or disposed of in one way or another however, they provided a very comfortable bed.

Of course the girls, being older than Earl Lee, were prone to exaggerate tales they had heard concerning the straw tick. They liked to discus chiggers that had, all but covered their bodies one time, while sleeping soundly on fresh straw mattresses. Though they had never come in contact with a single little red blood sucking insect at night, made no difference to the boy, he detested even the very thought of the tiny microscopic pests, having encountered them many times while picking blackberries. The severe itching that followed was enough to drive one out of his mind, for several days.

Earl Lee hated them, almost as much as the ticks that the girls talked about. Helen told him of one that got on her back one time and she didn't know it for several days. By then, it had grown almost as big as the ball Earl Lee played with. Papa had to pull it off with a pair of pliers, which left a hole in her back.

"If it left a hole, let me see it," the boy said.

"Maybe I will sometime," Helen said.

"I'll bet you don't have a hole in your back, does she Millie?"

"Of course she does but, you don't believe her so that's why she won't show you. If you really believed her, she'd show you. I believe her and I've seen it lots of times."

"When do ticks get in the straw?" he wanted to know.

"Out in the field, silly." Millie replied scornfully. "Where else do you think they'd come from. You sure are dumb, Er-ly. Isn't he Helen!"

"Yes, boys are just not very smart," her sister agreed. "Why do you think they call them straw ticks."

"I don't know. I never thought of it before," Earl Lee answered.

"Well, that's the reason. There's always ticks in the new straw. But, don't worry about them too much," Helen soothed. "Maybe the snakes will keep them out. I don't think ticks like snakes."

"Snakes!" Earl Lee exclaimed.

"Why yes! Didn't you know snakes get in the straw stack to get out of the hot sun?" Helen said surprised. "Everybody knows that."

"I didn't know it!"

"You do now," Millie said. "People sometimes pick them up with the straw and not know it until they get in bed and it wraps around their ankle or something."

He pondered this for a minute, then called out, "Aunt Bessie, the girls are trying to scare me."

"You kids calm down now and get to bed," she said from the kitchen.

A little later, Earl Lee lay in bed afraid to move, less something grabbed him. Unable to sleep, he began to toss and turn until Law said, "What's the matter with you, boy? If you have to go to the toilet, get up and go."

"I think there might be a snake in bed," Earl lee replied.

"Where in tarnation did you get such a notion as that?"

"I don't know but, I think there might be."

"Them two girls must be telling you tales again. There ain't no snake in this bed. Now, let me sleep."

In the other room, the girls were having similar problems.

Millie nudged Helen. "I think I felt something move."

"Don't be silly!" Helen retorted.

"I did! Down by my feet."

Helen jerked her feet upward. "Grandma, can we sleep with you?"

But, Grandma was already snoring.

They were silent for a minute. "A briar is sticking me," Millie said. "I'll be glad when this straw gets old so the stalks won't punch me."

"Helen?"

"What!"

"Do you really think there are chiggers or ticks or snakes in here?"

"I hope not."

CHAPTER 11

The weather stayed hot and dry. It hadn't rained in over a month. Crops in the upland showed the effects of having no moisture and were beginning to turn brown, way before their time. Corn leaves in the bottom were curling up. Many of the shallow wells had gone dry and farmers were hauling drinking water. And most of the ponds had dried up too.

Lawrence Reynolds was once again thankful that he'd had the foresight years ago to spend a little extra time and money to have deep wells dug. He had learned not to be too thrifty or cut corners, if he expected to succeed and last as a farmer, while all around him, men were failing and going broke. His wells had plenty of good water, both for household needs and also for livestock.

His main pond however was a different matter. Being dug long before he purchased the farm, it had gradually filled in with dirt from runoff. Now, it was dry with only a small puddle in the deepest spot. So, naturally it was the ideal time to dig it out and go deep enough to hold all the water that he needed for livestock.

He borrowed two slip-scrapers from the county barn over on the main road and they began digging out the pond. Law, Leonard and the two hired men worked the scrapers behind the teams of mules, moving dirt. They were a little awkward at first but, became more proficient as they went along. The smaller scraper went in first, being easier to handle and able to dig down into the soft dirt better. With the initial rut dug out across the bottom of the pond, the large scraper went in and carved out an even bigger one, carrying with it seven feet of mud.

The slip scraper was the common method of use in digging ponds and ditches. They came in different sizes for different kinds of work. Perhaps the best way to describe them is they resembled a large bucket made of heavy steel, flat on the bottom and open on one side, with an extra layer of metal on that side, serving as a bade. When pulled forward, this blade dug into the ground and scooped up piles of dirt into the bucket. It was controlled for depth by two handles, which were fastened on each side and extended to the rear. The driver of the team raised or lowered the handles by hand. In this way he could scoop out as much as he wanted with each pass through the pond.

Upon reaching the destination of the dirt, the driver merely flipped up one of the handles and turned it over, thus dumping the load. Law purposely wanted two different sizes of slips. The smaller of the two would carry four and a half feet of dirt was better to loosen up the hardpan of the earth, once they removed the soft dirt in the bottom of the pond. The larger size carried seven feet with each pass as it picked up the loosened dirt.

The three children spent hours playing nearby and watching as the pond grew bigger and deeper. Each time the men and mules went into the pond, they seemed to go deeper.

The earth became harder and the mules strained against the harness, pulling the loads up the sides and unloading back away from the digging. Men and mules seemed to reach their rhythm after awhile and the work progressed without incident as they moved back and forth.

While the two hired men handled the scrapers, Leonard began leveling off the loose earth on the banks with a team and blade.

One end of the pond was dug deep, while the other sloped more gradual, allowing the workers easy access in and out. When Law was satisfied it was deep enough to hold water even in a drought, he had them remove all the loose dirt from the bottom.

When they finished, he had them take several scraper loads and scatter in low spots in the barn lot and road. The rest was spread and leveled over a wide area around the pond, leaving gentle slopes on all sides for livestock to come drink when water came. By the following spring, it should be filled!

The rains were long in coming, as though lost forever. The earth seemed to be drying up and the temperature stayed above the hundred mark for days at a time. Little relief could be expected, even at night, making it difficult to find restful sleep. Most of the smaller streams and ponds had dried up long ago.

Law sat on the front porch of his home, contemplating the situation. He never liked not being in control of things, but even he was not able to combat what God placed on the earth. Twice in two years he had lost control of his destiny. Last year the floodwaters had sent him to high ground where he was obliged to sit on his hands and wait helplessly. This year the drought had caught him in a similar, yet almost opposite, situation. He knew though that he would fare better than many of his neighbors if it continued, but that was of little solace to his mind.

When the air was still, it sometimes was difficult breathing. When the occasional wind blew, it stirred up the dust and scattered it about, in one's eyes and nostrils and into the open doors and windows of the house, settling over everything and into the food on the table. The wind often made a dry, rustling sound as it passed through the cornfield.

A whirlwind danced erratically across the field, winding to and fro, kicking up dust devils among the plants. It entered the road, blowing clouds of dust and leaves skyward, as though searching for water to satisfy its needs. Failing in this, it finally found its way back again across the shallow ditch and into the field, where it disappeared on the far side. This seemed to be a common occurrence each day. At first, the children enjoyed the phenomenon and raced down the road after them. Now, they showed them no interest whatsoever, because of the heat.

There were times when the sun was nearly obliterated in the gray sky by the dust and haze in the air. Some days, men wore handkerchiefs over their mouth and nose to keep out the dust, making it hard to breathe and accomplish much work. At first, feed sacks and strips of cloth were put around inside the doors and windows to keep out the dust. However, this proved futile as the dust seeped through any way and it had to be removed, to let air into the house.

The air smelled of dust and was hot and stinging to one's eyes, nose and mouth.

Millie and Helen spent more time doing the chore they hated most, that of pumping water for the livestock. As the trough filled, the cows were let in. Drinking greedily, the trough emptied quickly, to be pumped full again. Dust settled on the surface if it sat for any length of time and cows nuzzled and blew it away before drinking.

Even walking to the mailbox became a chore. Walking through the thick, chalk like dust was hot to the hard, dry callused soles of the children's feet. Spurting up between their toes, it drifted out several feet, before settling back slowly to the earth. They waited until they saw the mail carrier coming in his buggy before going down to meet him.

Everyone's nerves were on edge and people were getting short tempered. Law found more fault than usual with his son, Leonard.

The day came when Leonard lost his usual cool mannered temper. Bending over to pick up a stick lying on the ground, his father's horse, Prince walked up and bit him on the shoulder. There was no reason for the attack, if one could call it an attack, the horse had never done such a thing before. Being a normally gentle beast, it was completely out of character for him. Being more surprised than hurt, Leonard whirled around with the stick in his hand and struck the big white horse across the shoulders. At that precise moment his father stepped out of the barn. Witnessing the one, single blow, he flew into a rage of fury. Grabbing the stick out of Leonard's hands, he began flailing him with it. Trying to defend himself by holding his arms over his head, he was backed up into a corner of the barn and an open door. He tried unsuccessfully to lash out at his father who only grew more angry and the best he could do was cower down and take the punishment.

Luckily, Earl Lee came by and saw what was happening. He ran screaming to the house.

"Aunt Bessie, Aunt Bessie," he yelled, "You better go out to the barn, quick. Uncle Lawrence is whipping Uncle Leonard. I think he's trying to kill him."

She gathered up the bottom of her apron and rushed outside. Upon seeing the spectacle, she hurried towards the fray, yelling at her husband. Like a man obsessed, He paid her no heed. Realizing that talking was out of the question, she grabbed his arm. He all but lifted her off the ground as he struck out again, freeing his arm. She braced her feet solidly on the ground and grabbed him again and literally took the stick out of his hand.

"Calm down, Lawrence, calm down," she said in what she considered a soothing voice.

"I-Gawd, what are you trying to do, kill the boy!"

"He hit ol' Prince," he retorted fiercely.

"That's no reason to beat him to death," Bessie told him. "You think more of that animal than you do your own son."

"He should know better. I wanted him to know what it's like to be whipped."

Millie and Helen came out and stood staring at their father, still cowering there on the ground. His cap had been knocked off and cuts on his head were running blood, as well as the places on his face. His left shoulder seemed to be hurt, judging from the way he held his arm. Millie thought that when he looked up at her, he was crying. She had never seen him cry before. There was so much sadness and hurt in his eyes! In that moment, she almost hated her grandfather. She felt a great compassion for her father and longed to go put her arms around him.

He got to his feet and stumbled over to the pump, where he washed his head and face. Then, he went to the shed, got out his car and sped off down the road.

Later that afternoon, the rain came. Clouds began forming in the west and moved slowly over the Bottoms. They were small clouds at first, then came together in huge black masses until the sky was filled and the sun blotted out. A stillness came ahead of the clouds, one that was eerie, for lack of sound.

The trouble by the barn was forgotten as Law and his family stood in the yard and watched the gathering of impending doom, or so it seemed.

"I'm scared," Millie said. "Why is it so quiet?"

"It'll be all right," Grandma consoled her. "Just looks like a little storm brewing."

"I'm scared too. Look at the cows, they're all acting funny," Earl Lee said.

The cows were milling about, nervous and lowing.

"I've never seen them act that crazy before," Grandpa said. "I don't like the looks of this at all."

The horses and mules had become skittish, and he hurried out to lock them in the barn before the storm arrived. It became so dark that the chickens went in to roost.

A rumbling of thunder sounded in the distance with a little breeze following, a cool, welcome breeze. The leaves stirred on the trees and the haze began to lift and the air felt almost clean again.

A sharp bolt of lightning and loud clap of thunder sent them all scurrying to the house, where they waited for the next clash. It came soon enough, followed by another and yet another. The wind began to blow and the much needed rain came. With it, the drought ended.

Law sat at a window on the leeward side of the house, watching as the water fell. The wind reached storm strength for a while, along with lightning and thunder, gradually settling down to just a downpour.

In the beginning, the big drops sent puffs of dust outward with each contact, leaving small holes where they landed. A musty odor filled the air as the water mixed with the dust. Then it became clean and fresh smelling. As the tiny holes filled in with the spattering raindrops, the dust flattened out into mud. The water fused together until there was enough to run through the dust. It made its way slowly at first over the surface of the road, edging along towards the ditch. The tiny rivulets picked up speed going down hill into the bottom of the ditch. Before long, the ditch filled with water.

Great sheets of rain blew through the yard and slammed against the house and barns. Some of the corn was flattened by the onslaught. Water poured down the roofs of the buildings and the rain barrels at the sides of the house filled and ran over.

After a few minutes, the storm passed over and the rumblings were far distant. But, the rain continued steadily for some time. Water stood in the fields, between the cornrows and low spots of the pasture and filled the ditches. The air felt clean and fresh! The world was good again!

That night, sleep came easily because the air was cool and the frogs sent forth their steady chant and the night birds sounded all around. It was peaceful and all was well!

Then the world fell apart. Well into the night, a car came down the road and turned into the yard. Thinking it to be Leonard coming home, Bessie rolled over and went back to sleep.

A minute later, a horn sounded and then a pounding on the door. It was loud enough to wake the entire household.

"Open up, Law, this is the sheriff," called a voice from outside. "This is Billy Tate. Get up and open the door."

Law got up and opened the door, standing there in his long underwear. Bessie was beside him in her nightgown with her long hair hanging to her waist. Three children stood behind them in various forms of nightdress.

"What in tarnation is going on, Billy?" Law glared at the sheriff. "Can't a man get himself a decent night's sleep any more!"

The sheriff held his hat in his hand. A deputy stood behind him. "Howdy, Law. Evening Bessie. I'm sorry to have to do this." He hesitated a moment, trying to find the right words. "It's about Leonard," he said.

"What's that fool boy got hisself into now?" Law demanded.

"It's nothing like that, Law," the sheriff said. "He got killed awhile ago."

Law stared at him dumbfounded. "How do you mean got killed. What happened?"

"He got run over by a car up on the main highway, right in front of the Hang Out."

The Hang Out was a restaurant of sorts, on the main highway, where the Blairsville road ended. It was a one story brick building with plenty of space around it for cars, horses and wagons to park. It had become a favorite meeting place for some of the local men to go, relax and discuss various topics of the time, after a hard days work. It's true that it was a restaurant, they served sandwiches, coffee, pie etc., the usual things that a small place served. However, the main attraction was they also sold boot-leg whiskey and home-brew. The authorities knew of this illegal activity, but did nothing about it, letting things go along quietly, so long as there was no trouble or complaints. Few people even knew of the liquor being sold, since the patrons kept still about it and seldom mentioned it.

Law stood silent, thinking!

Bessie asked, "What happened, was he in his car?"

"No ma'am, he was afoot," the sheriff replied.

"Why in tarnation would he be afoot when he had his car there?" Law asked.

"I'm not real sure, Law. I haven't had time to get all the details yet. The way I gathered it so far though, Leonard must have been in the place a long time." He glanced at Bessie. "I guess you know they sell moonshine there?"

"Yes, I know."

"Well, they said he'd been there drinking most of the afternoon and night. Boot-leg whiskey mostly! He didn't seem to be that drunk though, according to witnesses. He finally got up and left. Everybody thought he was coming home. A few minutes later they heard this car out on the road slam on its brakes. It must've been travelling pretty fast and couldn't stop in time. It hit Leonard and knocked him clean over into the ditch."

"What was he doing walking on the road in the dark?" Law asked.

"That's a strange thing," the sheriff answered. "The driver says he waited until he got close, and he just walked right out in front of him, like he wanted to be hit. Now, why do you suppose he'd do a thing like that, unless of course the driver was lying. He seemed sincere though."

Bessie looked at her husband who stood stoically, his face pale in the lamplight. "So, this is what it comes to," she thought.

The children began crying as they realized the impact of what had happened.

"What did they do with him?" Bessie asked.

"They took him to the undertaker in town," Billy Tate told her. "You can go in and make arrangements tomorrow."

Law's jaws developed a nervous twitch and he walked out into the yard without a word, leaving his guests standing in the kitchen.

The arrangements were made the next morning and that afternoon Leonard's body was brought home, for the wake. Being placed on its catafalque in the front room, the coolest place in the house, it remained open for viewing.

Word of the accident spread over the county and neighbors brought in food to feed the grieving family and visitors alike. So much of it, in fact, there was no room to for it all. Vesta Kincaid and Lottie Reynolds and Kate Quigley each carried over several kettles and dishes of food, only to return home with more than they brought, to make room for new arrivals. To leave so much there, it would spoil long before being eaten. Everyone who came went away with a full stomach.

Friends came from all over the county, farmers and businessmen from Mcleansboro. The wake lasted all night, as it was the custom. The closer friends, who knew him best, sat with the family. Many came to pay their respects, make the appropriate comments, eat, sit around and talk to friends and then leave. At this time, children were allowed to stay up past their normal bedtime, all night if they wished, but few were able to do so. By midnight most were in bed.

Millie, reluctantly at first, went to see her father and then refused to leave. She stood staring down into the still, white face for a long time. He looked so young, she thought, more like a boy with a smile on his face. She touched the cold, callused hand, but drew back immediately and never touched him again because Papa's hands were always warm and firm. He was always a good father, though not one to openly display much emotion. She knew he loved her, and Helen too. Tears filled her eyes, knowing he'd soon be gone forever and a great sadness descended upon her.

When people began coming in, she placed a footstool in the corner of the room almost behind the coffin, out of the way of everyone. There she sat quietly, with her own private sorrow, listening to the comments of friends and neighbors as they approached the coffin and stared down at the man lying there.

As in most similar circumstances, only the good was brought out in the conversations. Even if one tried though, it would be hard to find many negative things in Leonard's life because he had been a good man.

Sitting there, staring up at the mourners, Millie listened silently to their comments as though through a haze, like a part of her was gone forever.

Vesta Kincaid commented, "My, don't he look nice though!"

Another, "Such a pity, he was such a nice young man."

Aunt Lottie, "I just knowed somebody was going to die. I dreamed of muddy water the other night. That's always a sure sign."

"Look how he's grinning at us."

Uncle Sidney, "I remember when he was born, like it was only yesterday."

"I didn't know he was bald!"

"Sure, that's why he always wore that cap. Never seen him without it. Must've been a trait on his mother's side."

"He was a nice, easy going guy who never hurt nobody."

"He was a good friend."

"He was too young to die that way."

Cousin Reuben and Lorna seemed to be the most sincere and grief stricken than anyone. Millie knew they had been good friends to her mother and father all through the years.

Lorna said, "He'd never been happy since Mabel left him. He always seemed so sad."

Reuben added, "I kept trying to get him to find another wife but, he just wasn't interested."

Many pleasant memories were brought back to Millie as it went on and on. At last she became too weary to hold her eyes open any longer and she fell asleep about midnight, sitting there on the stool, much earlier than she expected to but, later than she was accustomed to. Grandma picked her up in her strong arms and carried her in to bed.

Because of the hot weather, the funeral took place the very next day, on the advice of the undertaker. Brother Josh Smith gave the eulogy at the graveside ceremony in Pleasant View cemetery over near Belle Prairie. So, at last Leonard Reynolds would rest in peace, there beside his real mother.

After a few days, the family settled down into a routine that was changed forever. Millie somehow managed to get her father's watch, the Klicker, given to him by her mother, long ago. It remained in her possession for the rest of her life, as her most treasured memento. Occasionally she wound the stem a couple of turns and it continued to be in working order.

After Leonard's death, Bessie decided to learn to drive the car, since Law simply refused to get behind the wheel. Bert Schultz, one of the hired men, set out to teach her. On the first and only lesson, she raced the motor and ran the car across the ditch, into the orchard.

Gripping the steering wheel with both hands, Bessie shouted, "Whoa, whoa there. Bless my stars and garters, I said whoa there, I-Gawd."

Hitting a big apple tree, the car bounced off and circled around and back into the ditch before Bert got her foot off the accelerator and stopped the car. She never tried to drive again! Law chose Bert to chauffeur them around whenever the need arose.

Law said of the incident, "Danged fool woman should know better. Never trusted the confounded contraption anyway. Besides women just don't have the temperament to handle such a thing!"

Law's sister came immediately from Mt. Hebron, upon word of Leonard's death. He always had been her favorite nephew, having helped raise him for most of his formative young years. She stayed at the house several days afterwards. During that time, she came up with a proposition that met the approval of Law and Bessie, but not necessarily the girls. Not at first anyway. The girls would go live with her, just before school started and remain during the entire school year, except of course Thanksgiving and Christmas. They would go home to the farm for the holidays. And they would spend the summers at home also. Lucille agreed to raise them as her own.

"Let them live with me and get a good education and up-bringing," she reasoned. "The farm is no place for two bright, pretty little girls."

It would certainly be different than what they were used to but, they'd miss the farm and Grandma and Grandpa and of course Earl Lee.

It'll only be for a month or two at a time," Helen pointed out to Millie. "And we'll be back home all summer. It might be fun."

So they became excited and began making plans!

Now, it had been two months since the girls left. Law's rheumatism had been acting up lately, making it a little more difficult to get out of bed in the morning. Besides that, things hadn't been going too well since Leonard was laid to rest. He now had more details to work out and take care of that he didn't have before. He blamed that on his son. It was very inconsiderate of the boy to go get hisself killed that way. It put an extra burden on him. When he was young a little extra work didn't matter to him, but things change when one gets older.

After Leonard, he lost the girls. Oh, he had been agreeable to Lucille's offer to take them. They needed to go to school in a bigger town all right. They'd get a proper education, but he did miss the little tykes.

What bothered him as much as anything perhaps, was the fact that they were the only link he had with Delcie. And that was Leonard's fault too. If he hadn't died, he'd still be here carrying his share of the load and so would the girls. With him around, there was a strong connection to the past and Law had someone to whom he could vent his frustration, using Delcie's death as a reason to blame him for many things.

Making his rounds of the fields as he always did, approaching harvest time, he stopped Prince on a slight rise to survey a field. The big white stallion stood hip-shod, waiting for the next command to move forward, apparently content with his lot. Law decided that the corn yield would be better than previously expected but, he hesitated about moving on. Something had been nagging at the back of his mind for a long time. He finally allowed it to come to the surface and out in the open.

He made what he considered to be an honest assessment of his life, these past several years.

He'd come a long way since Belle Prairie and Delcie. He was well known throughout the county and respected, too. Oh, he'd stepped on a few toes along the way, maybe, but that was to be expected. If they didn't move over, step on them, to his way of thinking. He had always been fair and honest in his dealings and everyone said he could be trusted. His word and his handshake were his bond. A written title or agreement wasn't always necessary, legal maybe in most cases but, he still believed in a good old-fashioned handshake. He had his own code of ethics and never cheated anyone. This fact was well known, yet he might take advantage of a loophole, if it suited his means.

He wondered how things would be now if Delcie had lived. Certainly, life would be much different. Likely, he wouldn't have this farm. Delcie just wasn't the type to live in a log cabin in the beginning as Bessie had been and without that there would be no farm here. He never could have prospered over around Belle Prairie. There hadn't been any land for sale there. That left only two options. He'd ended up by renting and being a poor dirt farmer like his father and never get ahead. Delcie would never have been happy that way!

The other option, he might have gone to work for Mr. Graves at the mill. They'd live in a nice little house in Belle Prairie, the kind that fitted her. She'd like that and so would her folks. But, Law would hate that lifestyle and never be happy and things wouldn't last for them.

Law looked back at his barns in the distance and the nice, white house and felt proud of what he'd accomplished in life. He admitted now, to himself, he could never have done it with Delcie. He'd go to his grave still loving her and only her, but all he had was because she had died young. She had been too delicate to withstand the rigors of real farm life, living as a pioneer in the early going.

He admitted now, for the first time, that without Bessie and Leonard, he wouldn't be sitting here surveying this property. Bessie was the type of woman it took, working alongside him from the very beginning. He realized that she had worked just as hard as he over the years, and what they had done, had been done together. Delcie would never have lasted.

Law admitted too, at least partially, that perhaps Leonard had been helpful in obtaining some of the holdings. He realized it now more than ever before since so much more had fallen on his shoulders. Not being as young as he used to be, it was harder to keep up. In the old days, he'd just take up the slack and move ahead. He had been dependent on Leonard, more than he realized. Maybe he had been a little harsh with the boy, now and then but, that was only natural, the way a father should be.

Yes, he saw much now, that he hadn't noticed before. Leonard probably had been of some help after all. Now that corn shucking time was coming soon, he had to take care of many things he'd left to Leonard. Of course, he had the two hired hands and they were capable, dependable men but, not like family. And, he'd have to hire an extra helper to replace Leonard this year.

Pulling on the reins, he turned Prince around and headed back to the house.

Aloud, he said, "I'm going to miss you, Boy!"

The End

Printed in the United States
33794LVS00003B/49-102